WINNING MARS

WINNING MARS

Jason Stoddard

PRIME BOOKS

Winning Mars

Prime Books
www.prime-books.com

For more information, contact Prime Books.
prime@prime-books.com

ISBN: 978-1-60701-216-0

For Rina, who tolerates my insanity.

Acknowledgements:

Thank you to the following individuals and organizations. Without their support, this book would never have been written:

• TTA Press, for publishing the first novella-length version of *Winning Mars* in *Interzone 196*.

• Andy Cox, who was the first editor to really believe in me.

• Jetse de Vries, who has made everything I write better.

• Rina Slayter, for her patience and understanding.

ONE: MOTIVATION

Pitch

"Of course, someone is going to die. Probably lots of someones."

Jere Gutierrez had heard a lot of stupid pitches, but most of them didn't start so bluntly. He glanced at the old guy's name and CV, scrolling in his eyeset: EVAN MCMASTER. His last show: *Extreme Losers*.

"Death is a legal problem," Jere said.

"For Neteno?"

"Neteno doesn't do snuff."

Evan gave him a thin smile. "What about the Philippines?"

"That was news."

"How about the Three-Day Fever?"

Jere just looked at Evan, waiting for him to look away. Evan looked fifty, meaning he was probably at least seventy, scraping the last of the best med-tech before the docs threw up their hands and said, in fatalistic voices, *We're not miracle workers here!*

While he waited, Jere skimmed his CV. Evan's career started in the mythical hegemony of the 1970s, when television was God, and audiences sat rapt on their cheap sofas scarfing down microwave dinners, going to work the next day brimming with the warm commonality of experience. From staff writer for *Five in a Room*, he went on to produce a bunch of mindless crap to fill thirty-minute second-slots in the eighties and nineties. He'd been exec producer on one of the first reality shows, *Endurance*. From there, Evan's work descended completely into the ghetto after the dawn of the internet era, and he'd done nothing past the aughties. The usergab on *Extreme Losers* pegged it a timewaster of the worst sort, a parade of physically unfit people put into situations where they were sure to kick it, except for some heroics at the end to save them. Most of the time.

Jere realized Evan was still looking at him.

"Make your pitch," he said.

Evan just smiled, but said nothing.

"I'm amusing to you?"

"Not at all. I respect what you've done with Neteno." Zero expression. Eyes like lead.

Jere turned to look through the window and out over the gray concrete expanse of Old Hollywood to the smog-brown west and the invisible Pacific. The view from Neteno's office at the top of what had once been the Capitol Records building was always soothing. A reminder of how far he'd come.

"Are you going to pitch, or are you going to leave?"

"It's a simple idea," Evan said. "We resurrect the reality show. And we take it to Mars."

Jere snapped back to look at Evan. To see if he was smiling, ha ha, good joke there. He wasn't.

"Resurrect the reality show?"

"Yes."

"And take it to . . . Mars? As in, the planet?"

"Yes. The planet."

"For real? Not CGed?"

"For real."

Jere stopped again. You gotta be fucking kidding me, he wanted to say. But . . . but it was a damn good idea. Except for the fact that it had to be colored all shades of expensive.

"I have data," Evan said said, waving a tiny projector. "Can I show it?"

Jere nodded. "Lights down, screen down" he said. The window dimmed to twilight, and the room light ramped down, turning and blue as the screen descended.

There were brief flashes as the projector's lasers found the screen, then garish graphics lit. *WINNING MARS,* it said, *A Proposal for Neteno.*

"First, let's dispense with the death thing," Evan said.

"Sponsors don't like it."

"Don't lie. Sponsors love it. They just look properly horrified and give some insignificant percentage of their profits to the survivors and everyone's happy. Your big problem is legal, and that can be surmounted."

"And budget, I bet."

Evan's cocky expression wavered for a moment. He turned to the screen. "Let's start with the reasons, first."

Jere's screen lit with colorful data, demographics, charts, multicolored peaks spiking like some impossible landscape. Standard 411, Inc. audience-inference data: size, engagement, propagation ability, monetization effective-ness. All stuff he'd seen before.

But this . . . this was wacky. Way out of proportion . . . Jere took a screengrab with his eyeset and blinked it out to 411 for verification. A message from one of their IAs shot back: YES, THIS IS OURS.

Evan zoomed in on one of the datasets, labeled POLITICAL/SOCIAL FACTORS. "First reason: the Chinese space program."

"Didn't the Chinese stop at the moon?"

"Yeah. But they said they'd go to Mars, and a whole lot of Chinese still want to go to Mars. And Koreans. And Japanese. And Americans." Evan pointed out separate spikes on the chart, big, rabid, we-care-about-this-like-crazy spikes.

"Another reason is NASA. They're gutted. After the Economic Rethink, everything's de facto under Oversight. And if it ain't promoting stability or leading to a shiny happy lower-consumption future, or helping someone get reelected, it's a permanent deader. But there's still an itch. People still want to see some great endeavor. Deep down, they dream about escape. It's the Frontier Factor."

"Never heard of it."

"Henry Kase. Started on YouTube like you, but from the brainiac side. He's been invited to the TED conference eight times, got a standing ovation from Zuckerberg at the last one. His algorithms found the guys planning that DC nuke. The Frontier Factor is his latest hobbyhorse."

Jere's eyeset barfed up lots of Kase video, but he blinked it away. "Go on."

"Third reason, the Rabid Fan."

Jere nodded. Everyone dreamed of creating a new *Star Trek*, still in syndication after all these years, or a new *Simpsons*, or a new *Buffy*. A show that made people dress up, go to conventions, meet in real life, invent languages, change dictionaries, and, most importantly, spend money in numerous ways.

"They'll think this is too game show," Jere said.

"Yeah. But they'll watch. They'll bitch, they'll moan, but they'll watch. All the trekkies and sci-fi nuts and people who dream about getting out, getting away, people who hate their lives for whatever reason, they'll all watch. Look at the numbers."

Data zoomed, showing tags of AUDIENCE STICKINESS and INFERRED ENGAGEMENT, peaky and perfect and tantalizing. If they could create something like that . . . Jere sat silent for a long time, thinking, dreaming, imagining himself in control of a neverending, ever-licensing franchise.

Evan stole a glance at Jere, his eyes cool and calculating in the reflected laserlight.

Jere let him wait. Even though he was thinking about all the things he could do with a project like this. Selling ads was only the start. What would it be worth to have your logo on Mars? To have contestants drinking Starbucks and eating Marie Callenders? To have exclusive coverage of the tech? Reality advertising with the contestants? Hell, how many trillions of impressions would they have for lead-up, and what kind of money could they make with user voting?

"Show me the budget," Jere said.

Evan licked his lips, and his eyes stuttered sideways before fixing on Jere. "First, let me show you the vision."

The screen switched to renderings of spacesuits with Nike logos, and something that looked like a big hamster wheel with a spacesuited person inside it, bouncing over the surface of Mars. The hamster wheel sported a Toyota logo. More data appeared: suggested sponsors, customized programs, and the like.

"I get the vision," Jere said.

"The revenue possibilities—"

"I get that. The budget."

"But I think we've found some additional opportunities—"

Jere just looked at Evan and waited. This time, Evan dropped his eyes. The slides flickered forward to black and white numbers, prettified by more renderings.

"We're using Russian tech, the kind they're using for the quarter million-dollar weeklong orbital packages. And we're pushing it even farther, so we have some significant economies of scale—"

Jere laughed, long and hard.

"I don't think you understand—"

"Oh, no," Jere said. "I understand. I get it. I totally get it. And, you know what, I really like the idea. But that budget is bigger than the biggest of the massively multiplayer online games, and we're stick down here in the linear narrative ghetto. Hell, that's our topline for all of Neteno."

"I think you're missing out on the revenue opportunities, which counter-balance the investment."

Jere glanced at the screen, expecting to see king-sized cost-per-impressions, exaggerated audiences, and sponsorship fees blown out of proportion.

But the numbers were solid. Evan hadn't fudged. For a moment, Jere wondered: What if?

"It's a show that could double the size of your network," Evan said. "It could *be* your network."

"Even if I said yes, our bankers would laugh us out of the room."

"There are other ways of raising capital," Evan said. "I would throw in personally."

"How rich are you, Evan?"

Evan looked away. After a few moments, he turned off the projector.

"Lights up," Jere said. The room brightened.

Evan turned to look at him, defeated. In that moment, he looked every bit of seventy, like something old and cold and prehistoric, dredged from the the La Brea tar pits. Evan didn't wear animated clothing, didn't have any visible tattoos, didn't wear an eyeset. His jacket was black and boring and imperfectly tailored, as if it had been made by real, imperfect humans somewhere in the world, rather than grown to his shape. He wore a gray collarless shirt underneath, devoid of even a corporate logo. He even had a big clunky metal watch, one of those awful things that throbbed and ticked on your wrist like a bomb.

"I thought Neteno took chances," Evan said.

"What?"

"I thought you still wanted to push the edge."

Jere flushed, the hot stab of anger like a Buffy-stake in the heart. "We've pushed it." Farther than you think, old man.

"I thought—"

"You're not going to guilt me into this," Jere said. "I told you how I feel. It's a great idea. But the numbers don't work."

Evan opened his mouth as if to say something. Then he closed it. He put his little projector away, went to the door, and walked out without a word. He left it open as he slouched down the hall.

For a moment, Jere really felt sorry for him. It would've been a fun project.

But it just didn't add up.

Scare

The Mississippi Chimera fiasco wasn't much of a thing, but it was a thing Patrice Klein could play with.

Or, more accurately, it was something Yvette Zero enjoyed.

And Patrice was definitely YZ today. Business YZ. Not a popular YZ. Most players of the Zero's One MMO would much rather see Date YZ, wearing something low-cut and slinky. Or Adventure YZ, wearing short shorts and a top that left nothing to the imagination. Or Bedroom YZ, wearing nothing at all. Or YZ with Master Chief, unmasked. Or ten thousand other authorized and unauthorized variations. When Patrice Klein created Yvette Zero back in her freshman year at UCLA, she never imagined she'd become the most popular female MMO character in the world.

Of course, Patrice never imagined she'd get plastic surgery to look more like the character she created, either. But life was strange, and you had to hang on to the fun.

So here she was, on a wet November day, stumbling around backwoods Mississippi dressed in a skintight light blue Dior business suit and expensively inappropriate shoes. She nearly tripped as she entered the remains of a shitty little chimera crèche, and automatically adjusted her polished platinum Gucci eyeset.

She was late. It was two days since the story hit the mediascape as a single lifenote, and twelve and a half hours since viral spread had peaked. The big infovultures were gone, confident that their exposure value had been maximized. Glowing crime scene tape remained draped between trees, but even the cops hadn't thought it necessary to leave a guard.

The crèche was hidden below a weathered, swaybacked hunter's shack buried in woods so deep you almost had to use flashlights in the daytime. Inside the shack, the camouflage was near-perfect. The stink of decay and disuse hung on everything. Unpainted wallboards were relieved by a single dirty window, and the only furniture was a thrift store table and a rusted Sterno stove.

The table had been shoved aside, exposing a solid wooden trapdoor. Patrice lifted it and gingerly descended the metal ladder to the cellar. The lab.

Here, decay gave way to a newish utilitarian space, concrete walls and floors with big metal-grate ventilators that probably dumped somewhere far out in the woods. The faint tang of antiseptic and ozone stung her nose.

Patrice's eyeset automatically adjusted to the gloom. There wasn't much left, just a few lifeless scraps of flesh in transparent tanks, things that probably would never have grown to maturity. Her eyeset tagged the abandoned equipment as several generations old. Just some good ol' boys playing with cheap Brazilian tech and dreaming of perfect angelic fairies, or sexy cat-girls, to help them through the chill lonely nights. Something moderately more interesting than moonshine. Nothing like the big Chinese or Russian cartels that promised to deliver whatever you wanted.

If I'd made YZ a chimera, would I be tempted to go transgenic? Patrice wondered.

The metal ladder rattled as two men climbed down it. The first stepped away to allow the second room to land. Patrice's eyeset tagged the first as a Mississippi State biohacker specialist, with the truly amazing name of Reynauld Peregrine. He wore a tan uniform with one of those Smokey the Bear hats. He was hot.

The other man was tagged, very simply: CONTACT. He wore the same uniform with a blinking red hatcam and carried a shotgun.

Reynauld said, "Not even an atomic mapper or an atom-laser setup. It's pretty amazing they got anything done."

Contact nodded, but didn't comment.

Reynauld finally saw YZ in a dim corner and stopped short. Contact bumped into him. Reynauld cursed and got out of his way.

"Who are you?" Reynauld said. "We're closed down here. No more press."

YZ smiled, and Reynauld's eyes went wide.

"She's Yvette Zero," Contact said.

"I . . . yeah," Reynauld said. His eyes jigged around the room, as if expecting to see a camera crew pop out of nowhere.

"I'm sorry," YZ said, coming close to Reynauld. Very close. Close enough so that he could feel her body heat. "You don't mind if I look around a bit? I'm interested in this."

"Uh, I—"

"Research on a new game?" Contact said.

She grinned. "Something like that. Is it safe?"

"We hosed it down earlier," Reynauld said, looking down the deep V of her top.

"Oh. Good. I won't be long. Do you mind if I take some pictures?"

Reynauld looked stunned for a moment, as if trying to imagine how he could tell her that was against the rules. Patrice wondered how many times he'd played Zero's One, and how far he'd gotten with YZ.

Finally, Reynauld shrugged. "It doesn't matter. Media's been here."

"Thank you," Patrice said, blowing him a kiss. She went around the room, taking pix with her eyeset. A red flag popped up: ACTION IMMINENT.

"Nothing hidden?" she asked Reynauld. "No rooms with semi-human sex slaves, no closets with living fetuses bubbling away in vats?"

He looked at her a long time before speaking. "You're an odd woman," he said, finally.

"So, nothing hidden."

A headshake.

"No Russian ties, no Boston corporates hanging about?"

"No, no."

Patrice frowned. "Boring."

Reynauld said nothing.

Patrice sighed. "I think I'll head into town. Maybe talk to some people there who knew the guys. Can someone give me directions?"

"Sure," Reynauld said. "You walked in?"

"Yeah."

"You might need someone to walk you out. Don't want the second news story of the day to be a big massive multiplayer star getting lost in the woods."

A snicker from Contact. Reynauld snapped a "shut-up" look back at him. Patrice smiled. She loved it when they fell for her.

The red flag in her eyeset began to pulse. Any second now.

"I'd be happy to accompany you, Mr. Peregrine—"

Something heavy slammed into the building above them with a deep bass thump. Weathered timbers shredded with a sound like tearing paper. Dust sifted down through the open door. A high yodeling cry that didn't sound even remotely human reverberated eerily through the lab—the essence of sadness, of frustration, of anger.

"What the hell?" Reynauld said, as Contact cowered in fear and backed towards Patrice.

A huge clawed hand—purple-veined and roped with wiry muscle—reached down into the cellar lab, clutching at equipment and knocking it over. As it momentarily withdrew its arm, Patrice caught a glimpse of a head like a naked bear, with translucent flesh hanging in folds over well-muscled shoulders.

Tearing the trapdoor opening wider, it plunged both arms, its monstrous head, and wiry torso into the cellar. It slashed at Reynauld, saber-sharp claws threatening to shred both uniform and flesh. Reynauld skittered away, scrambling to unholster his gun. Contact bumped into Patrice, eyes wide in realistic terror, still holding the shotgun.

YZ ripped the gun out of his hands and fired. The chimera screamed and drew back, then lunged through the opening again. Its eyes were big, blue, and surprisingly human.

Patrice fired again. Again.

The chimera's cry dissolved into a shrieking wail, and it drew back. There was a scrambling in the shack, and then whimpering cries, trailing away into the woods. The wrecked trapdoor jaggedly framed only tree branches and slowly falling mist.

Reynauld stared at Patrice. Smoke still curled from the barrel of the shotgun. He'd never gotten his gun out of his holster. His eyes were wide with embarrassment.

"I . . . I . . . "

"It's all right," Patrice said. She handed the shotgun back to Contact.

She realized she was out of breath, and her heart was pounding. That thing was terrifying. Even though she knew it was just a guy in a Japanese mechasuit and silicone exoskin, surplus from some planned experiential reality interactive that never made funding. With a few quick changes by aging real-effects guys, who would work for nickels and not talk for dollars, it was now the "Terror of the Woods."

"Are you okay?" Patrice asked Reynauld.

"I . . . I'm fine." He bent over, put his hands on his knees.

"Are you going to faint?"

"No, no."

"What do we do now?"

Reynauld stood, swaying, gray. "We need to track it. And get you out of here." He glanced from her to Contact guiltily.

"Not so boring now."

Reynauld just looked at her, his eyes darting, suspicious. Had she gone a bit too far this time? Patrice felt a quick shiver of excitement.

But no . . . he shook his head, grabbed the ladder, put it in place, and went up.

Contact and Patrice climbed out of the cellar and remained standing in the remains of the shack until Reynauld returned with more state troopers. Neteno camera crews followed, flushed with excitement. One crew and two state troopers escorted Patrice—YZ, really—back through the woods.

She knew how it would go from here. Neteno would cover the hunters who hunted the monster. First there would be glimpses, then brief encounters, perhaps a skirmish or two. One courageous hunter (whose friend was hospitalized in critical condition due to the Terror) would almost track it down . . .

They would have to avoid killing anyone, but that was a piece of cake. The aerial surveillance would even give them a great excuse to drop battery packs to keep the mecha going.

Next: the hunter finding its lair. The little crevice in the rocks, decorated with strangely relevant posters and scraps of still-glowing wallscreen, and seeded with bits of a bear-human hybrid genome that would never live, but would make it seem real. And people would scream and cry, and say: It was human, how could you hunt it?

Maybe there'd even be a brave child who befriended the Terror, though that was such a stereotype. They would have to find someone not well-liked, rebellious, and pay for a trip to Brazil for memory repatterning.

And then, finally, the big mystery, when it disappears as if it never existed. Just some tracks, leading off into the distance. Ending at a stream . . .

Or something like that. Half the audience would celebrate, half would cry, a few would say it was a fake all along, but that was okay. A new legend would be born. A legend Neteno would own.

A message appeared in her eyeset: GOOD WORK. WANT TO GRAB DINNER? Jere.

WE SHOULDN'T, she eyetyped.

COME ON, I'M IN TOWN.

For a long time, Patrice didn't respond. They really shouldn't see each other. It was too close to the show. Jere should know that.

But that was the thing about Jere. He wasn't the brightest star in the firmament. And he didn't always do the right thing. But that was why he'd turned a crappy YouTube channel into a major network at age twenty-five, which is why he was still rising now on the eve of thirty, when others were falling, which was why he—

Why he was hot.

SEE YOU THERE, she sent.

Toast

"What you're saying is, stick a fork in Neteno, we're done," Jere Gutierrez said.

The two 411 dataspooks didn't react. They just sat in their thousand-dollar visitor chairs and looked at Jere. Suddenly he felt naked behind his five-thousand-pound solid granite desk. This is my fucking office, he wanted to say. I pay you. Tell me what I *want* to hear.

One of them finally spoke. "What we're saying is that meetings like the one with Ms. Klein strain the credibility of your impressed-reality shows," said the first dataspook. Jere's eyeset tagged him as Richard Perez. Of course. He would be a Dick.

"People are noticing your stunts," the other said. His name was Edward Woo.

"Which makes your shows less credible. Which reduces value to your advertisers," Richard said.

"So I'm not dead yet, but everybody's started buying their black suits."

"You simply need to moderate your impressed-reality shows and move to more conventional forms of linear entertainment," Richard said. "You also may need to reduce the scripting used within Neteno personnel's lives, since there's a sixty-six percent probability someone will be able to infer the writers within the next three years."

Jere sighed, looking at the parasites in their too-perfect suits, as if pinstripe double-breasted was their natural pelt. "Anything else I need to do?"

"Selling of wholesale sponsorship packages, such as disaster relief, are also showing in the too-obvious feedback, with additional commentary on frequency of sponsor logo placement. That would have to be minimized as well."

Great. All the biggest money makers for Neteno. All the stuff 411 shouldn't even know about.

Jere stood and turned to look out the window. It was the end of the day, and charcoal Hollywood stood out under brilliant orange sunset skies. The

Neteno logo rotated in perfect holographic space outside his office window, ringing the cylindrical building like a wreath. Jere cast his eyes upward in time to see the ENO scroll lazily past, and the NET begin again. The colorful lights were pleasant, like a childhood memory of Christmas lights.

"Revenue breakdown, sales, and profit by sector," Jere said, softly. His eyeset streamed visuals that confirmed what he knew by his gut: without his tricks of impressed reality and scripted lives, Neteno was just like ABC or CBS or FOX or any of the other linear networks—scraping by on old-fashioned impressions, unable to compete with the engagement of EA and Gen3 and the other MMO giants.

"We'll have to work up some new tricks," Jere said.

Richard shook his head, sadly. "Public awareness of your manipulation is already starting to peak above the conspiracy theory reality line. Any further games will spike it into levels that can't be sheetrocked."

"People are hypersensitive to Neteno's actions," Edward said.

"Can't we pay to bury this?"

"No organization can stand against the customer. Look at Google."

Jere nodded. They'd covered that. Had a good story impression at the top-level, some docs of the Evil/Not Evil variety. It was one of the things that had launched Neteno.

Edward sparked up a projector, and charts lit on the screen. It showed Neteno revenues stabilizing and falling, costs rising, and the two lines flirting between black and red no man's lands. It stretched out, ten years into the future, slowly fading away.

"Following our best inference, you can still be in business a decade from now, making a reasonable profit relative to your industry," Richard said.

"Our industry doesn't make a profit."

Richard shook his head sadly and sighed, as if he'd just discovered the entire world was a cheat, and both he and Jere were set up for the worst rogering. Jere just looked at him. Richard couldn't get a job acting in zero-budget student linears for in-dorm streaming.

"Bullshit!" Jere slammed a hand down on the desk, then stood and paced. He was wound up with nervous energy, an overcharged battery, hot and ready to burst. The two dataspooks watched him like a tennis match.

"It's really your only choice," Edward said. The projector image changed. This time it showed revenue continuing to climb for about a year, then sharp downward spikes as sponsors dropped out and lawsuits hit. In less than two years, they were bankrupt.

"These are guesses."

"No. These are certified models from Four-eleven's enterprise-level inference algorithms. They are our best view of the future: ninety-one-point-three percent accurate over a sixteen month window, and exponentially increasing. The most solid, stable, and trusted brands use Four-eleven, from Toyota to ExxonMobil. Oversight came to us for our modeling prowess. We are the future." Richard grinned, dick that he was.

Jere recalled the day that really launched Neteno. Shelly, his girlfriend at the time, remembered his dad had said at some family dinner that they should watch *Casablanca*. She'd accessed it one night, when Jere was too tired to do much other than complain through the black-and-white titles, and make fun of the cigarette smoking. But when the movie was over, Shelly was crying, and even Jere was feeling something that he hadn't felt from the morass of user-generated and found media, or from interactives and even professional linears.

Holy crap, he thought, If this eighty-year-old film with guys in funny uniforms can affect me, maybe this is the story thing that dad always talked about, the thing he said we lost back when the age of television got eaten by the internet.

And, after a few YouTube experiments with impossible stories and heart-wrenching exclusives, it exploded into Neteno the powerhouse, Neteno the savior of linear entertainment, Neteno the spirit of television risen. All without a dime of Dad's money.

"I understand how you feel," Richard said.

"No you don't!" Jere said.

"It's really not so bad. You can make a good life from this business scenario."

Except it wouldn't be Neteno.

"We can help you maximize the potential of negative growth. There are many opportunities to—"

"What if I don't go along with it?"

Richard's lips pursed, like a teacher who'd just found a student watching RedTube on his tablet. "Everything is risk management. If you don't follow our recommendations, your business is higher risk."

"So you'll put out the word, and banks won't lend to me anymore." And without loans, Neteno was done. They couldn't fund forward from cash flow. Not at their growth rates.

"It's not that simple. But yes, I think raising capital will be more difficult, and the loans you get will be considered high risk, which demands higher rates."

"And today's currency market is highly fluid," Edward added. He changed the slide. "The new dollar is destabilizing against the Yuan, while Walmart Rewards Points and Gen3 VBux are rising again. Small changes in risk may net you loan rates that are simply unsustainable."

Sharks in suits, is what these guys are. Smiling sharks sailing down the sea of stability.

"There's already a small increase in rates baked into the long-term, stable scenario," Richard said. The hard sell. Of course that's how it would go.

No matter how it goes, they're squeezing my nuts. "What do I have to do, if I want to move forward?"

"On which path?"

"The . . . safe one."

I thought Neteno took chances. Echoes of that old asshole from the other week.

"We can have a provisional business plan ready for you to follow in a couple of weeks. Of course, this will increase our engagement with you. I'll have a proposal for that on your desk tomorrow."

Jere went back and sat down at his desk. "Why?" he asked.

"Why what?" Richard, sounding happy.

"Why do you still want to work with me?"

"Because, Mr. Gutierrez, there's always risk." Jerome again. It sounded like he was speaking through a smile. "It just has to be measured in terms of reward."

When they left, Jere looked up at the glowing Neteno sign, suspended in space. Little bits of dust sparkled in its smooth perfection. Below, Hollywood seemed to look up and laugh.

Safe

It was Patrice Klein's second Christmas bash with Jere. A reminder that she'd been seeing him for over a year. Not that it was an exclusive thing, but she did keep coming back. Jere wasn't scared of YZ. Jere was always fun. He always *went there*.

Except tonight. Even though she was full YZ Party, in a low-cut shimmering silver dress that showed off her curves (and even augmented them in a couple of places, thanks to new smartfabrics), Jere was quiet. He didn't even react when a publicity-bug jumped out in front of them to grab a photo at the intersection of Hollywood and Sunset.

Patrice knew she could ask. But YZ wouldn't ask. If Jere didn't de-morose, YZ would find someone more interesting at the party. And YZ would have no problem leaving with him.

The bash was at Jere's dad's house. Ron Gutierrez was old school. He lived in a sprawling gothic horror of a house on top of the Hollywood Hills. Built in the boomtime eighties with studio money flowing free, it looked like something you'd use for the set of a turn-of-the-century English boys' school. It rose—gray, stony, and severe—from among transplanted pines and impossibly perfect grass. From the circular drive in front, you could see the lights of the San Fernando Valley, glittering like so many pieces of junk jewelry on cheap black velvet. From the back, you could stand and look out at the towers of downtown Los Angeles, just waiting for the Big One to bring them down. Sometimes you could hear the popping of machine guns from South Central or spot fires where a microriot was breaking.

And Jere's dad loved Christmas. Not because he was religious, but because he was able to show off. He could get the house up in the most outrageous decorations (including, this year, a robotic free-range Santa, mingling with the guests like a spastic non sequitur-spewing rendition of St. Nicholas with a floating "Merry Christmas" circling his head). He could wear stupid outfits, like brocade smoking jackets and knee socks with cigars on them. He could eat to excess on pheasant and Belgian chocolate and crispy cinnamon churros and it was all okay because it was Christmas, the season of excess and indulgence. But most of all, he could show off, and dispense his largesse to kid, grandkid, uncle, aunt, cousin, or nephew—always with a degree of staging that managed to put all eyes on Ron Gutierrez.

Which was probably why he didn't like Jere so much. Jere had made it on his own, and drew too much attention with his success.

Patrice and Jere ducked inside through a side door, dodged the robot Santa ("Holiday blessings, young men," a deep voice said, as they passed it), and slipped into the kitchen, where Jere's mom, Sonya, was presiding over a staff of five kitcheneers. The smells of turkey, pheasant, goose, stuffing, homemade noodles, mashed potatoes, and fresh cranberries bubbling in a pot the size of a small bathtub, all brought instant memories of holidays past.

Jere snuck up behind his mother, grabbed her by the arms, and said, "Boo!"

Sonya shrieked, jumped two feet in the air, and spun, beating at Jere with a wooden spoon. With a grim sidewise glance at Patrice, she chased Jere through the dining room and into the living room. Patrice followed. Assembled kids giggled and adults smiled as the chase continued. Sonya had had a respectable career as an actress at one time and enjoyed her own style of theatrics almost as much as her husband.

Jere came up short at the big picture window that opened onto the balcony and held up his hands. "Hey!"

His mother whacked him with the spoon.

"Stop it!"

More whacking. Patrice felt eyes fall on her as she crossed the room to join Jere.

"Mom, is that thing even clean?"

Sonya stopped. Glared at the spoon, glared at him, then gathered him up in a big hug. Jere hugged her back, hard. Looking over Jere's shoulder at Patrice, she narrowed her eyes threateningly, but with an unmistakable twinkle. "You're supposed to make him behave," she told Patrice.

"I think you have mistaken me for someone else," Patrice said.

Mom blew out an exaggerated sigh and released Jere. "Then *you* behave," she said, waving the spoon.

Jere's grin suddenly disappeared. "That's what everyone keeps telling me."

"What?"

"To play by the rules."

His mother gave him a glare that was supposed to look menacing. It looked like a Chihuahua trying to stand down a Doberman. Patrice tried not to laugh.

"Patrice," said a voice, behind her. "Or should I say, Yvette?"

Patrice turned. Samuel Cho stood there, with a painfully slim, dark-haired woman on his arm. She had worked with Samuel briefly at Gen3 after they'd bought Yvette Zero. He was a bulky man, with a square and perfect face, like he'd bought it out of a magazine at the Cosmetic Surgery Outlet—but inside he was ethically small and far from perfect. He'd made a pass at her. More than a pass. Once.

"Samuel," she said, extending a hand to avoid his hug. "How's life after Gen3?"

"Not bad," he said. "I'm working with EA now."

Patrice nodded. EA was the big time. But the "working with" was carefully worded, which meant he was probably just a contractor. She wished YZ had been gauche enough to wear an eyeset to the party.

Samuel's eyes flickered from Jere to Yvette. "How's life with the king of linear entertainment?"

Patrice smirked. "Maybe you should ask him how life is with the queen of MMO."

Samuel opened his mouth, but no words came out.

"Hey Samuel. Why don't you introduce my sister?" Jere asked, nodding at the slim woman.

Samuel blushed. "Oh. Uh. Yes. Patrice, have you met Evi Gutierrez?"

"Not until now," Patrice said. "Nice to meet you, Evi. That's a brilliant dress."

Evi went from grumpy to gleaming. "You really think so?"

"I never say something I don't mean."

Eyes wide. "Oh."

"Evi's in interactive," Jere said. "Creative side."

"So you know me," Patrice said.

"Everyone knows you."

Samuel, forgotten, frowned and shifted his weight. He was getting bored, which wasn't good. Bored people ruined parties.

You don't fuck up a dad party, Jere had told her. And she knew he was serious.

As if reading her mind, Jere's dad breezed in from the balcony, trailing the reek of cigar. He wore a bright red smoking jacket, embroidered with electronic reindeer, flashing red noses and running simple animations. Patrice's nose tickled, but she didn't react. She never got used to the smell of smoking, whether it was cigarettes or cigars. The one time she'd tried smoking a cigarette, she'd gotten light-headed and puked. That was the end of any fascination.

"Jere," his dad said, clapping Jere on the shoulder. Jere shrugged off the hand and gave his father a forced smile. "And Patrice. Or should I say YZ? Good to see you both."

"Great party," Patrice said.

"Yeah, it's always fun. Want to come out for a few?"

Jere looked uncertain. "Uh. Sure."

Jere glanced back at her, shaking his head, before Ron popped back into the room and said, "You can come out too. No family secrets here."

Patrice joined them on the balcony. The towers of Los Angeles glowed in the distance, resembling a complete set of futuristic nosehair trimmers. Patrice heard a party horn, loud and long, coming from down in Hollywood, over the rush of traffic on Highland.

"What's up?" Jere asked.

Ron went to the railing and leaned. He picked up a cigar, drew deep, blew out smoke. "What do you mean, what's up? Can't a dad talk to his son?" The animated reindeer turned to look at Jere and Patrice.

"You mean, talk *at* me?"

His father's expression hardened instantly. "How'd I raise you to be so suspicious?"

"Oh, I don't know . . . " Jere shot a glance at Patrice and said nothing else. The silence dragged out. Drunken whooping from a house down the street filled it.

"Shoot," Jere said, finally.

"You saw a friend of mine the other day. Evan McMaster."

"Evan McMaster . . . ah, shit, yeah." Jere nodded.

"It's a good idea."

Jere pinched his mouth shut. For a long time, Patrice thought he'd say nothing. Then: "Yeah. It's a great idea. It's also too big. Way too big. There ain't enough money in my universe to buy that kinda big."

"You've done big things before."

"No."

"You won't even think about it?"

"No."

Ron sighed. "I thought Neteno took chances."

Jere's hands tightened on the railing, and he squeezed his eyes tight shut.

"I thought you, of everyone—"

"No!" Jere said. "No no no no no! Can't do it. Won't do it. Won't even think about it." He looked up at them, his eyes full of tears.

Tears.

Jere didn't cry. Patrice knew Jere didn't cry. He was on top of the world, always a lot of fun. She'd never seen him cry. Patrice felt she was, somehow, intruding and wanted to slink back into the party. But she was too far from the door.

Instead, she reached out and took his arm. Jere jumped. "What happened?" she asked.

"Four-eleven assholes," Jere said.

"Four-eleven, as in the risk managers?"

"As in the sharks, as in the fucks, as in the you-gotta-ramp-it-down dickweeds," Jere said.

"What'd they do?" Patrice asked.

"I have to be good. Or nobody will lend to me."

Suddenly everything made sense. Nobody bet against 411. They were the datagods, they set the odds for nearly everything, especially since the Second Great Recession. No wonder Jere had been so grumpy.

Ron nodded, as if none of this was a surprise. "Cut off the money and the network is dead. That's one thing that'll never change. What about alts, though, gamebux, indiefunds, have you thought of that?"

"Of course."

"And?"

"And what happens when they see Four-eleven's reports? They'll get right the hell out. All bow to Four-eleven now."

Ron turned to look out over LA. "I see," he said, after a while.

"I see what?" Jere asked.

"I see you giving up."

"I'm not giving up."

Ron said nothing.

"If I don't play it safe, Neteno is dead in two years."

Nothing.

"I have to do this."

Nothing. Then, a slow turn. Movie-perfect. Ron said, softly. "I see a kid who never thought he had to do anything. I see a kid who wouldn't take money from his dad. I see a kid who made the TV-is-dead pundits eat their words."

Jere stood, open-mouthed.

Ron unfolded a smile and aimed it at Patrice. "We should go in," he said. "Mingle."

"But—"

"No buts. It's getting towards dinner, and you need to show off this beautiful girl."

"Dad—"

Ron held up a hand. "No." His voice was firm. He pushed Jere towards the big glass doors. Warm light lit his face with a devilish glow. He gathered Patrice and pushed her ahead, as well.

After Jere had gone in though, Ron leaned close to Patrice and whispered. "Don't give up."

She started to turn, but he pushed her through the doors.

Call

Glowing on turkey and pinot noir, Jere braved his old bedroom, set at the top of Dad's house where cell reception was best. It had been made over with half-wall wood paneling and light blue wallpaper, and housed a frilly bed and white-painted shelves. Not a trace of Jere remained.

He put on his eyeset and found Evan's number. Eyetyped it. Waited. Expecting to get the old man generic message.

But Evan picked up.

"Hello!" Evan yelled. Behind him was the crunch of music. It sounded like a titty bar.

"It's Jere Gutierrez."

"One sec!" A curse and some banging and the music faded away to a tolerable level. "There. That's better. You—"

"Let's move forward with *Winning Mars*," Jere said.

Silence. Music swelled to fill it as the microphone struggled for words.

"You're assuming the project is still available."

"Can it, Evan."

"I've been working with—"

"I'll hang up the phone right now."

More silence. Then a sigh.

"Okay."

"You said you'd throw in."

A beat. Then, "Yes."

"All of it?"

"Yes."

"You'll sign a personal guarantee?"

A longer beat. "Yes."

So the old asshole really believed in it. "You mentioned alternate funding. What sponsor connections do you have?"

"Quite a few. Some are stale, but I can—"

"So nothing."

"No, not nothing!"

Jere sighed. "Start making a list. Start with the ones with the deepest pockets and biggest balls. I mean, like hit-the-doorframe-when-they-walk-through-doors balls."

"I will. When do you want to meet?

"Be in the Neteno office tomorrow a.m. And, uh, Evan?"

"What?" His voice quivered with excitement. Jere pictured one of those spastic little purse-dogs, wiggling and pissing on itself.

"Nobody is going to die."

Silence for a long time. Then something: a snort, a laugh.

Jere sighed. It didn't matter.

"Fuck you very much, Four-eleven," he whispered.

Riches

Patrice Klein lay beside Jere and looked up at the fake stars glittering in his ceiling. She was naked, just Patrice. Not any flavor of YZ. Because she needed a break from YZ. She couldn't be YZ all the time.

Or so she kept telling herself.

And it was okay. Because Jere loved YZ, but Jere also loved Patrice. Or at least liked her. She could see the relief in his eyes when she stripped off all the costumes and pretense.

Jere was on his side, softly breathing into her ear. His flesh was smooth, cool. His body temperature always seemed to run at least five degrees cooler than her's—really the only thing about him in bed she didn't like. They were in Jere's highrise condo, all concrete and colorless and spiky and grim. Jere lived like a college kid that who that had come into a lot of money. Which, more or less, he was.

Even that was okay, because Jere was Jere again: happy, going places, ignoring her, then loving her. She didn't know what he was doing. Her only clue was the name "Evan McMaster" and her eyeset came up mainly blank on him. He'd produced some TV shows she'd never heard of, way back. And of course, there was no public data on Jere's deal with 411.

"What are you doing?" she said, softly. She didn't expect a response. Jere slept like the dead.

Jere didn't move.

"What's your new game, Jere?"

Jere turned to look at her, eyes wide open.

"You're awake," she said.

He nodded.

"You don't have to answer me."

Jere stood up, naked, and walked through the darkened room. Simulated starlight chased down his slim but well-defined legs. Patrice liked to watch him walk.

He snugged on his eyeset. "Sweep room. Highest level scan."

After a moment, he seemed satisfied. He took off the eyeset and came back to bed, kneeling on the covers like a little kid. "We're going to do the biggest thing in the history of entertainment."

"No, really. What are you doing?"

"No, really." Jere's eyes locked on hers, dead serious.

She waited.

"We're bringing back the reality show, and we're going to Mars."

Mars. Mars. For a moment, it didn't register. Then, thoughts ricocheted: Mars? Mars the planet? Ares, ancient god of war?

"Simulated?"

"No."

But that was ridiculous! Suddenly she wanted her eyeset. She wanted to run the numbers—space travel was for governments and gamers and gangstas, not for television.

"That's crazy!"

"I know," Jere said.

"Is this why Four-eleven wouldn't back you?"

Jere sighed, shook his head. "Four-eleven happened before. This is . . . this is my way of saying 'fuck you' to them."

"Tilting at windmills."

"What?"

Patrice shook her head. Jere wasn't a literati. "Do you realize how insane you are?"

"I think so."

Neither said anything more for a long, long time.

"Why?" Patrice said, finally.

"If I'm going down, I'm going to go down big."

And that made her happy. Because that was Jere. Jere who *went there*.

"Do you need investors?"

"Of course. The numbers are runaway silly." He gave her a quick little glance, as if asking, Is this an offer?

He probably didn't know how much money she had. Nobody did, really. Her wealth was entirely private. Most of it in Gen3 VBux, which was one of the strongest currencies on the market. It killed the dollar in the last down rally. Gen3 had replaced their stock with it.

She remembered an economics professor from way back had said that today, currency valuation is a function of people's belief. A whole lot of people wanted to believe in Gen3's fantasy worlds, rather than in the grim reality of modern deficits and rebalancing and sustainability calcs and GNP-slimming. The real power was in the story, which Jere knew so well. Even if he couldn't articulate it.

But she had wealth. Enough to knock off eleven of the one hundred richest people on the planet, according to *Fortune*. Unless there were other icebergs like her, hidden. And of course there had to be. She wondered how many there were.

She almost asked him: What are the numbers like?

But she didn't.

"You could be on it," Jere said.

"What?"

"Be a contestant."

Patrice went cold.

"YZ, the first significant character on another world," Jere said.

In that moment, she saw herself, strapped into some silly spacesuit, running across a dim salmon-colored landscape, full of rocks and rivulets. She saw herself falling. She heard the crunch of her leg, breaking. She saw YZ, losing. For all to see.

And that wasn't fun.

"No," she said.

"It would help with the publicity—"

"No!"

Jere drew back. "I'm sorry. I just thought you'd like to—"

"No."

"Okay. Sorry." Jere looked confused.

Ask me for money, she thought.

But he didn't.

Orbit

Man oh man do they have this flyover country thing down, Jere thought, after hours of Russia. Ain't got nothing but.

Beside him, Evan rattled on about hotels rooms he'd trashed, women he had fucked in cabs, deals he made with nothing more than a napkin and an pencil and a whole lotta balls. He eyed the female flight attendants, even the ugly ones. He blew his old-man breath on Jere.

I'll make sure our seats on the flight back are far apart, Jere thought.

Krainly Airport could have been Austin or Burbank. Just another regional airport. The only differences were the English tags floating over the Cyrillic characters on all the signs and ads in Jere's eyeset.

A tall, stocky, dirty-blond man wearing the largest and shiniest chrome-and-wood eyeset that Jere had ever seen waited for them in baggage claim. Jere's own eyeset stubbornly refused to tag him. He held a hand-lettered sign that read: McMASTER/GUTTEREZ.

His eyes lit when he saw Evan. "Good morning, Mr. McMaster," No-name said. He spoke English with only the slightest trace of a Russian accent. "Mr. Guterrez."

"Gutierrez," Jere said, emphasizing the *i*."

The blond man gave him a moment's blank stare, then shook his head. "Of course. Sorry."

"It's all right," Evan said. "Valentin Ladenko, Jere Gutierrez."

"Call me Leninsk."

"Leninsk?" Jere said. The name sounded familiar, but his eyeset revealed no wisdom.

Evan burst into a big old-man barrel-laugh. "Stop kidding, Vally," he said, slapping the other man on the back. "You'll confuse the mark."

"Mark?" Jere said.

The two men both laughed.

"I'm not a mark," Jere said.

Evan laughed again. "Lighten up. Let the old farts kid around a bit. Vally, any chance we can partake of local hospitality before we launch?"

"I would prefer Leninsk to Vally."

Evan just cocked his head.

Valentin looked heavenward. "To answer your other question, no. Your launch is in three hours. I have already had to bend the rules to get you in without orientation."

"There are rules?" Evan said.

"Yes."

"Funny, never got the manual."

Valentin frowned. "I will wait until you get your bags."

While they were waiting for their luggage, Jere leaned close to Evan. "Who's that?"

"Vally. The guy I've been working with."

"Why isn't he tagged in my eyeset?"

Evan looked skyward.

"Is he . . . ?"

"*Organizatsiya*? Sure, why not."

"I just . . . I mean, they're sending us up free? As a teaser? Is that how it works?"

Evan squinted his eyes shut, as if the question brought him physical pain. "They really want our business," Evan said. "But, if we decide not to do it, I think we'd want to find a way to get these very nice people some very nice gifts."

"Gifts?"

"Specifically, the kind that are paper and printed with green and black ink."

It took a moment to decode Evan's oldmanspeak. He was talking about money. Untraceable multicolored bills, most likely yuan. Not nice easy-to-follow VBux or EAkash. Gifts.

It felt like a baseball was stuck in Jere's throat. He swallowed it. "Evan, I don't know about this."

Evan shrugged. "What's done is done."

"What does that mean?"

Evan leaned a little closer. "It means, don't even think about backing out now."

Jere shivered. Great. What am I getting into?

He was very happy when the bags arrived.

Valentin had a new Mercedes, a big gasoline S-Class, waiting for them outside, idling. In front of the airport. With nobody in it. He piloted them past more big Mercedes, Tesla limos, Daewoo microcars, and the odd goat on the road out of the airport. Jere didn't even realize he'd seen the latter until they were on a narrow, cracked highway, leading into more of the bleak land.

"Goats?" Jere said.

Evan chuckled.

"We are very cosmopolitan," Valentin said, flashing laser-white teeth in the rearview.

Ahead of them, a bright light bloomed, illuminating far mountains and low clouds. A roar soon followed, and a brilliant spark began climbing into the sky.

"Was that ours? Did we miss it?" Jere said.

"I think that was a SpaceX flight," Evan said, squinting up at the now rapidly disappearing dot.

Valentin nodded. "SpaceX."

And we're not approaching SpaceX. Why? Jere wondered. But he instantly knew the answer: Too expensive, won't deal, too interwoven with 411, yada yada.

As they got closer to their destination, Jere noted a bizarre mix of vehicles More big S-classes, BMW Ms, Lexuses, and Cadillacs competed with fuel cell personal transports and solar-powered Chinese Tsos. What little they saw of the town of Baikonur was a jumble of grim multi-story apartments and shining fanciful new hotels, including the Sputnik II, which looked like it had been braided out of glass ribbons.

Evan saw where Jere was looking. "Lots of space money coming in here," he said.

"Including the world's first trillionaire," Valentin said. "Fyodor Pushkin, creator of the *Star's Wars* games."

"*Star Wars?*"

"*Star's Wars,*" Evan said. "Space-based MMO with virtual currency, the Ruro, has been doing very well on the currency exchanges the past couple of years." A link appeared in Jere's eyeset.

"Where does game money intersect with space?" Jere asked.

"When there's nothing else to spend it on," Valentin said, chuckling. He dodged a suicidal goat. "You could say there would be no space without fake money."

At Baikonur Cosmodrome, they drove past a big mural of a man in an old-fashioned spacesuit, spreading his arms wide. Evan explained it was called "The Fisherman," after a cosmonaut who was bragging about a fish he caught in a nearby river. At that moment, Jere decided that Russia was nothing like Austin, nope, no way, no how.

They had the RusSpace terminal done up in orange-tinted concrete, with uncomfortable furniture that looked like Chinese knock-offs of old Eames designs. It offered a good view of the RusSpace rocket. Old style, as they said. Jere remembered seeing pictures of the old space shuttle, and other delta-winged sketches of fanciful spacecraft, but RusSpace had none of that. It was just a slim needle, bulging slightly towards the top, with a row of tiny dots near the front that Jere figured were portholes.

The terminal smelled of good espresso and vodka, but their escort hurried them along. As soon as they arrived at the RusSpace customer service counter, a woman started yelling at Valentin in Russian; he responded with shouting of his own. The exchange ended when he handed Jere and Evan off to her. She rushed them down a long tiled corridor to an elevator that took them up to the passenger capsule of the RusSpace craft—where every face turned to look at them, all angry.

Jere heard a babble of comments in various languages. The ones in English were not exactly complimentary.

"What's wrong?" he asked the woman.

"You one hour late!" she said.

"Oh."

She helped them climb in and set their straps. They were in something that looked like a cross between a commercial airliner and a bus. Five rows of four across seats with high, flat backs were bolted to the vertical interior of bare aluminum. The seats pointed skywards, and they had to climb to them at the top of the cabin using handholds and footholds. There, they could sit back and look upward. It was a vertigo-inducing experience, and Jere knew why people glared. He tried to smile at the couple sitting opposite them, two middle-aged, very elegantly dressed Asians. They ignored him, just staring straight ahead.

Jere sighed. I'm with you. Let's get it over with.

But there was one difference, he realized. Until they had to wait an hour on their backs, they were probably here to have fun. To have a great experience. To spend a whole lot of money. They had every right to expect it to be perfect.

"Isn't Valentin going?" Jere asked.

Evan shook his head. "You think they have any spare seats? Every one of these go up full."

Twenty people, twice a week. Five million a launch. Jere ran the numbers in his head. Five hundred twenty million a year. Not exactly huge numbers. No wonder they were interested in the Mars project. Though . . .

"I'm hearing that the numbers you gave me might be very optimistic," Jere said.

"What numbers?"

"For our current project."

Evan's eyes got wide. "You've been asking around? Are you insane? Three words in front of the wrong audience, and we're blown—"

"Give me some credit. I just had my sister's friend's kid look it up a bit, like he was doing a paper or something."

"Oh." Evan looked a little surprised.

That made Jere feel good. So you don't know all the tricks, he thought. Jere waited.

Evan licked his lips. "We'll discuss cost later. Just know there's a lot of sources out there, most of them for only a single purpose: to keep you from ever wanting to do what we're doing."

"Is that true?"

Evan nodded. "Yes. It is." And he said no more.

Less than five minutes later, the pilot gave a brief welcome in Russian, followed by Chinese and English versions. There was a minute's worth of countdown, mirrored in the flatscreen at the front of the cabin, and Jere felt something like an earthquake. He was pushed back in his seat, hard, like several bags of cement had suddenly been piled on top of him.

The roar and vibration drowned all of his thoughts but one: I never asked Evan how RusSpace's safety record was.

Jere saw motion and looked over to the side. His head snapped violently down, pulled by the force of their acceleration. He felt a sharp twinge of pain, and closed his eyes. When he opened them, streamers of mist were threading in complex patterns outside the tiny portholes. The sky was a deep blue-black.

Jere tried to look back upwards, but his neck howled in pain. He relaxed and watched the portholes. The streamers fell away, and the sky slowly changed from blue-black to entirely black. He could see the pinpricks of stars.

Space, Jere thought. I'm in space. This is insanely stupid. Why am I here?

A small voice in the back of his head provided a sarcastic response: Be glad you didn't blow up.

The roar and vibration stopped, all at once. Jere felt the crushing weight fall away. He looked back towards the front of the cabin. Another sharp twinge in his neck, but otherwise he seemed functional.

Jere felt . . . light, real light, like an express elevator nearing the top of the building. The cabin did something odd. He'd been looking up, but it wasn't up, it was forward. It heeled over again, and he was staring down a long metal tube, falling, seemingly motionless.

They were falling towards Earth! Jere gripped the arms of his chair.

"Evan, uh," he said. The words squeaked from between his clenched teeth. "We're falling."

Evan didn't look at him. "Of course. That's why they call it free fall."

"I, uh, oh, shi—" Jere said, as half-digested airline dinner hit the back of his throat.

"Use the bag!" Evan said, pushing himself away from Jere. Jere saw pens floating in the air, in the seats ahead of him. A kid, maybe eleven or twelve, had unbuckled himself and was floating in air. A flight—space?—attendant worked her way back to him, pulling herself by the railing on what was now the ceiling.

Evan scrabbled through the seat-back pocket and extracted a bag. It still bore a United Airlines logo. He thrust it at Jere, just as the airline food exited his mouth at what seemed like about a hundred miles an hour. Jere watched a red-brown gush fly into the the cabin, fascinated and horrified at the same time at the floating mess.

The attendant squinted at him as if marking him for some terrible punishment, and chased the puke. She held something that looked very much like a butterfly net but with translucent plastic in the place of netting. Jere had to laugh. It echoed over the expressions of disgust as the vomit hit the wall near a porthole. Part of it rebounded, but the stewardess caught it with her net.

"Bag!" Evan said. "Before you do it again."

Jere realized he was still holding the bag. He popped it open and held it to his face. He didn't feel like he had to puke again, but better safe than not.

"Gross!" the kid said, disappearing down beneath his seatback. Assorted adults glared at him.

"It's okay," the stewardess said, her expression saying it was anything but. "These things happen."

"I'm sorry," Jere said, into the bag.

He only had to use the bag once more before they docked with the RusSpace/Hilton Hotel, even then it wasn't so bad. He was by a porthole, watching as they approached the slowly spinning wheel, and he thought, God, it's like those old movies, those ones where we fly around the universe, a fucking space station, really.

But then he saw the RusSpace and Hilton and Scaled and Boeing and Starbucks logos, and he thought, Holy shit, this thing will really work. As the the shuttle wheeled around, his point of view changed, and he grabbed for his bag before he had a chance to see more remains of his dinner.

They wheeled towards the end of the hotel, spun the shuttle to match it, and slotted in with a metallic clang.

Pretty professional, Jere thought. As he climbed out of the shuttle, he noted a wall-mounted caulking gun with a tube of GE silicone sealer in it. His eyeset tagged the Russian lettering on the case: FOR LEAK USE.

The hotel was small and cramped, with hallways that seemed to curve upwards forever. Jere felt disoriented, and had to use another bag twice before he got to his room. The girl who escorted him—and had provided the bag—seemed genuinely concerned. She spoke English with something of a Midwest twang.

"You're American?" Jere asked.

"Yep," she said. "Nebraska."

"Why are you here?"

A grin. "Anyplace is better than Nebraska."

"No. I'm serious. Why here?"

She stopped for a moment, and turned to face Jere. "Beats getting an accounting degree to count some almighty's money."

Jere nodded. That was a sentiment he could agree with. He wondered, idly, how many young accountants had thought about killing their whales, just to get the money back into circulation, just to free up some assets.

"What do you do?" she asked.

"I run Neteno. We're . . . uh, we produce television shows."

A frown. "Television? I thought that was . . . well, not doing so well."

"We're not doing bad."

She turned back, took a few steps, then stopped and looked at him again. "Seriously, I'm here because—because it's space! I'm on a real space station! When I was a kid and America stopped shuttle flights, it was like we gave up a dream," she said, with a cool intensity that made her look ten years older than she was. "That's why I'm here. This is the future. This is what matters."

Fuck, Jere thought. It was like the early years of the internet. Like those interviews of all those young kids who thought they were changing the world.

This could work.

Evan came down the hall towards them, probably back from settling into his own room. "Getting lined up?" he said, looking from Jere to the hostess.

"No," Jere said, as she looked away, with a frown.

"They're all available, don't let them tell you they aren't. I already negotiated down from the ratesheet."

Jere just looked at Evan. He wanted to tell him to shut up. But he said nothing.

Evan slapped him on the shoulder and slid past, down the narrow hall. "See you in the bar."

"I'm sorry," Jere said to the girl. He didn't even know her name.

His hostess led him the rest of the way to his room in silence.

He tipped Miss Nebraska, smiled and thanked her, hoping she'd realize he wasn't an asshole like Evan, and entered his room.

Jere sat on the narrow little bed. There was another tiny round porthole, just like the one on the shuttle, where he could see the Earth below. He looked until he felt queasy again.

The wallscreen displayed advertising in English for the EarthView Bar and Grille, with sky-wide panoramic window. Jere shuddered, and hoped there was another place to eat.

A week of this. Dismal thought. But he also thought of his unnamed hostess, full of idealism and intensity. If this enthusiasm could reach Nebraska, he could reach half the world.

And make them believe in Mars.

Leak

Patrice found Jere in the London Underground, a pub-themed restaurant stuffed into an old basement under Sunset Boulevard. It was a dark place, lacking both light and reception. No wimax, no gigacell, no connectivity, period. Wrapped in copper foil and scanned every minute for microbugs, the pub proudly displayed mediascape flatlines on the big wallscreens. Discreet signs warned "no phones, no photos, no video, no tagging, no kidding."

Real stars went there when they wanted to be dark. Wannabe stars hung out, pretending they were important enough to follow. It was all very cool, so cool that it didn't even have flatscreens for real-time exchange rates. People had to take a chance if they wanted to order a beer with dollars or EAkash.

Heads swiveled when Patrice entered, and eyes continued to follow. Today was a full YZ day, YZ Vamp, YZ to show off for the bigwigs from China from whom Gen3 was courting money. She had no day-to-day duties, but they expected her to be available for important appearances.

Which made it all the more uncomfortable when 411 showed up, asking questions.

Jere was buried at the end of the bar, head down over a Guiness. He cocked an ear at the old guy he was doing the *Winning Mars* deal with. What was his name? Patrice's eyeset had gone red-tag city when she stepped into the bar. She had no idea. She'd have to fake it.

"—thought we'd have more—" Jere was saying, as she walked up. He saw her, stopped, and did a movie-perfect double-take.

"How'd you know I was here?"

"Little birdies."

"That's not funny! This place is supposed to be dark. Has Four-eleven been bugging me?"

Patrice shook her head. "Sorry. There's no intrigue. Your assistant at Neteno likes me, is all."

A nod. "Patrice, we're busy."

She nodded in return. "I just thought you might want to know Four-eleven came to see me this morning."

"Shit," the old guy said. Evan, she suddenly remembered, *that* was his name. He shook his head in disgust, his eyes never leaving Patrice's cleavage.

"What'd they want?" Jere asked.

"They wanted to talk about a new show of yours."

"Ah." Jere didn't look surprised.

"They knew what it was."

"Oh."

"They weren't happy."

"Yeah, we know," Jere said. "They had China Bank freeze our main line of credit."

Evan laughed. "They got our attention."

"Yes, indeed they do." Jere's voice was dead flat, the kind of dead flat Patrice had heard only once before. The night of the Christmas bash. The night at his dad's house. And she knew what it meant: Jere was considering throwing in the towel.

Patrice hated it when he was like that. Jere was Jere because he thought he could do anything, and since he thought he could do anything, most of the time he could convince enough people he could do anything, and then he ended up doing it, even though every sane person knew it was impossible.

Yet here he was, holding 411's leash, getting ready to put their collar around his neck.

"We should call them," Jere said, softly.

"And tell them what?" Evan asked. "Pretty-please, give us back our money? Please don't put our plan out for everyone in the world to see? Don't put us at the bottom of your investment picks and pans, together with a neat little notation, 'Unnamed Space-Based Campaign, Mars.' Because once any potential sponsors see that, you might as well forget that end-run, might as well give up going direct, because we're toast, stick a fork in us, done."

"Yes. I know."

"So—tell them what, then?"

Jere said nothing.

She knew he was thinking of packing it in. Patrice couldn't let him do that. She had to say something, even something stupid. "What about your dad? Can he help?"

Jere's knuckles whitened on the thin pint glass. Patrice expected to see a shower of blood and Guinness. "No," he said, finally.

"You're sure?"

"Yes."

"Jere."

"Stop!" he said, loud enough for other patrons to turn and look. He glared at Patrice. But his eyes had lost the dead flatness. They were blazing again. They darted back and forth. Jere spun his glass. For a long time, there was no sound except the murmur of the other customers.

Then: "Does everything have to be measured and rated and scored?" Jere asked. "Somehow, we got through the twentieth century without Four-eleven being rammed down our throats. We even had, what, the radio and TV and internet booms. How did they do it? They must have had whole lots of people telling them, 'Wow, that's a dumb idea, why would you do that?' But there was someone out there who would take a chance."

"Lee Iacocca did it," Evan said.

"Who?"

"The guy behind the Ford Mustang. In the sixties. The beancounters came to him, a year before launch, and said, 'Where's the research? Show us this'll be a hit.' So he made it up. All the research. Just fucking faked it. End result? One of the two most popular cars in the world, still. They sold over a million of them in the first two years. Twenty million to date."

"It's a different world now." Patrice, playing the foil.

Jere flushed red with anger and took a long drink.

"Can we turn it into a populist campaign, a crowdfund?" Jere asked. "I mean, there's what, four hundred million people in this country? Or hell, open it up worldwide. Eight billion people, get a few bucks from each."

Evan shook his head "No. You'll never get even ten million to give you a few hundred. Not in time. Not before they start wondering what's happening with the money, before the IRS comes in and starts auditing. Taking money from banks is one thing. Taking it from peeps opens you up. You remember the Big Wall?"

"Yeah."

"Same thing."

Patrice remembered the Big Wall. They'd even started building it down on the Mexican border. There were still a few rusting steel plates left that hadn't been stolen.

"Fuck, what about Cameron?" Jere said. "Can't we convince him that he's gotta shoot his next techtacular there?"

Evan shook his head. "Already talked to him."

Jere slumped in his stool, but almost immediately straightened up. And laughed.

"The rabid fan," Jere said "There's gotta be big businesses owned by geeks who get off on space exploration."

Evan nodded. "It's the wrong sponsorship profile, though, tell you that right off. You ain't gonna nab Proctor and Gamble or Starbucks by betting the CEO's a geek. More likely technical, software, engineering, stuff like that."

"So?" Jere said. "Maybe they can help us build it too!"

"They aren't populist, though. Nobody will recognize the logos."

"So what? You think anyone watches this shit for the logos? Come on, Evan, the brandistas have melted your fucking brains."

Evan sat back and nodded. "You may be right. Fuck. Maybe we have them build it, get some momentum, add bigger guys later. Promise them a making-of special, something where all their techies can smile and show their bad teeth. Yeah. They might even go in bigger, 'cause they're the ones making it."

Jere leaned over the table, clenching his fists. "And we tell them, right up front: Four-eleven thinks we're crazy, and it'll never work. That they've already dismissed it, filed it away, put it in the shitcan."

"Shitting on their dream," Evan said. "That'll drive them nuts! We do this right, and our financial problems are over."

Jere high-fived Evan, then hugged Patrice, whirling her around in a circle. She screamed. The bar stopped to look at the crazy men and the video-game superstar in fishnets and a mini-skirt. Lots of people saw her underwear. For once, Patrice was happy this place was dark.

But Jere had a plan. That was what mattered.

I hope it works, she thought.

Fish

They even dressed the part.

Jere wore a thrift store white shirt with a thin black tie, ten years out of date, with zero-prescription glasses in the thin-rimmed style of five years ago. Evan wore a sweatshirt with a ragged Linux penguin on it. Jere worried that it was too much, but Evan had told him: *It's never too much, that's how these people are.*

Their target was Edward Muchney, of Muchney CarbonWerk, the guys who were trying to get the space elevator working, fer sure, you betcha, just one more test this time. In the meantime they'd managed to get a whole bunch of Asian cities, from Guangzhou to Osaka to Manila, to go for their carbon nanotube high-wire taxis, so you could hire a little car and float serenely across the city, above the packed traffic below. Thousand-foot-high concrete and nanotube pylons, spaced more than a mile apart, held the ultra-tough cable. They'd tried to get LA to buy into the idea a few years ago, but NIMBYs scared of earthquakes had scotched the plan.

But despite the LA setback, word was that Atlanta was gonna buy, and maybe Sao Paolo, and so Muchney Carbonwerk was riding high.

Even more importantly, Edward was the peak of the peak of their target audience, a rabid fan who didn't even try to hide it. He owned something like a quarter of *NextLife*, the favored hangout virtual transhumans preparing for the Rapture of the Nerds, as well as half a dozen VR communities, where he passed out favors, such as flying and private islands, to his friends. He was a member of the Mars Society, the Planetary Society, and the OffEarth Militants. He'd been to the Russian orbital hotel eleven times, and he'd tried to bribe the Chinese to take him to their base on the moon. He even wrote very bad science fiction that rotted on an old-fashioned textblog he'd last updated in 2019.

Edward was a tall, thin man who sat in the grim aluminum office of a low industrial building in Mojave. He sat back in his creaky old brown vinyl desk chair, eyeing Jere and Evan suspiciously. He wore two of the latest eyesets, shiny silver teardrops from the Indian company *Fruta*, promising full retinal coverage and bone-conduction sound in a single package. There were whispers that it was available with either a sensory block, for full-immersion viewing, or somatic integration, so the user could experience a full range of sensation in their worlds.

And if anyone has it, Edward does, Jere thought.

"I have no social graces," Edward said. Then he stopped. Nothing in the room moved, except for the dancing data reflected from the man's eyes.

Jere was first to speak. "I. Uh. I'm sorry, I don't understand."

"That was a warning," Edward said, closing his eyes. "I'm getting bored."

"Mr. Muchney, I—"

"Why do I have to always do this?" Edward said. "Get to the point."

"We want you to finance our Mars expedition," Evan said.

Edward leaned forward, his forehead furrowing. "I thought it was that. No."

"But—"

"No."

Jere expected this. He stood up. Dragged Evan to the door, over the other man's protests. He opened the door, paused, and said, softly, "I'm sorry. They win, Evan."

He was halfway through the door when Edward called out, "Who wins?"

Jere didn't dare smile. He turned back to Edward. "The little minds. The safeniks. The crying whining fucking babies who live in their safe little suburbs and keep us from becoming everything we can!" He let his voice rise near the end, and the last word echoed through the barren office.

Silence for a moment. Jere turned and made to leave.

"Wait."

Jere stopped and turned.

"This is all an act."

"No it isn't," Jere said, going back to his seat, leaning forward, his voice low and hard. "Of course, you think it is, because Four-eleven has crammed you full of lies."

"Four-eleven is the most reliable information network and risk—"

"You're spouting their fucking slogans!" Jere said.

Edward's mouth clicked shut.

"How did you make it?" Jere said, leaning forward conspiratorially. "By listening to what they said you could do, what was safe?"

"Of course not, but—"

"There's no *but*. You didn't even give us a chance to show our hand. We were going to tell you that yeah, Four-eleven is against this, they say we're full of crap, they say you'll lose all your money if you throw in. And that's exactly why you should do it."

"Why?"

"Because it's going to work. And Edward Muchney is going to have his name plastered all over our expedition, you're going to be on Mars, standing there, with nobody else!"

Edward said nothing for a long time. He licked his lips. His eyes darted this way and that, scanning realtime data.

He wanted it, oh . . . how he wanted it.

"The numbers don't make sense," Edward said. "Nobody has any correlations."

"Five years ago, would $250k for a week in orbit make sense?"

Edward shook his head. "But this is a matter of scale. It's new. Nobody has ever done this before."

Gotcha.

"Exactly!" Evan said, coming to stand next to Jere. "The feds promised by 1980. They could have done it by 1970 with Orion. Then they promised 2018. And the Chinese said they'd do it by 2015. Even the Japanese and the Euros had their timeline. Virgin's made some noises, but they and the Russians are too busy scraping the money out of nouveau-riche assholes to worry about going deeper than orbit. So, who's going to do it?"

Edward just stared at them. Finally, he reached up and turned off his eyesets, *pop, pop,* and looked out at them through clear, steady gray eyes. He looked relatively young, in the way that people who never saw the sun looked young. Pasty-white and baby-like.

"You call this an expedition. Others say game show," Edward said.

"Does it matter how we get there?"

Edward sighed. "I feel like I'm being manipulated."

"Of course you are!" Jere said. "We're manipulating you. But so is Four-eleven. Where would you be, if you made all your decisions based on their recommendations?"

"The numbers are incredibly loose."

"We know that. This is an evolving thing. But if we commit to this, we can do it. Jere and I have committed. We want you to, as well."

A nod. Then silence. Then: "How much do you want?"

"All of it," Jere said. "We're in at two-fifty. We need a billion."

"Not possible."

"Don't you want to go farther than orbit, before you die?" Jere asked. "Wouldn't you like to set foot on Mars yourself? An entire new world, open before you."

"You're offering a slot as a contestant?"

"If that's what it takes."

Edward smiled. "I would have to be more than a contestant, if a whole new world was open before me."

"We—"

"Yes. I know. You'll promise me everything. Stop now. You've convinced me you're for real, despite your really bad costumes. How much do you want? Really?"

"All of it," Evan said.

"Please."

"As much as you can. We have one shot at this. It has to be a big number. A big number gets attention. Attention gets us sponsorship."

"Attention makes the show," Jere said.

"I need to discuss this with my wives," Edward said.

Oh, shit. The Wife Defense. The Real Decision Maker Ploy. Jere knew they were cooked. Nothing stood against that. He'd seen it a million times, growing up. Dad always hauled it out when he wanted to get rid of you, so he could call you back with a *Man, I'd do it, but I'm so sorry, the wife just won't let me.*

"I would expect a decision maker such as yourself—" Evan began. Jere kicked him in the shin.

"I understand," Jere said, standing. "You know how to reach us. Can I ask for a decision by tomorrow?"

Edward nodded. "Of course. I'll let you know. One way or another."

Evan stomped out to the car ahead of Jere, his shoulders tense. The searing Mojave sun baked shimmering heatwaves off his black sweater. Sweat instantly rolled down Jere's chest dappling his polyester shirt.

At the car, Evan whirled and grabbed Jere by the collar. "You let him go! I could've—"

"You could've done shit," Jere said, pushing Evan back. "He pulled the wife routine. He either wanted us gone, or he really is that whipped. There're other fish."

"We coulda landed him!"

"You want to go back in there?" Jere asked. "Go right ahead. Don't expect to be part of Neteno when you come out."

Evan grumbled, but settled down. Then, the big shit-eating Evan-grin: "Wonder what he meant by 'wives'?"

Back in the Neteno office, Jere found out what Edward meant. Apparently he had seventeen wives, one real, and the rest virtual. There was a lot of speculation which of the virtuals were actors and which were just bots. Jere scrolled through the images of Edward's wives, smiling faintly. What a strange world they lived in.

Since you've shown an interest in Edward Muchney, his earbud whispered, *new media is available to purchase.*

A list scrolled in his eyeset:

ARGUMENT WITH BETTY (ARCHIVE, 10 MINUTES AGO)

ARGUMENT WITH PRISCILLA (ARCHIVE, 3 MINUTES AGO)

ARGUMENT WITH SAMIETHA (ONGOING)

AVAILABLE ON GEEK ALERT NETWORK, $150 EACH

Jere looked at the list, for a moment not knowing how to feel. Then he sucked in his breath. Could that mean what he thought it meant?

He sighed and looked up at the big Neteno sign. And waited.

Seventy minutes later, Edward called.

"I can't do a billion," he said. "But I can do four hundred million. And I may have contacts that can leverage the rest. But I have no social graces."

"What does that mean?"

"It means I don't want to be on camera. But I want to go."

"Get us the rest of the money, and consider it done," Jere said. He disconnected.

And then he sat there, not taking the calls from Evan, thinking: This was incredible stuff, this was powerful, this was insane. To trump not one wife but seventeen.

This is how we do it, he thought. This is the Neteno way.

Game

Patrice dragged Jere up to Big Sur.

It was obvious he didn't want to go, pleading he was too busy, that they'd lost a couple of big fish, that they had to keep making the deals, getting the commitments. His eyes darted side to side, as if searching for a threat. Worried Jere. Focused Jere. That was the way he got when he was in the middle of something. It was why he got things done.

It was also damn annoying.

They went up the 1 in Patrice's little BMW convertible, top down, the rush of the crisp sea air a counterpoint to the late-afternoon sun slanting in from the Pacific. She let her newly-cropped hair whip free, for once not caring what it looked like when they arrived. She was Patrice today, not YZ, because YZ really wasn't that interesting to Jere, not any more. The shine had worn off her costume, and he was starting to look at the person within it. Unlike many of her beaux, his eyes weren't wandering away from who he found.

Will he be the one?

She batted the thought away. It was likely there would never be a one, there would never be a little house with a white picket fence—or a big architectural in the Hollywood Hills, with carefully matched kids dressed in Dior and Armani—because even though she could dream about it, she could never really see herself as The Generic Woman, a cloud in a dress, a not her.

Jere was looking out the passenger side window, pretending not to be using his eyeset.

Damn irritating.

"Any good messages?" Patrice asked.

"No service here."

"Really?"

He turned to her, stripped off his eyeset, and dropped it on the center console.

"This'll be worth it," Patrice told him.

"What?"

"This. Getting away. With me."

Jere's boyfriend reflexes kicked in, and he gave her a forced smile and a pat on the shoulder. His hand was tense and cold. She could tell he was still thinking about work.

At Big Sur, they checked into a weathered cabin with an interior done in Modern Log, as if a Hollywood set dresser had been given the instructions: Small, homey, woodsy, but not too much Smokey Bear. Jere threw his bag beside the bed and fell on the too-perfect quilt, staring up at the ceiling.

"Come on," Patrice said, offering a hand.

"Where?" Jere didn't look at her.

"Take a walk. You know, exercise. That thing some people do to stay in shape?"

"Some people are crazy." But he got up.

Outside, dusk had fallen, bringing a sudden chill. Giant redwoods stretched upward, carbon black against the purpling sky. The creek chuckled sluggishly along at their side, mingling the scent of algae with the organic pine-cleaner smell of the trees. Patrice leaned against Jere. He put his arm around her and sighed. Some of the tension had gone out of his body, but he seemed more resigned than relaxed.

"Any service here?" she asked.

Jere laughed. "I didn't bring my eyeset."

"And you didn't check?"

"No."

"Do you want to?"

Silence.

"It's okay. You can admit it."

A sigh. "It's not you. It's just . . . I have too much to do. This project is, well . . . not a lot of fun."

Patrice knew about Jere's latest losses. They'd finally gone to SpaceX, but Elon was busy with his third divorce, and not as idealistic as he'd been in his youth.

"Maybe I can make you feel better." They'd reached a stretch of river where campgrounds lined the banks. They were spotted with off-season campers huddled around brilliant orange campfires. An old Coldplay tune came softly from one of the larger hydrogen-powered RVs. Tents lit from within like jack-o'-lanterns seemed oddly festive.

She pulled him away from the stream. "Let's get off the beaten path."

"Ohh . . . kay." His tone indicated he thought he knew what was coming. She knew he didn't.

She led him up a steep slope, to a place where an old oak canopied a low rise. They were up high enough to see the gray-silver of the Pacific through the redwoods on the hillside opposite them. The cold sea breeze stirred the oak leaves, smelling faintly of salt.

"Sit down," she told him.

"What?"

"Sit down." She pointed at a large gnarled root.

Jere looked confused, but complied. "What do you—?"

"Shh."

Jere's mouth clicked shut.

Patrice pulled out a small pocket-projector. "Now, pay attention."

The projector flared, brilliant in the twilight. Its lasers searched for the nearest vertical surface, found the embankment, whirred a bit as it adjusted and focused the image.

An image of people in fanciful spacesuits running beneath the pink sky of Mars was rendered on the natural screen. The title read:

WINNING MARS
THE GAME
A PROPOSAL FOR NETENO FROM GEN3

"What's this?" Jere asked.

Patrice pulled out a baseball cap with the Gen3 logo on it. "I have to wear the company hat for this one."

"Patrice, what the hell?"

"Shh. I told you this'd be worth it, right?"

"But—"

"But nothing. I am authorized by Bob Petracio, the CEO of Gen3, to bring you this presentation. To make offers. To close deals."

"Patrice!" Jere's face was drawn down in a deep frown. His eyes bounced from the projector's image to Patrice's face and back again.

She clicked the projector. Another view of Mars, new words:

> IF NETENO LICENSES *WINNING MARS* AS A GAME,
> IT WILL MAKE MORE MONEY ON THE GAME THAN THE SHOW.

"I don't want it to be a game!" Jere said.

Second slide. It read:

> IF YOU DON'T LICENSE IT AS A GAME,
> YOU'RE GIVING UP 75%* OF YOUR POTENTIAL REVENUE.
> (*PER AVERAGE CONCEPT-TESTED GAME NET,
> GIVEN CURRENT VIRTUAL CURRENCY EXCHANGE RATES.)

"It's not a game!" Jere's face was red, even in the twilight. "It shouldn't be a game!"

Patrice clicked.

> AFTER ALL, IT'S ALREADY A COMPETITION.
> A GAME SHOW.
> A GAME.

Jere opened his mouth. Closed it.

Patrice let him sit a while before she advanced to the next point. Dusk was turning to full night, and the words glowed more clearly on the embankment:

> CONCEPT SIMULATIONS SHOW TOP-QUINTILE REVENUE POTENTIAL
> AS WELL AS 94.2% INCREASED AWARENESS OF THE SHOW
> IN THE TARGET AUDIENCE.
> (AND DID WE MENTION IT WILL MAKE A PILE OF MONEY?)

Jere sat on the root, hands in lap, saying nothing. His mouth hung open as he looked at the slide.

"I," he said. "I. Ah. It should be a show."

"Why?"

"Because. Because the value is in doing it for real! We could CG this easy, make it a dumb movie. But we're doing this. For real."

"The game doesn't stop you from doing that."

"It blunts the impact!"

"Of really sending people to Mars?"

Jere shut his mouth. Patrice hid a grin. Jere was talking about something grand. A world-changing thing. Maybe he was finally realizing it.

"I don't know," he said.

Patrice changed to the fifth slide. It had the numbers on it.

Jere looked at them for over a minute.

"Are these real?" he asked.

"As real as we can project. And our projections are 91% accurate."

A pause.

"This is revenue in to us?"

"Yes."

"Damn."

"On average, gamers invest 271 US dollars in each of our releases, when all expansions, options, and in-game purchases are counted. Our bigger titles do ten to twenty million in unit sales. Patrice said. "What's your CPM again?"

Jere's eyes were glass. Faraway.

"And in your case, we have a lot of potential spikes to hit. First release, launch of the real rocket, start of the real game."

Patrice clicked once more. The final point, simply:

SOUND GOOD?
LET'S DEAL.

"What do you think?" she said, softly.

"I think you were right," Jere said.

"About what?" Although she knew.

He stood. Gathered her in his arms. "This trip was worth it."

Need

It was official. Jere didn't like Russia.

This time they were in Moscow, in the Universe Hotel, a horseshoe-shaped thing of chrome glass decorated in late-1980s style. Jere wondered if there was a time, a few years back, when that era had come back in style again, or if it was a fanatically preserved relic of those last go-go days before the Internet Age.

And he hated negotiating. After yesterday, they were exactly nowhere. Valentin (of whom the mediascape was ominously silent, even when presented with current video for facial analysis) and his goons had looked at their plans, conferred gravely, and named a price that was ten times their highest projections. Now he and Evan were drinking Stolichnaya in the disturbingly eighties hotel bar, leaning on a bright chartreuse railing overlooking the dining room.

Evan stared down hungrily at a trio of blondes in a nearby booth, who studied menus wrapped in eye-searing purple vinyl. Jere's eyeset tagged them with unpronounceable Russian names and safe, green-lit CVs. They weren't deal-skewing plants from their sponsors, at least as far as he could tell.

"Promise them more flights," Evan said.

"We don't have any," Jere replied.

"It doesn't matter. Make them up."

"We can't just *bluff* the friggin' Russian Mafia, can we?"

"They're bluffing too."

"What do you mean?"

"They got shit. You saw the shuttle. I coulda gone to school on that bus back in the sixties. They do tourist crap. They don't know Mars. Hell, they haven't even been to the moon."

"Yes they have," Jere said, thinking of that caulking gun and the tube of silicone, of those hard vinyl seats, of all the exposed aluminum, worn shiny in places from use. And yet they hadn't fucked up. They could do launches. They were doing half a billion dollars a year from stupid rich fucks who wanted to go up a couple hundred miles and look down on everybody and get spacesick and complain about the crappy food. And nobody had yet been blown up on the launch pad, or depressurized in the *Special! Value! Spacewalk!* in ill-fitting old spacesuits that smelled like farts and BO. Yet.

Evan turned around and leaned on the rail to stare at Jere. "They've been to the moon? When?"

"Uh, like, after us. Seventies?"

Evan smiled. "You kids. What do they teach you with in school these days? Bananas and inner tubes? Nope. No Commies on the moon. Just us: 1969 through 1972, six manned lunar landings."

"The Russians did it too!"

A smug head shake.

"Didn't they?"

"Nope. Never. Not unless you counted unmanned. Once we landed on the moon, they dropped their program and just did unmanned probes. Said that sending actual people, real humans, was a showboating capitalist move. They wouldn't stoop to it."

Evan threw back the rest of his double and waved the waiter over for another drink. The impossibly perfect man studied Evan with unconcealed disdain and pretended not to understand his order.

When the waiter was gone, Evan continued, "You just need to know what we're dealing with. It's a poker game. And they're bluffing."

"If you don't think they can get to Mars, why are we here?"

"I think they can make it to Mars. They're just talking like its easy, like they did it a hundred times, like they already have the stuff on the drawing board. But it won't be easy. It will be hard. Especially on our budget. And they know it."

"So what do we do?" Jere said.

"We bluff right back. Tell them we're going to do this every year. Every three months. Every shittin' week if that's what it takes. Tell them what they want to hear. Then they'll tell us what we want to hear."

Evan's drink came. It was a big pink concoction in a glass the size of a Big Gulp. Evan looked sideways at the waiter and let loose with a burst of Russian that made the man redden, stand straight, and rush off.

Jere only partially noticed. He had visions of black-clad thugs, maggots in suits, showing up at his high-rise condo.

"We're going to lie to the *mafiya*?" Jere asked.

"That's the idea," Evan said.

Jere shivered. "No way."

"I thought Neteno was the big maverick studio, willing to take any chance. With the biggest thing in the history of entertainment coming."

"We are."

"Then act like it, or I'll take it to Fox."

A rush of anger coursed through Jere. He opened his mouth. Closed it. Because that was the one concession he'd given Evan. His contract said he retained rights if the deal fell through.

And the networks knew he was doing something with space. The trend in the mediascape was low, below the radar. But the studios knew, and the net regularly picked fragments of space-related convos from the Eatin at the Y restaurant, and Puck IV, and all the other lunch places in town. Not enough to spawn any rival plans. He hoped.

But enough that Evan had him by the nuts.

"How do I do this?" he asked. "And live?"

"They're gonna have their setbacks too, stuff we can put them over a barrel for. Once we've primed the audience, they have to meet our schedule. Or all the advertising for RusSpace goes out the door. Because people get nervous, and they might want to go Virgin next time, 'cause they meet the deadline. Why did you think I went to see the Branson?"

The waiter returned with a bottle and two glasses. "And a round for the ladies," Evan said, turning around and nodding at the blondes. The man ran off again.

"We can't afford Virgin."

"I know. I know. But that's what RusSpace is looking for: lots and lots of publicity for their space tourism biz. They want to send a hundred thousand people up, not two thousand. They want to send people to the moon. Hell, they may even want to build hotels on Mars for all I know. That's where they'll make their money. If they can do this and not go completely bankrupt, they'll be smiling."

And you think you'll draw them into some big web, some big thing where all paths lead to Evan, Jere thought. "I wish I had your confidence."

"It's my life too," Evan said.

Yes, Jere thought. And you're more visible than I am. He'd need to have some private meetings with their *Organizatsiya* friends and drop some hints about how the disappearance of a high-profile network CEO wouldn't be ignored, and how the concept was all Evan's in the first place.

I will make sure it is your life. First, you fuck. First.

"Okay," he said. "We bluff. Now, what's this the lawyers have come up with for the contestant contract?"

"Aha," Evan said. He pulled out a palmtop and scrolled through a long document. "Eighty pages of gibberish. Printed, that is. They want real signatures in real ink."

The drinks arrived at the blondes' table. Their eyes followed the waiter's pointing finger to Jere and Evan. One looked directly at Jere and asked something. One looked from Jere to Evan and back again, with cool assessing eyes. The third one just glanced and frowned.

"Come on!" Evan said, pushing off the rail to head down to the blondes. Reluctantly, Jere went to follow.

But before they got down to the dining floor, they'd pushed the tray of drinks away. The now-smirking prettyboy waiter brought the drinks back up to Evan and extracted a signature from him in exchange.

"What does it say?" Jere asked, when Evan had returned to the railing.

"What?" Evan said, scanning the room for more targets.

"The contract."

"Oh. Yeah. Essentially, it makes the contestants legal wards of Winning Mars, LLC, a wholly-owned subsidiary of Neteno, Inc. They state they are of sound mind and body, and they've designated us as their sole legal representatives and conservators. They renounce citizenship to whatever country they're coming from, and cannot claim such of any country on the Earth. That keeps the governments fighting and tied up in court while we launch."

"What do they do when they come back? Live in airports?"

Evan grinned. "Not my problem."

"Fuck," Jere said.

"You worry too much."

Jere shook his head, finished his vodka.

"One other thing. The lawyers say we absolutely, positively cannot spin this. We have to tell people they are signing up to get killed."

"There are always volunteers."

"The lawyers had one other suggestion."

"What's that?"

"Start in the prisons. Public reaction to a death will be less if they have a record, even if it's a nonviolent crime."

Jere's vision of beautiful, YZ-quality contestants went floating away. "But they'll have less buy-in."

"Yeah, that's a problem. Do you think we can spin it?"

"Maybe. Depends on the person."

Evan grinned. "Translation: Depends on what they look like."

"I'd be happier if most of them were genpop. And at least one an aspirational. Celeb, maybe."

"Patrice, maybe," Evan said.

Jere shook his head. The waiter came back and looked at Jere's empty glass questioningly. Jere shook his head.

"I'm surprised she isn't first in line," Evan said, after the waiter left. "YZ on Mars. That's gotta be worth a billion or so right there."

Jere said nothing. There was only the sound of murmuring patrons, rattling glassware and an argument deep in the hotel, maybe from the kitchen.

"Why?" Jere said, finally.

"Why what?"

"Why are you doing this? The money?"

Evan sighed and looked away, to a slim brunette, who'd just entered the restaurant. He sagged when she went to join a dark-suited guy in one of the booths.

Then Evan looked down at the table and said, "After a while, you get used to it. Not the money. The other shit. Having dinner with Bill Clinton, 'cause you have your hand on the throat of the public. Fucking Courteney Cox, since you pay more attention to her at one premiere than her husband does all month. Picking up your office phone and asking for anything and getting it, 'cause you're on top, you're on fire. Why else?"

Jere's eyeset had to give him context on names. But even then, he didn't understand at all. His reasons were totally different. Starting with: Because you don't want your dad to look at you with that look, that you-fucking-pussy look, ever again.

They went back to serious drinking. Later, Evan would find his women. Later still would be more negotiation. Endless rounds. Bluff and dare.

The real product of Hollywood.

Phone

"What the hell is this?" Jere was yelling and holding up a phone. In the crappy frame rate, Patrice caught only a glimpse of bright pink graphics.

"I can't see."

Jere brought the phone closer to his eyeset. It showed jerky graphics of a Martian landscape, with overly processed graphics of a man in a clean white spacesuit ascending a canyon wall. Beyond the phone, the sci-fi skyline of Shanghai sat layered under smog.

"Doing another deal?" she asked.

"Damn it, Patrice!"

Patrice pursed her lips. She was clearly YZ. YZ evening; YZ the diva for the annual meeting of Gen3's virtual billionaires. They were doing the deal at the restored (again) Palladium this year. The room was full of fat guys in pirate costumes, shy thin dudes dressed all in black, chubby goth-chicks with too many piercings and bad tattoos wearing gear left over from the last Ren Faire, suit-and-tie executives from the Midwest who tried to shrink into the shadows, embarrassed and out of place. Tags floated like butterflies in Patrice's eyeset, showing name and avatar name and net worth in both Gen3 Bux, dollars, and RMB. Not one person in the room was worth less than fifteen million dollars, even after the exchange rate had shot skyward by 8.6 percent that day. The dollar was unaccountably strengthening, the most visible evidence of the invisible machinations of the current administration. The next day it might plunge 12 or 15 percent, or it might be another Blue Thursday, and dollars might as well be pennies. But that was the modern currency market. You took your chances. Not that anyone in the room would be hurting. Their Gen3 Vbux were convertible at 98 percent of the nation's stores, and easily exchangeable for whatever government currency was strong at the moment. They were people who could buy beach houses and personal assistants.

And they all had their eyes on YZ. She wore the classic Yvette Zero, Version 1.0 outfit: a purple man's tuxedo with a low-cut white blouse, plunging to reveal square inches of sideboob. The pants were tailored, skintight. Her lips, bright crimson. A look almost ten years gone. All new again if YZ wore it.

"Patrice!"

Patrice focused on the video in her eyeset and sighed. "What?"

"What's with this game? Why didn't you tell me it was going to be out?"

Patrice shrugged. That was business stuff, and it was hard to care about business when she was being YZ.

"Patrice!"

"I didn't know," she said.

"You didn't know!"

"It's just a casual game," Patrice said. "I don't really follow the casuals."

"The game is shit! It's terrible! The graphics are—"

"Casuals aren't graphics-driven or character-based," Patrice said. "They're really not immersive."

"But this is a shitty game!"

"Does it matter?"

"It's the same name as the show! Who said you could use the same name as the show? Who said you could do a crappy phone game?"

"Your contract," Patrice said. One of the shy Midwest guys was eyeing her, and he was hot. Jere sounded very far away. Very unimportant.

"Damn it, Patrice!"

Patrice called up the ratings and user commentary for *Winning Mars* (casual handset game). The average user rating was 4.1, comfortably above their average of 3.7. Negative comments were almost all about graphics and lack of depth. They wanted to play it, and play it some more. That was good. She tried to explain that to Jere, but he didn't want to hear it.

"Your users are one thing," Jere said. "But this has Four-eleven putting things together again. And they're not thrilled."

"Can they stop you?"

Jere shook his head. "I don't know."

"Why worry, then?"

"Because . . . there's a lot of gab. And . . . and this game looks like shit!"

Patrice laughed. "Of course. It's just a hack-and-reskin. Just something to get the idea out, to whet their appetite. Have you seen some of the highest-karma user comments? 'Brilliant chit, manga, together in ancient videorites with spaceploration.' And 'Reality is dead, but reality taken this far is greatness.' Then there's: '*Survivor* in space, whoa.' You have huge mindspace in the high-rep realm."

Jere went silent. In front of him, diesel taxis cruised, spewing pollutants.

"How are sales?"

Patrice took a look. And told him. Jere frowned. "That doesn't sound good."

"It's about middling. Maybe a little lower."

"Should I be worried?"

Cute Midwest-guy had found enough courage to sidle up to Patrice. She grinned at him and pointed at her eyeset. He made apologetic gestures and began to back away.

No, stay, she mouthed.

Cute Midwest-guy raised his eyebrows. Her eyeset identified him as Leon Athenae, founder of the fashion house Athenae's Delights in the freeform world of Pax Verbis. He pulled in about ten million dollars last year by selling virtual fashion to female avatars.

"Don't worry," she told Jere. "You're just getting started."

And so was she.

Team

Dad was sitting out on the upstairs balcony of his Hollywood Hills house, looking out over Los Angeles. April had gotten warmer, and he was wearing an old short-sleeved T-shirt inscribed with the name of some long-dead band, Weezer, who looked like a bunch of skinny geeks more likely to be beaten up than rock stars. Jere's eyeset offered to sell him a complete set of every song they ever recorded plus exclusive bonus material for only 39 VBux. He blinked it away.

Dad glanced at Evan, smiled at Jere, and said: "I want in."

For a long time, there was no sound except the rush of traffic from the freeway, far below. Ron smiled and looked from Jere to Evan and back again, as if they were all old friends.

"You want in on what?" Jere said.

"The show. *Winning Mars.*"

Jere risked a glance at Evan. Evan, open-mouthed, looked back at Jere.

"You want in?"

"Yes. Hello! Is my own boy thick, or what? I. Would. Like. To. Become. An. Investor. Thank you."

"What about the family?"

"What about them?"

"Their security! Your money!"

Ron looked away. Down below them in Runyon Canyon, the dudes who owned the Lloyd Wright were having a party. Toned, naked men splashed in the pool, or lounged concreteside. Two of them shaded their eyes to peer up at the dad house.

Dad waved back to them, then turned back to Jere. "I want in."

Ah. No explanation. The assumptive thing. Dad wants in, so you let him in.

"What if we don't want you in?" Jere said. Beside him, Evan made a little gasp of protest.

"So everything's suddenly sunshine and roses?" Ron said. "Your big bombs in China aren't any big deal? The magical virtual currency deal with Gen3 is gonna finance the whole schmear?"

Jere shook with anger. "Where . . . how . . . who's telling you all this?"

A smile. Reptilian. All knowing. Like when Jere said he was quitting school. Like when Jere said he was starting his own company. Jere's fists clenched involuntarily.

"I have my sources."

"Four-eleven?"

"No."

"InfoPlex? Mediascape Analysts? IntelAdvance? Or do you have your own algorithms cooked?" Jere said, tagging Dad's last words and sending it to the office, where a Neteno intern could beat the Russian dataminers into finding the leaks. Hopefully. They didn't have much budget, even for interns.

Dad's face crumpled into a mass of quivering wrinkles. He laughed. He bent over. He laughed some more. In the end, he walked over to Jere, put a hand on his shoulder, and laughed some more. Jere shook him off.

"What?" Jere said.

"You kids. Algorithms this, predictions that. I had a couple lunches, talked to a few people. They told me."

"You're kidding."

"It's about who *you* know," Dad said. "And what *they* know."

"I don't believe you."

"They have human-equivalent algorithms yet?"

Jere grunted. Shook his head.

"That's what I thought. Don't count people out. They're still damn smart." A pause. "Even if they've already been counted out."

"We don't need your help." Jere could sense Evan staring at him. But he didn't understand. If dad was in, there was no way he could ever look at the old man and say, *I did this myself.*

"I can help," Ron said. "More than investing. I know 411 has a hard-on for you. Your exec profile with them is, well, how can I say this . . . less than stellar. Whereas mine—"

"Is insane," Evan said, licking his lips.

"That's what fifty years in the biz will do for you."

"Experience isn't everything," Jere said.

"Yeah, but that's how the game's called. You want to go face-to-face with the ref?"

Jere said nothing. What do you do about this? he asked himself, turning to face the basin. LA itself stared back at him, its great blank buildings glittering through the omnipresent gray smog. Far out, he could just barely see the curve of the Pacific Ocean.

A sudden thought came, strange and powerful. Someone had looked out over this vista when there wasn't a damn thing here, what, four, five hundred years ago? Now it was the epicenter of entertainment for the entire world, more powerful, in its way, than London or New York, or maybe even Shanghai and Mumbai. Their contestants would look out on that same vista: an empty world, full of infinite potential.

"Please," Dad said.

Dad pleading. As alien as Dad crying. Jere closed his eyes. He was, for the first time, truly scared. This was never supposed to happen. What was he going to do?

"May I talk with my business partner privately?" Evan said.

"Of course."

Jere followed Evan into the living room. The house was vault-silent, the scent of wood-polish and leather defining its whole world.

"Have you seen his connections?" Evan whispered. "He could get us in—"

"I know."

"Then why are you being such a dick?"

"I just . . . you wouldn't understand."

Evan leaned close. "Take his help."

"No."

"Without his help, we may not make it."

"We could fake it, CG it," Jere said, softly.

Evan paused for a moment, then looked at Jere intently. "Yes. We could. I can call Virtefx and we can stage the whole thing. Do you want me to do that?"

Matter of fact. Like it didn't make any difference. That was Evan. He was surely thinking: *If it makes me powerful and it's cheaper and I can use someone else's money—then that's fine, let's do it, call it a day, and be done with it.*

But that wasn't Neteno. Neteno was going against the popular wisdom, using data in different ways, taking chances. That was what Neteno was about.

And maybe, just maybe, it was something more.

"No," Jere said.

Evan waited, tapping his foot on the hardwood floor.

"We'll let him in," Jere said.

"Yeah!" Evan said, pumping a fist in the air.

"Don't be so happy."

"Why not?"

"Now it's not our show. It's Dad's."

Evan shrugged. "Depends on his percentage, doesn't it?"

Jere laughed. "You don't get it. You don't get it at all."

They went back to Ron, who hadn't moved from the balcony. As if he was expecting this. As if he planned this. He smiled at them and said he envisioned them having a great business partnership. Said he was happy to be getting back into it, after so many years.

Jere accepted with as large a smile as he could. It felt like his face was being stretched in strange and terrible dimensions.

"So what do the contestants look like?" Ron said.

And there went the afternoon.

TWO: AUDITION

Paul

Keith Paul woke that morning, stared at the gray paint flaking off the cracked ceiling of his cell, and thought, One hundred ninety-one days.

I could do that standing on my head.

Still, one hundred and ninety-one days of eating bologna and white bread sandwiches, smelling the farts of Jimmy Jiminez in the bunk below him after a dinner of bland beans and fried chicken, and playing nice with the guards so he could spend a couple of hours a day in the exercise yard was one hundred and ninety-one days he would not spend in a bar, or in his own apartment, or with Jimmy Ruiz and Keira Montoya and Britney Jackson and George White, and certainly not with the open road before him, beckoning.

He licked his lips.

Of course, one of his friends might have been put away. He hadn't kept up. He didn't like to use the computers here. They looked at everything. And, every once in a while, they'd call you away and say, *You know, that stuff you were selling on eBay didn't really exist.* And *Oh by the way, you have won another six months in our establishment.* Or *No, you only thought you hacked the cam network. Don't try again. One more year for you.*

Or Jimmy or George might have a good game going. One that would work. If they hadn't been so greedy last time, they probably could've milked that offshore bank-spoof for another year. Maybe enough to step away. Maybe enough to be satisfied.

One hundred ninety-one days. He could remember that. He was always good at math. Numbers weren't bad. Unlike letters, which would slip away when made into words.

The snail mail guy came down the corridor, banging once on the steel bars in case anyone was asleep. Keith ignored him. He never got any snail mail. That was for the guys not smart enough to get out before they got old. He stared at the ceiling and thought, for the millionth time, of what he was going to do when he got out. Find the nearest bar. Jaegermeister. Unless Keira or Jimmy would pick him up. Find a decent terminal with an earpiece so he could listen in private. That would be a good enough start.

Bang! The bars clanged.

Keith sat up in bed, almost striking his head on the ceiling. Jimmy looked up at him from the bunk below and shrugged. The asshole guard—a new one, Keith didn't recognize him, but they cycled in and out quickly—with his stupid little paper cart pointed at him. Keith.

"Got the wrong guy," Keith said.

"Nope. It's for you." Asshole mail guard shoved a big, thick envelope through the bars and waggled it impatiently.

Keith hopped down off the bunk and reached for it. The guard drew it back. "Not so quick. Sign first." The guard stuck a tablet with an attached blunt plastic stylus through the bars.

Keith scrawled the little house-with-family that served as his signature. Asshole mail guard looked at the glowing sketch on the screen, then to the big envelope, then to Keith, and raised his eyebrows.

Yeah, fuck you, I can't read, Keith thought. But he said nothing. Guards talked to guards. He didn't need to get on their shit list. Or one hundred ninety-one days would become three hundred seventy-one days in a real big hurry.

Asshole guard shoved the package at Keith. "Enjoy that now, y'hear," he said.

"Fuck you," Keith said, when asshole guard had gone on down to the next cell.

"What is it?" Jimmy said.

"I don't know," Keith said. The envelope was already open. Keith shook his head. Like they could send him a paper gun, or cardboard knife. He reached in, pulled out a quarter-inch thick, stapled sheaf of cheap paper, fronted by one creamy-smooth sheet with a familiar logo on it: the stylized Neteno *N*, above an old-timey media player timeline.

"So what is it?" Jimmy said, looking over his shoulder.

"Something from Neteno." The rest of the pages were filled with close-packed text, with numbers in front of every paragraph. Keith recognized that. It looked like stuff he signed when he got credit cards. A legal contract.

But credit contracts didn't have thirty-eight pages.

Click. Something connected in Keith's mind. The kiosk. That was it. Their wacky show. Almost six months ago, the guards had brought in a shiny aluminum kiosk, like the kind they use for making alibis to your wife or girlfriend. It had a deep purple camera eye on an articulated stalk and a big flatscreen. They'd set it up in the lunchroom for about a week and let people talk to it—all the while flanked by Richey and Washington, the two most assholish guards in the entire prison.

There was always a big line for it. The dudes who'd talked to it said the girl they talked to was smoking hot. But that could be a chatterbot. So Keith had ignored it for six days.

Then Washington and Richey came to get him. They dragged him in front of the kiosk, where the purple camera eye followed him, like some creepy alien in a sci-fi show.

"You want pretty boys, here's the prettiest," Richey told the girl on the screen.

Keith smiled. He knew he was good-looking. The girls always liked him. They said he had broad shoulders and a Dudley Do-Right chin, whatever that was. They were always wanting him to take off his shirt and walk around like that.

And the one on screen was noticing too. She was a cute little blonde, that white-blond hair like you see on some Swedish girls in pornos. Keith wondered what color her bush was. She wasn't smoking hot like everyone said, but nice, with a round face and full pink lips. The monitor cut off just before her tits.

She looked him up and down. The purple alien eyeball followed her gaze. She looked at him for a long time, her mouth slightly parted.

"So why do you want to be a contestant for *Winning Mars*?" she asked.

"Is that what you ask all the men?" Keith said, sliding into his sexy-deep voice. Even though he couldn't read, he'd always had a wonderful ability to parrot. It had kept him from being thrown out of many hotels he shouldn't have been allowed into in the first place.

The girl laughed. "Actually, yes."

"I'm afraid we haven't been formally introduced."

The girl paused, and her eyes widened, just for an instant.

Point to me, Keith thought.

"I'm Cassandra Wasserman," she said. "And you are?"

"Master Keith Paul, at your service." He gave her a comically low bow. The eye followed him. He had a sudden urge to snap it off its arm.

She giggled. "You're courteous, at least."

At that moment, something passed between Richey and Washington. They looked at each other, bottom lips slack as if held down by invisible fishing-sinkers.

"Hey, step it up!" Washington said. "There're other suckers."

"Yeah, get to the point," Richey said.

Cassandra cleared her throat. The camera turned to look at the guards. They crossed their arms and tried to look tough.

She turned the camera back on Keith. "So, why do you want to be a contestant?"

"It is my highest ambition, dear lady! Anything to be next to your radiance!"

Another laugh. "I'm not going."

"Then I shall hear none of it! I refuse!"

"You don't want to be a contestant?" Cassandra looked disappointed.

"Not if it takes me out of your sight."

She shook her head. "I don't know what to think of you. But I like. Can I put you down on the list?"

"If it makes you happy, yes."

"Great!"

"Are you done yet?" Washington said, hanging over the screen.

"Yes," Cassandra said.

"Goodbye, fair one," Keith said.

Washington came around to escort him back to his lunch, glowering with promised future revenge. "What was with all the flowery talk?"

Keith just shrugged.

"Fucking ham."

"Sometimes the spirit—"

"Ah, shut up," Washington said, pushing him down onto the bench. Keith let him do it. He watched Richey and Washington drag a few more guys over, but the shadow of Cassandra's face never seemed to smile as much as it had for him.

She liked me.

But what had she said? *Winning Mars?*

Keith shook his head. He only had three hundred fifty-seven days before he got out of East Valley Correctional. That was what mattered, not some tart in a box.

"It's the show!" Jimmy cried, bringing Keith back to the present. "You're on the show!"

"What show?"

"*Winning Mars*."

"What's that?"

Jimmy's face closed up as if he'd just bit into a lemon. "You don't know what it is, and they want you?"

"Just tell me."

"It's a reality show."

"Reality show? Like, old-time TV?"

"Yeah. They're bringing it back. But they're going to space. To Mars."

"To Mars? The planet?" Keith felt something like a cold hand grip his guts and twist. And they were picking prisoners? That meant everyone was gonna die. And there was probably no way out of it. He riffled through the meaningless words.

"Whatsa matter?" Jimmy asked.

"Mars? Space? They're sending us to die."

Jimmy looked surprised, as if he'd never thought of that. "But if they pick you, you get out early."

Early? As in less than one hundred ninety-one days? Keith stood up straighter. And if he was out, that didn't mean he *had* to go on to Mars. Might be ways around that.

"What does it say?" Keith said, handing the documents to Jimmy. Jimmy looked at it and shook his head. Pointed at the camera in the cell. "Sorry, man. Too many assholes watching. I tell you the wrong thing, they have my nuts."

"What'm I supposed to do?"

"Take it to the library," Jimmy said.

"We have a library?"

Jimmy just looked at him and shook his head.

At lunch, Keith discovered they did have a library. It was a tiny room, lined with terminals, and stacked floor to ceiling with antique discs and cards. It was staffed by a young guy with a big mop of black hair who was actually reading an old-fashioned book. He took one look at Keith's papers and pointed at the back of the room.

"You lucky fuck," he said. "Reader's over there."

The reader was an old cranky thing that didn't even explain the big words. But it did tell Keith he was accepted as a contestant on a show called *Winning Mars*, and if he signed the papers, he would be out of jail in a week.

There were lots of words he didn't understand, but he didn't care. He took a real live pen from the real live librarian and signed his little house-and-family mark to it.

Seven days. Seven was better than one hundred and ninety-one. And he was sure he wouldn't have to go to Mars.

Not a chance.

Play

Ron made them fly out to Detroit, sketching on napkins the whole way. Jere sat back and closed his eyes, willing sleep. This is Dad, turning my shit into his own, he thought.

Evan leaned forward and asked questions, as if he was really interested.

"Why Ford?" Evan asked. "Aren't they number three?"

"Three or four," Ron said. "Doesn't matter."

"Why not Toyota or Hyundai for a partner?"

"These aren't sponsors."

"What are they?" Evan asked.

"Partners."

"What's the difference?"

"Partners are gonna develop technology. Plus pay for logos."

"We have technologists."

Ron snorted. "You got college dropouts who lucked out, threw some stupid yackware together, and made a few billions. You got other dewy-eyed dreamers milkin' the VC and promising magical materials that will never break and will also do the dishes. You got shit. People at Ford actually have to make things that work. They get to show up in federal court if they don't. These are the partners you want."

"So why not Toyota?"

"Don't know anyone at Toyota. And I'm in no mood for Japanese politeness. I don't need someone smiling and saying *yes, yes, yes,* when they really mean 'get the fuck out of my office, you uncultured round-eye asshole.'"

A pause. Then, Evan's voice: "You have the connections?"

"Of course."

Jere seethed, but said nothing. That was Dad. Fingers in everything, doing nothing. He'd never appeared on a screen in his life. It was all about having a drink, playing golf, having dinner.

"After Detroit, we can head to Chicago," Dad said.

"Why?" Evan said.

"Talk to Boeing."

"You know someone there too?" Jere asked

"Of course."

When they got to Dearborn, though, Ron's connection just shook his head. Henried Wenger, the Senior Vice President of Vehicle Development, Specialty Division, North America, was a squat fireplug of a man who looked like he'd been poured into his seventeen thousand-dollar suit. His office overlooked most of Detroit, surreally resurrected in colorful, sustainable, artsy style by the neo-settlers who got in during the First and Second Great Recessions, buying homes for pocket change.

"Mars?" Wenger bellowed. "Are you kidding? What's your budget?"

Ron's smile never wavered. "This is a great way for you to prove reliability in tough environments. Imagine what it would do for your image. You should be paying us."

Henried's expression went dark. "You're expecting us to pay?"

"I expect that having your branded vehicles on the surface of another planet would inspire some real creativity in your engineering staff. Not to mention the marketing potential."

"Marketing would tell you to go pound sand," Henried said. "This new experiential advertising . . . they aren't spending much on new programs. Put a few cameras in cars, give 'em away, pay some people with high attention index, call it a day. It's too easy. Plus, the fanboy rallies are always good."

"When Pathfinder ran way past its rated life, do you know what that did for NASA's image?"

"They ain't around today, are they?"

Ron shut his mouth with an audible click. Jere had to stifle a smile. Seeing his dad shut down was funny.

But it also meant a door had just closed in his face.

"We'll have to take it around," Ron said. "Toyota. Hyundai."

A shrug. Then a sigh. "If you expect to get my blood up with rah-rah Americana, it ain't happening. We still have a permanent US Government Oversight staff here, and we still never took any money from the Great and Wonderful Oz. They'll have a shit-hemorrhage if they hear anything other than building more electric-powered balsa cars."

"We could spin it as advanced R and D. You know what Apollo did for the technology of the era?"

A headshake. "Sorry, Ron. If you gotta shop it, shop it."

"I'd really rather it be here."

Another shrug, and a perfectly manicured smile, somehow sad.

"Think on it," Ron said. "We'll call back tomorrow."

"The answer'll be the same."

Out on the pavement, on the muggy August day, Ron clenched his hands into fists. "Fucker!" he grated. "He's still pissed about that little exposé NBC did, a million years ago."

"What was it?" Jere asked. "Can we use it?"

Ron looked at him. "At least you're thinking in the right direction. But no. It's not a big deal now. Employee sex workers."

"At Ford?"

"No, at a big law firm he used to be at."

Evan stirred. "He was a lawyer?"

"Yeah, why?" Ron asked.

"You aren't gonna sell a program like this to a lawyer. He's thinking about how many ways his friends in Ford Legal can nail his ass to an Oversight clause for fun and advancement."

Ron sighed. "There's one other possibility."

Evan stopped and turned back towards the office. He looked confused when nobody else followed. "What are you waiting for? Let's get back in there."

"This guy, you don't meet in an office."

"Who is he?"

Ron shrugged. "An ops guy, but a higher-up. But he doesn't meet in his office. Not if you want to do real business."

Evan sucked air through his teeth. "Golfcourseware," he said.

"Not exactly," Ron said. "More like stripclubware. And we aren't selling CRM, anyway."

"What the hell are you talking about?" Jere said.

The two older men looked at him, shook their heads, and went back to their conversation.

Which is how they ended up in Fast Eddie's, a shitty little strip club built into the usable half of a half-burned apartment building in downtown Detroit, comfortably hidden from the new friendly face of the city. Tattered

"Urban Renovation" banners hung from the roof. A multicolored neon sign hung in one cracked window.

"He comes here?" Evan said, looking doubtful.

Inside, though, the runway was beautiful polished marble, and the bar was a chrome and glass artwork. And the girls were as perfect as surgery could make them. Flyeye-zappers popped in every corner of the bar, and heavy lead foil offered some proof against line-of-sight wireless. Jere made himself drink a single beer, slowly, away from the dancing flesh.

Their whale came in at 10:30, and a whale he was. He was a large African-American man wearing a gold-trimmed red jogging suit and a very large gold Rolex.

"That's him?" Evan said, when Ron pointed him out.

"Yep."

"What is he, a mob boss or something?"

"Oh ye of little faith. Just remember this is a chance meeting. Take my lead. Don't go off-script."

Evan just looked at him.

"Got it?"

"Ye-es," Evan said, drawing it out.

"Go," Ron said. He stood up, then suddenly threw open his arms in a big expression of surprise. "Thalos!" he shouted. "Thalos Winnfield, is that you?"

Thalos looked up, frowned for a moment, then broke into a big gold grin. He stood and lumbered towards Jere, in the strange and graceful way that very large people sometimes have. They met in the middle of the room, a collision of flesh, with Evan and Jere orbiting like little moons.

"Ron! What brings you back?"

Ron looked sheepish. "Business, actually."

"Business? With who?"

"You, actually."

"Me, as in Thalos?"

"You, as in Ford."

"What you doing with us?"

"Turns out nothing," Evan said. "Let me introduce my colleagues—"

Thalos held up a hand, his face clamped down into an exaggerated mask of concern. "Wait. What do you mean, 'turns out nothin'?"

"Thalos, it doesn't matter. Probably best we go to Toyota anyway. We already met with your VP of Special Vehicles, and he said—"

Thalos held up a big hand. "Wait! Wait! Toyota? What's this shit?"

"Well, they have motivation. The Chinese on the moon and all . . . Thalos, this is a long story."

"And I'm gonna hear it," Thalos said, gathering Ron in one big arm and herding him towards his table.

Once seated, and introductions made, Thalos ordered a bottle of thirty-year Macallan and sat back. "So what's this crap about Toyota?"

"Thalos, it doesn't matter. You probably wouldn't be interested, anyway. I bet Ford engineering has its hands full, just trying to keep up."

A nod. "You said it. Hybrids, hydrogen, fuel cells, cold fusion II, geez, whatever happened to good old gas? But you're still gonna tell me what you're doing."

"We're sending people to Mars, and we need vehicles for them."

Thalos's face went completely slack for several long moments. Then he guffawed. "Oh. Man. You had me going."

"No. We're serious."

"Wait. Wait. You work for NASA now? I thought you were just a Hollywood asshole."

"I'm still a Hollywood asshole."

"No. Wait. Wait. Hollywood is going to Mars, and you want Ford cars for product placement?"

"No. We want you to design special vehicles. And build them."

Thalos sat back, suddenly serious. "You're not kidding."

"No."

Silence for a time. "Fuck. Wow. You're right. Toyota would do it just to spit in the chinks' eyes."

Ron let Thalos sit. The big man shook his head and chewed on a thumbnail. "What's the real catch?"

"We want it for free."

"That's all?"

"We'd like sponsor participation as well," Evan said.

A look from Thalos. "Don't press your luck."

"But the rest, yes?" Ron said.

A nod. "Tell the engineers it can't be done, and stand back."

"And you can you get it approved? On the up-and-up?"

Thalos nodded. "Yeah. Shit, you should see the money we piss away for schools and their engineering programs. Yeah. We can do it."

"Even with Oversight?"

"There's always a spin. How do you think the CEO made a billion dollars last year?"

Ron gave a sigh of relief. "We have a deal?" He held out his hand.

Thalos's hand ate Ron's. "Deal. Come by tomorrow, we'll talk to the techies. Fair warning, though—whatever you get won't look like a car."

"We're not expecting it to."

They stayed. They drank. They groped.

And, when it was all done, Evan asked Ron, "What does Thalos do?"

"As little as possible," Ron said.

"What's his title?"

"Chief Operations Officer, Vehicle Line Assembly and Liaison, Reformed UAW."

"Can we trust him?"

Ron smiled. "If he says it can be done, it'll be done."

Indeed, the next day, they had ink on paper, and even a press release. Jere could already see the headlines: *Ford Sponsors Mars Shot,* or something like that.

But it made him feel even more lost, behind the great wall of his father.

Patrice

Patrice's locator found Jere at the Porsche dealer, buying one of their new little gumdrop cars. Patrice wrinkled her nose. She never understood what Jere saw in the stupid things. They were expensive, but they were uncomfortable, and small, and loud, and fitting any kind of luggage in them was nearly impossible, which meant he had to take the Caddy SUV on long trips anyway, and . . .

But that didn't matter. She got in her own little BMW and paid maxtax to take the Fast405 down to Newport Beach, pushing the warnings that flashed when she hit 88 miles an hour, threatening tickets for another mile an hour over. It cost her over $160 to go from Westwood to Newport, but it was worth it, because she caught him, stylus poised over a signscreen, with a rack-suited salesman trying to hide a grin, behind his big aluminum desk.

"What're you buying?" Patrice asked.

Jere dropped the pen and looked up, his eyes wide like a kid who got peeking up skirts. "I, uh . . . "

"I thought you had to save money."

"He qualified," the salesman said, giving Patrice his God-I-hate-wives-and-girlfriends look. Just as quickly, his eyes went wide in recognition. Patrice was Yvette Lite today, just the makeup and the skinsuit, but she was still YZ. The salesman's eyes ping-ponged back and forth between the Courageous Television Exec Who Was Taking Us to Mars and The Über-Heroine of the Interactive Age. For a moment, he seemed at a loss. Then his sales instincts kicked in. He picked up the stylus and held it out to Jere. "Just one more signature."

"I thought everything was going into *Winning Mars*," Patrice said.

"I can treat myself now and again," Jere said. His voice was soft and rough and low. His I-just-had-a-fight-with-Dad voice.

"With all the publicity?" *Winning Mars* had broken out of the geekspace of BoingBoing and io9, and was racking the mainstream buzz. She glanced at the realtime data. Gab about the show had even cracked her own attention index. She felt a mild buzz of irritation.

As she watched, new tags floated in: *Jere/YvetteZero/dealership/Porsche*

She looked around. Outside, a crowd of gabbers had gathered, pointing eyesets and handsets and chatting furiously into their real-time feeds. Jere was big news. She was big news. Together, they were even bigger news. Anything to feed their popularity.

"And is it so bright, doing this in front of a crowd?" she asked.

"What?" Jere said. He looked up, through the glass, at the crowd gathered in the bright sun. An enterprising salesman went out with a Newport Beach Porsche sign and URL to hold in front of the gabbers. "Ah, shit."

"Just one final signature," the salesman said. His eyes never left the pen in Jere's hand.

Jere just looked at the crowd.

The salesman sighed and sat back in his seat.

Jere scrawled his name on the sales contract.

"Jere!" Patrice said.

Jere shook his head. She could almost hear his thoughts. Yeah, I could run the numbers through Four-eleven and find every reason not to get this, I could be responsible and save money, I could be like everyone else wants me to be. But I won't.

He looked up at her. She smiled.

"You're mad."

"A little," she said. Smiling.

The salesman grabbed the sheets and did a little dance. "I'll get the car prepped."

"This is idiotic," Patrice told him. But so was spending twenty thousand dollars on a dress. Or getting cut up to look more like a video game character.

I understand, a voice said, inside her. A familiar voice. YZ's voice.

Patrice shivered. In her eyeset, Jere's attention index peaked even higher, as the news of his purchase (and her presence) ricocheted from ScreenTime to Hollywood411 to TimesNow. There was a lot of negative chatter tagged with the purple of jealousy, but overall the mood was bright.

As if they're rooting for him.

Patrice followed Jere out to see his silly little car. It was bright blue. It was pretty, in a way. But it was just a thing, nothing exciting, nothing special.

A quote from an old movie came back to her: *The things you own, end up owning you.*

Real

I can't believe I'm doing this again, Jere thought, as the chill Russian stewardess strapped him into the vinyl school bus seat of the spacecraft. The cabin still smelled of raw aluminum and grease, and, faintly, of puke. Jere wondered if it was his.

This time, he was the only one on board.

The attendant made sure his belts were tight and went forward into the pilot's cabin. When she didn't come out, Jere realized she wasn't a flight attendant. She was a pilot. Just Jere and the Russian ice queen, headed for the Hilton-RusSpace Hotel. In the interactives, a setup for a kinky time with the ice queen. In reality, Jere's hands were too slick with sweat and his heart was pounding much too fast to think about any kind of tryst.

He could think about only one thing: Kevin Cho.

Jere'd watched the Kevin Cho thing evolve over the last weeks with half an eye, wondering if Neteno could do something with him. Kevin was a biological virtuoso. He'd designed the little mini-Godzillas that swept Japan and the United States. From lizards, or something. But they stood up on their hind legs and waved their little arms at the kids, and even voiced tiny little cries that were high-pitched echoes of Godzilla's famous scream. That was the kicker. The animals themselves were cute, but the scream was what made people run to the pet stores and buy them in droves. And they bought the accessories—little model cities with little model cars and little model people that their mini-G could stomp around in, microcams so they could record its adventures, memberships in videocommunities where people shared their best stuff and rated it, or even paid to be on the mini-G channel. It had made Ling Kung Biodiversity billions of dollars, and even managed to melt the icy Chinese-Japanese relationship for a little while.

Maybe it was the billions that set Kevin off. Maybe it was his boss, driving up to work in his multimillion-yuan custom-made Ferrari, that did it. Or maybe he was just an idealist from the start. Maybe he wasn't just marking time in Ling Kung. Maybe he'd been learning to do what he really wanted to do.

The media had tried to spin it both ways, pointing to old blogs where Kevin talked about how there was no reason for us to need or want oil any longer. But Jere looked at those, and they seemed to be just college venting, the shit you did when you were a little too full of facts and idealism and too dumb to know you couldn't really change the world. It didn't seem to be the work of a man who had a deep-seated need to take down the world economy.

But, whatever the reason, he'd taken a little trip to Iraq and injected a petroleum-eating bacterium of his own design into one of their most prolific oilfields.

They didn't find out about it until days later—when all that came out of the pipes was thin brown slurry, like melted chocolate ice cream. Analysis revealed the bacterium. Oilfield video revealed Kevin Cho planting it.

And, in one moment, Kevin had succeeded in becoming The Most Hated Man in the World, with Muslim extremists and the Chinese Premier and the American President and the various parliaments of Europe all calling for his head. Russia, self-sufficient on oil, had made a few rude noises, but the damage was done. Kevin had already booked a weeklong visit to RusSpace's orbiting hotel, territory that no country claimed. And he'd brought weapons. Bio-engineered handguns that looked almost alive—maybe were alive—that shot black greasy stingers full of curare.

Jere watched the American nukes blow in Iraq, *flash flash flash*, three in quick succession, to sterilize the oilfield to a depth of twenty thousand feet. Flying cams showed the ground rippling like the sea, ahead of the blast, as the brilliance seared their pixels to black. And the Iraqi government, profusely thanking the United States for their help. Surreal raised to the power of infinity.

And the scary thing, the newscasters and inpersons said in hushed tones, is they didn't know how deep the bacteria had gotten, or how interconnected the oil fields were, or if the nukes would really sterilize it. And they wouldn't know for many years.

Up in orbit, Kevin said we should have let the bacteria take its course, how we shouldn't be dependent on oil, how the sooner we moved to a true sun-based bioeconomy, the better it would be for the planet. And he reiterated his desire simply to stay there, to become Earth's first expatriate.

RusSpace made noises about wanting him out of their station, but they were selling media rights for bigger numbers than their weekly ops. *And they know this is the best publicity in the world,* Jere thought. *When this is over, they'll have a dozen orbital hotels. Hell, they'll have fucking resorts.*

After his statement, Kevin stopped talking. He said he'd speak to only one person.

And that was Jere Gutierrez.

And now here he was, going to talk to the nut. A huge hand pressed him back in his seat. He was ready for that. He was even ready for the sensation of falling. He felt the room flip. He felt his stomach flip. He filled the bag twice before they docked with the RusSpace hotel.

He went forward to the hatch without waiting for his pilot. She joined him there with a wry smile. Probably thinking he was going to get killed. Or maybe drawing some kind of bizarre connection between Mississippi and the Oilfield Incident. There was a lot more chatter about Neteno these days. That was one thing, at least, that 411 had been right about.

When the hatch opened, though, she waved him on and crossed her arms, clearly unwilling to go any further. The hatch slid shut behind him.

Jere trudged through the sickly centrifugal gravity and found the lobby. The terrified Russian behind the counter—a portly man so pale he almost matched the white plastic paneling—waved Jere down the main corridor.

"In cabin! Three-dash-four."

Jere checked his gear, a little head-mounted camera that connected to his eyeset. Which, itself, connected to nothing. The pathetic network connection between the hotel and Earth had been severed. Which was fine by him. Because they couldn't exactly sell the footage if it was beamed all over the net.

Jere still remembered Evan and Ron, eyes wide, lips slick in anticipation of money. *What do you mean, you don't want to do it?* Evan had asked him. *That video is worth tens—hell, hundreds—of millions. Because we're the only ones who have it. Nobody else. This shit never happens, not anymore.*

It'll make up for the Porsche, his dad said.

And so now he was standing outside the door of a madman's cabin. It was the same one he'd stayed in on his first visit. Jere's heart pounded, and he heard his breath rattling in the back of his throat.

He knocked on the door.

"Come," said a voice within.

Jere pushed through. The door seemed to swing in exaggerated slow motion, as if time itself had become unbuffered. He half-expected to see a muzzle flash, and feel a bullet slam into his body like a wrecking-ball.

But there was just a man—tall, slim, dark-haired—sitting hunched-over on the little bed. Something that looked like a gun, if guns were grown in fields on big gnarled gun-trees, lay in his lap. He didn't even look up at Jere.

"May I come in?"

"Please." Looking up at him. The man had strange brown-green eyes that didn't show well in his publicity photos, sunken cheeks, and a mouth that curved down at the edges in a permanent frown. His dark hair was ratty and thinning, even though he couldn't be more than thirty-five years old.

Jere slipped into the room and propped himself in a corner. He put his hands behind his back to hold himself away from the wall but still be as far away as possible from the thing on the bed.

"Thanks for coming," Kevin said.

Jere just looked at him. *Questions, anytime now, he thought.* But his mouth remained stubbornly closed. He imagined himself silent through the whole interview. Boy, would that footage would sell.

That did it. "Why me?" Jere said.

"I thought that was obvious."

"It isn't."

"You're the visionary. You're the one leading us to Mars."

Jere's mouth dropped open. That was the last thing he'd expected to hear. "It's just a reality show."

Kevin's downturned mouth spread into a wide grin. "That's okay. Keep telling them that."

"We could be faking the whole thing," Jere said.

"I looked into it. You aren't faking a thing."

Jere shook his head. "I still don't get it."

Kevin gave him several seconds of that surprising grin, then sighed. "Ask your questions. The ones everyone wants answered."

Jere nodded. "Why'd you do it?"

"I already explained that."

"So you did it because you think we shouldn't be using oil?"

"Mainly," Kevin said.

"Over fifty percent of the world's energy still comes from oil," Jere said, reciting statistics that were stored locally in his eyeset. "It would be an irrecoverable shock to the world economy to lose that overnight."

"It wouldn't be overnight. And it wouldn't be an irrecoverable shock. Oversight would celebrate. Or should celebrate. It would get us several steps closer to sustainability." Kevin gave a wry, sad smile.

"It's a hell of a thing to force sustainability."

A wry smile. "What do you think Oversight is doing?"

"Huh?" Jere forced himself to come out of the corner. Kevin's eyes were big, expressive, and very convincing. Whatever kind of nuts he was, he believed it. Jere needed to move a little closer to him; it would show his commitment in the video.

Kevin tracked him with his eyes, apparently not afraid at all. "With Oversight, the timescale is just a bit longer, is all. Too long. So long we'll get used to it. In sudden change, there's hope. Hope of brilliance. In gradual change, there's only decay."

Jere said nothing. Kevin's soft-spoken words hit him, hard. Because that's what 411 wanted for him. Gradual change and ultimate decay.

Kevin stood up. "You see it, don't you?"

"See what?"

"What you're doing. How it's different."

"I don't know . . . " Jere said, his voice not much more than a whisper.

"Yes. You do. Don't ever give up on that dream."

Those eyes. Those confident, knowing eyes. Kevin seemed so rational, so logical, so well-balanced.

"So . . . so you want to stay up here the rest of your life?"

"No. I want to go farther."

"The Chinese moon base?"

Kevin snarled. "The Chinese will never let me on the moon. I'm still an American to them. I don't wear a uniform. I'm not a party member."

"Where, then?" Jere's voice was soft. He knew the answer.

"Mars."

There was silence in the small room. For a long time, the only sound was the rush of air in the ventilators. Kevin was the first to break it.

"I want to be a contestant," Kevin said.

"We aren't going to stay. On Mars."

Kevin looked at Jere. His eyes appeared to be focused on something very far away. "I might."

"You'd die there."

"That's okay." Silence again. Then: "Make me a contestant."

Jere sighed. He imagined whipping out a contract and having Kevin sign it, right there and then. Spin that, Evan, he thought. He imagined Oversight officers surrounding Neteno. He imagined a brief, bright nuclear flash.

"I can't do it."

"Yes you can! I read your contact! You're making expats. They're your wards. I can sign it and stay right up here until it's time to leave for Mars. I can even help you build your transport. You're assembling in low Earth orbit, right?"

It would be the biggest publicity to ever hit Neteno. It would be the end of Neteno. Because no matter what Ron said, there *was* such a thing as bad publicity. When it got so big it ran you over and flung you out like a bag of trash on the freeway, it was bad.

"I can try."

"There's no try," Kevin said. He raised the little wood gun and pointed it at Jere. Jere's heart thundered, a million miles an hour. He noticed the barrel glistened wetly.

"I . . . "

"You'll do it!" Kevin screamed, leaping off the bed. He took the gun and pressed its muzzle against Jere's neck. The barrel was warm and slick. Jere felt his gorge rise again.

"Say it!" Kevin said. "Give me your word! Say it! We don't need paper! We don't need screens! Your word is good enough."

"I . . . " Jere began.

There was a sharp *ping* from somewhere in the cabin, then a scream like a giant teakettle. Kevin made a small noise, deep in his throat. His weight fell against Jere. He wrapped his arms around the other man to hold him up, and felt something warm and wet spreading on Kevin's back.

"Kevin!" Jere called, as the other man's legs buckled. His eyes were wide and blank.

Jere pushed himself away. Many things hit him at once as Kevin crumpled to the floor. His hands were covered with blood. The teakettle noise still wailed. His ears popped, and he felt light-headed. There was a tiny little hole in the aluminum wall, right below the porthole. And something, gleaming and metallic, floated outside the porthole itself.

There was a hole in the wall. The shriek of air escaping.

Jere's eyes flew wide, and he scrambled out into the hall. He could feel the air flowing towards the cabin door. He shut it, but it buckled inwards and didn't stop the flow.

In the lobby, the pale Russian attendant shrieked like a girl when he saw Jere's blood-soaked hands. "We're leaking!" Jere cried.

"Leak?" the attendant said. "You shoot?"

"No! Someone else shot Kevin. Through the wall. From outside."

"Outside? Is not possible!"

"Is possible," Jere said. "Now go fix!"

The blond pilot came running down the hall, carrying the caulking-gun, silicone, and a roll of plastic. The two took off towards the room while Jere collapsed into a lobby seat. His hands made bright red prints on the white vinyl.

When Jere was back on Earth, the video sold for fifty-seven million dollars to the WarnerNetflix studios, which posted 745,000,000 paid accesses in the next twenty-four hours.

"There's the size of your Mars audience," Evan said.

"Or bigger," Ron said.

But when Jere went online, the boards fed disturbing things to his eyeset.

Of course, it's a Neteno thing, they said. *Does anyone ever believe them anymore?*

Probably orchestrated the whole thing. I bet Kevin never existed.

But the bombs.

Were YOU there? Easy enough to hack the Found Media.

But Kevin existed. He did the mini-Gs.

Do we know that, for sure?

And, most disturbingly: *I bet their whole Mars thing is a load of shit.*

Glenn

When Glenn Rothman got the big thick envelope from Neteno, he knew what it meant. He didn't even bother taking it up the drive to the house. He tore it open right there. Old Lady Pellerman, his crazy next-door neighbor, watched him from her mailbox across the street.

I'll sign it right here, he thought. Sign it and show Alena. Once and for all. He'd look down at her from Mars and thumb his nose at her. She'd hate that. She was the first to go for the flightsuits through Manhattan gig, she was the one who insisted they do the ice climbing on Jammu; she was more competitive than he ever was.

And this was the big one. Bigger than anything. The fifty million prize didn't mean a damn thing. Well, maybe it did. But being able to say, hey, I ran this course on another planet, where nobody had ever thought of being before, where no human foot had ever touched—that was the big deal.

He pulled the letter out from a big paper-clipped bunch of legalese.

Dear Mr. Rothman,
    We're pleased to accept both you and your wife Alena as contestants on our upcoming show, Winning Mars. . . .

Glenn's brain went full stop. *Both?*

During the course of our review, we found that both you and your wife had applied to our program. . . .

Oh, shit.

We're pleased we can accept you both. Your accomplishments in the field of action sports are extremely impressive, and we believe you will be a very competitive team.

Shit oh shit.

Please note that this offer is for both you and Alena. If either of you decline this offer, please consider it void. The contract is only binding with both of your signatures. Although we do not anticipate that you will have a problem with this stipulation, we did want to clarify. Please sign, notarize, and return these documents by the date specified.

Sincerely,
Jere Gutierrez
CEO, Neteno, Inc.

"Shit!" Glenn screamed.

Mrs. Pellerman halted her snail-slow mailbox routine, and put her hands on her hips, glaring at Glenn.

He didn't care. "Fucking Alena!"

"Watch your mouth!" Sharp, in that squealing old lady tone that drove Glenn insane. She used the same tone when she gossiped with the other blue hairs about the "colored couple in the neighborhood." That was back when Glenn and Alena were together.

"Watch your hemorrhoids!" Glenn snapped, and raced back up to the house.

Glenn called Alena's office. No answer. Just the smooth impersonal voice of her attendant. Of course. Probably because she knew it was him. He called her home number.

No answer. Another attendant. Fuck, couldn't Alena have a little bit of personality and use her own voice?

Glenn paced back and forth in his little home office. He should call Neteno. He should get them to reconsider.

But they would never do that, would they? They were Hollywood. The more Springer-esque they could make it, the more they would. He re-read the letter, grinding his teeth at the assumption in the last paragraph. They knew this would turn him inside-out. The story on him was all over Facebook, all over the mediascape.

He twisted the simple gold band he still wore. It was polished smooth, inside and out, by all of his twisting. Would Alena do it, even if he were part of the package? If he could speak to her in person, he could tell her: *It's not like we're married. Just a business thing.*

Because this was the biggest thing out there.

If this is the biggest thing, go bigger, Glenn thought. That's what Mr. Henry, his high-school track coach and mentor, had told him. Track was just a thing. Mr. Henry had really been into rock climbing—and that was what had led Glenn into action sports. That, and meeting Alena.

Glenn sat down at his computer and paid a locator a hundred bucks to get a GPS read on Alena's phone. It mapped to a location at the foot of Boulder Canyon. Sat photos showed it to be a parking lot. The parking lot where they left the car, back when they used to do Lady of the Light on Solar Dome. Glenn remembered those climbs well. The up-and-out, the rock alive under his fingers, just inches away from the end. His heart, like a well-tuned motor. Alena, above him. And then finally at the top, alone, looking out over Boulder and the foothills to the plains. On a clear day, it was almost as if they could see Nebraska. Sitting through sunsets with Alena, huddled close as the sky pulled the heat from the rock.

She was climbing.

Glenn slammed the Neteno contract down on the table, turned to the back where the signatures went, scrabbled for a pen, and scrawled his name. He would take it to her, already signed. He'd say: *All we need is a signature. Just one signature, and we've done the biggest thing in the world. Off the world. If you can't do it for me, do it for the endorsements. Do it because it's something nobody else can do.*

Glenn shoved the contract into his back pocket, grabbed his bag of climbing gear, and headed out for the trailhead.

Two hours later he was watching Alena try to kill herself.

Of course, she wouldn't see it that way. For her, it was just being aggressive, just going max-out. That was the way she was. She always pushed it. Whether it was Tibet, or Scotland, or just a little climb right outside their hometown, she always tried to do more. Climb once, time it, try it again. Try to make that time better. Try a harder route. Or do stuff like she was doing now.

Glenn stood on the ledge to the right side of Solar Dome, looking up at Alena scrabbling on the clean steep face of the Lady of Light. Not an insane route, not by a long shot, but challenging, mainly edges and side pulls with a long crux reach rightward for thin fingers. The stone was decent, nothing more. Careful and slow, it was safe as houses. Fast and loose, like Alena liked to do it, and you were looking at turning yourself into ketchup right quick.

Fast and loose on a winter day when the sun was warm but the rock was cold, where there were still little pockets of ice gathering in cracks and crevices, was insane.

The sun may be warm, but the rocks know the weather, Mr. Henry's voice whispered to him, from the distance of many years.

Glenn wanted to shout. But he knew you didn't shout. Not even if you thought you had to. He imagined her starting at the sound of his voice, slipping, falling . . . there would be nothing he could do but watch.

A terrible little voice said: *She can't sign if she's dead.*

Glenn pushed that voice away and set to climbing. Starting was difficult, blank for the feet, and he had a terrible moment when his fingers seemed to find purchase, then peeled rock when he started to shift his weight. He pushed hard against the cold stone. He imagined he could hear it, laughing at him. Slow and go, slow and go.

When he chanced his next look upwards, Alena was moving through the narrow slot that led to the top. She looked down at him, her eyes dark beads. But he knew she saw him.

She sped up her pace.

Great, Glenn thought, and continued climbing.

The slot was icy, and Glenn's numb fingers felt nothing as he pulled himself up. Footholds slipped and peeled. The rock itself seemed to be against him. He paused and panted, waiting for Alena to look down at him again. He imagined her standing there, hands on hips.

But she never looked down, and a grimmer thought came to him. Maybe she was already on her way down. Avoiding him.

Glenn climbed a little faster.

When he reached the top, Alena was sitting on the cold stone, pants flapping in the wind around her slender legs. She looked out over the foothills to Boulder, hands wrapped around her knees. Like those nights he remembered.

Except now she was alone.

Glenn went to her side, but she just looked up at him and said, "Stop."

She was so beautiful. Big dark eyes set in an elfin face with high, perfect cheekbones. Skin on the darker side of caramel, a shade lighter than his own. Arms like a dancer, with powerful muscle hiding close under flesh. She'd cut her hair shorter than the last time he'd seen it, and it fell in playful chocolate-highlighted waves, tousled from the climb.

"I know what you're going to say," Alena said. "You almost killed yourself, blah blah, you need to be more careful, gnar gnar."

Glenn started to sit down.

"You can't sit by me," Alena said, scrambling to her feet. She backed away from Glenn, as if they were two prizefighters circling each other in the ring.

"What are we going to do, then?" Glenn asked. "Dance?"

Alena tossed her head. "I see you're still wearing your wedding band."

"Some of us can hope."

Alena blew air out her nostrils. "I got the contract too."

"All you have to do is sign," Glenn said. "Then we're going to Mars."

"They're playing us. It makes me sick."

"Alena . . . " Glenn started, then a flare of anger made him say, "Why'd you even have to enter? I would have already been signed and on my way to LA!"

"Don't be so confident, big man."

"Why'd you have to enter using our last name?" Glenn said.

Alena stopped pacing. "Labels don't matter."

"Is that it?"

She laughed. "Don't read anything into it. I'm not pining for you." She held up her hands, bare of rings. "And, speaking of that, why'd *you* enter? I'd be signed and on my way to Hollywood, if it wasn't for their stupid pair-or-nothing clause."

Glen just goggled at her.

"They did it on purpose," Alena continued, pacing from one side of the rock to the other. They saw both of us, said, 'Hey, this is a great-looking couple, and we can check the African-American box too.' Then they saw we were divorced, and said, 'Now, this is absolutely perfect. Get them fighting too."

Glenn nodded, remembering his earlier thoughts. "You think we're a good-looking couple?"

"One of us is."

For a while, there was only the sound of the breeze, and the faint hum of civilization, far below. Alena went to the edge of the dome and looked down on the valley below.

"If they're rigging the game, there's only one way we can play," Glenn said.

Alena frowned. "Sign it and act the happy couple, you mean." Alena sneered.

"Act like two people in business together," Glenn said. He reached around to his back pocket and pulled out the contract, now rumpled and sweat-stained. "I've already signed. All it takes is one more signature, and we're on our way to the biggest thing ever."

Alena looked at the contract, and cocked her head at him, as if amused.

"Bigger than Everest, bigger than free climbing Half Dome, bigger than marathoning the Utah desert, bigger than swimming the English Channel."

Alena sighed.

"If you won't do it for me, do it for yourself."

"Have you read it? The contract?"

"No."

That amused look again.

"Don't fucking laugh at me!"

Alena laughed. "I'm not." She reached into her bag and drew out a sheaf of papers, neatly folded. "It's just that I was going to say the same thing."

On the back page was her signature, neat and clear.

Alena Rothman.

When they'd signed each other's contracts, Alena went to sit down on the rock. Glenn made to sit down beside her.

"No," she said.

"You're kidding."

"Not at all." Smiling up at him, in mock innocence.

Glenn stood by her for a few minutes, then started back down the rock. He wanted Alena. He wanted her more than ever.

But, for the moment, the signature was enough.

Science

"I thought they found life on Mars," Jere said.

Evan rolled his eyes heavenward. It was 3:47 a.m., and they were screaming down the 5 at triple-digit speeds in Jere's Porsche. The scrub brush at the side of the road whipped by, ghostly gray streamers disappearing into taillight-red twilight. They were in that no man's land between Stockton and Santa Clarita where the land falls away and you could believe you were the only person in California, at least for a time.

Jere frowned, seeing the look out of the corner of his eye. It was Evan Shows Off time again. He loved to do that. "What? They didn't? Talk, you fucking know-it-all."

"They still don't know," Evan said. "There were those meteorites, but they're still arguing about it. Some of the scientists say that the microstructures they're looking at resemble ancient bacteria, and some of them say it's wishful thinking. Typical science tempest in a teapot."

"What micrometeorite? They brought something back from Mars?"

"They found it in Antarctica."

Jere frowned. He couldn't wear his eyeset at night, not in the car, so he couldn't ask it to confirm what Evan had said. He hated being disconnected. It was like losing part of your mind. "What does that have to do with Mars?"

Evan shrugged. "Scientists say it was a piece of Mars, blown off the planet by a meteor. It eventually landed in Antarctica."

"And they can tell that shit? That it's from Mars? How do they do that?"

"I don't know the details."

Jere snorted. "I thought you knew everything."

Evan went silent for a long time. There was nothing but the hum of the tires and rush of the wind and song of the engine. Just when Jere thought he was going to let it go, he cleared his throat and said, "What's important is that the scientific community is interested and wants to give us a bunch of money."

"Funny thinking of Mars as a science thing."

Evan shook his head, and then said, almost gently, "It's too bad we can't wait a couple years. Do it in 2026. The whole fiftieth anniversary thing."

"Fiftieth anniversary of what?"

"Viking. 1976."

"What's Viking?"

Evan shook his head again. "Viking 1 and Viking 2 were the first probes we landed on the surface of Mars. We, the United States, that is. In 1976. For the bicentennial. They did some experiments that, again, some scientists say indicated life, some say they didn't. Later, we went and found water, and methane, and lots of stuff that indicate life, but there's never been any definitive word."

We put shit on Mars fifty years ago? Jere thought. What the fuck happened after that? Have we had our thumbs up our asses for that long? He remembered seeing grainy video of American astronauts on the moon, jumping around like the Chinese were doing now. That was even earlier, wasn't it?

"We're still on for this year?" Jere asked.

"So far."

"You don't sound so certain."

"They're being a bit cagey. I think they're still trying to cope with the business after you and the Kevin stunt."

It wasn't a stunt, Jere thought. The United States was still denying having killer satellites, or satellites full of killers, in orbit. But Jere knew what he saw, and someone had clearly shot through the cabin from the outside. Someone who didn't care very much whether it ended in explosive decompression.

I could have died.

More silence. In front of them, nothing but darkness and stars, and the dim outline of mountains. Jere pushed the car to 130, 140, 150. The blur became a haze of motion, almost surreal.

"So what do you think about the Berkeley proposal?" Jere said.

"It's crap."

"Why?"

"Like, duh. Berkeley probably can't even design the right experiments package. They're a liberal arts school."

"Why'd we bother seeing them?"

Evan gave Jere his don't-be-stupid look. Jere recognized it, even out of the corner of his eye. "Because they asked. Because if we're talking to them, others'll be interested."

"So we get another school."

"No."

"What?"

"We might see some other schools," Evan said. "But we fish from industry. That's where the money really is."

"Who?"

"Siemens. Or IBM. Maybe Nanoversics. Someone big, with deep pockets."

Jere nodded. Berkeley had offered them quite a bit of money. With someone like IBM in on a bidding war, how high could the stakes get? God knew they needed the money. Expenses kept creeping up, especially now they had to start thinking about training, launch, and ongoing support.

"It's coming together," Evan said. "You're getting some great contestants lined up, now that we're off the convict frequency."

"I didn't know Keith and Samara would be so problematic."

"Nothing you could do. At least we still have one. And the Glenn and Alena thing is brilliant. This is just like the shit we used to do, back in the day."

Ah. Now the Congratulatory Evan. The politician, the manipulator. He should run for Congress after this was all over.

Still, Jere couldn't help smiling, a little. "It'd be great if Glenn and Alena got back together, then won." A storybook ending.

"What do you mean, it'd be great?" Evan turned around in his seat, so he could look directly at Jere. "I thought that was what you were planning. Give 'em a cash offer to for kissy-kissy, then make sure they finish first."

"If they win, they win."

Evan's mouth popped open. "You aren't going to run this real, are you?"

"It *is* a reality show."

"That doesn't mean it's real. Fuck. Run this real, Keith is gonna win." Pissed. Angry. The real Evan, at last.

"You don't know that."

"Yes. I do know that. That's how it works. Nice guys finish last. Assholes finish first. And Glenn is the fucking definition of a nice guy. Fucking pussy-whipped nicey-nice asshole. I'd've thrown his bitch wife off the rock a long time ago."

"Whoever wins, wins. I won't game it."

"You're being stupid."

"That's fine with me."

"Then get prepped to see Keith standing on the podium. How're you going to spin that?"

"If he wins, I'll think of something."

Evan turned back in his seat, and slumped down so his knees hit the dash. "Better start thinking now, then."

Silence. Nothing but them and the open road.

Scarce

Bob Petracio, CEO of Gen3, was blunt. He was always blunt—at least when he was safely alone in his office on the top floor of One Wilshire, sitting behind a big expanse of gauche mahogany desk. For someone not yet forty, he had the taste of Patrice's grandfather.

"You need to stop seeing Jere for a while," he told her. Behind him, tinted floor-to-ceiling windows admitted a fraction of the bright clear day, as fluffy white clouds piled in a bright blue sky above the slate-colored Pacific.

"Why?" Patrice asked.

A pause. The pause of a guy who wasn't used to explaining himself. "He's become too controversial. That Cho affair keeps bubbling up."

"I don't see anything in my contract that prevents me from seeing my friends."

Silence for a while. Patrice waited, arms crossed.

"You are supposed to act 'in the best interests of Gen3,' and not directly jeopardize our position as the North American leader in interactive entertainment,'" Bob said, his eyes glassy as he read from the eyeset.

"*Directly* is the key word here, I think."

Bob sighed. Drummed fingers on his desk. "The lawyers can fight over that one for months. In the meantime, I'd prefer—"

"No."

A nod.

Patrice turned to leave.

"Wait," Bob said.

"Why?"

"Because I must insist." Patrice's eyeset floated a red IMPORTANT MESSAGE alert. It was from Bob. It was a simple legal document, only a couple of hundred pages.

"What is this?"

"It's an injunction," Bob said.

Patrice laughed. "Go ahead. I don't need any more money from you."

"This isn't just forward-looking. We'd want reparations, as well."

Patrice stomped to Bob's desk and leaned over. "What the fuck, Bob?" Bob's expression didn't change. He waited a long time to speak. When he did, he sounded bored.

"Bottom line, Four-eleven doesn't like the connection between you and Jere. They don't like the negative spin of the Cho incident, they don't like the ongoing speculation. Their analysis shows it having downward pressure on our sales, specifically your titles, in the range of eleven to thirty-eight percent. Big numbers. Numbers that are eminently avoidable."

And that's all it is to you, Patrice thought. Cooking the numbers. Maximizing the revenue. All the boring crap. Business.

"You're bending over for eleven percent? *Maybe* eleven percent?"

"Eleven to thirty-eight percent. And I trust the Four-eleven numbers."

Of course you do, you whining asswipe, Patrice thought. She remembered again why she liked Jere so much. He'd see those numbers and laugh.

"So that's it?" she asked.

Hands spread. A weak smile. "I have no choice."

Patrice thought of telling him to stuff his contract up his ass. Patrice thought of storming out of the office. She thought of finding a superstar lawyer of her own. She thought of immediately going to Jere and the media.

But she could lose it all.

And she could not see YZ in the world with no money. YZ with no money was YZ in prison, YZ on a leash, YZ the pet. And Jere hadn't even yet asked her to throw in. But she could play it.

"What do I have to do?" she asked.

A smile, broad and genuine as a car salesman. "Just stay away from Jere."

"For how long?"

"For a while. If his enterprise goes well, there is a point where it will be advantageous for you to step back in."

Patrice nodded. She stood up. She left.

In the hall, she said, softly: "Asshole."

Mike

This is less of a party than a wake, Mike Kinsson thought, as he stepped out onto the back porch. But at least his parents had gotten the banners right:

Farewell Mike!
Win Mars for Us!
Upward and Onward!

His parents' yard was done up in a cool motif, with fresh-printed *trompe l'oeil* canvasses of Martian terrain covering the normally bright green grass, and panoramas of Martian sky and horizon hanging at the back of the yard from the tall juniper trees. They'd set round tables with brilliant blue tablecloths in the middle of the Martian scene, in an almost surreal contrast to the reds and salmons and pinks of the printed landscape.

They'd even gotten the music right. As he walked out onto the porch, the bump of old style rap was replaced with a redo of Gary Numan's famous song, "Cars."

"Here on my Mars, where everything has gone right . . . " Numan's electronically smoothed voice rang out across the yard, turning heads. Eyes settled on Mike. He shrugged, feeling a small thrill of fear. Time to run the gauntlet.

The crowd was a mix of neighbors and relatives. Neighbors because you couldn't have a party anywhere these days without offending someone, so you had to have the invitation trail, and the disclaimers, and the legal notices that you might play music at a level where others might hear, and that you could not guarantee they might not get offended. Had to invite the key opinion-leaders and gabbers in the hood. Apologies in advance to all others, best with a small cash donation.

Mike's parents lived in a small, flat neighborhood of fifty-year-old ranch houses in San Jose, part of the first wave of building when the city was starting to be known as the capital of Silicon Valley. It was a pleasant enough neighborhood with mature trees and ruler-straight streets and homes set back behind broad expanses of front lawn, with generous-sized back yards they'd build two houses on these days. Most everyone there was old and conservative and remembered the days when you tolerated a little stupidity from the neighborhood teens now and again. But you never knew, so you invited them anyway.

Mike nodded at the neighbors, shook a few hands, and took a few perfunctory congratulations. Most gave him that close stare that people used when they were inspecting something unusual and maybe a little dangerous, like a jeweled seventeenth-century dagger or a vial of the Three-Day Death. Mike remembered almost none of them except for the Ettslers, who had become gray and stooped in the years he'd been away. He remembered Mr. Ettsler as a tall, gaunt man with salt-and-pepper hair. Now his hair was completely gray, and he stooped almost to the level of his wife, who blinked out at him through amazingly clear blue eyes.

Then it was on to gauntlet number one. Grandparents Part Uno: Mom's mom and dad sat at one of the circular tables, drinking some kind of straw-colored drink. Mike looked up to see his dad happily bartending behind an antique fake wood grain portable bar, running margaritas in a blender. Dad didn't drink, but he enjoyed getting other people drunk.

"So it's off to Mars, is it?" Granddad Murray said.

Mike tried to smile at them. It felt like he was trying to stretch a wooden mask.

"Why?" Grandma Murray said.

"Yes, off to Mars."

"Astronauts used to do that," Granddad said.

"Not you," Grandma said.

"It's a different world."

"Ahem. Yeah." Granddad Murray had found a groove he could fall into, like a vinyl record on an old-fashioned turntable. "Can't say I understand a whole lot about it anymore. Can't say I like it that much."

"We were talking about Mars!" Grandma said.

"Oh, yeah. Mars."

"You talk him out of it!" Grandma said, glaring at Mike.

Granddad blinked and focused. "I wouldn't do it," he said. "Not if someone put a gun to my head. And I was in 'Nam."

Mike rolled his eyes. Anything to get Granddad off *that* frequency.

"I can't," Mike said. "It's a done deal. I signed the papers."

"It's never done," Granddad said. "It's a damn movie studio, not the government. It's not like they can put you in jail."

Mike frowned. You didn't see what I signed, Granddad. You don't know what they can do with me. "It doesn't matter. I want to go. I'm going."

"It's dangerous," Grandma wailed. Heads turned towards them, then quickly snapped away.

Mike knelt down to look in her eyes. "I know. But it's something I believe in."

"We should fix the problems here at home first," Granddad said.

"Then we won't ever go anywhere!" Mike said, standing again. He'd heard all arguments before. First from Gina. Then from his boss. Then over the phone from family. Now in person.

"You don't have to shout," Grandma said.

"I'm sorry. But I'm doing this, and nothing's changing my mind."

Granddad nodded. "It's good to have something to believe in."

"Right."

"It's just, well, it's too bad yours is so *out there*."

Mike clenched his fists. Yes, I know. I should've become a stockbroker or a lawyer or something safe like that. You've been telling me that since I was old enough to understand. Maybe longer, for all I know. So why don't you go back up to San Francisco, to your safe house, and your safe life, and don't worry about me?

"Yes, I should stay here," Mike said. "And make sure I follow all the Oversight guidelines."

Granddad pursed his lips, and he jaw worked, but he said nothing."

Mike looked up at his dad. "Oh. I think Dad wants to talk. I'll be back later."

"We may not be here," grandma said. "We have a concert in the city in a couple of hours."

"Yeah, the Second Stones are playing."

Barf, Mike thought. And they'd probably have him do that, have implants to get Keith Richard's canned thoughts running around in his head, so he could ape his work.

Dad was mixing some kind of nuclear orange-colored drink when Mike walked up. "Martian Sunrise," he said. "Want one?"

"No."

"Your loss." He set it on the bar. It was soon scooped up by a passing neighbor.

"You didn't have to go all out like this," Mike said, gesturing around at all the Mars decor.

"Of course we did," Mom said, coming up behind Dad. She smiled brightly and batted her eyelashes. She was still a very attractive woman, though in the last few years she'd decided to stop battling the gray that streaked her hair. It made her look ten years older than Mike remembered. He thought it was a little sad.

And what she said was spot-on. Of course they had to go all out. This was what they did best. The guilt. *See what we do for you,* they were saying. *How can you leave us, how can you go against our will, when you see all we do for you?*

"Are you ready?" Dad said.

Oh yeah, and we won't mention it, so you'll feel even guiltier.

Mike sighed. "I know you're worried."

Mom and dad exchanged glances. "We're not—" Mom started.

"What about your job?" Dad said. "Can you get your job back when you return?"

"No." Apple had been very clear on that. Even thought they'd sponsored other employees to vblog from Africa, or explore the Antarctic, or five dozen other stupid things, they had no interest in Mars.

"That's too bad," Dad said. "Though you could probably get a job pretty quick with the experience you have."

"I guess."

"If he gets back," Mom said, her face crumpling into an agonized mask. "You might die!"

"I know."

Silence for a bit. Then, Dad: "Do you really? Have you looked at the odds they're giving for this thing?"

"No."

"You should."

Mike shook his head. He'd never looked at them, but he knew them, because people spouted them all the time. But those were the odds the bookmakers made, the guys who looked at horses or athletes or any of a dozen other things that had no real investment in winning.

When you care, it's different, he thought. He looked around the perfectly manicured yard, to the perfectly-kept little house. It wasn't much, but it was worth millions.

Why chance it? friends had asked. *Hang on, take the house when they're gone, call it a day. You're an only child.*

"You should think of us," Dad said.

"You should think of me."

Mike's parents stared at him, open-mouthed. Which was the perfect entrance for Grandparents Part Dos, the Kinssons. Grandpa Kinsson was a large, red-faced man. He sloshed the remains of one of Dad's Martian Sunrises in the general direction of Mike. Mike was able to avoid the stream of orange liquid. "What's the prize money up to now?" Grandpa Kinsson asked.

"I don't know. I'm not in it for the money."

Grandpa Kinsson gave a big, roaring, boozy-smelling laugh. "Right, right. I think it's what, forty million?"

"Closer to fifty," Grandma Kinsson said.

"That's enough to tempt anyone. Smart boy."

Grandpa Kinsson owned parts of seventeen wineries in the Sonoma and Russian River Valleys. He'd been nothing until the California wine collapse. Then he'd gambled, and won big. Now he drove a white Ferrari, like the ghost of improbable TV shows past.

And you're one to talk about improbable TV shows, Mike thought.

"Excuse me," Mike said.

"We're offending him," Grandpa Kinsson said.

"No. I've got to take a leak."

And he did. But on his way to the bathroom, he passed his old room. His ten-by-twelve universe, where he would stare up at the glow-in-the-dark star chart that Grandpa Kinsson had got him one Christmas before he was rich. Where he slept under covers printed with aliens from old science fiction movies, watching those same movies on his prized iPod. Because even then he could look out over that perfectly manicured lawn and walk down the plastic-covered carpet of his perfectly manicured house and sit at the dinner table where you ate slowly and carefully because that was what was mannerly, and that was what you did. Because he knew everything was safe, even then, and he wanted to get as far away as possible. Even though they made fun of him for doing well in science. Even though they called him geek and nerd. Even though he had to struggle ten times as hard as the real brainiacs to do well in math than in English or even Chinese.

All that was gone now. His room had been wiped clean, painted in a light lavender color, with a frilly white bedspread on his old twin bed. The ceiling had been scraped clean of that cottage-cheese stuff they used in very old houses, and was now a flawless matte white. The closet door, formerly pocked from thumb-tacked posters, had been replaced with floor-to-ceiling mirror-doors. A thirty-something guy wearing Dockers and the *Winning Mars* gimme-shirt looked back at him. A guy with a face too round to be conventionally attractive and thin brown hair already receding. Nothing special.

Mike went to the closet and opened the door. It was empty, except for three unused hangars. It smelled like new paint.

He shook his head, feeling hollow inside. His childhood was wiped clean.

When he rejoined the party, he pushed his face into a smile and held it there. He even accepted one of the sickly-sweet Martian Sunrises that Dad was pushing on people. He couldn't finish it, but it made the smiling a bit easier.

Only one more gauntlet left.

Mike sat and waited for Gina, smiling. He was determined to be smiling when she came. She was late, but that didn't mean anything. She was always late.

When his dad came out of the house, shaking his head, Mike knew something was wrong.

"Come on in," Dad said, beckoning at the house. "You have a message."

"Gina?"

A nod.

Inside the house, Gina looked out at him from his parents' tiny thirty-inch flatscreen.

"Gina, if you can't come, I—"

"Mike, I'm sorry I can't make it—" Giggling in the background. Gina clipped on an earring.

She was getting ready to go somewhere.

"—but I wanted to say goodbye, or farewell, or whatever—" more giggling interrupted her, and she turned to look at whoever it was. "Stop it! I'm talking to Mike!"

He was watching a recording.

Unintelligible conversation from the side. "Okay. Mike. I mean, good luck. I hope you win. See you when you're back."

But I won't miss you in the meantime, she was saying.

Mike stood and watched the recording, all the way through. By the time he was done, both mom and dad were watching with him.

"Weren't you going to give her a ring?" mom said.

Mike nodded.

"I'm sorry," she said, her eyes filling with the first real tears.

I'm not, Mike thought. Hurt, yes. Sorry, no.

He stayed. He drank. He got in arguments.

Finally, when it was night, he stood out in front of the house and looked back at its clean and tidy façade. Clean white light spilled out from the windows onto the front lawn. The walkway, flagstone, had razor-sharp edges. Not a blade of grass was out of place.

From inside the house, his mom noticed him looking, and raised a hand in tentative wave.

Mike waved back at her, then turned to where his ten-year-old Corvette waited at the curb. It was weighted down with everything he felt he had to bring. He'd be in LA for three months, training.

Then off to Mars.

To *Mars.*

Sponsors

"It seems like a lot of work for just a show," said the asshole from Proctor & Gamble. He was your typical lifer executive, baby-smooth hands and a soft voice and lacquered-in-place hair and an oh-so-conservative black Armani suit that probably exactly matched the dozen-or-so black Armani suits hanging in his closet, and were trusted only to the highest level of bioproof, DNA-sampling-insured cleaners. He tapped his perfect shiny nails on the model of the Can, sprouting its ring of eleven transport pods.

God save me from execs who think they're smart, Jere thought. Send them to the golf course and the cocktail lounge, where the conversational bar is comfortably low, and they can dazzle the gold-diggers with boring tales of imagined high adventure in the boardroom.

But they didn't really have a choice. It was scrape-the-bottom time. Pitching to anyone who might be interested in having a logo on the ship, or product placement at convenient places throughout the voyage. A step up from in-stream advertisers, but not much. Today was the big-box guys. Proctor & Gamble, Altria, Johnson and Johnson, even Foodlink.

They were in the Neteno boardroom, which had been transformed into a neomodern interpretation of a 1970s NASA workroom, redone on a much greater scale and budget. A moving-ink banner was cycling though imagined Marsscapes and the logo for Neteno's *Winning Mars*, and models of the Can, the drop and transpo pods, the kites and the wheels and the returns hung from the ceiling or were suspended with cheap magnetic trickery.

"Are you launching from Russia?" said the Foodlink rep, a young thin guy in an uncharacteristically rumpled gray suit.

"That's the plan," Jere said.

"You're sending up this entire thing from the ground?" Foodlink-guy said. Jere glanced at his eyeset display and saw his name was Paul Morees, and that his background was red-flagged with tech markers. Degrees in chemical engineering and financial analysis.

Fuckasaurus. A ringer. He was trained in more than the art of taking other people's money. Jere eyeblinked over to the current *Winning Mars* mission plan.

"We're doing a distributed launch, multiple modules to low Earth orbit, then assembly and launch to Mars from there."

"With gravity slingshot?"

"If we tried that, we'd have to scrape the top of Everest to get the velocity," Jere said. Paul gave him a thin grin, as if saying, *Point to you.* The other executives looked at each other and shrugged, or pretended not to hear.

"Your mission plan has changed, what, seven or eight times since announcement?"

Jere nodded. He forced a smile. "One of the main differences between show business and industry is our flexibility. We have a show time, we have a packed house, and the curtain is going to open at a set time. We do whatever it takes to ensure that the show goes on."

"Even if it means sacrificing safety?" Paul said. The other execs leaned forward, lawsuit-senses tingling.

Jere forced his face to stay neutral. "Not at all. Every single contestant gets shuttled to orbit by the most reliable transport system ever designed: the RusSpace Orbiter."

"What about the rest of the flight?" Paul asked.

"We're using the most conservative, most-tested technologies available. Take the ring. It's a standard component of the new RusSpace orbital hotels. And we're saving four module drops by incorporating all the return pods into a single big softlander. The transpo pods are as simple and reliable as they get, just a big bouncing ball. Almost everything we're doing has been used—and proven—multiple times. We're using some of it in new ways, but never in ways that will compromise safety."

"Probably what they said about the *Titanic*," the Proctor & Gamble exec said.

Jere forced his smile wider. *Of course, someone's going to die,* he wanted to say. *Probably lots of someones.*

"Of course we don't claim infallibility," Jere said. "Unexpected things can happen."

"In which case, what's our recourse?" Paul said.

"We have extensive hold-harmless clauses," Jere said. "In the case that any contestant could manage to bring suit against us."

"I've seen your contract," Paul said, his eyes focusing on the floor.

And you're not complaining, Jere thought. Don't think we don't notice that.

"Who's signed so far?" Paul asked.

"I'm sorry, but that's confidential. If you want to buy into a prospectus package, we'll discuss that further."

Paul nodded.

And you aren't saying anything about that, either, are you? Jerry thought. Because you know this is the deal of the century. Even if it goes bang on launch, it's worth it. And if we make it all the way back, you have more publicity than you've ever dreamed.

"What you don't see is the most important part," Jere said. "The personal touch. The people who will actually make this happen."

"You already have your team picked?"

"No. Not at all. I just want to show you what the teams might look like. Because I know you have this idea of a bunch of spacesuit-clad guys hopping around on a dead planet. Boring, right? Well, no. Our friends at Nike outdid themselves on this one. Evan?"

Evan McMaster entered the boardroom through the double doors at the back, accompanied by a trio of young women wearing cosmetic squeezesuits and headers. Brilliant white and crystalline transparent, they looked like nothing more than young women strutting in leotards wearing plastic bubbles on their heads. The suits hugged every one of their curves, making them seem impossibly perfect, unattainable, and unreal.

There was a collective gasp from the execs, and Jere smiled. It always worked that way. They didn't expect this.

"I don't see how it will work." Paul again, of course. "You're trying to use mechanical compression to eliminate the need for a pressurized suit? Won't that kill the wearer?"

Jere draped an arm around one of the women and smiled. "Do these ladies look dead to you?"

"No, but . . . those aren't real suits, are they?"

Jere smiled. He'd memorized this one too, but he usually let Evan take it—because he could be so condescending. It stopped more questions.

"They use the same principles," Evan said. "And it is a very old idea."

An image of a Space.com article, circa 2005, appeared on the Neteno screenwall. Contextual tags highlighted the most important points of the article, and an overlay showed a comparison between the imagined suit in the article and Neteno's version.

"Oh," Paul said. His voice was soft, almost inaudible.

Gotcha, Jere thought.

"I still don't get it," Proctor and Gamble's asshole said. "Why don't they look like the Chinese astronauts on the moon? Their suits are huge."

"The moon is a vacuum," Evan said. "Mars does have a thin atmosphere."

"So?"

"So it makes our job a lot easier. We can provide pressurized air through a small backpack only to the face, which makes the whole suit much less bulky. The pressure required to maintain body integrity is provided by the special form-fitting polymer of the squeezesuit."

"Showboating," muttered one of the other execs.

"No," Evan said. "Not at all. Which would you rather look at—this, or some old Chinese taikonaut in a wrinkled-up old body sock?"

"Your contestants may not look that good."

Evan smiled. "The squeezesuit is of variable thickness. We can make a wide variety of body types look good. And it provides an excellent palette for logo placement."

He snapped his fingers, and logos appeared at strategic spots on the suits. Spots with high visual magnetism, to use the geek phrase. One of the girls spun to reveal a P&G competitor's logo emblazoned over her buttocks. All the better to remind them that if they didn't take the chance, someone else would.

Oh, they loved it. Jere could see it in their eyes. They were sold. They would talk tough and haggle and try to make friends and wheel and deal, but they had them. They'd try to score some free rounds of golf at the best LA courses, or nights out at Matsuhisa, or dark times in dens like the ones under Wilshire, but in the end, they would buy. Just like Panasonic and Canon and Nikon fighting over the imaging rights, Sony and Nokia and Motorola fighting over the comms deal, Red Bull and Gatorade fighting over the energy drink part of it, hell, damn near every single nut and bolt was being fought over.

Go ahead, Jere thought. Talk. Then shut up and give us your fucking money.

Nandir

For Nandir Patel, coming back to Hollywood was a little like coming back to his hometown—and discovering that it had been populated by the undead.

He'd grown up in Studio City, in the San Fernando Valley, the huge suburban sprawl that crept north from Los Angeles like a scruffy sweater made of houses and single-story industrial parks. As a kid, he'd cruised with friends down Sunset Boulevard until it turned into Highland and plunged into the heart of Hollywood. He'd smiled at pretty girls from the backseats of cars, and, sometimes, once in a while, met them later at a party or a bar. Once in a very long while, he had taken them home, to crawl through the screenless window to his bedroom. Where every movement seemed to make the tiny fifty-year-old house squeal like a car alarm, and his parents' room, all the way across the house, seemed much too close for comfort.

Because Mom and Dad believed. They believed in the old ways from the old country, things Nandir had never seen. They even believed in all the United States crap. They'd come to the States in the 90s, before it had gone insane. Before 9/11 and Homeland Security and the Three-Day Death and Oversight. Before the first and second Great Recessions, before the Economic Rethink and the money crash. The New World they'd come to was one in which Nandir's millions would have carried him through the rest of his life, instead of being just enough to make others jealous and leave him unsure of how long it would last.

Even now, his parents still believed. They said, *This is a great place to live.* They said, *Our son is so successful.* They said, *We're so grateful for everything we have,* in their soft voices that they'd tried to scour clean of any trace of Indian accent. And they still lived in the same little house in the same flat part of the Valley, and still worked for the same software company that Nandir had once almost bought, just because he could.

The Hollywood he remembered had never been so clean, so bright, so tourist-oriented. As if everyone had been swept away and replaced by robots that only knew how to smile and say, *Yes ma'am,* and *Yes, sir.* As if hordes of feral Roombas crept out at night to polish the glittering sidewalks, the shining bronze stars, the perfect blacktop.

IT IS PERHAPS RELATED TO THE HOLLYWOOD REWOUND BRANDING CAMPAIGN CURRENTLY RUNNING IN MAJOR MEDIA CHANNELS, Nandir's earbud whispered to him.

Nandir was startled. It was the first time his experimental inference software ever correctly guessed his thoughts. But why was it talking like some demented UCLA professor?

"Informal voice mode," he said.

SURE, his earpod said.

A young girl from a tourist family, fat and unstylish in that inimitable flyover-state way, turned to look at Nandir. Her eyes flickered up to his eyeset.

"Daddy, is he an interactivemaker?" she said.

Dad, clad in a multicolored, horizontally striped shirt and black sweatpants, turned to look, open-mouthed, at Nandir. His bottom lip curled down like the business end of a pitcher. He blinked at Nandir, perhaps running him through some mental database of people seen on the late-night shows.

"Nah," he said. "He's nobody."

Nandir smiled at them as they walked out of the lobby of the Hollywood Roosevelt and onto the street. The girl stared back at him, but when he waved, she snapped her eyes forward.

"What's 'rewound'?" Nandir asked his inference software.

IT'S A TERM THAT REFERS TO THE PROCESS OF RETURNING A MAGNETIC TAPE TO AN EARLIER TIME-MARKER.

"I thought I put you in informal mode."

SURE.

"What's 'rewound'?"

IT'S A TERM THAT REFERS TO THE PROCESS OF RETURNING A MAGNETIC TAPE TO AN EARLIER TIME-MARKER.

Nandir sighed. "What's 'Hollywood Rewound'? "

IT'S A BRANDING CAMPAIGN THAT AIMS TO RETURN HOLLYWOOD TO AN IMAGINED GOLDEN AGE OF HIGH SOCIAL AND MORAL STANDARDS.

"Wow."

The software said nothing, which Nandir thought was probably for the best. He still had a lot of work to do before it was even a tenth as good as

InPersonator, the software he'd sold to WeRU two years ago. If it weren't for the big Neteno dinner, he'd probably be coding.

They'd said to meet at six-thirty in the lobby. It was 6:43 by Nandir's eyeset, and he was still the only contestant there. Unless he'd missed someone in the briefing that morning. Which was entirely possible. He had a poor memory for faces.

At 6:50, one of the other guys arrived. He was a tall, thin man with dark hair and glasses. The universal sign of the geek. Nandir smiled at him, wishing he remembered his name.

"You're the owner of InPersonator, aren't you?" the guy said.

"Was," Nandir said. "Sold it two years ago to WeRU."

A nose-wrinkle. "I don't like their system as much."

Nandir nodded. "It has its drawbacks."

"Yours was more flexible."

"You were a user?"

"Evaluator. I worked for Apple." Eyes cast down, as if embarrassed.

"Worked?" Nandir said.

"Yeah." A pause. The guy held out his hand. "I'm Mike Kinsson."

Nandir took it. His hand was warm and slick with sweat. "Nandir Patel."

"Nandir. Yeah. I remember. But didn't you make a lot of money? Why are you here?"

Why am I here? Nandir wondered. Because even with my pile of money, I don't think I'll be able to live the rest of my life comfortably? Because my current software is a little, well, undeveloped? Because no matter where I go, whether it's here in California or New York or even my little research park in South Carolina, I just can't seem to get comfortable?

"Twelve months of uninterrupted coding," Nandir said.

"Oh. Yeah. Wow, you could probably get a lot done."

"Why are you here?"

Mike looked away, and pulled his bottom lip between thumb and forefinger. "I . . . it's what I always wanted to do."

"Be on a reality show?"

A head shake, violent and decisive. "No. Go to space. Mars."

"A true believer."

Mike took a step away. "You think it's funny."

"No. I think it's admirable." Just like his parents coming to the United

States. Admirable, even if the country they ended up with wasn't the one they expected. What could they do on Mars, with nothing to stop them at all?

Mike looked at Nandir for a long time, studying him with his dark eyes. "You really do?"

Nandir nodded. "I really do."

Mike closed his mouth, as if he didn't know what to say to that. Finally, he nodded.

And, as if the affirmation had been a cue, the rest of the contestants descended upon them. They walked, en masse, across the rough Spanish-tiled floors. Nandir recognized the hard-looking man that everyone said was a convict, the two pretty blondes that everyone said were lovers, and the business-suited blonde from Neteno.

YOU SHOULD COMPLIMENT THIS PERSON, AND ASK THEM OUT TO A NEUTRAL LOCATION, SUCH AS A COFFEEHOUSE, Nandir's earset whispered.

"What?" Nandir said.

YOU SHOULD COMPLIMENT THIS PERSON, AND ASK THEM OUT TO A NEUTRAL LOCATION, SUCH AS A COFFEEHOUSE.

"What what?" Mike said.

Nandir held up a hand. "My software. It needs a little work. Inference software, why did you suggest that . . . your last suggestion?"

YOU APPEAR TO BE ATTRACTED TO THIS PERSON.

Nandir felt a blush warm his face. "I'm not."

YOUR AUTONOMIC REACTIONS APPEAR OTHERWISE.

"I'm not. That was an incorrect response." Nandir looked at Mike, then quickly glanced away.

CORRECTION NOTED AND INCORPORATED INTO THE DATABASE. THANK YOU FOR YOUR INPUT.

Nandir rolled his eyes. He was about to apologize for his software when the business-suited blonde announced, "Okay, we're heading out to Miceli's. Anyone who doesn't know where it is, make sure you're with someone who does."

"Do you know where it is?" Mike asked.

Nandir nodded. "Yeah, I grew up in the Valley."

They ended up with one more guy, a stocky Asian who ran after them as they headed out the doors of the hotel. "I go with you?" he asked.

"Sure," Mike said.

They walked for a while in silence, then the Asian guy said. "I know you, you the software guy."

Nandir rolled his eyes, then turned and gave the guy a smile. "Yeah. And you?"

"What?" the man looked confused.

"What's your story? Where you from?"

The man beamed. "Philippines," he said, nodding vigorously. "I'm Romeo Torres. Wanted to go to space for long time."

"You should talk to Mike, here. He's always wanted to go to space too."

Romeo looked at Mike, beaming. "You did? You see future?"

"I'm not a fortune-teller."

Romeo looked confused.

They ended up that night on one side of a long table, in a restaurant hung with thousands of basket-embalmed wine bottles. A buffer of one chair on either side of the table separated them from the rest of the group.

Geek repellent, Nandir thought. It's like anti-gravity. We drive back everything near us.

INSECT REPELLENT CAN BE PURCHASED AT MOST MAJOR SPORTING GOODS STORES AND A LARGE PERCENTAGE OF DRUGSTORES. THE CLOSEST CONFIRMED STOCK IS AT HIGHLAND DRUG, APPROXIMATELY 0.15 MILES AWAY.

Nandir smiled. "That is an incorrect response," he told the software.

Both Mike and Romeo looked at him, then went back to their conversation about the Chinese on the moon, their moon base, where they were going, diverting asteroids, terraforming Mars, and lots of other things that Nandir didn't really understand.

They were crazy.

And, he knew, they were probably the people he'd end up being teamed with.

Play

Patrice bounced over the surface of Mars in her Mars rover. Ahead of her, two other rovers threw up rooster tails of pink dust and larger pebbles. The debris pattered on her visor as she was thrown violently side to side against the sparse tube-frame of the rover.

There was the roar of an engine behind here. A sudden force shoved her forward. She was spinning, then tumbling, across the cold surface of Mars. Straps dug into her shoulders as the rover tumbled. She saw pink sky and rough Earth, alternating. Finally, she landed upside-down, dizzy and disoriented. Rovers roared by her, engines screaming, towards a red-and-white striped arch, barely visible in the distance. The finish line.

Crash! Patrice's vision spun wildly as another rover bounced off of hers, sending it spinning. As she came around in a complete 360, she saw the rover flying through the air, then bouncing and tumbling. It came to rest on its side. The driver scrambled out of his seat and pushed frantically on the Rover's frame, trying to right it.

I should be doing that, Patrice thought. I should be getting back in the race. But she couldn't summon any interest. She was content for a while to lay upside-down in the cold sand, and watch the race scream by her.

As if mocking, the *Winning Mars* holobanner flickered to life above the finish line. Yvette Zero's perfect face blew kisses from above the banner. Patrice shook her head.

"Reset," she said.

The rover flipped itself over and suddenly she was back at the beginning of the race. Upright, engine idling, a long flat desert in front of her. A long row of contestants stretched away on either side of her, names glowing faintly above their heads. Behind them was the Winning Mars Saloon, where players could buy a virtual drink and talk to other players.

Patrice sighed. The game wasn't bad, but it wasn't good, either. It played well, at least on the full-immersive rigs at Funimation in Santa Monica, where they'd built the actual rovers and flyers and you wore fake Tyvek spacesuits, just as she was doing now. They'd done a good job on the rendering. The landscape was absolutely real. The hardware had that scratched and battered look that came from actual use. The pink sky was otherworldly and dim. She could actually believe she was on another planet.

But most people wouldn't play it on full-immersive. That was reserved for only a tiny percentage of folks. Most people would play it as fake in glasses, or flat on a screen. For them, they'd worked in a lot of social spaces, both on the Mars Explorer in orbit and on the ground, as well as a leveling option that allowed them to start their own gaming leagues and run their own contests. Eventually, they'd even be able to add their own style of competitions to the *Winning Mars* circuit. The hook was that some of the user-generated competitions might be used on a future show.

There was also a "Play with YZ" hook running, since she was the nominal leader of the expedition. So, sometime soon, she'd have to run through the teamwork parts of the game with some panting fan. Which was okay. She liked panting. She liked it just fine.

But she wasn't playing as YZ today, or even Patrice. She'd created an ironic username: ZerozOut. A common enough play on Yvette's memes. She'd seen a thousand variations like it on the username rosters. She'd even set up her character to look a little like YZ—but had made her breasts a little bigger, as if she was a female fan trying to outdo the original. Playing incognito was strangely fun. She hadn't done it for ages.

When the starting gun went off, Patrice let the other rovers rush ahead of her. She took off slow, then turned off the course, towards the east. The game didn't complain. One of its selling points to the geek-tech demographic was that it accurately modeled the entire surface of Mars. You were free to explore.

(And she was sure somewhere on the surface of Mars there was an easter-egg that hid the entrance to underground warrens, where the last remnants of an ancient race toiled on crystalline machines of unimaginable complexity.)

Patrice checked her inventory. In it was a little device named FriendDetector. She smiled. She still had friends in the Gen3 development staff, friends who wouldn't talk to the asshole Bob. She pulled FriendDetector out of inventory and attached it to the tube-frame of her Mars Rover. It lit up green, like some ancient radar screen, and showed a tiny blip, far ahead and farther to the east.

Patrice floored the rover and headed for the blip. She bounced over ground strewn with boulders and cut into rivulets. Nothing moved. There was not a single bit of green. Not a single blade of grass. Patrice shivered. Thousands and thousands of miles of barren world.

Ahead of her, a tiny fleck of white. The blip on her FriendFinder flashed bright green.

As she got closer, the fleck of white resolved into a man in a spacesuit. He stood at the edge of a deep ravine, looking out over hundreds of square miles of alluvial plain. The dust here was more yellow than pink, and the hazy sky had shaded to a light blue. They could almost be in an Earth desert.

Patrice pulled up next to the spacesuited man and stopped. Over his head floated the username "J_wins." He turned to look at her. He was wearing a standard "jim" avatar with no customizations. She felt a pang of disappointment.

"Jere?" she said.

The avatar didn't react. Of course not. If he hadn't spent any time customizing the avvie, why would he set up a webcam to mirror expressions?

"Don't log out," Patrice said. "It's me. Patrice."

"Patrice?" He hadn't even disguised his voice. It was Jere.

"Yes. I'm sorry I haven't been able to—"

"How do I know this is really Patrice?"

Patrice thought. "You bought the Mississippi Monster mechasuit from your friend Jose, who got stiffed on the purchase by Warner Brothers."

"You could get that by digging."

Patrice sighed. "I sold you on this game with six display points, under an oak tree."

Jere said nothing for a long time. His avatar stood, expressionless, like a wax figure.

"Jere?"

"Yeah."

"You believe me?"

"This game is all wrong," Jere said.

Patrice said nothing.

"What happened?" Jere said finally.

What happened with the game or what happened with us? Patrice wondered. "You shine too brightly. Bob said to stay away. For a while."

"And you did."

"I'm sorry! They had me on the hook for financial impact."

"I thought you didn't care about money."

Patrice shook her head. It was easy to seem like you didn't care about money when you had it. "It wasn't just money. IP. They technically own YZ. They'd have me on a leash." And I wouldn't be able to help you when you need it. Amazed she was even thinking that, planning that. What did that mean?

"Will I see you again?" Jere asked.

"Yes!" Of course! Couldn't he see that? Didn't her being here say that, loud and clear?

"When?"

"Soon! The Cho incident is washing off, the *Winning Mars* game is ramping up—"

"—and you're just waiting for His Master's Voice, Four-eleven, to clear it." Rough, angry.

"Don't be like that!"

Jere said nothing for a long time. She wished his avatar would emote. Or at least pace back and forth. Or clench its fists. Or do something.

Finally: "This game is all wrong."

Patrice could think of nothing to say.

"The rovers are wrong. We're not going to use tube frames and little tires, too easy to get stuck. The spacesuits are wrong, we have a whole new design for that. Your planes are all wrong, way too small, and with no downthrust. Your ships are all wrong. We can't afford something that big. And don't get me started on the finish lines, or the tents where you can take off your suits, or—"

Patrice laughed.

"What?"

She imagined the confused expression on Jere's real-world face and laughed even harder.

"What's so funny, for fuck's sake?"

Patrice laughed so hard she couldn't answer for a while. When she could, she had to speak through gasps: "You . . . you're a . . . television executive . . ."

"So?"

"Complaining about . . . how realistic something is."

For a moment, Patrice thought that Jere's avatar actually looked stunned.

Then Jere started laughing.

It sounded so good to hear him laugh.

It sounded so good to hear him, period.

Geoff

Geoff Smith's friend Dave was cool with letting him stay in his apartment in Hollywood while he picketed Neteno about the show. But now that *Winning Mars* contestants were slated, Dave dropped a comment every morning about how it'd be nice to get his apartment back to himself again.

Geoff could see it, a little. The apartment was tiny, muggy, and had that old apartment-smell, like a mixture of ground carpet and wet dog. He had to sleep in the living room. So yeah, it would probably be better for Dave to get the place back to himself. But Dave also worked all day, sometimes twelve or fourteen hours, wrangling computers for some insurance company or something like that. So he really wasn't home that much.

And when he wasn't home, why should he care that Geoff was around?

Truth was, Geoff didn't want to go home. His mother had a little house up in Palmdale. And Palmdale sucked. And living with Mom sucked. Of course, it was only temporary. As soon as he got a job paying a reasonable wage, he'd be out on his own. Maybe even his own condo where he would have his own kitchen, his own dining room, his own game room, his own console, and his own subscription to EA's interactive library. He might even be able to invite Laura, the waitress at the Lancaster Café, down for a game of *Winning Mars*. Maybe. If she didn't expect him to be all romantic and smooth, like the guys in the movies.

At first, his plan to get on *Winning Mars* seemed to be working. He did a video of himself explaining why he should be chosen for the show—not the real reasons, of course, just the ones he thought they wanted to hear—and sent it to Neteno. A few days after uploading it to Neteno, portions of the video mysteriously appeared on YouTube set to 80s music. Eurythmics. 'Til Tuesday. Things like that. People made fun of him in the video comments. But that was okay, because a whole bunch of people got together and lobbied for him to be on the show.

Fat Guy Goes to Mars, they called the cause. Not exactly flattering, especially after he'd lost ten pounds, but Geoff didn't really care how he got on the show. He agreed to a Fat Guy Goes to Mars interview, and talked earnestly about why he wanted to go. But then an even stranger thing happened: Fat Guy Goes to Mars membership shriveled. They left nasty comments about how he wasn't funny without the music.

That was when Geoff went a little nuts.

He filled out every form on the Neteno site. He wrote stories about what he would do when he got to Mars, with realistic scenarios about him dying from lack of oxygen. He did a little machinima thing about him going to Mars and meeting the Martians. He started his own Help the Fat Guy Go to Mars crowdfund site, and he showed up in a fat suit at the Palmdale mall, wearing a sandwich board. People laughed and pointed. Some of them signed his petition. He forged a lot more himself.

When he wore the same board at ComicCon in San Diego, people booed and threw food at him. Just jealous. Most of them wanted to be on the show, Geoff was sure

The only good thing about ComicCon was Gen3 had a thing with YZ pimping out the *Winning Mars* game. Their booth was mobbed. And YZ was stunning, even more beautiful than in her games. Geoff stood for a long time on the sidelines, getting jostled and bumped by the pressing crowd, but he couldn't make himself go any closer to her.

Eventually, he braved the scary vinyl and leather-clad crowd and stood in line and waited. And waited. When he was finally shoved forward to meet YZ, she was frowning at her little plastic jellybean watch. But then she turned to him and smiled, and Geoff knew what he had to say.

"I have to go to Mars with you," he said.

"You're direct," she said. The crowd tittered, as if they'd heard what she said.

"I have to go! I'll show them there's life on Mars!"

Patrice looked surprised. Geoff rushed ahead. "They're hiding it all. NASA. The Russians. Everyone who's been there. Ask Arthur Clarke. The trees. They have pictures of the trees. There's life, and I'm going to prove it."

Patrice's eyes went wide, but she said nothing.

"Clarke's dead, dumbass," someone called from the crowd. And Geoff realized, right there, what he'd done. Their words were being amplified and played into the crowd. He'd told them all the *real* reason he wanted to go to Mars.

Geoff turned to face them, open-mouthed, just as something smacked him in the face. At first, all he felt was cold and pain. He wailed and clawed his face. Then he saw the remains of an ice cream cone laying on the floor, and the trail of ice cream (it looked like chocolate mint chip, but he wasn't about to taste it, oh, no) dripping down his shirt, and realized what had happened.

"Get outta here, nutcase!" Jeers. Laughter.

Geoff looked from them to YZ. YZ had gone back to the back of the stage. She held a hand over her mouth, as if she was trying to keep from laughing.

Geoff pushed his way through the crown and ran.

He spent the rest of the day berating himself. Now, hundreds of people knew the real reason why he wanted to go to Mars. Some of them might even be from NASA or other government agencies. There was no way they'd let him on the flight now. Because he knew they were covering the truth up, and now they knew he knew and was out to expose them.

Geoff closed his eyes, thinking of all the brilliant things he'd done to get chosen for *Winning Mars*. Spending a day in Neteno's waiting room. Coming back for three days more. Using his game projector to show his vids to the secretaries. Arguing with security when they took him out of the building.

Geoff carried a sign: WILL GO TO MARS FOR FOOD, and paced back and forth in front of the Neteno building. The police came and told him to leave the property. He sent them photos of himself, with Mars 'shopped into the background. He played lots of *Winning Mars*. At night, Dave helped him put his story on the nets. But the story fell on a dead network. Nobody seemed to care.

When they put all the contestants up at the Hollywood Roosevelt, Geoff thought of taking his sign down there. But he knew the police would put him in jail if he tried it, in a cell filled with rapists and murderers and drunk drivers. So he went down to the Roosevelt and sat in the lobby and watched the lucky ones stroll by him.

Now they were at some super-secret training facility. Geoff had watched the bus leave the Neteno building and head up the 101. Knowing that was the end. Knowing he was never going to be on the show.

Knowing, now, that he really had to go home.

There was a sharp knock on the door.

Geoff froze.

Maybe Dave hadn't paid his bills. Geoff held his breath.

Muffled swearing came from outside the door. Then, harder: *Knock knock knock.*

A voice: "We know you're there, Geoff!"

A thousand images cascaded through Geoff's head. The police had found him. They were going to take him away. They'd found out about his little AnOther World scam. They were going to put him in a jail cell with rapists and murderers and drunk drivers.

Then, an even more frightening thought: Maybe it was NASA, come to put him away. That would make sense. It took them a long time. But they were the government. Kind of slow. They'd finally realized they couldn't have him saying there was life on Mars and that he was going to prove it.

Geoff went to the window. Outside, there was an old-fashioned fire escape. He tried to push open the window, but it wouldn't slide up more than four inches. He slid it down, then up again, banging it against the top of its frame.

"We hear you in there! Come on, Geoff!"

Geoff banged the window, but it wouldn't budge. He went into Dave's little bedroom and checked the window there. Same thing.

He went back into the main room. Everything was silent. He went to the door and looked through the little fisheye lens. He saw no one in the hall.

Geoff went to open the door, then shook his head. No. Oh no. That was what they would expect. That was what stupid people did in horror movies. He went to the window and tried to figure out why it wouldn't go up.

He'd just found the clamp on the counterweight line when a key scratched in the lock and the door opened. Two men in identical gray suits stepped in the room. Geoff gave a startled little-girl cry.

"Are you Geoff Smith?" one of them asked.

"No!" Geoff said.

The other sighed and looked at a handscreen. "Yes you are."

Geoff felt his heart hammering. "So?"

"*Winning Mars* had a contestant drop out. If you're still interested, we have a contract for you."

"You . . . you do?"

A smile. "Yes. Hell of a thing, finding you. Ever heard of cell phones?"

"Mom doesn't believe in them."

One of the suits looked puzzled. "How old are you?"

"Thirty." Geoff answered automatically.

"Wow. Anyway. We have a contract. Are you interested?"

Geoff took the contract from them, half-expecting it to be a trick, for them to try to put handcuffs on him. But it was just a contract. On paper, like they said it was. He scanned it quickly.

It was real. They wanted him! For *Winning Mars*!

"Give me a pen," he said, in a quavering voice.

They watched as he signed the contract on the greasy bar. Dave would be so happy to get rid of him.

Geoff smiled. And I'll do it, he thought. I'll *prove* there's life on Mars.

Astronaut

Russia was getting to be almost normal.

Jere almost didn't feel the awful winter chill in Moscow, or notice the goats on the road at Baikonur. He didn't mind grabbing cold-slick vinyl seats as the cars' drivers deftly steered around potholes on the treacherous black-iced roads—potholes that looked as if they could hide black bears, potholes that looked like they could swallow the car, potholes so big and deep and dark they might have gone straight through to some beautiful tropical beach in Brazil.

Now they were back at Baikonur for a meet-and-greet and get-some-video with the guy who was really gonna run the show, John Glenn. Not really John Glenn, of course, but that's what everyone called him, 'cause he was old and happy in that creepy way that fit old people had. His real name was Frank Sellers, another good generic white-boy name, like most of the other astronauts who had ever come out of NASA.

Jere and Evan and Ron and the cameraman waited in the awkward RusSpace lounge for Frank to show. But the time ticked by, and there was no Frank. Evan had the cute RusSpace receptionist page him. After half-a-dozen tries, a gruff voice barked out of the speaker.

"What do you want?"

"It's time for your interview, Frank," Jere said.

"What interview?"

"Remember Neteno?"

"Who?"

"The guys who're paying your salary?"

"I got problems here. Your talking-head stuff can wait."

"No it can't. We're flying back today."

A sigh. "Look. That stuff doesn't mean anything. You want to fly, I need to work this through."

"I thought you were a pilot, not ground crew," Evan said.

"I do what I need to do."

"Tomorrow?" Jere asked.

"Doubt it. I gotta go to orbit soon, to work the problems I'm trying to work down here for real."

Ron leaned forward. "What kind of problems?"

"Crap. Where do I start? The Can's a mess, and we haven't even got the pods on it. Electrical is fubar, we're having some hull integrity challenges, and they're arguing about whether or not the air system is robust enough, to start."

"Air? On a journey this long?" Ron said, his face drawing down into a frown. He looked at Jere as if it was his fault. Jere silently cursed himself for allowing Ron to come along.

"Yeah, yeah, the length's the problem. Longer the voyage, the more pain to start. But we always work through it."

Ron turned to Jere. "Let's go film him in place."

"What? You mean like, documentary style?"

"Yeah. We shoot it no sound, as he's doing . . . whatever the hell he's doing, then do narration. The heroic Frank Sellers, giving his all for the cause."

Evan nodded. "It could work."

Frank, from the speaker: "What are you guys mumbling about?"

"We're coming to see you," Ron said.

"I don't have time for your interviews!"

"We don't need an interview. We'll shoot around you, documentary style. We won't even get in the way."

⋯⋯ Then: "Make it quick."

next launch, an aged RusSpace freight
ere had the cameraman take video
on it were the *Winning Mars* logo
ne money from the Roddenberry
ched to orbit, the cargo container
f the *Winning Mars Interplanetary*
ke the contestants from Earth to
e name, it looked like a big trash
e Can.

array of flatscreens. Some of them
Some of them showed 3D charts
them showed an interior shot of

something with a spaghetti-mess of cables floating in air. Blobs of something like water or oil also floated in air. Two VR-goggled Russians wearing those funny fur hats they liked were sitting next to Frank, and mumbling in Russian into throatmikes.

Frank looked at each of them in turn. His mouth was turned down at the edges in a perpetual frown. His gaze flicked mechanically from person to person, as if assessing each of them for signs of weakness.

Jere knew that Frank was ex-military, Air Force. He'd been in the astronaut program back in the Shuttle Days but he'd never actually flown a mission. Something about a shuttle blowing up in 2003. So he wasn't really an astronaut, he was a wannabe-astronaut. Jere smiled as Frank looked at him.

"Do your shot," Frank said, and turned back to what he was doing.

"Perfect," Jere said. "Stay right there." He went to tell the cameraman to get set up, but he was already doing so.

"Is that the Can?" Ron said, stepping forward to lean over Frank, pointing at the interior shot on one of the screens.

"I thought you weren't going to bother me," Frank said.

"Dad, get out of the shot!" Jere yelled.

Ron and Frank both glanced at him, then glanced away. "Is it the Can?" Ron asked again.

"Part of it," Frank said.

"Doesn't look too safe."

Frank made as if to stand up, then sat down again. "Of course not. It's not finished."

"Is this mission safe?"

Big smile. "Of course."

"Then how come you're having so many problems?"

"Ron—" Jere began.

"Shut up," Ron said. Even the Russians stopped chattering and looked up.

Ron turned back to Frank. "I'm concerned."

Frank shrugged. "They'll make it work," he said.

"Not very confidence-inspiring, is it?"

Frank laughed. "If you could have seen half the stuff I saw behind the scenes at NASA, man, you wouldn't worry. These are good guys. Smart. They'll figure it."

"That's why they need your help."

"Look. I don't have to do this. I'm helping. 'Cause this is what I love to do. You're making me love it less."

"Ron, let it go," Evan said, putting a hand on his shoulder. "Let everyone do their job."

Silence for a moment, his dad's body spring-loaded under the pressure of Evan's hand. Then he relaxed. "You're right. I'm sorry. Please continue."

White-hot anger surged through Jere. Evan and his dad. Like old pals. Listening to Evan. Not listening to him.

He pushed the anger down and worked with the cameraman to set up the shot. Frank scrolled through other images on the flatscreens as they shot, sometimes speaking Russian on his own throatmike, or taking long pulls from a bottle of vodka covered with Russian lettering. Jere shook his head. Just have to edit it out.

A little more softly, in the back of his head: He's our fucking pilot! Should he be drinking?

But there weren't any other options. If there were, Neteno would have taken them.

The cameraman got his shots and they headed out.

When they were back out in the freezing cold again, and well away from Russian ears, Ron turned to Jere and said, "Would you fly in this thing?"

"Of course," Jere said. Not a bit of hesitation. Not a bit. He knew how to deal with his father, and uncertainty wasn't the way to do it.

The older man looked up and down the *Enterprise 7*, standing like a dirty needle on the launch pad, and shook his head, but said nothing.

"We're on schedule?" Ron asked Evan.

"So far," Evan said.

Even later, when they were back in the car for another freezing, terrifying ride back to the hotel, Ron spoke again.

"Do you get the feeling that Frank wants this to work a little too much?"

"How's that?" Jere said.

"He was an astronaut. But he never flew."

"So?"

A frown. "So maybe he wants to fly now. Really bad."

"Sometimes a little enthusiasm is a good thing," Evan said.

Ron turned to Jere. "What do you think?"

Jere pretended to consider, and then made his answer: "I think it's good we have someone who loves what he does."

Silence from Ron. Then: "I hope you're right."

Loner

"Help!" Geoff's voice came faintly, far behind Keith Paul.

Keith smiled. Fucker was probably stuck in that chimney of rock back there. Worthless lump of lard. Ahead of Keith rose another steep slope, and beyond that, the little white flags that indicated the finish line. He didn't dare glance at his watch, oh no. He was faster yesterday than the day before, and he'd be faster today than yesterday.

Because I'm going to win.

"Help me! Keith!"

Keith shook his head. Like he was gonna turn back. *I don't need a fucking teammate,* he kept telling the contest pukes. *I put Grimes in the hospital, you want me to do that to this one too?*

As he started scrambling up the loose rocks, faintly he heard Geoff call, "Mr. Paul!" The rocks rose up sharply near the end, but Keith pushed hard with his legs, dancing as the rocks shifted under him. He stayed hunched over, so the fifty-pound pack wouldn't pull him back and send him tumbling backwards down the slope, like the first day he'd run the course. It was larger than a normal pack and top-heavy, which made it tricky.

They said the actual packs would be lighter on Mars, and that he would be lighter too, and that they might have to relearn everything they were doing here, but Keith couldn't worry about it. If he did well here, he'd do even better on Mars.

He was going to win the thing.

Up and over the top. The big gray shadow of Denali rose in the distance, bisecting a passing cloud. The sky was a cheery deep blue, like the kind of shit you saw in postcards and travel snaps from boring assholes. The air was cold. Keith shivered and pushed on, fast down the slope. The flags at the end of the route fluttered happily in the breeze. One of the showpukes sat on a folding chair, behind a table with plastic jugs of Gatorade on top of it. He looked up at Keith as he made his way down the slope, then took a little handscreen and wrote something on it.

Fucking prick, Keith thought. Probably something about Geoff not being with him.

Well, you shoulda given me someone who can keep up, he'd tell them. *You're not gonna slow me down with this lardbucket.*

The action-sports assholes came over the ridge ahead of Keith, moving fast in their funny little spandex suits. The chick was a hot one, if you liked them like steel, with corded muscles that stood out on her legs and arms, and a tight little round ass and decent-sized tits. But she was a monstrous bitch, wouldn't even talk to him. Not even when he was being nice and asking about all the climbing and shit she did. She just looked at him in that fucking superior way, just like the blue-haired bitches buying groceries at the Ralphs where he'd worked for a summer. *No, puh-leez, not a store sack—here are my reusable totes,* they'd say, all high and hoity, pushing their organic cotton bags at him as if they could make up for their lumbering Lexus SUVs parked outside the store.

Keith sprinted towards the end flags, even though he knew they were on different timetables, and it didn't matter at all who got there first. But seeing the buffed-up couple running for it, he couldn't help running for it too. Especially that bitch. Her long legs pumping fast, muscles bunching like steel cable. Keith caught the flash of her eyes, briefly, as she looked up at him.

She pulled out in front her so-extreme dude. He reached out for her as she passed, as if to hold her back.

Keith smiled. How's it feel, asshole?

One hundred yards. Keith was slightly ahead. He thought. It was hard to judge distance. The bitch had pulled twenty feet in front of the dude.

Fifty yards. No. She was closer. Shit. Keith leaned into it, pushed his screaming muscles even harder, felt them turn into something like red-hot lava in his legs, burning.

But he didn't seem to run any faster. The bitch was closer to the ending flags. She was, dammit.

Come on! Come on legs! Keith pleaded with his body.

Twenty yards. Ten.

The buff bitch ran through the flags. She threw her hands high in victory, and high-stepped off her velocity, her feet throwing up little puffs of orange dust.

Keith and the extreme-sports dude almost collided as they went through the flags. Dead heat. No winner.

No, you're a loser, he told himself, looking at the spandex-suited woman, now bent over and panting in the scrub.

"What was that?" the showpuke said. He wore a name badge, but Keith had long since stopped trying to decode them. It didn't matter anyway. "This isn't a race! There isn't a winner here!"

Keith smiled, taking big whooping breaths.

"It was fun," action-sports bitch called, still bent over.

Showpuke frowned and tried another tact: "Where's Geoff?" he asked.

"Fell down . . . a hill . . . died," Keith said, between huge breaths.

"He . . . what? He did?" Showpuke said. His hand jerked towards his handscreen.

"Yeah . . . big mess, *splat!*"

Handscreen went to mouth. Showpuke's eyes were wide. In the distance, the dude and the bitch were circling each other, like fighters in the ring.

"No," Keith said. "Not dead . . . got himself stuck. What was my time?"

Goggle-eyes from the showpuke. "You . . . what . . . time?"

"Yes." Keith tapped his watch. "Time."

"What about Geoff? You have to go back and get him!"

"I don't have to do shit. Time?"

"If he's stuck, he might be hurt."

Keith nodded. "It's possible. Time?"

"No! We have to go get him."

Keith pretended to look thoughtful. "If you tell me my time, maybe I'll get him."

"Okay—12:08.5," the showpuke said.

"Cool," Keith said. He'd shaved another fourteen seconds off. Progress, progress, progress. He grabbed a Gatorade and headed for the Neteno van, parked in the shade of a large boulder.

"Hey!" Showpuke said. "You said you'd go get Geoff."

"I said 'maybe'," Keith said, not turning around.

"But . . . you said—"

"I changed my mind." Keith said, smiling into the distance.

He heard the showpuke arguing with the extreme-sports assholes. From the tone, they were telling him to fuck right off. That made Keith's smile grow. They got it. They were the ones to watch. It was always good when the competition got obvious.

Because hey, you never knew when your climbing gear might have a little problem. Or when someone might be just a little ahead of you on the course, setting up some little surprises.

He remembered Jimmy, trying to talk him out of staying on the show. But that was stupid. They paid Jimmy more to sit on his ass than Keith had ever made. And there was the big prize, the thirty million or whatever it was supposed to be now.

One chance in five isn't bad, Jimmy had agreed.

One chance in five, hell, Keith said. *I'm going to win it.*

Can't count on that, Jimmy said.

But Keith had just grinned. He was going to win. He knew it. He could feel it. Everyone else here was soft. While they were going back to get team members who'd fallen down, he'd be moving ahead. While they were arguing which way to go, he'd be getting farther in front.

Eventually, Geoff made it over the ridge, and the showpuke stopped chattering into his handscreen. His gray clothes were streaked with orange dirt, and his hair stuck out in odd spiky angles, but he didn't seem hurt. He walked, slowly, down the slope towards the finish flags, casting low-lidded glances in Keith's direction from time to time.

Maybe he'd quit today, with the big boo-hoo face he was wearing.

If not today, soon.

Schedule

"What the hell does Timberland know about making space suits?" Evan said. He shuffled through the documents on his deskspace, arranging and rearranging them as if trying to make them into something he wanted to read. Hollywood was dark behind him, save the streetlights and glow from the buildings. Lots of late nighters. Evan's office was a floor lower than Jere's in the Neteno building, but it was set up like a newbie's cubicle: spare of all decoration, no personal touches at all.

Evan rubbed his face, pulling it into a comic mask of fatigue and frustration. Jere didn't care. He was so beyond caring. "Nike dropped out."

"Why?"

"Legal got nervous."

"Shit," Evan said. "You're supposed to keep their legal from getting nervous. That's your job."

No, that's not my job, Jere thought. It was never my job. I just want to make cool stories. I don't want to be the drink-buying, golf-playing, kid-asking, fake plastic salesfuck. That. Is. Not. Me.

Plus, Jere had to keep Neteno running. The Cho thing was dead and cold. Nobody believed anything Neteno did now, not fully, and the revenue numbers reflected it. Nobody believed in anything Neteno did—except *Winning Mars*, and that was only because there was so much coverage, so much hardware, so much crap running around that you couldn't *not* believe it. Even then, they were running odds that it wouldn't get off the ground.

So. Fuck you, Evan. Fuck you very much.

"Another prime sponsor."

"What, like you're suddenly worried about our contestants?"

Evan shrugged and stood up to pace. "RusSpace finally got back to me."

"And?"

"And, we're fucked."

For a moment, the word didn't even register. Then he heard the phrase like a physical blow. "Fucked! What does fucked mean?"

"Fucked means fucked."

"Come on, Evan! Fucked like they won't do it? Don't tell me they're pulling out. Don't tell me we just boosted a ton of shit into orbit so they can make another goddamn hotel at cut-rates, when our whole show turns to shit."

"No, no. They still want to do it. But it's going to cost about fifty percent more than we thought."

Jere's stomach surged and bucked like a roller coaster—fifty percent more. That was impossible. They were shaking down their biggest sponsors for all they were worth. They were taking loans on the future value of Dad's house. The advertising had been forward sold so many times it might not even own out. They were taking reduced forward moved residuals to keep things running.

And to boot, the big money was getting cold feet. Ford and Boeing pulled out when the schedule last slid. So now it was Kia and Cessna for the wheels and the kites. Good names, yeah, but not blue-chip. Maybe it would boost the ratings, that bit of risk, that added chance . . .

Evan nodded. "Yeah, it's a shit cocktail, all right."

"We can't do this," Jere said. His voice sounded hollow and faraway.

Evan shrugged. "We have to."

"No. You don't understand. We can't do this. Unless you have a bunch of money hid up your ass, we're toast. RusSpace gets their orbital hotel on the cheap. And we get shit."

Evan was silent for a long time. Finally: "There's no more money."

Jere tugged at his hair and paced the room. He looked up at the scrolling Neteno sign, but it was long-gone, reprogrammed and sold to another company.

"What's the problem this time? RusSpace lied again? They fucked up? What?"

"No." A sigh. "Frank ran the analysis. For once, the basic designs look solid. It's the testing that's killing us. Five drop modules, five backout pods, five wheels, five kites, the big package of return pods, a ship with a fucking centrifuge, for God's sake, goddamn, it's a lot of shit to do!"

"So what do we do?"

"We scale it back." Evan said, looking directly at Jere.

"What? Take it to three teams?"

"No. Scale back the build and the test. Leave out the backout pods, for example."

"What happens if the team can't make it to the returns?"

A slow smile. "Tough snatch, said the biatch."

"What?"

"Before your time." Another shrug. This one slow, lazy, nonchalant. "If they can't make it to the return pods, they probably can't make it back. Plus, they signed the waivers."

"But . . . will this get us to budget?"

"I don't know. But we could do more."

Jere's gut felt like a giant spring, knotted and twisting. "What?"

"Skip final test of the kites and the wheels. All they are is a bunch of fabric and struts anyway."

"And?"

"Leave the centrifuge off."

"How are the contestants supposed to stay in shape if they don't have gravity?"

"We'll put in a whole lot of Bowflex machines. They can exercise. And we get another sponsor."

Jere felt his lunch straining to come back up on him. How much more can we sell out? He wondered. "And?"

"And, that might get us back on track. Or so say our formerly communist friends."

"Will they guarantee it?"

"They aren't guaranteeing anything anymore. But I think it's a lot more likely that we'll make the budget if we drop some of the fluff."

Fluff. Yeah, fluff. Just a bunch of safety gear. Nobody will notice.

"We have to make a decision," Evan said. Jere stopped and looked at him. Now, there was no uncertainty. No hint of doubt. No humanity at all in his leaden eyes.

"I don't know," Jere said.

"It's this, or bankruptcy. You said it yourself."

Jere felt something in his eyes. He rubbed it away. "We're gambling with people's lives."

"Someone's going to die. Probably lots of someones," Evan said, softly.

Exactly the same thing he said when they first met. Exactly the phrase that had resonated through Jere's mind for the past year and a half. Was this all grandstanding from the start? All an act? Orchestrated and manipulated to achieve the desired result?

He opened his mouth. Closed it. Of course it was. That was what they did.

"It's a huge chance. A fucking huge chance," Jere said.

Evan shook his head. "What's a bigger chance? Going BK, trying to find more money, or making a few changes?"

A few changes. Nothing big. Nothing major. Nothing we won't be crucified for if someone dies and it comes out that we did this crap at the last minute. Their trial might have a bigger audience than the whole *Winning Mars* thing. Maybe they could forward sell the rights to that too.

"Can we do this clean?" Jere said. The words seemed to come from very far away. "Can we make it look like we never had plans for the centrifuge, the backout stuff, all that?"

"I'm sure we can arrange something."

"Are you sure?"

"Russians are some of the best data manipulators in the world. I hear they helped the president with that little indiscretion she had last year, the one you can't find on Found Media anymore."

Jere let the silence stretch out. Evan watched him intently. In the dim light of the office, his weathered features could have been the craggy face of a demon.

"Do it," Jere said finally, quietly. Hating himself.

Wheel

Mike Kinsson bounced along Movie Trail Road outside Independence, riding inside something that resembled a hamster wheel wrapped in cellophane. The bright California sun beat down on a landscape that looked like something out of a science fiction movie.

Mike supposed that their wheel might make sense on Mars, where they had no idea what kind of terrain they'd encounter, and there was no weight budget for anything like a conventional rover. But it did look stupid. Every day, a carload or two of tourists and locals would come out to point and laugh.

One thing was for certain: the wheel was damn uncomfortable. Beside him, Julie Peters and Sam Ruiz grimly hung onto their harnesses, as every shock and jolt was transmitted directly through the frame to their perch. The hydrazine engine they would use on Mars had been replaced with a small gasoline engine, which buzzed like a gigantic insect near Mike's ear.

To top it all off, their miracle dust-won't-stick-to-it polymer was indeed attracting dust, as well as being scratched and hazed by the rocks they passed over. Seeing through it had become more and more difficult. Mike tried to duck his head outside the spinning rim, to get a better view of the trail they were following, but couldn't quite reach. He squinted and sighed. Off-road probably wasn't all that different from the rutted trail.

They crested a rise and caught a brief moment of air.

"Hey!" Sam said. "Be careful!"

"I know, I know," Mike said, squeezing the brake to slow their descent down the hill. Rain had cut deep channels down the middle of the trail, and at their right side as well. Mike steered them over towards the left side of the road.

I am definitely getting the hang of this thing, he thought.

They hit a little gully where a small stream crossed the road. There was a metallic groan that Mike heard even over the buzzing of the engine.

Then he was falling toward a crumpling mess of plastic sheeting and buckled aluminum struts. It happened so fast it almost seemed as if the wreckage was flying at him. Mike put out his hands, as the knee of a bent strut came up at him . . .

He hit the ground, hard, pain exploding as he took the knee of the strut in his stomach. Julie screamed. Sam Ruiz cursed. The gasoline engine screamed for a moment as it freewheeled, then went into shutdown.

Suddenly there was silence, except for the soft rustling of the plastic sheets. Mike rolled over on his side, hands clutched around his belly. Above him, dirty plastic colored the blue sky a dull gray.

He looked down at his stomach, expecting to see a metal strut poking out of it. There was nothing. He pulled up his shirt. There was one small red mark, nothing more.

"That'll be a fucker of a bruise tomorrow," Sam said, unhooking himself from his harness. He'd come out of the crash without ever hitting the ground.

"Julie," Mike said, and turned. She was on all fours, still harnessed in, groaning.

"Alive," she said.

"Need help?"

A glare. Julie was a cute girl, long black hair framing a perfect oval face and big gray eyes. Her athletic figure was a more attractive one to Mike than the current emaciated ideal.

Sam pushed past Mike to help Julie up. Julie didn't glare at him. Sam was one of those wiry-thin vigorous guys with a face like something out of the *Interactive Plastic Surgery Guide to Looking Like the Perfect Man*, so he wasn't surprised.

But still, nice to be surprised now and again, Mike thought.

Once he was out of the wreckage, Mike stood with hands on hips, frowning at the shattered remains of their wheel. The winter breeze was chilly, but he had to wipe sweat out of his eyes. His hands still shook.

"Oh, shit, now I'm worried," Sam said, emerging from the pile of struts and plastic. He led Julie by the hand.

"What do you mean?" Julie said.

"Mike looks worried."

"I don't get it."

"If a True Believer looks worried, I should be worried too."

An instant flash of gray eyes and perfectly-plucked brows. "Huh?"

Sam ignored her. He dropped her hand and went to stand by Mike. "Are you worried?"

"This is the second time our wheel crapped out," Mike said.

"So we walk back."

They were still three miles out from the pickup point on Movie Trail, which was still ten miles outside of Independence. But that wasn't what made Mike frown.

"What if it breaks on Mars?" Mike said.

"They said these were specially made for Earth, bulkier, or something."

Mike nodded. The point had been made that these wheels were intentionally made heavier to withstand Earth gravity, but inertia was inertia, wherever they were. What if they ran into a ravine—on thinner struts—and the wheel left them stranded on Mars? The whole thing was a tensioned space frame. One weak link, and the whole thing came down.

"If it breaks on Mars, we're done. There isn't any truck to walk to."

Sam was visibly shaken. "They'll come pick us up."

"No. They won't. You saw the plans. There's no backup."

"But they have to pick us up!" this from Julie, arms crossed.

"No. They don't."

"We can fix it," Sam said.

"With what?"

"I . . . shit, they've gotta give us duct tape or something," Sam said.

"I don't think that would do it," Mike said. They didn't understand. They would never understand. There was a very real possibility they could all die on Mars.

Oddly enough, the more he thought about it, the more he was okay with it. *Here lies Mike, who gave his life to pioneer humanity's path to other worlds* sounded a whole lot better than, *Here lies Mike, who worked for Apple for forty years and managed to put enough money away so he wouldn't starve when he was old.*

At least part of his feeling was his last conversation with his parents, who had appointed themselves the official Negative News Gatherers for *Winning Mars.* Every phone conversation ended shortly after they said, "Oh, yeah, and I don't know if you heard, but . . .

" . . . Neteno's in financial trouble, that's what they all say . . . "

" . . . the Russians had their first little orbital accident; it only killed one of their staff, but we worry about you . . . "

" . . . buzz is Oversight is looking into *Winning Mars* . . . "

And so on.

"What are you trying to say?" Julie asked.

Mike looked away. "I'm not trying to say anything."

"He's saying, if the wheel breaks while we're on Mars, and there's nobody around to pick us up, we might as well pack it in. We're dead."

Silence for a time. Julie took a step towards Sam. Another.

"You're trying to scare us off," Julie said. "You want to be like that Paul guy. Have the prize all to yourself."

Mike just looked at them. He didn't know what to say.

"Is that it?" Sam asked.

"No!" Mike said. "I wouldn't be able to assemble everything in time. Keith Paul is a bear!"

"So you've thought about it?"

"Not until now, no."

Sam retreated to Julie and put an arm around her. She leaned into him and glared at Mike.

"Look. I just want us to win. To win, we have to stay alive." Put it in terms they'll understand.

Julie and Sam shared a glance, but relaxed visibly. "So what do we do?" Sam said.

I could offer to help them with the design, Mike thought. Except for the one little fact that he didn't know anything about mechanical engineering. But Sam and Julie were probably sufficiently uneducated to think that, since he was a techie, he could probably help.

Or we can just say fuck it, pack a roll of low-temp duct tape, and take a chance, Mike thought. But they wouldn't like to hear that, either. They probably had plans for their lives, plans that probably involved having kids and going out to dinner and spending the thirty million dollars they'd win, throwing parties for friends and flying to trendy places in France and New York and St. Bart's. Anything that might interrupt that kind of grandiose dream, they wouldn't want to hear about.

But it's the explorers who are remembered, Mike thought. The people who made a difference. Columbus, not the people who financed him. Lindbergh, not the people who built his plane. Armstrong, not Mission Control. Edison, not the millionaires he made. Einstein, not the people who used his physics.

But they wouldn't understand that, either.

Would you, dying under an alien sky?

"I don't know," he said, finally.

They trudged back to the pickup point. In the low-slanting light of the afternoon sun, their shadows were cast before them like giants.

Oversight

They came on a rainy November morning, less than three months before launch.

Jere was in his office, arguing on the phone with a fucknut from McDonalds who was pissed about *Winning Mars* hitting the August sweeps instead of February.

"*The Reporter*'s projections show an even more dominating position against other networks in August, and you can hit the Christmas market on access passes, physical media, and promo items that tie into the February landing back on Earth," Jere said.

The fucknut wouldn't hear it. "No matter how you slice it, there's less audience in the summer! I was sold a show for February. Now it's August. I want concessions!"

Jere sighed. The fucknut was right. It didn't matter that *Winning Mars* wasn't like a regular show. It didn't matter that it had problems way bigger than having an actor walk off in the middle of the project. It didn't matter that they were doing something entirely new, and having your fucking McCafe onboard for product placement was ten thousand times more important than all the smiling know-nothing asshole celebrities on all the biggest billboards in the world. They'd promised one thing, and delivered another, and there'd have to be kickbacks.

That was when Dad came hustling into Jere's office, eyes wide and heel-toeing it as if someone had a gun to his back.

Jere pointed at the phone. Dad grabbed it out of his hand and slammed it down in the cradle.

"Dad, that was—"

"No time!" Ron said. His face was old, twisted, alien.

"What's happening?" Jere asked.

"We're having a meeting," Ron said.

"With who?"

A quick glance towards the door. "Don't let them kick me out. You need a witness. Play along."

"With what—"

Dad said, loudly: "The hell with the sponsors, let them whine about prices!"

"Dad?"

His father gave him a desperate, wide-eyed look. Little beads of sweat stood out on his brow.

His father was afraid.

Giant cold fingers grabbed Jere's stomach. Dad didn't get scared. It simply didn't happen. Ever.

"Yeah," Jere said. "Let them complain, where else they gonna get this deal? Metrics don't line up with anything out there."

Dad nodded, smiling grimly. "Offer them something, buy them tickets—"

Two men walked through the office door. Which in itself was wrong. They couldn't afford receptionists any more, but their automated security system shouldn't have let anyone through without a keycard.

The two men wore identical khakis, forest-green polo shirts, and cheap plastic Dell eyesets. They smiled, displaying perfect orthodontic work and recent laser whitening. They looked for all the world like a pair of old friends, come for a casual chat. But their eyes darted calculating glances at Jere and Ron, like facial-tracking cameras. Their shirts bore identical embroidered logos: the cheery bisected globe-and-eye of US Government Oversight.

Oh holy fucking shit. Oversight was the holy arm of the United State's official Department of Sustainability. They could go into any business or organization at any time, examine any record, stop any executive and question them under oath. They were empowered to make instant decisions and mete out any necessary penalties. They operated above any law, secure in their higher purpose to move every US citizen forward into the bold new future where everything was happy, everything was green, and everything was sustainable—even if it meant sacrifices.

"Mr. Gutierrez?" One of them stepped forward and flashed his ID. It was one of those overdone holographic things. On it, the Oversight symbol morphed from a colorful globe to a stunning iris, and back again. Jere supposed there was a name on the card, but he never noticed it.

"Mr. Gutierrez?" the first agent asked, again.

"Yes." Gut-churning fear made his voice high and tight.

The first agent turned to his father. "And you, sir?"

"I'm Ron."

"Ron . . . ?"

"Gutierrez."

"Ah. Yes. Minor stakeholder."

Ron's lips grew thin and hard, but he said nothing.

Silence. Agent One turned to Agent Two, who pursed his lips. "We'd like to talk with Jere Gutierrez alone."

"No," Ron said.

"We can have you removed."

"Because I'm, such a threatening old man? A *minority* shareholder, at that?" Ron said it with undisguised disgust.

Silence for a time. Data danced in Agent One's eyes, reflected from his eyeset. Finally a nod. "You may remain."

Jere blew out of breath. Make nice. These guys can make you disappear. "Would you like a seat? Coffee?"

Agent One sat. The other remained standing.

"What do you want to talk about?" Jere asked.

"Your program. *Winning Mars.*"

"Would Oversight like to become a sponsor?"

No reaction. Not even a glance. Agent One said, "There will be no *Winning Mars* program."

"What?" Jere and Ron said in unison.

Agent One continued to stare at them, his expression neutral. "We will not permit the launch."

Jere forced himself not to react. "We've already launched the majority of components for assembly."

"The remainder of the launches will not occur."

Jere shook his head. "Our launches are on Russian soil. How are you going to prevent them?"

Agent One cocked his head. "We have interlocking jurisdiction with all world sustainability cabinets, departments, and agencies. RusSpace will comply."

Nobody said anything for a long time. In the silence, Jere could almost hear Evan asking if they'd be reimbursed. Because that's all that mattered to him. Jere's face went hot.

"Why?" Jere asked.

Agent Two smiled. "Our projections show that this program of yours has already consumed several hundred thousand lifetime equivalents of resources, based on the median average world product per person. It's practically the definition of unsustainable. You don't seriously think we'd allow it to continue?"

"Silly us, thinking that we could freely use our own time and money," Ron said.

Jere's heart thudded, thinking, Shut up, Dad!

"This program has gone far beyond you and your company. You've involved many international corporations, both as donors and as partners."

"Silly us, thinking they could freely use their own time and money too."

"Ron!" Jere said.

Dad didn't even glance at him.

"This program is over," Agent Two said.

Over, Jere thought. Just like that. Turn a switch. Over.

Ron nodded, sudden understanding gleaming in his eyes. "China. China's bitching, aren't they? They want the United States to continue sliding net worth to balance the global productivity numbers. Stirring up investment isn't exactly good for that, is it?"

The agents glanced at each other.

"And I bet they're more than a little pissed that the miserable USA is turning their Mars dream into a TV show."

Agent Two shrugged. "That's speculation."

If it's us against China, this is just another business deal, Jere thought.

"What do you want?" he asked the agents.

Agent Two looked politely confused. "I don't understand."

"What do you want from us?"

A headshake.

"What's it going to take to make the launch happen?"

Agent Two leaned forward. "This isn't a negotiation. However, there's a chance that the program would prove sustainable on a R and D and general public investment basis if it was turned over to the US government."

"And then was allowed to become an international governmental program," said Agent Two.

Aha. And there it was. Simple as that. Thanks for doing the work. We'll take it now. "No," Jere said. Dad snapped around to stare at him.

"We're not here to negotiate," Agent Two said

"Our sponsors and partners will come for our heads. That includes *Organizatsiya*." Thinking, this is fucking crazy. Oversight could do anything they wanted. He could be picked up and whisked away and never seen again. He could have everything taken from him piece by piece, a Job job. Or worse.

Agent Two offered him something that approximated a kind smile. "Face it," he said. "It's over."

Over.

Over, just like that. After all this time. After standing up to 411. After making all the impossible deals. After doing everything people said was impossible. And fuck! Even after putting stuff in fucking orbit!

Anger surged through Jere. Suddenly, he didn't care what Oversight would do. It didn't matter. He stood up and yelled, "So what! So fucking what! Does every dream have to die under your boot heels? Do you get off, crushing any chance of doing something amazing?"

Both Oversight agents stepped back and looked at him in wide-eyed wonder. Even Ron had his mouth open.

"And what if we took that microscope and turned it around?" Jere said. "Are all the Chinese city redevelopment programs sustainable? Is an R and D effort to develop a new kind of toothpaste sustainable? Is Oversight itself sustainable, or would we be better off if all of you fuckers found real jobs where you made something, rather than sticking your nose in other people's business?"

There was silence in the room for a solid minute.

Then Ron stood up, his face thunderous, so red it was almost purple. Ron stuck his finger in Agent One's chest. "We're not going to Mars to plant fucking flags! Did the fucking pilgrims come to plant fucking flags? No! They came to get away from bureaucratic fucks like you! You assholes had your chance. How many billions did we give you shitheads? What did we get for it? Our lunar rovers in Chinese museums! A bunch of rusting hardware crash-landed on Mars. Thanks. Thanks a lot. Now it's *our* chance!"

Jere watched his dad, frozen in place. What had he started? They were dead, unless they could take the car down to Mexico . . .

"You really want to make a stand on this?" Agent One asked. His voice was low and deadly. "On a show? On a publicity stunt?"

"That's not all it is," Jere rasped, his voice low and deadly. "If it was, you wouldn't be here."

Agent Two stepped forward quickly and put his hand on Agent One's shoulder. He bent and whispered something in his ear. Agent One nodded and stood. Both of them addressed Jere.

"So you refuse to turn over the program, as directed by Oversight?"

"Yes. I refuse."

The two swiveled to look at Ron. "Both of you?"

Jere looked at his father. Ron looked back steadily, intently. He nodded, just a fraction.

"Yes."

The agents stood there for a moment longer, their expressions unreadable. Jere couldn't stand looking at them.

"Get the hell out of here," Jere said.

The agents turned and filed out. Ron looked up at Jere, the ghost of a smile on his face.

"It . . . it was the right thing. We did the right thing," Ron said, grasping the chair arm with trembling fingers. On his face was a strange expression. It might have been something like love.

I hope you're right, Dad, Jere thought. Otherwise, we're both dead.

Kite

Nandir Patel imagined flying his kite as something akin to being suspended over the desert in a hang glider. He'd seen films shot from hang gliders, and had always secretly wanted to try one. But that would mean taking time away from the company for training, for test flights, for selecting the right glider, for packing it up and carting it to the foothills—all for an hour or two of silent flight. His time was worth more when he worked on software, or on the company. That was what mattered. Making enough to step off the treadmill. Then he could sigh in relief, take a breather, learn to hang glide, write a novel, or just sit in Peet's and drink tea all day, waiting for the perfect woman to come along.

But he didn't expect to be shipped down to El Segundo, and hung up in a small blue cylindrical room in the far corner of a large concrete tilt-up building. There was something similar to a treadmill below him, set on the floor.

"Is this the test flight?" he asked the woman who had strapped him in.

"It is." She wore a white T-shirt with a faded logo of Moto Robotics on it, over tight blue jeans. Long brown hair cascaded down her back.

"You're a technician?"

"Engineer," she said.

"So this is a simulation?"

"Kinda," she said. She went on to explain that the model kite was one-quarter scale, so it could fit in a barometrically controlled wind tunnel. They'd take the pressure down to Martian levels, run the tunnel, and use force feedback from the model to provide him with realistic control inputs on his full-sized harness.

"What about my teammate?"

A quick grin. "Simulated."

"So they aren't going to build a full-sized test model?"

"Can't. There's so much more air here on Earth, tests would be meaningless. Or we could fly in the stratosphere, but then you'd have to wear a spacesuit."

"Squeezesuit," Nandir said, frowning, remembering his fitting for the thing. He would be happy never having to wear one again. When he first slid it on, he thought, Oh, hey, this isn't bad, kind of like long underwear, but when they'd activated the fabric, he felt like it had become a giant snake, and was squeezing him to death. He could feel the catheter, digging into the skin of his crotch.

And you have to wear that for days on Mars, he thought. He wasn't looking forward to it.

"Have a good time," the brunette engineer said, waving from the door. Nandir waved back.

The room went dark, then lit again, this time showing an immersive of Mars. Nandir smiled. It was good. Really good. The illusion was almost seamless, except for some light-spill where the vertical wall met the ceiling and floor. If he looked straight ahead, he could imagine he was suspended over Mars. Orange, arid rocks beneath him, pink sky ahead.

"We'll start the simulation now," the woman's voice said. "First we'll do steady-state, then landing, then takeoff."

The buzz of an engine came through the speaker. Nandir supposed it was to simulate the sound of their hydrazine motor. The ground unrolled under him quickly, and the airframe became live in his hands.

Nandir pulled the control bar forward, dipping the nose of the kite. The ground quickly rose up to meet him. He pulled up. The kite jerked up. He saw nothing but sky. Then the craft heeled over and he saw nothing but ground. It came at him, fast, stopping with a comical crashing noise.

"Easy!" the engineer said. "You need to be gradual with the control inputs. You're flying pretty fast and low to get lift, remember. There isn't much margin for error."

"What about automatic control?" Nandir said.

"You should be able to limit control input to defined parameters."

"Oh."

"Now, let's try it again," she said, and the ground unrolled under him.

Nandir eventually got the hang of the controls, and the extremely light touch they required. When he got used to that, they had him do landings. After the seventh crash, he finally was able to bring the craft down to a smooth landing. The harness lowered with him, allowing his feet to run on the treadmill. The treadmill moved too fast for him, and he lost his footing three times before he managed a successful landing.

"Not bad," the engineer said.

"As compared to?"

"Betting pool," she said. "You're the first. The rest of your friends come later."

Compared to landing, taking off was relatively easy. The only catch was angling the engine's thrust; it had to be at full speed in order to give them enough lift to take off. When he finally managed it, Nandir earned a round of applause over the speaker.

The convict asshole was next. He glared at Nandir when he walked into the little room. "This is flyin'?" he asked.

Nandir smiled. "Indeed. This, sir, is flying."

Another glare. Nandir ducked out of the room, chuckling.

Freedom

When Oversight came back, it was with two grinning NASA executives and their own camera crew. Following them were a hundred and fifty thousand people, jamming the Hollywood streets in cars and on motorcycles, and on bikes and on foot, holding banners saying FREE ENTERPRISE! and NEW FRONTIERS, NOT NEW OVERSIGHT! and of course, EXAMINE EVERYTHING, EVEN SUSTAINABILITY!

It almost didn't work. It *shouldn't* have worked. Oversight should have noticed Ron's prosthetic eyecam and plucked it right out of his head. They should have destroyed the recording. But they missed it. Because nothing is perfect. Not even a grand plan for a happy and sustainable future.

Within a day, Ron's video of the Oversight shakedown had gone viral, posted on a thousand online video networks, rebroadcast from tens of thousands of backyard producers, reflected on a million blogs, and shared by over a billion people. Even Oversight couldn't move fast enough to stop the spread.

They tried. Wait Wednesday, they called it, as video widgets all over the world spun beach balls of death, and begged off due to network congestion. Oversight intervention slowed the worldwide internet to pre-dial-up speeds.

But even at 2K downloads, it got through. It went out via ancient flash drives and on ad hoc community networks. It hit the never-go-down servers of the Open Source Alliance. Servers that, on that afternoon, almost went down.

Almost.

And the rage rose.

From one of the top-ranked opinion leaders in France, a scathing diatribe against the "Sustainability Stalinistas," and a grim question about how we could entrust our future to a regime of absolute control, no matter how well-meaning.

From Japan, questions about the transparency of their own Sustainability Minister resulted in fistfights in the streets, forty-seven minutes of compromising video, and a quick reorganization of the government.

From tiny Iceland, effigies of government figures burned around boardroom tables, and citizens waved signs decrying backroom deals.

In the US, the video sparked bonfires throughout the political spectrum. Republicans railed against the ongoing "power grab" of the Democratic Party, and promised to purge the world of their socialist ways by lowering taxes and reinstating the Department of Homeland Security. The Democrats pretended to be aghast at the discovery of corruption in the system, promising to purge evil, self-centered people like the two agents caught on tape. Charges were filed. Motions were made. Legislation was drafted for an oversight of Oversight.

From the Green side, a great wailing about how the program didn't go far enough rose in the networks.

And from the Libertarian ranks, noise about the importance of individuality and Constitutional limits. And, of course, gold and guns and pot.

Survivalists polished their weapons and streamed out of the Sierras and Appalachians and half-forgotten Nebraska missile silos to demonstrate. TrekCon turned into a huge caravan that converged on Sacramento, trapping senators in the capitol, demanding that the governor secede so that Neteno could go about its business. Joined by people from other states—over a million people of them somehow converging on Sacramento—they held the capitol for three days. Some were dressed in overalls, had prickly beards, and were armed with shotguns; some wore Klingon outfits; some were science fiction writers; some were housewives in SUVs; some were business people who worked in aviation, space, and engineering. All had a glint of adventure and discovery and progress in their eyes.

In three days, two slogans were posted at over one hundred million websites, plastered on bumper stickers, hung from suction-cups behind windows: *Free Enterprise*, and *Give Us New Frontiers*.

In five days, Henry Kase's new e-book, *Kase for Audacity*, asked—in close to 200,000 words—the very serious question: Has limiting the scope of human endeavor, at any time in history, ever resulted in progress?

That was when Jere received a discreet phone call from a higher-up at USG Oversight.

The higher-up made him a very generous offer.

Jere politely refused and made his own counteroffer.

A day after that, he received another phone call, politely accepting the prime sponsorship for the mission, for a price that was a significant fraction of the monies they'd collected to date.

The launch would go forward as planned. Jere and Ron and Evan were still the controlling shareholders. The only real differences were that there would be one NASA observer present at the launch, they would carry some NASA interferometers and measurement gear, and there would be another discreet logo added on the ship and the suits.

Jere watched Evan and Ron as the NASA muckety muck spouted off about a "New Partnership with Business," and how wonderful this opportunity was. The crowd looked happy, vindicated, relieved. As if they were thinking: Good, good, we still have the power, we still live in a free country.

"We are proud to be able to support this effort," the muckety-muck proclaimed. "For less than the cost of our robotic Mars missions to date, we are sending the first manned mission to Mars. With this mission, we have again leaped ahead to lead the world in space exploration. We see this as a model for future exploration of space: Oversight and private industry, working hand-in-hand to accomplish our goals."

Some applause, some boos, some catcalls. But it was done. They were back on track. It even got them their advertising hooks: *Free Enterprise,* and *The Newest Frontier.* Both were really catching on in a big way, buzzing around the net. Some studios even floated ideas for competing programs.

So now it's more than a game, he thought. It was a demonstration what people would need to do to conquer the red planet.

Or at least they'd spin it that way.

He looked at his dad. He'd taken the biggest chance. If Oversight had managed to kill the video, they'd probably both be in a very small cell in a very remote part of the country right now.

Fucking showoff, Jere thought. But it was a kind thought. For now, at least, his dad was okay.

Not like Evan and his hard, unblinking eyes. To him, it was all still just a game.

A game played hard, winner take all.

Teams

"I expected you to sell the naming rights," said Wende Kirschoff, when Neteno's program coordinator brought up picking team names. "We'd end up as 'Walmart Team' or something like that."

Geoff nodded. He didn't know why he was nodding, but he expected it was because he was being teamed up with two women. He was pretty excited about that, even though it seemed like they only took him on because he was running the IBM experiments package, and that bought them some extra time. Wende was rounder and cuter, with a few extra pounds on her frame and dirty-blond colored hair cut shoulder-length. Laci's features were thin and sharp; she always looked like she was smelling something bad, but she was still attractive, tall, and blond. Criminal Keith kept referring to them as "the lesbians," but Geoff couldn't really see them that way. Keith was probably just being a jerk.

The teams hadn't ended up as they had hoped, though Neteno tried to play it off. Geoff had seen the docs. Originally there were fifteen slots: five teams of three each. But they hadn't found fifteen acceptable contestants who would agree to the contract. Then criminal Keith wouldn't play nice with him, or Sam, or anyone, but he'd aced the physical and aptitude trials, so he was going it alone. Glenn and Alena Rothman had said they didn't want a third, and neither did Nandir and Romeo. So that left Julie and Sam and Mike as the only other threesome.

So here they were, eleven tired contestants in a Neteno conference room, overlooking drab Hollywood and Los Angeles beyond. Geoff shivered. He didn't like cities. Didn't like so many buildings, so much traffic.

But if it meant he got to be the guy who discovered life on Mars, he could live with it.

"I'm sure we looked into selling the names," the program coordinator said, completely passing over Wende's sarcasm. He was a gung-ho guy in his early twenties, wearing a wrinkled white button-up shirt over jeans. He'd mentioned his name, but Geoff had forgotten it. "For whatever reason, though, they're going to let you pick your own team names."

"Budweiser," Keith said.

"What?" the PC asked.

"My team. Budweiser Team."

The PC shook his head. "No brands."

Keith frowned. "Paul. Just Paul."

"Paul," the PC said, his fingers tapping his slate. "Next?"

His eyes found Geoff. Geoff's mouth went completely dry. "Uh, uh—" he stuttered.

"Ride," Laci said. "As in Sally Ride."

"Isn't that a little obvious?" Wende said.

"No historic figures, no politics," the PC said, frowning.

"Trailblazers," Laci said.

Wende nodded. Even Geoff approved. They didn't look at him. The PC scribbled it down.

Mike, Julie, and Sam were next. Mike muttered something about Mariner, but Julie jumped up and said, "Money team! Money because we'll win!"

Mike shook his head and started to say something, but Sam chimed in first. "Money sounds good to me."

The PC scribbled.

The Rothmans made brief eye contact with each other. "K2," Alena said. Glenn nodded in assent.

Nandir seemed nonplussed by the question. Data danced in his eyes from his eyeset. Romeo Torres cleared his throat and said, "Sarimanok."

"What's that?" the PC asked.

Romeo blushed a deep purple-red. "Sarimanok is a mythical bird that brings good luck to anyone who catches it. In Filipino mythology, that is." He looked at Nandir, who nodded absently.

"I meant how to spell it."

Romeo spelled it out for the guy, who scribbled dutifully. Then he went to the front of the room, to turn on a projector. Its laser brilliance etched the screen with a 3D landscape of Mars, with a diagram of the Can, the return modules, and five different drop points, each with a dotted line leading first to blips labeled "transpo pod," then through different terrain to the "return modules."

"Second, rules. There aren't many. We drop your team at one of these five points. You run for your transpo pod. Find it. Get the kite and wheel out. The first time to make it to the return modules wins the fifty mil. We're firm on that now, you'll see the numbers in the ads."

"What if the dollar exchange rate changes?" Nandir asked.

The PC just looked at Nandir, as if to say, *Not my problem.*

"Second, let's go through the routes. The eggheads have done some tweaking, so look 'em over well. We're gonna do a first-pick, second-pick, third-pick lottery thing here later, but check 'em out, then think what you want to do. Some are closer, but more strenuous, some are farther away from the return modules, but easier. Make sure to note the flying, rolling, walking parts."

"This one," Alena said, going to the screen and pointing to a short one with a big cliff.

"This one," Julie said, picking a long flat one with lots of flying.

"What do you think?" Geoff asked Wende.

"It doesn't matter," Wende said. "As long as we get there."

Geoff grinned. He liked Wende. Wende was okay. Maybe she—

"Speak for yourself," Laci said. "I'd like to win."

"Just getting there proves—"

"Proves we can be poor and famous," Laci cut her off. "Might at least try."

Popularity

Tonightshow.com was one of the survivors of the Golden Age of Television, even if most people now watched it on some screen other that a television's.

Jere supposed it was appropriate to appear, but it still seemed strange. *The Tonight Show* was where the up-and-comers and just-over-the-hills came to get skewered, gently, by the perpetual and ageless Jay Leno. Jere wondered how much technology had gone into maintaining his appearance for the last couple of decades, how many little trips out of the country he'd taken, and how many hairs of his familiar salt-and-pepper coiffure were made of some synthetic fiber.

I shouldn't be here, Jere thought, as the makeup guy worked on him in the cramped dressing room.

But on the other hand, on his way to the studio, he'd passed a mural of Mars, drawn by locals with UV-active paint, so it sparkled and morphed in his Porsche's HID lights. On the Hollywood and Vine macrodisplay, promos for *Winning Mars* chased across the giant screen. His earbuds whispered that Ho-Man's "Spirit of Mars" was currently playing on the Hip-Hop (light, positive) channel, and The New Daves' "Fuckin' Mars" was playing on the Mashup channel of the A-only nets.

It was just like Evan said. Just as the charts showed. They'd done more than touch a nerve. They'd gone live wire. The world turned around Mars, at least for the moment.

Part of it was their famous Oversight video, 21.5 billion views and counting. But it was more than that. Jere sampled their fanmedia. Housewives yelled at aging NASA scientists, who in turn were verbally razored by nineteen-year-old kids with animated tattoos. Engagement was off the scale. There were over 1700 sites dedicated to tracking progress on the *Mars Enterprise*. Time-lapse footage of its orbital construction played on over a hundred million desktops. Proctor and Gamble had started doing Mars-themed advertising, even though it wasn't a sponsor. He had to hand it to him: Evan's projections had been absolutely right. This was the biggest thing in entertainment in the twenty-first century. Maybe the biggest thing, ever. *Star Trek, Star Wars, Terminator, Battlestar Galactica, Stargate, Avatar, Dr. Who,* hell, *Futurama* . . . Neteno could eat all those old franchises without even a twinge of heartburn.

But if anyone dies, we're fucked. Jere didn't want to think about the compromises. Oh, the compromises. So many compromises. If people died, forget the Russians. There was no place on Earth he could hide. He'd have to go to Mars himself.

The makeup guy finished and made a half-hearted pass at Jere. He was a good-looking kid, probably not more than twenty-one. Jere politely declined.

When they took him to the stage, Jere was surprised. It was done in warm reds and inviting earth tones, and the familiar cityscape had been replaced by a giant mural of Mars from orbit, cast against a background of brilliant stars. The ruddy planet glowed down on the stage, throwing warm shadows.

Before he knew it, they were live and on the air. Jere endured the entrance, the brief intro, the good-natured ribbing about Neteno CGing the whole thing, about them acting out the whole Oversight thing, about their impressed-reality work in the Philippines. Lightweight stuff. Stuff to get Jere off his game, because the only thing Hollywood liked better than making someone was breaking them again. Two for the price of one. Two opportunities to ride.

And he was the prime target, the Big Kahuna.

Leno leaned forward, suddenly serious. "I just have one question: Why?"

Aha. The open-ended question. The one Leno hoped to hang him with. He could answer like any other butthole, say something like, *Because it was there,* or *Because it's space, the final frontier,* or *Because it needed doing.* But those answers would make him look like another self-satisfied executive asswipe that'd just lost fifteen percent of his brain cells by climbing Everest without oxygen. Audiences would make the connection, pronto. Oh yeah, another parasite sucking our wallets dry, not enough real work to do so he's gotta play.

No. Turn it around.

Jere leaned forward. "May I ask you a question, instead?"

A look of momentary surprise flickered across Leno's face. He shrugged. "Sure."

"When you were just getting started, did anyone tell you, 'Don't bother, kid, that's a dumb idea, you'll never make it.'"

Leno laughed. "Lots of people."

"Anyone big? Anyone important? Anyone so important, so powerful, that you couldn't ignore them?"

Leno's brows drew down fractionally, and in his bright eyes there was a moment of genuine emotion. "Yes."

"And you did it anyway."

Leno licked his lips. For several long moments, there was quiet on the set. The audience stirred and looked around, recognizing that something had just happened. Maybe not even fully understanding it, and yet, deep in the brains of thirty million current viewers, a connection had been made.

Blink. "So you did it just because, what, someone told you not to?" Leno looked nervously to his side.

"And you did this just because someone told *you* not to?" Jere said, spreading his arms to encompass the totality of his career.

Blink blink. "Not entirely."

Jere's heart hammered. He felt light-headed. He had Leno on the defense. He had the most powerful talk show host in reverse!

"So when the time came, you ran all the calculations and determined that your version of *The Tonight Show* would be the best possible show of its kind, that it was exactly the kind of information that your audience would need to become good enlightened citizens?"

Laughter from the audience.

"Or you called Four-eleven and had them run a what-if to determine the most profitable path for the studio, based on trillions of datapoints of demographic data?"

The laughter got louder. Leno's jaw set grimly.

"Or you went in front of Congress to get your comedy bailout with the stamp of approval from Oversight?"

Even more laughter.

Leno didn't look happy. He didn't look happy at all.

Jere grinned and leaned forward, as if he and Leno were old buddies. "I'm not here to jump on your nuts."

Leno found his voice. "Coulda fooled me."

"Come on, man, you know how this goes. This is show business. This isn't about numbers and quotas and doing the Right Thing for Our Time. This is fun. And people need some fun."

"Some people say this is pricey fun." Leno's voice strengthened.

"Some people say this is a stupid timewaster of a show, and that we should all be growing planet-sized brains playing instructional MMOs twenty-four-seven."

The studio audience barked a laugh, and Leno echoed them. For a moment, he seemed content to let Jere go.

"Okay," Jere said. "Time to get serious."

"Oh, did we suddenly become *Wikileaks*?" Leno interjected.

"Ha. No. Really. A lot of money for fun, some people say. But I think that's because fun is dangerous. Fun makes people dream. And we can't have any of that, can we?"

Silence from the audience.

"And that's what it comes down to. We can run the numbers, follow the lines, be good little kids. Or we might be able to dream."

Out in the audience, eyes sparkled, welling with tears. In that moment, everyone was remembering one of their dreams. A love lost. A business never started. A trip never made. A chance they never took. In that moment, Jere knew, they'd follow him anywhere.

Leno sat back in his chair, shaking his head and smiling. He looked at Jere with genuine admiration. After a couple of more half-hearted jabs, he brought in an Oversight wonk who chattered about how they were the ones who were saving the world, and a science fiction author who speechified about how they were always the real pioneers. The audience barely noticed.

Outside the studio, Jere clipped on his eyeset. It swam with messages. Most prominent was one from his dad. It said, simply: YOU WERE FUCKING BRILLIANT. GRATS.

And one from Evan: THAT'S ANOTHER HUNDRED MILLION IN THE BANK.

But through the haze of messages, he also saw something else. Someone else. Someone who leaned against his shiny perfect Porsche as if she owned it.

Patrice.

Rebound

Jere stopped ten feet away from Patrice. In the orange sodium-lights of the NBC parking lot, his eyes were dead black, unreadable.

"So you can see me now?" he asked.

"I don't know."

"I thought you'd get in a lot of trouble if you saw me."

"I don't care."

They stood, miles apart, watching each other.

"What about your grand and glorious leader?"

Patrice shook her head.

Jere made a small sound deep in his throat. He took three big steps and gathered her up in his arms. He was wearing that some unfamiliar cologne, lightly, over the acrid smell of terror.

"I saw you," Patrice said.

"On Tonightshow.com?"

She nodded. "You tripped the master."

Jere nodded. And for a long time, he stayed like that. Motionless in her arms. Then he said: "We should celebrate."

Patrice didn't say anything. She didn't want to go out to some big trendy place and endure the crowds and gabbers and media wonks. She wasn't in that mode. She wasn't in character. In fact, she wasn't wearing a single thing of YZ's. In the past couple of weeks, she hadn't felt like being YZ. Not at all.

"Nothing big," Jere said.

She said nothing.

"Maybe nothing other than a walk on the beach?"

"Yes," she said.

They took Jere's little gumdrop car over Laurel Canyon and through the sweeping curves of Sunset Boulevard towards Malibu. On the way, a giant carload of kids paced them, yelling, "Hey Marsman, hey YZ!" But their faces were bright and open and smiling, and soon they roared off to whatever club would serve as their home for the night.

I should be in character, Patrice thought. But she couldn't make herself care. She realized, for the first time in years, how she could never completely separate herself from YZ, no matter how hard she had tried. But now there was a dividing line; everything was suddenly compartmentalized: crystalline and clear.

Patrice shivered.

In Malibu, they parked in an empty parking lot and went to walk on the deserted beach. The half moon shone down on them through a gathering mist. Patrice took off her shoes and let the cold sand slip between her toes.

They weren't the only ones on the beach. A bunch of kids, no more than high-school age, lounged around a rough shack. Above it hung a handcarved sign:

Robot Ike's Sushi

Standing behind the shack's serving counter was one of those robotic Japanese sushi chefs. Fish chilled under glass, set with mathematical precision. The kids were trying to get Robotic Ike to drink a beer.

Their attention turned quickly to Patrice and Jere.

"Oh god and goddess of our age, welcome to our humble abode," said one. He was the stereotypical California surfer, deeply tanned and flushed with freckles, his blond hair bleached beach-sand white, and wearing only a bright teal pair of surf shorts.

"This is your restaurant?" Jere asked.

"Oh hardly a restaurant, just a place for good company, informal delights. Sit a while and share with us."

Patrice pulled Jere away. "We have other plans."

"Oh great goddess, we understand."

The kids laughed as they walked away. But there was no knowing edge to it. It sounded completely open and good-natured. It was as if nothing in that night could go wrong.

A magical night. Patrice shivered again, harder.

The dark beach led down to an ocean done in charcoals and blacks. They walked down to a point where the lights fell away completely, as if they were walking into an art exhibit made entirely of coal. The only lights came from homes, high on the hill. The only sound was the crash of the waves. It was as if they were the only people left among Los Angeles' twelve millions. It was as if, just for a time, the universe revolved around them.

It was a night that Jere could ask her anything.

She waited.

Eventually, he said, "I'm glad you didn't go to Mars."

"I'm happy too."

"I have to go to Russia tomorrow."

"I know."

"I'll be back."

And I'll be waiting, Patrice thought. Though she couldn't bring herself to say a thing.

Launch

Russian summer was the same as Russian winter, except that the black ice had been replaced by mud. Depressingly familiar to Jere, now, as was the grin of Valentin Ladenko. Who drove a new Mercedes S-class, this one hydrogen, as if change for the sake of change was all that mattered.

It was an entire caravan this time, reporters and pundits and hangers-on, all loudly complaining about the facilities. Baikonur was overwhelmed by visitors. The space hotels were long since filled. Reporters were sleeping in taverns, in houses, in barns, in the street, maybe with the goats. No Food signs hung from many of the restaurants and bars.

"Should they pay us extra for the tourism, Vally?" Evan said, watching a gas station gleefully quintuple its price.

"Leninsk," Valentin said.

"It won't last," Jere said.

"Sure it will," Evan said. "There are enough bored reporters around here to crank out fifty thousand local interest pieces. And people will travel anywhere. They don't care what a craphole it is."

Maybe he was right, Jere thought. Public support for *Winning Mars* had risen to an insane pitch following his routine with Leno. The peak of the Gaussian consensus showed Jere as a reluctant visionary, too modest to express the depth of his conviction. Even 411 showed charts that painted him as some crazy hybrid of Churchill and Robbins.

Dad wasn't impressed. *People believe what they want to believe,* Ron said. *And they change their minds in an awful big fuckin' hurry.*

Now it was launch day.

Jere had seen a lot of launches. He'd been on a couple of them. It shouldn't be a big deal. Just another LEO shot for RusSpace, done it hundreds of times, no problem.

But he couldn't get the twist out of his guts. It was too big. Too important. Too many people watching. And when things got too big and too important, people fucked up. And when people fucked up, bad things happened. It would be a completely appropriate end to the show if the entire lot of contestants died on the launch pad. Not a great ending, but something you'd watch in a theater and think, Yeah, saw that one coming a mile away.

If the whole thing went up in smoke, public opinion would snap instantly, like a steel beam strained to breaking. His brilliance and selflessness would become a cold-blooded publicity stunt. He would be crucified. If he was lucky.

All because the public wasn't fed. Because they wouldn't get their daily dose of excitement.

A-muse-ment, Ron called it. Nonthinking. To muse is to think, and to *a*-muse was to not think. Which is what most people wanted. Give them a roof and food and someone to fuck, let them buy a few shiny things from time to time, and all they really cared about was filling the gaping void of their lives. They didn't want to "muse." They wanted to "*a*-muse."

And God help the person who promised a-muse-ment, and didn't come through.

The RusSpace orbital shuttle looked larger and dirtier than he remembered it. The Can waited patiently in orbit, but without the dozen contestants, it was nothing. They should have sent up the teams separately with Frank on his own flight. But the timeline. But the budget. Even the government money had gone fast when the Russians' bills came due.

The most expensive amusement ever created, Jere thought.

The ride to the launch pad was short. The crowd outside the gates parted reluctantly, pointing cameras. Grabbing that last glimpse of Jere and Evan and Ron. Getting that last bit of emotion.

In the little box at the top of the grandstand, Ron collapsed in his seat with a grunt. Jere and Evan plopped down next to him. They were sitting on camp chairs that looked like they could have come from a Napoleonic campaign. Perhaps they had.

"Crunch time," Evan said softly.

"Yes," Ron said.

"All or nothing," he rubbed his hands.

"Yeah."

"Anyone in a betting mood?"

"Shut up," Ron said, and Evan fell silent.

For once, Jere was glad to have the old man with him. Without Ron, Evan would have woven a web tighter and tighter, until he alone controlled the relationships with the sponsors and the Russians and even the public. Jere knew that now. But Ron had stepped in and helped even it out. Evan still held too many purse-strings, and hiding a lot of money, but they could deal with that later.

I'm really just along for the ride, Jere thought. And then, less bitterly: No. I'm not. I decided to do this. I went up against 411. I stood down Oversight. I dominated Leno. This was my baby as much as anyone's. No matter what happened now, Jere was proud of what he'd done.

Ahead of them, the ship towered over the bleak landscape like the last hope of humankind after a nuclear war. Gleaming steel and clouds of vapor, a high-tech needle aimed at the deep blue sky. At its apex was the last, and most critical component, of the needle: the passenger shuttle. Holding every single one of the contestants.

Which really was amazingly stupid, Jere thought. If that goes, we're done. Gone. We shoulda . . .

They shoulda done a lot of things. But, in reality, they shouldn't be here now, period. Not at all. He could spend the time second-guessing, or he could savor what he'd accomplished.

One minute. The few people left on the field scampered to cover.

Jere realized, Holy shit, I really believe in this.

Thirty seconds.

Jere basked in a strange disconnection. He didn't know how to feel.

Ten seconds.

Jere held his breath as the numbers flickered down on the big board.

There was an explosion of light and a mind-numbing roar. The Plexiglas windows of the booth jittered and shook. Jere held up a hand to shield his eyes. It's exploded, it's all over, it's done, I'm done.

But then the cheering of the crowd roused him. He looked at them in disbelief. What were they cheering for? Were they crazy? Did the fucking Russians actually want to see blood?

Then his father pointed and shouted, "Look!"

The needle was rising into the sky.

Slowly at first, then faster. It was a hundred feet up. Two hundred. Then as tall as a skyscraper, balancing on a long white tail of flame. The wind battered the grandstand and beat at the throng standing hundreds deep. The smell of burnt mud and concrete worked its way into the shelter. Sand and dust and grit pattered against the window.

My God, Jere thought, as the needle rose higher. Its flame no longer touched the Earth. It gathered speed like a jet, shrinking smaller and faster as it rose up and arced out.

Eventually, the roar reduced itself to a shout, then a mild grumbling. The passenger shuttle was a bright speck in the sky, like a magnesium flare.

Everybody was still cheering. Reporters looked around the crowd, dazed and blinking.

They'd done it.

We did it.

I did it!

When they were finally able to tear their eyes away from the pinprick, Frank was happily chatting away about " . . . a perfect launch . . . see you in a year."

Dad stuck out a hand. "Congratulations."

Jere took his father's hand and let it crush his own.

"Why?" he asked.

For a while, his father just grinned. A real grin. A happy, genuine grin. Then: "Because you did what everyone said you couldn't do."

Jere felt numb. Was his father actually praising him?

Ron squeezed his hand tighter. "Because there are lots of people who are trying to close the door on anything like this ever happening again. You snuck in right before the door went *bang*."

"I . . . " Jere could only manage the single word.

"Because," Ron said. "This *matters*."

"But . . . it wasn't . . . it was just a . . . "

Ron held up a hand. "Shh," he said.

Touch

Glenn Rothman grimaced as the RusSpace passenger shuttle pushed him back into his hardbacked seat. Beside him, Alena moaned softly. He could smell her sweat, not clean workout-sweat, but rank, sour, fear-sweat.

He looked over at her, fighting to keep his neck from snapping to the side. She had her eyes closed shut, tight, her eyelids folded into little piles of wrinkles.

Of course, Glenn thought. *She* can't control this. She can't even pretend to try.

He reached out with his hand. It felt like there was a fifty-pound weight hanging from his fingertips. He tried to softly place his hand on hers, but it came down hard.

Her hand turned under his, and gripped his briefly. Then her eyes flew open and she snatched her hand away.

"Alena," Glenn said.

"Don't do that," she said, yelling over the roar of the rockets. "Don't ever do that."

THREE: SHOW

Friends

Mike Kinsson brought his iStuff aboard *Mars Enterprise*. A hundred terabytes of books, movies, music, and interactives. It made sense. Six months in space. That meant boredom, even with his tablet. He couldn't lose himself in code like Nandir. Nandir was amazing. He hadn't brought a single book, magazine, movie, or game with him. Just his laptop and an eyeset paired to the machine. Nandir seemed completely oblivious to his surroundings. He sat in his corner and stared at his software all day, sometimes talking in low tones to his throatmike. For Nandir, that was happiness.

For Mike, happiness was floating down the aluminum handrail to look out through the rearmost porthole from the Can. Earth was only about thumbnail-sized, which meant they were past the orbit of the moon. Soon it would shrink to a fleck. Then just another point of light. A tiny blue star.

Even astronauts haven't seen this, Mike thought. It was a strange thought. Even the Apollo guys. Even the Chinese on the moon right now. He'd gone farther than all of them. They all had to look up at him now. At some point not long ago, a tiny entry had been made in the history books: Mike Kinsson, part of the first crew to go beyond the orbit of the moon.

On his way to Mars.

Mars.

It was an endless loop, playing over and over in his mind. One of his earliest memories was seeing an image from Mars Pathfinder slowly raster on his father's amazing new internet-connected computer with a 56k modem. Even as a kid, he knew he was looking at something millions of miles away. And yet . . . it looked so ordinary. It looked like a black-and-white photo of the Mojave. It looked like a place where you'd see sand rails and dirt bikes and ATVs.

He remembered thinking: It'd be fun to visit.

"And now I am," he said softly. Too soft—he thought—to hear above the wheeze of the Can's air-recycling systems. "I'm going there. I really am."

"What?" A voice, behind him.

Mike whirled. Julie floated slowly past him, reaching to catch the Can's rearmost rail. Mike looked forward. Nobody else was in the main cabin. Most likely in the bunkroom, or the kitchen, or the cramped little exercise space. All the fitness nuts had gone crazy when they hit zero-g and their bodies puffed up and started doing weird things. They spent most of their time in the exercise-space. It already stank like a middle school locker room. Mike wondered what it would smell like when they returned, almost a year from now.

"What were you talking about?" Julie said. Her pretty gray eyes scanned across his face. Mapping. Measuring.

"Nothing," Mike said.

Julie nodded and leaned close, pressing her face against the side of the cabin to see out the tiny porthole. Mike could feel her body heat. Her hair smelled faintly of some floral shampoo.

"It's really small now," she said.

"It'll get smaller."

"Will we still be able to see it . . . when we get there?"

"It'll be like a star."

Julie closed her eyes, her face still pressed against the cold metal. When she finally opened them, tears shimmered.

"I'm scared," she said.

Mike opened his mouth, but no words came out.

"I . . . I don't want to die. When I signed up, the money sounded so good, and even if I didn't get the money, I'd get the sponsorships, you know, that's what everyone told me, I'd be set, I . . . " Julie trailed off, looking away.

"It'll be okay. You'll be fine. We'll all be fine." Mike's words sounded hollow, fake.

"I want to go back!"

But you can't, Mike thought. You can't step off and take a taxi. You can't take the bus home. You're stuck here, whether you like it or not.

Mike put his hand on hers. "No. Really. They're exaggerating the danger—"

Julie twisted away from the wall and put her arms around him. Her body shook, wracked by sobs. She made almost no sound, except a low stuttering intake of breath.

Mike put his arms around her.

"He doesn't care!" she said.

"Who?"

"Sam! He says I'm being a baby."

Sudden realization dawned. Sam. Sam and Julie. Of course. Both of them spent all their time talking about how they'd spend their money if they won, and how they'd sell their story if they didn't. They didn't care about Mars. They didn't understand what a historic and amazing thing they were doing. In their way, they were as small-minded and self-centered as Keith Paul. Why couldn't he have been put on the team with Nandir and Romeo? Romeo's eyes shone every time he talked about space, about watching a crappy copy of the first Apollo moon landings as a kid, over and over, asking himself, why aren't we there now?

For a long time, Mike didn't know what to say. "We'll make it," he said, finally.

Julie pushed away and held him at arms' length. Her eyes jittered across his face again, as if searching for something they couldn't quite find. And in that moment, Mike melted. Selfish as he was, he couldn't just let her twist in the wind.

"I'll do what I can," Mike said. "For you."

"I—"

There was a bang from the front of the cabin. Julie pushed Mike away. Mike turned to see Frank Sellers, swinging from the foremost rail in an uncharacteristically clumsy manner. A toolkit floated beside him.

"Sorry," Frank said. Petrov Machenko followed him in. He was a big, chubby Russian who, from what Mike could figure, was the second-in-command, a production assistant/general do-it-all kinda guy. . They'd never been introduced. Frank and Petrov had been chasing down various bugs in the Can since launch, and only in the last couple of days did they seem less wild-eyed.

Frank thumbed his throatmike. "Okay, everyone," he said. His voice echoed hollowly throughout the Can. "General assembly in main cabin. Put down what you're doing, pause the movies, save your games, and get here on the double."

"What's going on?" Mike asked.

"Are we going back?" Julie said.

"You'll see, and no," Frank said, his gaze landing on each of them in turn.

The other contestants filtered in by ones and twos, until all eleven of them had arrived. Most went to the walls, but Glenn and Alena Rothman hung suspended, almost motionless. They were still dressed in the plain gray workout gear, showing huge sweat-stains at their necklines and underarms.

"We've been too busy for formalities, but now it's time to start the show," Frank said.

He opened the toolbox and withdrew three bottles of Cristal Champagne, holding them like a bunch of flowers.

"All right!" exulted Keith Paul, squirting toward Frank from the wall.

Frank pulled the bouquet of bottles away from Keith's outstretched hands at the last moment, and the man went hands-first into the opposite wall. He rebounded and thrashed about, looking for a handgrip. A couple of the contestants laughed, but quickly stifled their grins. Keith's expression was deadly.

The laughs came back when Petrov pulled a big bottle of vodka out from behind his back, and held it forth in imitation of Frank.

"Hey!" Frank said. "Where'd you get that?"

Petrov grinned. "Emergency fuel supply," he said.

More laughter. Frank's brow furrowed. Then he shook his head, as if deciding consciously to relax. "Okay, okay. I won't ask."

He turned to address everyone. "Before we 'par-tay,' I need to go over a few things with the group."

"Like what?" Keith said, still flailing.

Frank didn't even glance at Keith. "First and foremost, let me get this right out. We're going to be in this can for almost a year. A year, people. Three hundred and sixty five days, twenty-four-seven. That's a lot of time.

"Yeah, I know, you've heard it from the trainers and you've heard it from staff and you probably heard it from your mommy and your shrink, but I want you to really think about it. A year is a lot of time."

"I know," Nandir said, eye painted with data from his laptop.

The group tittered. "Don't laugh," Frank said. "I don't know about you, but me, I'd be one divorced SOB if I spent this kinda time in a can with my wife. We're going to get mighty sick and tired of each other. Simple things'll get stupid. Someone's gonna fart—and we'll all know whose it is—it'll be mighty tempting to pick up a wrench and have at 'em."

"Sounds like you've done this before," Alena said.

A nod. "Navy. Close enough. What you need to do, if that happens, is just get away, far as you can. Go remix your movies or look for that hidden level in your game. Check the tomatoes and the corn in the garden. Or just go look out a port and think about all that money you're gonna get from appearances and endorsements and crap when we get back. Laugh at Petrov and I for being antisocial assholes who haven't signed any juicy contracts, and won't be visible enough to make any money. It doesn't matter what you do. But get away from whoever is bugging you before you do something stupid."

Silence.

"Secondly, I don't give a fuck what you do while you're on this ship."

Keith smiled.

"Thirdly, I'm not here to be your mommy. Neither is Petrov."

Keith smiled broadly.

Petrov nodded, his teeth on the cap of the vodka bottle.

"Fourthly, none of that crap matters. What we are is judge and jury of this whole mess. Look it up in your contract. You've agreed to abide by our decisions. They're legally binding. So if we say you get chained in a bathroom the rest of the trip, that's what happens."

Keith's smile disappeared. "How is that fair?"

"It isn't," Frank said.

"Good luck getting me chained in a bathroom."

"You wanta go there now?" Frank asked, not looking at him.

Keith's mouth clicked shut. The rest of the group watched in silence.

"Point is, don't start whining when we tell you what to do. There's bound to be problems on a trip this long, so if we say jump, you say, 'how high?' "

Some nods.

Frank smiled. "Good. You're getting it. One final thing. Smile and wave. You're on camera."

Mike found his voice. "What do you mean?"

Frank pointed towards the ceiling, where a little black nubbin sprouted. "Since the beginning of the trip, the show's been running. I'm told the ratings are pretty shit so far, but I'm sure they'll pick up when we're on Mars."

"We're already on camera?" Julie said.

"Yes."

"All the time?"

"You got it."

"In the bathroom?" Julie wrinkled her face in disgust.

"No. But you can count on it almost everywhere else."

"Even when we're eating?" Julie said, looking almost as disgusted as when she was asking about the bathroom.

Mike tried to hold back a grin. There was laughter throughout the room, and Julie went red. That made everyone laugh even more.

"What if I don't want you assholes taping me twenty-four-seven?" Keith said.

"Then you better take a step out the airlock, because that's the only place . . ." Frank looked thoughtful. "Wait, actually, there's cameras out there too."

More laughter.

Frank grinned like a proud grandparent. "Okay. Now you know how it goes. They'll take the interesting bits, splice them together, and feed it to all the slack-jawed viewers. If you don't want to be part of the show, better act like Nandir here. Boring."

Nandir looked up. "I'm working on some very interesting software!"

Laughter.

"What about the internet?" Geoff asked.

Frank chuckled. "Our bandwidth is for sending data from the cams, not for feeding your porn collection. And it ain't that simple, even if we had a good connection."

"The delay is going to start being a problem soon too," Mike said. "Mars is about five light-minutes away from Earth, at the time of the show."

Frank nodded. "This isn't like calling your home service provider."

"It sucks," Geoff said.

Frank sighed. "Okay, enough of this crap. You're on a TV show, you're gonna be filmed. Get over it. Let's get this party started!"

Frank stripped the foil off one of the bottles of champagne and popped the cork. The champagne fountained out into the cabin. It coalesced rapidly into bubble-filled globes.

"Ah, shit," Frank said. "Shoulda thought of that."

Keith twisted to catch one of the globes in his mouth. He sucked it down and belched. Everyone laughed. Then the room was full of floating bodies, chasing champagne balls. Julie sailed past Mike, her face smiling and radiant.

Mike held back. Frank opened a second bottle of champagne and sprayed the crowd. Petrov sat with a bottle of vodka, sharing direct hits off it with Keith and Alena.

After a while, Nandir came to float by Mike. "You don't drink?" he said.

"Not now," Mike said. Julie and Sam were whirling in midair, as if dancing. She grinned and laughed.

"I agree," Nandir said.

"With what?"

"Not drinking now."

Mike turned to look back at the Earth. It was smaller. He was, slowly but surely, moving away. Moving out.

If only I could stay here, he thought.

"What have you been looking at?" Nandir said.

"Earth," Mike said, not turning.

Nandir craned his neck. "It's getting small."

Mike was silent for a long time, until his curiosity took him by the neck. "Don't you think it's strange?" he asked Nandir. "Leaving Earth? We're the only ones who have ever seen this."

"If you don't count automated probes."

"Yeah. But probes don't have emotions? What does it feel like, to you?"

"It feels like being stuck in a very small aluminum condo," Nandir said.

"That's all?"

"I am grateful for all the time to work on my software."

"No sense of wonder? Nothing?"

Nandir shrugged. "Things change. This is just another one of them."

Mike shook his head. Nobody understood. Not like him.

Julie ended up sitting beside Petrov and the others, drinking directly out of the second bottle of vodka he'd produced. She waved at him. Mike waved back.

Eventually, she came over to him.

"What's the matter?"

A wrinkled nose. "Stop looking!"

"At what?"

"Earth!"

Mike sighed. "I can't."

Julie looked at him a moment longer, then pushed off and went back to the group. She ended up drinking for the next hour, long after Mike had left the room and gone to his hammock. He lay awake for a long time. After a while, Julie and Sam came in and shared her hammock. Mike tried to ignore her soft cries. Mike tried not to look at them in the dim blue light. He ended up looking down at Keith.

Keith's eyes were open, and he was grinning.

"Friend zone, he's in the friend zone," Keith sang, softly, aping some song that was almost familiar.

Mike turned away and looked at the wall. Eventually, he slept.

Pall

It was as if Jere's life had rewound eighteen months. Here he sat, behind his big obsidian desk, with the Neteno sign spinning in the background again and gray Hollywood spreading away to the invisible ocean.

Revenues were decent, especially with the release of *Winning Mars II* from Gen3 and the solidification of the Gen3 currency against the dollar and RMB. The show itself was drawing okay viewership, even though it was just light drama in a can. The trip out to Mars was long and boring. The editors complained every day that there was little to work with, and bitched even more mightily when Jere told them, no, they couldn't have Frank and Petrov stir the pot; no, they weren't going to use any of Evan's ideas.

The world had flared again, as it always did. Extremist Muslims in France were threatening to nuke Paris again, and some fucking disease-for-profit asshole released his shit in Nebraska. Neteno had done well with those, because they were credible again, now people would believe anything they did. Even 411 had shut the fuck up, and sponsors were listening and nodding and making all those little buying signals again. There was still a black balloon of debt floating out there, but, at least for the moment, Neteno had some breathing room.

People were bringing him crazy ideas. *Winning Gold*, featuring a hunt for a mythical solid gold asteroid. *Kissing Venus*, some crazy kid's cloudsurfing idea. *Protecting Earth*, if they could figure out how to lob an asteroid at it. That one would be huge. Of course, if they messed up . . .

And now, he was listening to the craziest idea of all.

Horatio Wood was a familiar face to anyone involved in the currency exchange markets. His ME Platinum was the premier virtual currency in the world, trading at an average of 104.4:1 to Gen3 Bux. Horatio Wood was the richest man in the world.

Sitting in Jere's office, Horatio was not an imposing figure. He dressed in a conservative business-style, the classic black suit and tie, brown hair cropped short above a face plain enough to disappear in any small party. But his eyes were still and calm, as if they rested on something fifteen thousand feet away.

"I'd like to buy Neteno," Horatio said. He named an impossible figure.

"No," Jere said.

"Then I want to be a minority shareholder." He named the same ridiculous figure.

"No."

"I want to be a most valued partner." The same ridiculous figure, meted out over a number of key projects.

"No."

Horatio Wood sat back in his chair and put his hands together in his lap. His face showed no hint of emotion.

Tags floated in Jere's eyeset. HORATIO WOOD, FOUNDER OF MODERN ENLIGHTENMENT, INC. ESTIMATED MEMBERSHIP IN MODERN ENLIGHTENMENT. ESTIMATED NET WORTH IN SEVERAL WORLD CURRENCIES. PROJECTED GROWTH OVER THE NEXT TWENTY-FOUR MONTHS. It wasn't 411 data, because 411 didn't track churches or religious institutions, but Jere had no reason to doubt the numbers.

If you want to make some money, put on a good show, Jere thought. If you want to become the richest man in the world, combine virtual currency and religion.

Horatio shifted slightly in his chair. "It is a very generous offer."

"I'm not debating that."

"Then, why not?"

"I don't see the connection," Jere said. "We're an entertainment company. We work in the here and now. You are a religious institution, working towards . . . whatever comes after."

A smile. The same smile Jere had seen at TimeOnline. The same smile etched into *Wall Street Journal* art after a billion dollar donation to a small Mexican church. "That makes it all the more synergistic. We *operate* in the here and now, do we not?"

"Are you afraid we'll bring back evidence of life on Mars?" Tons of religious nutjobs had been freaking on that frequency since they launched.

Horatio laughed. "No. Not at all."

"Wouldn't that disprove your god?"

"It would only prove God more wondrous than we imagined. There is no incongruence. There's nothing but congruence. Our organizations can learn a lot from each other. Neteno inspires the spirit of the present. We inspire the spirit of tomorrow."

"*Winning Mars* is only a TV show."

Horatio shook his head. "And our churches are just buildings."

Images of Modern Enlightenment churches played on Jere's eyeset. Rapt believers, eyes wide in synthetic glory. Some of their heads were still shaved. Some still bore surgery scars.

"No," Jere said. "Thank you again for the offer, but the answer is no."

"You don't approve of our methods."

"I'm not here to judge."

A brief pursing of lips. Horatio nodded. "I can see from your vantage point. You think we have made salvation into a game of paint-by-numbers. You don't like to see the path to heaven well-lit and properly marked."

Documents from Modern Enlightenment scrolled in Jere's eyeset:

A GOOD DEED IS WORTH ONE SILVER COIN.

A TESTAMENT THAT SPREADS THE WORD AND GARNERS AT LEAST ONE HUNDRED THOUSAND MCCANN ATTENTION-POINTS IS WORTH ONE HUNDRED SILVER COINS

A CONVERSION IS WORTH ONE GOLD COIN.

PARTIAL DONORS ARE WORTH ONE PLATINUM COIN FOR EACH THOUSAND DOLLARS OF DONATION.

TOTAL DONORS ARE WORTH ONE HUNDRED PLATINUM COINS IF EMPLOYMENT IS RETAINED (SUBJECT TO REVOCATION.)

REFORMATION OF ANY OTHER CHURCH IS WORTH ONE THOUSAND PLATINUM COINS.

THE PORTAL TO HEAVEN COSTS ONE HUNDRED PLATINUM COINS OR ANY EQUIVALENT.

ACCESSING THE PORTAL TO PEAVEN COSTS ONE GOLD COIN PER MINUTE. (EXPERIENCE VERIFIED BY INDEPENDENT MINISTERS FROM THE MAJORITY OF LEADING RELIGIONS AROUND THE WORLD—CLICK HERE FOR A LIST.)

Jere stood and extended his hand. "Thank you for your generous offer, but Neteno is not seeking any additional investment at this time."

Horatio didn't stand up. "I urge you to reconsider."

"I've made my decision." Jere put his hand down, but remained standing.

Something flitted across Horatio's face, something that could have almost been anger.

"What about your partners?" he asked. "Would they be interested?"

"I'm the majority shareholder."

"Perhaps they are interested in moving on."

Jere thought of Evan. Luckily, Ron had insisted on a first-rights purchase contract for the majority shareholder based on stated value. "I'll pass along the information."

Horatio nodded, stood. He held out a hand. Jere took it. It was cold and limp.

"I hope to speak to you again," Horatio said.

"Goodbye," Jere said.

He watched on Neteno's security cameras until the man had left the building.

Jere shivered.

Fitness

"Alena, stop!" Glenn Rothman said

Alena floated rapidly down the short hall from the exercise room to the main cabin. He reached out and grabbed her arm. It was still slick with sweat. Alena twisted away effortlessly. She caught the handrail, whipped around to face him, and punched him, hard, in the stomach.

Glenn doubled over, his breath going out of him with a big "Whoo!"

He felt himself rebound from the opposite wall, and scrabbled for the handrail. He tried to pull in air, but it was like breathing through a straw. He opened his mouth and sucked, hard. A tiny bit of air slipped into his lungs.

"You see!" Alena said. "You're getting weak. Look at you, trying to catch your breath!"

Glenn pulled a little more air into his lungs. "Not . . . " Breath. "Because . . . " Breath. "Weak . . . " He reached out for her.

"Don't touch me!" Alena knocked his hand away.

"Alena—"

"I'm getting weak too." She rolled up the sleeve of her exercise outfit and flexed her arm. She pulled at it, pinching and stretching the skin. "I'm getting flabby. I work and work, but I'm getting flabby."

"Muscle loss is to be expected," Frank said, sticking his head into the corridor.

"It is? It is?"

Frank chuckled. "We've known about it for years. Decades."

"How the hell are we supposed to do a sheer climb?"

Frank smirked. "I'm sure the lower gravity will help."

"What about when we get back? What shape will we be in?"

A chuckle. "You should've read your contracts. Permanent bone loss, muscle loss, et cetera, I think we covered it all."

"You did?" Alena said. She turned to Glenn. "Why didn't you see that?"

"I . . . did," Glenn said. His breath came a little easier now.

"Why didn't you tell me?"

"You didn't ask."

Alena pulled herself close to the wall and closed her eyes. Glenn wanted to go over and comfort her, but he knew he'd just be thrown off. And she was right. He should have told her. She wouldn't have read down to page thirty-one, article one hundred-fifty-six. She wouldn't have read the bits after that, either, the ones that said they probably wouldn't want to have children after this, at least if they didn't want them to look like Kermit the Frog. Or the piece that outlined their increased risk of cancer over the course of their lifetimes. She wouldn't have read any of that.

He remembered the first time they did Everest. No oxygen, of course. It was a hell of a thing, a perk for winning the '19 X-Games, one of those group things where they'd send up cameras and cull it for a show later on. A hell of an opportunity. All for free. She'd signed the contract without looking at it. Glenn had done the same. Of course he would go with her. He loved her. They'd be married, and they'd spend the rest of their life together. That was the only way things could go.

On the third day of the ascent, white-out conditions drove them into their tents early. Glenn sighed and lay down with Alena, waiting for the burn in his muscles to subside. But it didn't. If anything, it got hotter. Alena rubbed her calves and arms too.

Glenn asked her what was wrong, but she said, quietly, *Nothing.*

In the morning, in the clear ice air, they discovered the reason. Their guide, a burly white guy who hid behind a full face-mask most of the time, just laughed.

Everyone gets that, he said. *Muscles, hurtin' for oxy. Crying out. Saying, you should be carrying a tank.*

Alena looked panicked, and asked if it would hurt her.

Not permanently, the guide said. *May even make you stronger, in the long run. Mind, that's another thing. Some people say you're dumber after you come down off Everest. Brain cells crying for oxy too. That's why it's so hard to think.*

But physically we're okay? Alena said.

And, with the guide's nod, that was that. They set off again.

Bad weather kept them from seeing the summit. Glenn had to drag Alena back when their guide said it was time to call it quits. Eventually, she'd looked towards the invisible summit, and said, in a voice low and determined, *We'll be back.*

"Don't know about the climb, anyway," Frank said, bringing Glenn back to the present.

"What does that mean?" Alena said.

"You may not even make it."

"We'll make it!"

"No. You're not getting me. You might not make it to the cliff. All the routes are guesswork and bullshit, based on photos from orbit. We know there's a mile-high vertical cliff there. We think we can land you near enough so you can do the climb. But if we can't, you get another route."

"We trained for this route!" Alena yelled. "I don't want another route!"

"If you're gonna splat face-first into a boulder the size of a house, you want another route."

"We'll take the chance!"

Frank shook his head. "When we get closer, we'll decide."

"But . . . "

"Alena," Glenn said.

"Shut up! Shut up! We may be losing our chance at the ridge!"

"We'll do everything we can to get you there," Frank said. "Trust me."

Alena looked from Glenn to Frank and back again. Then her face turned down into a deep frown. "What about me? What about my muscles?"

"You can work out more," Frank said. "That does slow the effects somewhat."

"What about drugs?"

"Drugs?" Glenn said. *Alena must be really desperate. Really scared.*

She turned to him, her almond eyes wide, frightened. "Yes, drugs."

Frank shook his head. "Nope. Not like there was a big call for it, before this mission."

"There's nothing?" Alena said, her voice rising into a wail.

"No pills."

"But exercise works."

"A little."

Alena clamped her mouth shut and nodded. She turned and went back to the exercise room. Glenn followed her, as she loaded the inertial machine with fifty kilos more than she usually did.

"What are you doing?" Glenn said.

"I'm going to stay in shape."

"You already spend more time in here than anyone else!"

Alena stopped. Looked at him. "I don't care if I'm in here twenty-four-seven."

Glenn turned away, sighing.

"You shouldn't, either," Alena said. "At least, if you want to keep up with me."

Glenn stopped, still turned away. What she was doing was crazy. They still had four months left. She'd kill herself.

After a moment, he turned and went to set up his own inertial machine. He smiled at Alena, but she didn't look at him. She was already in the routine, legs pumping, arms pulling, eyes straight forward, seeing nothing.

Stars

Patrice Klein stood in front of the small window and looked out at the stars. Even with the lights off, they were small and unimpressive. No better than *Halo Empire* on a 3D screen, and definitely no match for *Galactic Foundation* seen with immersive goggles or on a mid-price home wraparound.

Patrice sighed. But these are the real stars, she thought. The actual galaxy. From space.

But it didn't stir any feelings. Except for the starward view through the three-square-foot window, her suite in the Russian space hotel Stolichnaya could be a cheap cabin in a third-rate cruise ship. She'd paid more for that view.

She rested her forehead on the window to get a better view. She drew back, gasping, at the chill.

That was one difference. That was one shred of reality.

But the stars just weren't impressive. Yes, there were a lot of them. Yes, they stretched impressively deep. However, they didn't hit her like she expected them to.

We've gone beyond the real, Patrice thought. Our illusions are better than the actuality. I should be standing here in awe, like a Cro-Magnon discovering fire or the Montgolfier Brothers watching their first balloon rise. But no . . . it's something to grade and dissect like a second-rate game.

What had Jere seen, to make him want to gamble everything on the show?

On the narrow bed was a print copy of the Henry Kase's first fiction book *Out*. Patrice picked it up, flipped to a page, and read:

. . . was like a trap to him. Complexity formed the bars, process defined the boundaries, unquestioned belief this was not only the right way but the only way to do things kept him there. And yet, where would he go? Every place on the world was the same. The bars might be configured a little differently, the process might let him walk a few more steps, but in the end it was the same. There was no place where he could take his

blimx and say, "Yes, I know, this is a chance, but I'll take it, alone."
There was no place . . .

Patrice shook her head. She'd watched some fan-made rough cuts of
the book, which was supposed to be "a kaleidoscopic novel about breaking
free of the chains of modern life." But the rough cuts made no sense. Badly
animated 3D characters dreamed and worked, dreamed and worked some
more, and failed. The guy making the personal aircraft. The inventor of the
big IA recommender. The guy who wanted to walk around the world. The
kid working on the time machine. The woman who decided to erase her past
and go back, after all that surgery. The girl building a rocket in her backyard.
It made no sense. The rough cuts were scenes without meaning.

Reading the book helped, because it explained what was going on in each
character's mind. Yet their thoughts were so alien. Growing up, Patrice had
always had one thing in mind: getting enough to get out. But these people's
"outs" weren't defined by getting enough money. They wanted something
more. They yearned. They kept fighting, and they kept losing.

It was profoundly disturbing.

Because what did it say about her? She had everything she wanted. Even
after the wrist-slap from Gen3 for seeing Jere, she had more money than she
could ever spend. She didn't have to work. All she had to do was show up,
have fun, and look good while doing it. And looking good was something
she could do for the next twenty years at least. She was only twenty-nine. She
might even be able to look good for thirty or forty years more. The treatments
were getting amazingly good.

I might be able to do it for fifty years, she thought. Every day, some new
amazing thing came along. And the pace was picking up. A hundred years.

Suddenly, Patrice felt cold. The image of her, a hundred years from now,
descending on a party as the Once and Eternal YZ, the matriarch of Adventure
Game Characters, burned into her mind. It was as if a hole had opened up in
her soul, and she'd found nothing inside.

The room was too small. Patrice went out to the public areas on the other
side of the ring, where the earthward view illuminated romantic restaurants
and dark bars with brilliant blue light. Local time was 5:45 p.m. There were
only a few people out in the corridors and in the bars; the clubs hadn't opened
yet, and people seemed to dine late.

Patrice went into a place called the Rebel Bar and Grille. Its sign showed a Confederate flag with two pistols crossed in front. The proprietor stood in the shadows in the back of the bar, the lit coal of a cigarette illuminating his face in warm reds. From the stink, it was a real cigarette. Patrice went to a booth near a window and sat.

Outside, the Earth was painted three-quarters in sunlight. Fluffy white clouds spun over Europe and Africa. Asia was in darkness. The mega-cities of Beijing and Tokyo were faint sparks on a black canvas. The view was impressively dimensional and real—and yet, still no better than a midline immersive system with a second-tier game.

"You're YZ!" a young, enthusiastic, and female voice said.

Patrice turned. Bobbing up and down with excitement was a young girl, maybe twelve or thirteen, dark-haired, with a big gap-toothed grin. Behind her, a man, late thirties, wearing a polo shirt and glasses, looked embarrassed.

"I'm sorry," he said.

"But she's YZ!" the girl said, leaning over the table in her enthusiasm. Patrice couldn't help grinning back. She wasn't wearing a YZ outfit, she wasn't made up, she wasn't trying to be YZ, but that was okay.

"We should leave her alone," the man said.

"No! Can't we talk to her?" The girl was still bouncing with excitement.

"It's not polite."

"I don't care! It's YZ."

The man looked at Patrice with a helpless expression that said: *I have no idea what to do now.* An odd look, at a resort where only the über-rich could afford to stay. And he didn't seem rich. He didn't give off that busy-executive vibe, that captain-of-industry command, that I-built-myself-up feeling.

"I don't mind," Patrice said.

The girl didn't need any more encouragement. She slid into the booth, looking up at Patrice with round, amazed eyes. After a moment's hesitation, the man followed her.

"I'm really sorry," he said. "YZ is like a goddess to her."

The girl snapped a sharp look at the man. "YZ is my inspiration." Suddenly, she seemed much older and more serious.

"I'm Richard Soto," the man said, extending a hand. "And this is my daughter, Amy Soto."

"I won the Microsoft/MIT pseudolife challenge," Amy said.

"Wow!" Patrice said. She had no idea what Amy was talking about.

"She created a new virus," Richard said.

"From scratch!" Amy corrected. "It makes mice smarter!"

"And *I* inspired this?"

Amy nodded vigorously. "YZ can do anything. She can go anywhere. She's smart and she's pretty, and she's always doing something interesting. Whenever I got stuck, I asked myself, 'What would YZ do?'"

Patrice almost laughed, but Amy was earnest. Her wide eyes were completely honest.

"So that's why we're here," Richard said. "In space."

Amy frowned. "Mom wouldn't come."

Richard looked away.

"Dad almost wouldn't come."

Richard said nothing.

"They didn't want me to go!"

Richard looked back at her. "We were just worried. We didn't want you to be hurt."

"If you don't take a chance, you'll never do anything," Amy said. She grinned at YZ. "Or something like that. It's an old saying, and I didn't bring my eyeset."

"Amy—"

"And look," Amy interrupted. "YZ's here. YZ. She can do anything, and she's here. I bet you're not scared, are you, YZ?"

Patrice remembered dry-mouthed terror when the rockets lit. She grinned at Amy.

"I bet she's doing something really important up here," Amy said. "Something she can't even tell us about."

Patrice tried to keep her grin fixed.

Just trying to figure out what's in Jere's head, she thought. And what's in mine. And maybe who I am. Not important in the grand scheme of things, but important to me.

After a few moments, she nodded, as if admitting to a hidden agenda.

"See!" Amy said, lighting up.

And on the beaming face of the child prodigy, she saw it: Jere and Henry Kase and his crazy blimxmaker and the nuts in the Can on the way to Mars, the nuts who still might die, the nuts who might never come back to Earth. There were people like Amy, wide-eyed and brilliant, and there were people like Richard, worried and ridden, and willing to look for any excuse not to do something, any excuse to play it safe.

"I'll be like YZ someday," Amy said. "I'll go to Mars."

But I'm not going to Mars, Patrice wanted to say. Maybe Amy was just talking about the part of her in the game. The YZ part.

The better part.

Education

Keith was deep in an interactive, thinking of the lesbians. In the interactive, he was a walk-in with two sisters writhing on Mommy and Daddy's bed. He was supposed to be a plumber or something. The VR deck wasn't much good without the dick-sleeve and the little stick-sensors, but it beat whacking it in the bathroom with his eyes closed.

Laci and Wende, he thought, as he rounded the corner on the two sisters. They looked up at him, wide-eyed, shocked, gasping. But smiling too, as if they wanted it, like maybe being lesbians wasn't the best thing on the planet.

Or off. Though the lesbians here hadn't given him much of a show, so that he started wondering if they were even lesbians at all. But that was crazy. Two bitches not hot enough to be strippers, living together? They liked to talk about stupid shit like "empowering women" and "striking a blow through the glass ceiling," whatever that was. That wasn't exciting. That wasn't what normal chicks talked about.

One of the girls got up off the bed. She was perfect, slim, big tits, not sagging at all. Keith smiled and moved his POV forward.

His POV dissolved in a mess of blocks. The sound stuttered and jumped.

"No! Shit! Not now!" Keith growled, hearing his own voice over his earbuds. He shook the tablet, but the picture didn't come back. Instead, an angry red screen displayed some text below the international fuck-you icon, the exclamation point in the yellow triangle.

Keith pushed the reset button, but the red screen stayed lit. He'd just have to unplug it for a while.

"Shit," he said, stripping off the goggles and pulling out his earplugs.

"What's wrong?" a voice said, beneath him.

Keith jumped. He'd thought he was alone in the bunkroom. Or else he wouldn't have been pulling his dick. What kinda fag would be laying there watching? He looked over the side of his hammock. It was Glenn, the fucking action-sports Negro. Sweat ringed his workout gear, and his muscles stood out hard under his skin. Probably just back from the workout room, where he spent all his time with that chick who hated him. Dumbass.

"What's wrong with you?" Keith asked.

Glenn looked genuinely surprised. "What do you mean?"

"I mean, you walked in while I was pulling my dick. You mean you missed that?

But, Keith realized, it was entirely possible Glenn had missed it. The fucker stumbled around like a goddamned zombie, too zonked from working out all the time to do anything else. Keith knew he was getting a little flabby, but those two assholes took it way too far.

"Tablet," Keith said. "Fuckin' thing redscreened."

"Ah," Glenn said.

"Yours workin' okay?"

"My what?"

"Your tablet." What a dumbass.

"I didn't bring one."

Keith snorted. He *was* a crazy fucker.

Keith pushed off the bed, down the hall. Nothin' to do but wait for the deck to come back to life. He went to the exercise room, watched the wiry Alena chick go at it on the inertials for a while. He normally didn't like black chicks, but she was fine. Finer than the lesbians.

Alena raised sweat-matted hair and glared at him. Keith smiled back.

"What are you looking at?"

"You," he said.

Another glare, then she dropped her head and went back into it. She'd lost weight during the three months out, and thick muscles corded her arms and legs. Beneath her short top, he could see ribs.

Keith watched her a while longer, just to annoy her. He waited until she looked up again. Then he went down the hall. Almost everyone was in the common room, stuck behind a wall of eyesets or earbuds, or eating like robots. Because it was a fucking boring trip. Nothing to do, except run the same movies and games over and over. And think about the lesbians. Or not-lesbians. Or whatever they were. They were out of sight, which might mean they were in the pilot's cabin with Frank. Keith wondered what they did in there. And if Frank watched.

Back through the hall. It was almost an unconscious thing. The pacing. Nothing to do. Back and forth. Nothing to do. Back and forth. Keith felt rage building. Three more goddamn months. Then six months back. He tried to think of the money going into his account, automatically, every day. He tried to think of winning the fifty mil. But even that seemed pale and faraway.

But I will win it, he thought.

BFD, another voice said, as if he was having a conversation with himself. *It's three months till you win, then six months till you can go spend any of it. Like a whole fucking life.*

I could pay the lesbians to suck my dick all the way home. I could pay Alena. Hell, I could afford Julie.

Doubt that, the voice said.

Besides, he'd still be here. Keith shook his head and paced.

Low singing from the hydroponics room made him stop and look. Inside, Julie, the Mexican-fucker, was busy farting around with the tomatoes. She wore earbuds and was humming along to some dumbass tune. She was a good-looking chick, like someone out of those girl-next-door videos anyway, a decent ass and a mid-sized rack that looked pretty perky, but of course they all looked pretty perky with no gravity, and a face you wouldn't have to cover with a bag. The one geek had a thing for her, but he'd been fucked in the ass by the Mexican, who shared Julie's sack from time to time. Keith smiled, remembering dim glimpses of smooth flesh, and her moans, slowly rising in intensity.

She looked up and saw Keith. At first, she gave him that blank look, like a deer seen through a telescopic sight. Nothing going on up there, no idea of what would happen next.

Then her brows drew down in a deep frown, and she looked back down at her work.

Fucking bitch, Keith thought. Thinks she's better than me. Anger grabbed his gut with a sharp clutch. This time, he didn't try to push it away. He stepped into the room.

Julie looked up, her eyes going wide.

"How's it going?" Keith said.

She pulled the earbuds out, and dropped them, "N—nothing," she said, her eyes suddenly wide. She backed away from him.

Keith smiled. He liked her fear. "What you mean, nothing?"

Julie blinked, shook her head. "I mean, fine, I'm fine. How are you?"

Programmed. Like a fucking computer. "I'd be better if you came back and shared my bunk."

"What do you mean?" Julie backed away, bumping into the racks of cucumbers, or whatever they were growing back there. Eyes wide under the bright light.

"It means I want to fuck you," Keith said, moving forward again. He had her stuck in a corner. She looked around frantically and tried to push past him. He grabbed her arm and pulled her to him. She pushed at his face, flailing. Her feet tangled in the tomatoes and tore some vines free.

Keith batted them away and pulled her close. She squealed and pointed up at the little black camera eye above them. But Keith was past caring. Maybe, if he was really bad, they'd send him back. Maybe that was what he really needed to do.

Three more months. Then six more.

He clawed at her clothes. She yelled, but it sounded very far away, like a stereo just turned on.

"Come on," Keith said. "I just want to kiss you."

She paused for just a moment and looked at him, to see if he was serious. Keith laughed and tore her blouse open, exposing smooth white bra.

Like you need that in zero-G.

Something struck Keith from behind. It felt like an eighteen-pound sledge. It knocked him off Julie, and he went flying through the plants himself. He hit the far wall and turned in time to see Petrov launching at him.

Keith grabbed a rail and lashed out at Petrov. His fist whooshed through air, narrowly missing as Petrov ducked and spun around. He was tricky with shit like that.

Keith gathered himself to shoot through the door and into the hall. Frank's face appeared in the door, and he thought better of it.

Wham! Petrov's fist hit him again, sending him flying. Keith's POV spun wildly. He saw Petrov give up his grip on the handhold and launch after him.

Somewhere, far away, a woman was sobbing.

Oh, shit, Keith thought. I did that.

He hit the wall, grabbed a handrail, and looked towards the door. Frank hugged Julie close. Her face was red and streaked with tears.

I did that, Keith thought again. The last minutes streamed back at him, like a show on fast forward. He closed his eyes. It was like he was watching someone else entirely.

"I'm sorry," he said.

Wham! Petrov's fist hit him, again sending him flying. Keith crashed into Frank and Julie. Julie wailed. Keith wanted to say he was sorry, but Frank flashed teeth like a coyote and shoved her outside.

Petrov came up behind Keith and grabbed him with one hand. Keith turned to see him holding onto a handrail.

"I'm sorry," he said.

"Too late for that," Frank said. He pulled the door closed. It was the first time Keith had ever seen a door closed on the Can. He felt his stomach clench with fear.

"What're you gonna do with me?" he asked.

Frank gave him a terrible old-man smile and blew out terrible old-man coffee-breath. "Anything we want," he said. He raised a fist. It came down. It was nothing like Petrov. But he couldn't escape.

Eventually, Petrov took over.

The pain went *beyond*. Keith heard himself, yelling and crying. He saw the fists come down, again and again. It was like a business. One of them held him against the wall and the other hit.

In the end, they plucked him out of air filled with globules of red—his blood—and carried him to the door. Before they opened it, Frank leaned close to Keith's ear.

"Next time you do that, we won't hit you," Frank said. "We'll throw you right out the fucking airlock."

Keith nodded.

"Big cheers, audience says," Petrov added.

Three months.

Then six months.

Fuck.

Face

"Ratings are up, anyway," Evan said.

Jere sighed. Outside his office, the Neteno sign orbited as if nothing was wrong. As if Keith hadn't tried to rape Julie. As if Frank and Petrov hadn't turned him into pulp right after that. As if some dumbass editor hadn't put the unedited stuff up on the nets.

"Keith was your idea," Jere said.

"What?"

"You said to use convicts."

Evan crossed his legs, cleared his throat. "If you're thinking of scapegoating me—"

"No. I'm the face. I'm the one who has to stand up in front of everyone and take the beating. Just reminding you how it is."

"But the ratings are up—"

"Fuck the ratings!" Jere yelled. He came around from behind his desk to stand over Evan. Evan scooted back as far as he could in the chair. For a moment, his dead eyes almost seemed to show something, something that might have been fear. "If you paid attention to anything besides the raw numbers, you know ratings don't mean shit. The positives/negatives flopped from balanced to negative. Demo's gone to crap, we picked up pervs and lost females. Females won't let their significant others watch it, now. Ratings'll drop next day or two. Then we'll lose some sponsors, and then we'll be back in the same position we were a few months ago: wondering where all the money went."

Silence.

"Why?" Jere asked. "Why'd you pitch me this damn show?"

Evan just shook his head.

"Talk!"

Evan opened his mouth. Sighed. Looked up at Jere. "Nobody was ever supposed to say yes," he said.

"Everybody? You pitched this to other people?"

"Of course."

"Why? Why so big? Why Mars?"

Silence again. Evan shifted in his seat.

"Why, dammit?"

"Because big is the only thing that matters. I thought you knew that."

Jere shook his head and paced. "But Keith! Frank! Petrov!"

"Noise in the system."

"Noise that'll kill us!"

Evan shook his head. "I thought you were the visionary."

"As opposed to who? You?"

Evan laughed. "No. I never had any illusions about what I was."

"You're a fucking shill," Jere said.

"Guilty."

"You don't even care what you shill!"

"Guilty."

"This little . . . noise . . . might take us all down!"

"I know that."

"Then why?"

"Because once you've been at the top, you'll do anything to get back."

For one tiny moment, Evan was completely transparent. A terrible thing of gears and interlocking cylinders, calculating only one result: how high he could go. A thing that would destroy the world, if its destruction assured he stood on top of the rubble.

"When you signed the personal guarantee, you really signed everything over, didn't you?" Jere asked. "You weren't hiding a damn thing. You didn't have a backup plan."

Evan nodded. "Now you're starting to understand."

Plans

"We have much better data on the routes now, so we have what we think is the final drop plan," Frank said.

HE IS MUCH LESS CERTAIN THAN HE ASSERTS, Nandir's inference software whispered in his earbud.

Nandir nodded. That was no surprise.

Still, his software had called it, even operating without a connection to the global networks, using a relatively limited local database. That was pretty amazing.

They were gathered in the common room for the weekly "Briefing and Beating." Nandir was usually able to sleep through them. He was the boring one. He'd never tried to put on a squeezesuit and take an unauthorized spacewalk, he'd never groped someone else's girlfriend or boyfriend, he'd never even started singing, badly, in Tagalog, as Romeo had done once, at three a.m. ship time. He wondered if Romeo was still on antidepressants.

Now, only two weeks before Mars orbit, Nandir was annoyed. He was close, so close, to getting the inference software above fifty percent confidence. Fifty percent confidence was the golden measure. Nobody had ever achieved that goal before. Not even with a persistent connection to the unlimited database of the internet. Not even with processor arrays a hundred times better than he had. When Nandir went home and could use the eyes and ears of the net and a richer database, he might be able to get its score above sixty percent. That was when the software started becoming interesting. If it was more right than it was wrong, it changed from a toy to a useful tool. He could find investors. He could build another, bigger company. And maybe this time he'd make enough to step off the treadmill.

But that was for when he got back. There was still the show. In a couple of weeks, he'd have to put on a silly suit and go down and run and jump and fly. So people back on Earth could watch and comment. It seemed incredibly stupid. There was no way he and Romeo would win it. And it didn't matter.

He had no interest in winning. He'd be slow and careful and get back when he got back. If Romeo was angry, Nandir would offer him a job at his new firm.

He wondered what they'd do if he faked being sick on the day of the drop. Would they disqualify his team? Maybe. Romeo wouldn't be able to do the assembly by himself. Or would they send him anyway? That seemed a lot more likely. Being sick would just add a little more drama.

Plus, Frank seemed to have a reasonable amount of medical knowledge. He might know if Nandir was faking.

But what if I wasn't faking? What if I was actually sick? Nandir smiled.

"Why the grin?" Romeo asked.

THIS PERSON IS INTERESTED IN YOU SEXUALLY, his inference software said.

"Never mind," Nandir said, and turned back towards Frank. He was still droning on about the drop plan.

". . . upshot is that the drops'll be staggered over a seven-hour window. Laci, Wende, and Geoff are first, to allow time for the IBM experiments package—"

"We're not all dropping at the same time?" This from Keith Paul, the asshole.

THE SPEAKER IDENTIFIED AS PAUL IS EXTREMELY UPSET, Nandir's inference software said.

"Where have you been?" Frank said. "Schedule has been posted forever. We're just doing final tweaks."

Keith set his jaw and dropped his eyes. "How's that fair?"

"Of course it's fair," Frank said.

"Not if you drop the winners first."

Frank blew out a breath. "Do I have to go over this again? Fucking pay attention! The drops are staggered to compensate for the different routes. Trailblazer team has additional duties—namely, running the IBM experiments package—and Patel's team has the shortest and easiest route."

Keith frowned and looked away.

THE SPEAKER IDENTIFIED AS PAUL IS OVERCOME BY JOY, AND WILL AGREE WITH THE INTERPRETATION.

"That is incorrect," Nandir whispered to his software.

NOTED, the software said.

Frank continued. "Of course, this is all still best-guess stuff. The routes may be easier or more difficult than we think. But, hey, you pay your money, you take your choice."

"Same route would be fair," Keith said.

Frank's lips set in a hard line. "We can't do the same routes."

"Why not?"

"Because that's not how this show was planned. Programming is in place. We're not going to make this a free-for-all with everyone running the same route."

"It'd be more fun."

He's thinking about killing people, Nandir thought. He's thinking about whatever he can do to win.

Now, if his software would just say it!

THERE HAS BEEN A FATAL EXCEPTION IN MODULE INP66X0FB21, his inference software said.

Nandir cursed. "Reboot," he said softly.

REBOOTING, the software said.

"I'll bet Nandir doesn't have a problem dropping last," Frank said.

Nandir looked up. Frank pointed towards him. Nandir noticed how dirty Frank's long-sleeved shirt was. But everything was like that. Nissin Foods and TacoBell@Home and General Mills wrappers piled in drifts until someone got bored enough to shovel them away. Every handrail was dark with grime. The whole place needed hosing out.

"Who cares what the dot thinks?" Keith said. There were a couple of gasps from the other crewmembers.

We're all getting a little messy ourselves, Nandir thought. Messy in the head. If he hadn't had his software to work on, how bored would he be now?

"What?" Keith said. "I can't say that? Dot, dot, dot!" He pointed at Nandir. Nandir stifled a smile. It meant nothing to him.

Keith pointed to others. Romeo. "Gook!" Sam. "Beaner!" Glenn. "Nigger! I bet I can't say those, either! What do you think! I'll say them if I want! Give everyone a show! Fuck 'em if they can't take a joke!"

Frank nodded at Petrov, and the big man launched towards Keith. Keith's eyes went wide, and he cowered against the wall. Then, at the last instant, he launched out of the room and down the hall. Petrov tried to grab him and almost snagged a cuff. Petrov swore in Russian and squirted out of the room. Down the hall, they heard a crash and the smack of fists.

"Sorry about that," Frank said, turning to look down the hall.

THE SPEAKER IS VERY HAPPY, Nandir's inference software told him.

"That is in—" Nandir said, but then stopped himself. Frank might be very happy to see Keith beaten again. Nandir decided not to correct the software.

"Okay," Frank said. "Anyone else have questions about the drop schedule?"

Heads shook a negative reply all around.

THE SPEAKER IS INTERESTED IN BALLROOM DANCING, Nandir's software said. SUGGEST ASKING HIM/HER OUT FOR AN ACTIVITY.

Nandir sighed.

Then, softly, he laughed. He still had a long way to go, but at least he had something to do.

Romance

Jere took Patrice to Yamashiro, which was strange, because Patrice had heard him saying it was for tourists and people who wanted to get married. It was one of those showy places where you paid as much for the view as the food. Some producers had taken Patrice out there before, so at least some industry people went there. But in the strange ecosystem of what constituted cool in the world of studio luncheries, she knew the hot places changed every month. She favored the small places with flyeye-zappers the Oversight spooks hadn't shaken down yet, the funky places with active wallpaper and a few bar stools, a menu printed by an ancient laser printer, and maybe an engineered dog-parrot under glass, squawking out the dialogue from the hot game of the week.

Yamashiro was nothing like that. It was one of those Cal-Asian places that had been doing the jive so long that it seemed almost respectable. Quiet little booths with crisp linen tablecloths clustered around views of the Los Angeles skyline through the floor-to-ceiling glass.

"Thank you," she said.

Jere looked up from frowning at the menu. "For what?"

"Taking the time. Taking me out."

A start, and a guilty smile. "You're welcome." Jere went back to studying the menu.

"What are you having?"

"Oh. I don't know." Eyes on the menu.

"Will you order for me?"

"Sure."

"You will?"

Jere nodded. Looked at her. His eyes darted around, almost distracted. "Of course."

"What's the matter?"

Jere looked back down at the menu. "Nothing."

"Nothing? You can't even look at me!" Irritation rose in her, and Patrice heard her voice rising to a shrill note.

She expected Jere to explode, but he only sighed and rubbed his forehead.

"What's the matter?" Patrice said.

Jere looked up at her. For the first time, she noticed little beads of sweat standing out on Jere's forehead. As if seeing where she was looking, he wiped them away with a shaky hand.

"We're dropping tomorrow."

"I know."

"You know? Then you know how I feel!"

"I thought things were going well."

Jere sighed. "If by that you mean that there haven't been any more attempted rapes, or real rapes, or fist-fights that we couldn't convince the editors to leave out, or bullshitty snipes between the cast, or Frank getting drunk and singing "Rocketman" like William Shatner, or Petrov coming up with some issue that can't be fixed with silicone and stainless-steel wire, then yes, things have been going well. If you mean that the reports from the ship make me think we're going to do the drop without someone going *splat*, then that's a totally different thing."

I'm sure it'll go well, Patrice wanted to say. But that wasn't true. She had no idea how it would go. The words were meaningless, idiotic, something a telemarketer would say when they were trying to close the deal.

"It doesn't matter," she said, finally.

Jere's eyes snapped up. "What?"

"Even if they die, it doesn't matter."

"Are you fucking kidding?" Jere snarled. "If they bite it, we're done. Everything's over. Neteno's over. I'm over."

"But think of what you've done."

A momentary pause. A brief spark. Then Jere shook his head. "It'll still be over."

"You and your dad will be over?"

Jere glanced at her. Glanced away.

"You and I will be over?"

Jere's jaw moved, but he said nothing. Patrice let him sit there for a few moments. Then she softly said, "If you hadn't done this, what would you have done?" Jere shook his head.

Patrice waited.

"I'm scared," he said, finally.

"I'm glad you are."

A glance at her.

"Otherwise, you'd be Evan."

A snort. "Yeah. Evan would just be thinking how to spin it."

"Exactly."

Jere looked down at the menu, flipped back and forth a few times. His eyes were glassy, seeing nothing. "I'm still scared."

"And you'll drop tomorrow," Patrice said. "And it will go how it goes."

Jere sighed. He reached out and took her hand. He didn't look up at her for a long time. When he did, his eyes were bright, brimming with tears.

"Marry me," he said.

Patrice's heart thumped, once, in her chest, as if someone had hit her with a hammer. "What?"

"Marry me."

Patrice sat there, looking at him.

"Please," Jere said.

Patrice shook her head. "No."

Jere blinked and rocked back, as if from a blow. "Why not?"

Patrice just shook her head. Jere was great. Jere was fun. Jere took chances. But she saw the years stretching in front of her. She heard Amy's voice: *Someday I'll go to Mars, like YZ.* She saw endless parties, endless fun, bright and devoid of meaning.

"Why?" Jere asked, again.

"I can't."

"What's wrong? What did I do?"

"Nothing," Patrice said.

"I don't understand!"

Patrice took Jere's hand. It was cold and hard, but he let her hold it. "I don't understand, either," she said. "Not fully."

"Then—"

She held a finger to his lips. "Shh."

"But I—"

She covered his mouth with her hand.

Above her hand, Jere's eyes were almost relieved.

Falling

Being paired with Laci Thorens and Wende Kirschoff wasn't distracting to Geoff. During the long trip in the Can, they'd never been openly affectionate, and they'd never invited Geoff Smith to join them in any of their pilot's cabin activities. They dressed in shapeless clothes, and stayed away from the criminal and the other contestants as much as they could. And Geoff had his own thoughts, important thoughts, so far beyond sex that it didn't really matter who they were. And, when sex got bothersome, he had his own interactive library.

So he didn't really catch himself looking at them until the day of the drop, when they put on their squeezesuits. They came out to the ring where the drop pods were, looking like white-jumpsuited versions of Lara Croft, Tomb Raider. Perfectly sculpted buttocks, breasts that stood out full and firm (a little more full than the breasts he'd caught glances of on board, Geoff thought). Even their crotches were sculpted, hiding nothing. Which made no sense, Geoff knew, because even at their thinnest, the squeezesuits were at least four millimeters thick. Which was enough to hide any detail.

Maybe they did it to better balance the pressure of the suit on our skin, Geoff thought. Struggling not to look. Struggling to keep his racing thoughts on track. Because, suddenly, all the activities Laci and Wende took part in seemed to grow in importance, until they were all there was.

"Trailblazer team, sound off!" Frank said. "How's it hangin'? You ready? Time to win the good fight for all the oppressed feminists?"

Laci threw Frank a murderous glance. "This isn't a joke! This is—"

"This thing hurts!" Wende whined, rubbing at the front of her thighs with the heel of her hand. Her voice was tinny and compressed, coming over the suit comm.

"Did you use the depilatory?" Frank said.

"Of course," Wende said, still rubbing.

Frank frowned and looked back at the passenger cabin. Only the three of them were in the launch ring, per Frank's instructions and Petrov's enforcement. It made sense. The ring was a small, cold crawlway around the outside of the ship. There wasn't much room for even the four of them.

"It pinches," Geoff said, scissoring his legs. The suit was painful. Even after the depilatory and the whole-body lubricant.

"And you used the lube too?" Frank asked.

"Of course!" Wende said.

Frank looked at Laci. "What about you? If the suit is painful, that might mean . . . "

"I'm fine!" Laci snapped.

"Blistering, epidermal tears, internal bleeding, none of those show up in the dictionary of fun."

"I read the manual. I'm fine." Laci said, arms crossed.

"It's really painful," Wende said.

"Bad enough to lose our drop window?" Laci pointed at the blue numbers, flickering down towards zero. There were only eleven minutes left.

Wende frowned.

"If you got a problem, better strip and get it fixed," Laci said.

"No, no problem."

"Good," Laci said.

"If there's a suit fault, we'll blame you for it," Frank said.

Laci started. "What does that mean?"

"We have this all on film. You bullied her into going."

"We don't have time!"

Frank frowned and flew over to Wende. "If you've got a problem, let's get it fixed now." He popped off Wende's header and opened her suit, turning her away from Laci and Geoff.

Laci's frown deepened. "We don't have time for this."

"Shut up," Frank said, and his hands went back to Wende's crotch.

"Hey!" Laci said.

Red-faced, Frank pulled his hands out. "Got it," he said. "There was a small fold. I did what I could to smooth it out. You've lost weight."

Wende nodded, her face bright red.

"Come on," Wende said, from the door of their drop capsule. Laci followed.

"What about you?" Frank asked Geoff.

"I'm fine."

"You said it pinched."

"I'm fine!" Geoff tried to slide past the old man.

"Oh, no you don't," Frank said, grabbing Geoff's arm. "I'm not going to have you die down there, either."

"No, it's okay, really."

"Where is it?" Frank said, popping off Geoff's header and splitting the suit.

"I don't have a problem!"

"I can make you stay on the ship." Old gray eyes, cold and hard. Geoff didn't doubt Frank meant it. And he had no doubt Frank would do it, even if it killed Laci and Wende's chance.

And he'd have to share the ship with them on the way back.

Unable to speak, Geoff pointed at his groin.

Frank split the suit further and thrust his hand down inside it. Geoff felt his face go hot and red. *They're recording all of this*. Even if it doesn't go on the show, it's in a digital archive somewhere. Or somebody was intercepting it. They'd play this damn clip at parties until the end of time.

Geoff looked heavenward as Frank fingered his balls. He pulled out a hand. "I don't feel anything."

"It's not that bad," Geoff said. "It's better."

"Is it?"

"Yes! Yes!"

"Come on, for fuck's sake!" Laci called from the pod, gesturing frantically with her hand.

Frank chuckled as he helped Geoff get his suit sealed back up. "Go on," he said, shoving Geoff towards the hatch.

Laci grabbed him and stuffed him into one of the drop chairs. They were nicely padded with open-cell foam, and looked very comfortable until the top closed on him like a clam, compressing his body in a foam sandwich. The other lids flipped down. Geoff looked around. Laci and Wende lay on one side of him. Ahead was a tiny round porthole. It showed the blackness of space, devoid of even a star.

If I turned out the cabin lights, I could see stars, Geoff thought.

"One minute until drop," Petrov's voice came through the suit comm.

The pinching, tingling feeling in Geoff's crotch slowly came back. He grimaced. It would go away. It didn't matter.

Or maybe it would matter. Maybe he wouldn't be able to do anything. Maybe he wouldn't be able to do any of his experiments.

No!

"Thirty seconds." Petrov again.

Geoff wondered if Laci and Wende were holding hands, deep under the foam. He tried to wiggle his fingers, but they wouldn't move.

"Ten seconds."

The suit wouldn't be a problem.

"Nine."

Or maybe it would.

"Eight."

He'd be able to do the experiments. Even the IBM ones.

"Seven."

He'd prove there was life on Mars, once and for all.

"Six."

Or he wouldn't.

"Five."

Or the wheel would break, and they wouldn't go anywhere.

"Four."

Or they'd hit a little too hard, and they'd be stuck.

"Three."

Or the airbags wouldn't inflate at all, and they'd go splat.

"Two."

Geoff felt sweat crawl its way down his temple. It landed in his eye, stinging.

"One."

Explosive bolts went *bang!* and then they were turning, rolling. The pod hissed and darted this way and that as it maneuvered away from the *Enterprise*. There was a long hiss, and Geoff felt the little capsule accelerate. It was a strange sensation, to feel acceleration for the first time in six months. Geoff wondered how well he'd be able to walk on Mars. Or when he got home.

Then the capsule rotated around and Mars filled the little porthole, salmon-red and streaked with yellows and blacks.

This is it, Geoff thought. I'm falling towards another planet.

Falling.

Towards.

Another damn planet!

Geoff wanted to pump a fist in the air. Take that, NASA! Take that, skeptics! I'm here, I'm going to prove there's life here, and there's nothing you can do to stop me.

It was an indescribable feeling. A little like the day he got accepted to the show. But deeper, sharper, and edged with fear.

Because, of course, he was falling.

Towards another planet.

A lot of things had to go right before he stepped out of the capsule and onto the pink dust of Mars.

But in that moment, that was okay. Things would go right. Nothing would stop him. Geoff heard the echo of his breathing, high and fast.

Mars grew slowly in the porthole.

Bar

Jere suggested Harold's Under Melrose for the evening of *Winning Mars'* first drop, but Ron vetoed it.

"You have a higher composite profile than Ms. President. Or any current head of state," Ron said. "You can't hide. People are going to be watching your show, and they're going to be watching you too."

"They'll kill me if anyone goes *splat*," Jere said.

"That's a chance you take."

Patrice's words from last night floated back to him: *It doesn't matter. Look at what you've done.*

The three of them ended up going to The View, an ultra-touristy place filled with smartfog displays and ghost-windows and rent-by-the-minute somatics, as well as the latest not-yet-scheduled psychoactives, delivered in ultra-expensive cocktails. Evan found them, either by happy chance or by location service, and the four of them held down seats at the bar, just below the non-interactive smartfog display that kept cycling through various famous cityscapes. Just eye candy, marshmallow shapes of familiar spires, but something that the tourists liked to goggle at.

Jere sipped his dry space-distilled Stoli Orbit martini and tried to ignore the eyes. It was like he was on display, and everyone knew what was happening. He caught fragments of conversation:

That's Jere. That's him.

Winning Mars.

They start tonight.

He's here to be watched.

Fucking showoff.

Patrice sat pressed against him, her warm flesh mostly bare against his thin silk shirt. She'd chosen the most minimal cocktail dress she had, a tiny bit of silvered silk with some intelligence that kept it from revealing too many bits. Some YZ getup, obviously. He wondered how many they'd sold in the game.

He wondered how many they'd sold in real life. She was attracting as much attention as Jere.

That's YZ Extreme Barset, isn't it?

YZ and Jere. Like an attention nova.

Supernova, more like.

Yvette, what a showoff. How much is she getting paid?

Great idea, dad, Jere thought. If someone dies . . .

"If someone croaks, you're gonna get massacred," Evan said, leaning close. "You sure you don't want to visit the pisswall right about now?"

"I can't," Jere said. "I need to be seen."

"What, are you the fucking pope, raising the glad-hand?"

"Apparently." Nodding at Ron.

"Fuck the old bastard. They aren't going to rip *him* apart."

"You sound so certain someone's gonna die."

Evan shrugged. "Better safe than dead."

Jere shook his head. His eyeset counted down the final minutes. Near the end, The View made its smartfog go flat and projected a realtime of *Winning Mars* on it. Necks snapped up.

For a while, there was no sound. Just the image of Mars, huge and red. Then, soundlessly, one of the passenger pods flew out from their point of view, to drop towards the planet. The View changed to a camera on the pod. The planet slowly turned in their View.

"First contestant module released," Frank's voice came over The View's sound system. Jere jumped and looked around. Glittering eyes were fixed on him. He tried to smile at them. He turned back around to look at the display.

"Trailblazer team," Ron said, loud enough for everyone to hear. The music in back ramped down, so that soon the only sound in The View was the creak of the passenger pod and, later, the thin scream of the Martian atmosphere, as the pod went deeper into the atmosphere. The planet seemed to swell larger on the screen.

"Atmospheric insertion successful," Frank said, crackly through the speakers.

"As if there was any doubt," Evan said. "Those things are supposed to drop like rocks."

People at the bar heard him and turned around.

"Shut. The fuck. Up." Ron said, slow and deadly.

It was like watching your first landing at an airport. The planet drew closer and closer. More and more details became clear. The rate of change slowly increased. It was almost hypnotic.

"Following predicted course," Frank said. "Impact in thirty seconds."

"Impact?" someone at the bar said.

"They're bouncing," someone else said.

Now, the bar was quiet enough to hear the breathing of the contestants in the drop pod. Their breath came quick and sharp, as if they were afraid.

Of course they are, Jere thought.

The ground rushed by, faster than Jere had ever seen a plane land. It looked sharp and twisted and ugly.

This will never work, Jere thought.

"Ten seconds," Frank's voice.

A small whimper from the cabin.

We shouldn't be hearing this, Jere thought. But of course they *should* be hearing this. They should be *seeing* this too. They should have thought to put cameras in the drop pods. It was the money shot. It was what made people tune in.

And with that thought came another strange sensation. What a crass fucking thought. Always the audience, the money, the angle. Why couldn't it be something simple, like putting people on another planet?

Because they aren't on the planet yet, a little voice whispered, laughing, in the back of his mind.

"Five seconds," Frank again.

Over the whistle of the wind, loud bangs, screams from the cabin. People in The View looked around sharply.

"Airbags," Ron said, loudly.

"Three . . . two . . . one . . . " Frank's voice said.

A tremendous crash, and the picture dissolved into fuzz and static. People in The View stared up at the projection, mouths open, in that moment between shock and acceptance.

Are they dead? Jere thought. Please God let them not be dead, please make this work, please please I really do believe in this, please . . .

A murmur went through the patrons. It started small, but quickly deepened to ugly. After a moment, Frank's face appeared. He was thin and unshaven. "For those of you following the raw feed, this communication failure was expected. Telemetry indicates the module is intact. We should hear from them shortly."

For the next minute, nobody moved. Nobody raised a drink. Nobody even seemed to breathe. This must be important, Jere thought. They're not even drinking.

He looked at Patrice, but she didn't even look back. She saw only the screen, still displaying Frank's worried face. Her mouth was slightly open, as if in wonder. Jere still didn't know what to think about her. There were times when the curves lined up so well it was impossible to fight them. The curves pushed you along. And there were times when the curve fought one another, and nothing would make them line up. She was at the nexus of those curves. It felt right, in many ways. Jere smiled, trying to be happy.

The picture above the bar was replaced by an image of two people wearing squeezesuits and headers—a blond girl and a vaguely dorky-looking guy. There was the sound of someone blowing out a breath.

"Wow, what a landing," Wende Kirshoff said. "But hey, you know what they say, any landing you can walk away from . . . "

"And we're walking!" the dork said.

Behind Jere, a cheer rose. It was loud and happy and sustained. It made the hair on the back of his neck rise.

"Turn around," Ron said. "Take a bow."

"Why?"

"Because in this moment, you're a hero. You're the biggest fucking hero that ever was."

Jere stood up and turned. Every eye was on him. He'd addressed crowds before, but they'd never looked like this. Smiling. Open mouthed. Applauding. Looking at him with something like awe.

The cheer rose again. Hands pumped in the air. The crowd surged forward to meet him.

Their hero.

Death

Glenn Rothman was still shaking from his drop when he saw it. A thin white line, arcing through the light blue Martian sky. Like a single strand of spider-silk, glinting and gossamer. There was no sound.

Sarimanok team, Glenn Rothman thought. Nandir and Romeo. Named for that rooster, that bird from Romeo's hometown, the one that brought luck. He stopped to watch the thread disappear into the pinkish haze of the horizon.

Chatter from Frank in the can went softly hysterical. Sarimanok's drop had gone unstable and tumbled in the thin atmosphere. The airbags had never deployed. A software glitch. Or something in the hardware. They were trying to figure out the details. Glenn stood rooted to the spot, feeling a chill through the wet heat of his squeezesuit.

It could have been us. Glenn shivered. They'd almost picked Nandir's route, which seemed easier on the rolling and flying legs but more difficult on the Overland Challenge to the travel pod. Perfect for him and . . .

"Come on!" Alena said, over the local comm. She stood thirty feet in front of him, looking back, her face twisted into an angry mask.

"We just lost Nandir."

"I know! I can hear!"

"But . . . "

"And I'm going to lose you if you don't get moving!"

"Don't you care?"

An inarticulate growl. Then a sigh. They were, after all, on camera, all the time. "Of course I care. But I want to win. Come on!"

Glenn bounced over to her. Her face was flushed with exertion, but tears glittered in the corners of her eyes. She wouldn't look at him.

She's more scared than she'll admit, he thought. He tried to take her hand, but she pulled away.

"Stop that!" she said. Her dark eyes transfixed him for a moment, her full lips compressed into a thin line, the soft arcs of her face pulled into something harder and more brutal. The face he used to love. The face he still loved.

She bounded away, moving fast in the low gravity.

Glenn hurried to catch up. *I know how you feel,* he wanted to say. I know, and I understand. The stories about people losing brain cells were one thing, the brief acquaintances with half-remembered names in wheelchairs were another. Everything they'd done before carried risks, but the risks were well-quantified. Even their insurance agent had said, *Oh yeah, you do action sports,* and ticked off every one they did on the form before he submitted it. And with the bill came a surcharge, clearly outlined, that covered every single one of their activities.

But she'd never really seen someone die. And neither had Glenn. Suddenly it was like there was nothing inside him but a vacuum, looking to be filled. He thought, for a moment, Things will be different when we're back.

Then: If we get back.

Glenn caught up with Alena and tried to give her a smile. She refused to look at him, staring ahead grimly. The terrain was getting more rugged. Ahead of them rose the Budweiser Ridge, a three-thousand-foot near-vertical they would have to free climb to reach their transpo pod. The good news was that it looked climbable, especially in the low gravity.

The low gravity was both a blessing and a curse. Glenn was still getting used to what he could do. The squeezesuit and header made him top-heavy, throwing off his balance, but his total weight here was still less than half of what he was used to on Earth. Getting comfortable with taking eight-feet vertical jumps and twenty-foot flying leaps wasn't easy. Momentum still worked.

"More human interest," Petrov's voice blatted at him from his private channel.

Piss off, he thought. But he couldn't really do that. It was part of their contract. They had to do what they were told. Frank and Petrov reminded them, every time they had a chance.

"Glenn, we need to see Alena." Frank's voice, this time. Out of breath. Still edgy from Sarimanok. But doing his job. Frank was good at doing his job. On the way out, Glenn had recurring nightmares about Frank wearing a Nazi outfit and carrying a whip.

He plodded ahead.

"Glenn, we're close to contract breach." Frank, sounding sad.

"Shit!" he said, but turned obediently to focus on Alena. The squeezesuit clung to her curves, and the transparent header was designed to show as much as her pretty face as possible. Less attractive now, perhaps, with her hair hanging with sweat and her mouth set in a hard line.

"More," they said.

Glenn tried running in front of her and feeding the view from one of his rear cameras, but it was too hard to concentrate on the terrain ahead and maintain a decent frame. Eventually he dropped back to focus on the exaggerated hourglass shape of her suit.

I should be thinking about Nandir and Romeo, he thought. I should be worried about climbing the Budweiser Ridge. Instead, I'm a fucking soft-porn cameraman.

"Good," Frank said. "Stay there for a while."

"Okay," he said. *Assholes.*

Funeral

"Oh, shit," Jere said.

He was very, very drunk, and the ancient flatscreen seemed to float and dance a million miles away. He could almost tell himself it wasn't happening.

"Jere, did someone just die?" Patrice said. She leaned against him, warm and soft.

"Yes!" Jere snapped.

They'd agreed to go to a more private party from The View, invited by some investment assholes from New York who had a quaint old house near Ron's in the Hollywood Hills. Jere looked around the room. The investment assholes watched him in the reflection in the mirror on the backside of the bar. A couple sat in a loveseat, ignoring everyone but themselves. A very, very beautiful woman, dark hair and pale skin and strange silver eyes, who'd made a pass at Jere on the ride over, watched him through her eyeset, the white recording LED glowing bright.

"I have to go," Jere said.

"Yes, you do," Ron said.

Jere started. He'd forgotten Ron was there.

"Do you have to?" Patrice said.

"Yes."

"Can you get in front of a camera?" Ron said.

"I'm in front of one now!" Motioning at the silver-eyed woman.

"No. A real camera. Studio camera. Can you get in front of one now?"

Jere swallowed. I'm dead. I'm a zombie. I can do fucking anything. "Yeah."

"Can you look sober?"

Jere nodded. "Long enough to do what needs to be done."

"I'll drive you," Patrice said.

"I'll take you up on that," Jere said.

Evan and Ron bummed along on the ride to Neteno. Once in the car, Evan shook his head. "Rotten luck," he said.

"You said it'd happen."

"No. Not that. Nandir and Romeo. You lost the two most important demos for the Asian market. What a fucking bitch that'll be on the long tail."

Jere frowned. "Evan, you're an asshole."

Evan just nodded. "I know.

At Neteno, Jere downloaded an insta-script about sadness and loss. It read like utter bullshit. Total fakery. Computer-generated sugar and spice. He wanted to tear it up and sit there and look into the camera and say, *It doesn't matter. Look at what I did.*

But there was Ron, looking back at him and shaking his head. "Play your part," he said. "Play it straight. For now."

Jere looked at the camera and did his best to deliver the lines. The entire time he was on camera, he thought about Evan's words. And, he bitterly thought: Of course someone's going to die. Probably lots of someones.

When it was done, Jere expected to see crowds outside the Neteno building, holding torches and screaming for his head. But there was nothing, just the faceless traffic on Vine. Evan was gone. He thought of looking at his public ratings in his eyeset, but decided it wasn't a good idea. He turned it off.

"What do you want to do?" Patrice asked.

"Go home."

"Home?"

"If they're going to kill me, it might as well be at home." Jere popped his eyeset off his face and stuck it in his pocket. Patrice watched him do it with big, unbelieving eyes.

"Do you want me there?" she asked.

Jere looked at her. She was very beautiful. She could never understand. He didn't know what to feel.

"Please," he said.

Crash

"Pull it out! Come on! Pull!" Sam Ruiz shouted through their local comm. Mike Kinsson and Julie Peters tugged at the shattered plastic shell. Suddenly the whole side folded and twisted off, and all three of them ended up in a tangled heap on the dusty ground. Mike Kinsson noticed absently that the Disney and Red Bull and Walmart logos on Julie's suit were covered in dust, and reached out to brush them off.

"What are you doing?" Sam said, yanking Julie to her feet.

"Dust . . . " Mike said, and trailed off. It was stupid anyway. Why should he worry about their sponsors? Why should he worry about anything? They were dead.

Sam's team had picked the easiest Overland Challenge, essentially nothing more than a fast run over rocky ground, because they also got the toughest rolling and flying part. Soaring over the Valles Marinaris was part of their air journey, partly to make it more dramatic and partly to bring back some great images.

But after their brief Overland, they'd bounced up to the scene of a disaster. Their transpo pod had come down in the lee of a huge boulder, and had smashed itself in between the rock and the ground. Its smooth globular shape was now twisted into something resembling a crushed basketball.

It was supposed to hit and bounce, Mike thought. Which meant all the kinetic energy of the fall had been absorbed at once by the boulder, rather than a series of lazy bounces. A terrible design, something from last century's NASA that didn't work even then, despite triple-redundant systems and all the overbuilding the government could throw at it. Now, with Russian manufacture, the wheel and kite inside were probably . . .

"Junk," he said softly, as Sam and Julie began pulling out bundles of bent and sheared struts and shreds of fabric. It didn't look anything like the training. Not at all.

"Are you going to help, or not?" Julie asked.

Like a robot, Mike went and helped them pull out all the contents of the pod. He noticed that the big Timberland and Kia and Cessna logos emblazoned on the outside of the pod had survived intact, and he had to suppress the urge to laugh. He had to crawl inside to try to get some of the last pieces, but they had been wedged into the rock and wouldn't come out. He noted, with no great emotion, that one of the final items was the hydrazine engine intended to power both the wheel and kite. It was twisted almost beyond recognition.

"Where's the rest of it?" Sam yelled, when he came back out.

"Stuck."

Sam glared at him and crawled in himself. There was a great volume of cursing on the local comm network. When Sam crawled out again, sweat was running down his cheeks and there was a strange, faraway look in his eyes. Mike looked around at the twisted pieces strewn around them and shook his head. Sam saw it and grabbed him.

"What?" he said. "What are you shaking your head for?"

"We're dead," Mike said. "It's over."

"No! We can make something! We can do some hybrid thing, like a wheel." He began rooting through the wreckage, frantic, eyes bright and intent.

"Powered by what?" Mike said softly.

"We can power it! Or we can make skis! Or we can . . . "

Julie went over to Mike and laid a hand on his shoulder. As soon as he felt her touch, he stopped. He stayed still on his hands and knees, looking down at the rocks and dust, panting.

"Mike's right," Julie said. "I saw the engine."

"Then what do we do? Give up?"

"Rest, at least."

Sam stood up. The pale sun reflected off his shiny bronze face. He looked from the wreckage to the horizon and back again. "I don't want to stop!" he said.

"Why?" Julie said. "We can't win."

Sam looked at her for long moments, as if trying to decipher a strange phrase in an unknown language. Then he slumped. All the tension left him. He sat on a boulder and hugged his knees. Something like a wail escaped him. Under the cloudless alien sky, amidst a red desert unrelieved by water or leaf or lichen, it was a chilling sound.

"What do we do?" he said finally. "How do we get to the returns?"

"We don't," Mike said, standing carefully away. Trying to understand what the other man felt, what Julie felt. They'd talked about nothing more than money for the last six months. As if it were their magic, their touchstone, their love. Maybe it was. Maybe that's all they cared about. But he'd really cared. He wanted to make it, really make it . . .

And you did. You're here.

But in that moment, Mike realized: I want to go home too.

"We can walk," Julie said. "Jog. Run."

"We wouldn't make it," Sam wailed.

"There's not enough food and water," Mike told her.

"We'll eat less!"

"We can't cross the Valles Marinaris."

"Why not?"

"Mile-high vertical walls."

"The gravity is less—"

"We'll still go *splat!*"

Julie was silent for a while. "They'll have to come rescue us," she said finally.

"Who?" Mike said. There wasn't any backup. He knew that. He knew that very well.

"We've lost," Sam said.

"Wait," Julie said, grabbing Mike's arm. "What do you mean, 'who'?"

"They can't just come down and get us," Mike told her. "Other than our drops and the return modules, there's no way to get down here and back again."

Julie looked confused.

"They can't rescue us," Mike said. "They don't have the capability."

"They can't rescue us?"

"No."

"How can they do that? How can they leave us to die?"

It was all in the contract, Mike thought. But he said nothing.

"They can't leave us to die!" Julie yelled.

"What do we do?" Sam said.

Mike looked away. Even he knew better than to answer that.

Julie offered Sam her hand. After a moment, he took it, head hanging low.

Mike edged away from the two, not wanting to be part of any coming outburst. Sam was driven by a single purpose: to win his share of the fifty mil. That's what he wanted. Nothing more, nothing less. He hadn't disguised it, hadn't hid it. But now that was taken away. And what's more, his life was forfeit.

We knew the risks when we signed, Mike thought, walking farther away. Or at least he did. Sam and Julie were part of the walking dead, the people who never really thought much about life, who never really thought they could die. They really hadn't read the contract at all, just signed it and sent it off.

And I didn't care, he thought. All I ever wanted to do was to see another planet. All I ever wanted to do was to get away. To get away from Mom and Dad and their ideas about the perfect life, the planned life, the work-until-you're-old-and-hope-to-save-enough life, the life that most everyone took.

Thoughts came quick and bitter. He was still better off to die here. Earth was a dead-end world pursuing dead-end dreams, the majority of the population interested in nothing more than making money and amusing themselves. Nobody produced anything anymore. Nobody explored. Nobody took chances. There were no places to take chances in.

And yet I never did anything either, Mike thought. This is the only chance I ever took. Until this, I was too scared to give up my job, too insecure to let go of my condo, my 'Actives, my things. I was a geek. There was no other way to describe it. Endlessly yearning, but unable to commit.

And so, now this great leap.

And so, now you die.

Mike tried to make himself feel something, but he couldn't. It was too far away, too remote.

They had three days worth of food and water in their packs. Plenty for the show. Uncomfortably grim now. How long could they stretch it? A week? A week to live. The number seemed unreal, impossible.

Or you could just take your helmet off and be done with it.

It's too bad they didn't give the science pack to me, Mike thought. I now have infinite time to do the experiments. Or at least many days. But it had gone to the other asshole on the Thorens team. Too bad. It would have been good to have, THE FIRST MAN TO CONFIRM LIFE ON MARS, or something like that, on his headstone. They could put up a monument to him, when people came to Mars for good.

Or maybe they'd never come to Mars for good, Mike thought. Maybe this is the last shot, one stupid game show and then nothing. Everyone content to just do their thing, live their safe and planned life.

It wouldn't surprise him. First Sarimanok. Now them. Not exactly a rousing endorsement of interplanetary travel.

Mike wandered a hundred feet or so away from the couple when Frank's voice from the Can blatted in his ear.

"We're aware of your situation," Frank said.

"So?" he heard Sam ask.

"We're asking the Paul team to divert and rescue," they said. "We think he can carry you in his wheel. Is your fuel bladder undamaged?"

"Yes!" Julie said, hope rising in her voice.

"Good. We're transmitting the request to him now."

"Great!" Julie said. "Sam, did you hear that? We're going to be rescued."

"Nope," Sam said.

"What do you mean?" Julie's voice, edging into the strident.

"It's a request," Sam said. "Re-quest. Do you think Paul is going to give up his fifty million?"

Sudden silence over the comm.

"Do you think he'll do it for you?" Sam asked.

More silence.

"Did you have something so special with him that he'd throw away his chance to win?""

"Shut up! Shut up!" Julie screamed.

Mike couldn't help grinning, just a little. You see how your boyfriend is now, he thought. He wanted to go back to Julie and comfort her. She stood far away from Sam, pacing and wrapping her arms around herself. But there was no way Mike would get in front of Sam. That would just be a faster way to die.

"Keith might do it," she said. "He might!"

Sam's laughter reverberated inside their helmets.

Buried

"Don't be a baby," Ron said. "Get back on camera. Now."

"And tell them what?" Jere said, staring at the image of his dad, on the kitchen flatscreen.

"Now it's the time to play the curve."

"Curve? What curve? This isn't a curve. This is a break."

Ron grimaced. "Tell them there need to be sacrifices. If the next missions to Mars are going to mean a damn thing, you've got to scramble some eggs now. And you're on the cusp of that thing!"

"You're not making any sense," Jere said, puzzled.

Ron's face went bright red, and he leaned into the camera. His face turned beet-red. "Shut. Up. Stupid. Get on camera. Tell them something. You're blazing the trail. Whatever!"

"There aren't going to be any other shows."

Ron stared into the phone, his breathing rough and ragged. He said nothing for a long time. Finally, in a strange quiet voice, he said, "Yes. There will be."

"What do you mean?"

"Yours is the spectacle."

"What?"

"The spectacle isn't the end. The spectacle is never the end."

"Dad, you're talking crazy."

Ron shook his head. "It doesn't matter. Get on camera. Talk about new frontiers. You can do it. I know you can." Then he cut the connection.

Jere sighed. "Drive me back to the studio?" he asked Patrice.

Patrice shook her head. "No. Do it here. With me."

"Are you sure?"

Patrice reached out, squeezed his hand. "I'm sure."

They set up the camera to show them seated on the couch. Jere called into Neteno and had them set up a live feed. He didn't care what it looked like. He didn't care about scripts.

He sat down, faced the camera, and thought, Shit, eight hundred million people.

"Hello, everyone," he said. His voice was soft, low.

"I'm not going to apologize for the Ruiz team," Jere said. "I'm not going to read off a script. You don't need canned words to know I'm sad, I'm angry, I'm ashamed, and I'm scared.

"When I started this, I knew people could die. But while I was putting this all together, I discovered I felt that, hey, this is really important. Like, so important that maybe some people will die doing this, and so important that might just be all right and worth it."

A deep breath. "Yes. All right.

"I'm sad to see the Ruiz team stranded, but maybe it needed to happen. Maybe we needed to be reminded that life isn't all milk and cookies and picket fences and a career you can plot with a ruler. There are eight hundred million of you out there watching this. What are you feeling right now? Horror that a company like Neteno can put on a show like this? Or thrilled there are people on Mars? People, standing on another planet, and your watching them, live.

"When I started this, I didn't know that we had put probes on Mars in 1976, almost fifty years ago. Trillions of new dollars in government programs later, and we still hadn't put anything more than a few Roombas on Mars.

"The Chinese gave up at the moon, because it was more interesting to them to gather up the old United States stuff—now over fifty years old, think about it, that's half a century since we had people standing on the moon—and take down our flags than go on to Mars. You can see the Lunar Rover and the original flag from Apollo Eleven in a Beijing museum, I'm told."

"So, here we are. I ask you: are you outraged, or are you thrilled? I will do everything I can to get the Ruiz team, and all the other contestants, back to Earth safely. But they had the courage to sign up and go do this thing. They are on Mars right now, looking back at Earth from another world."

"I'm thrilled. I hope you are. If not, I understand. But, even if you are outraged, ask yourself one thing: if not this way, then how?"

Jere thumbed the remote control that turned off the camera. He wanted nothing more than to go to sleep. It had been a very, very long day.

Patrice held out his eyeset. Jere shook his head. He would find out what everyone thought eventually.

But not right now.

Offer

The only thing that kept Keith Paul from swatting the tiny cam away was the knowledge that it would destroy his chance at fifty million dollars. *Contract breach,* the asswipe Frank would say, in that gruff old-man voice of his. And oh boy would he be happy to say it to Keith. He'd be thrilled to say it.

Words from the training came back to him. You're all on camera, all the time. We can tap in at any time we want. You won't know when we'll be using your footage, but we'll always be watching.

Yeah, and I hope you get a shot of me taking a great huge shit, Keith thought. Broadcast that to a billion viewers. Here is Keith Paul, taking a dump on your ratings.

But they wouldn't do that. Oh, no. That might offend someone. Some fucking wanked-out chick might faint dead away at the sight of his weewee. They were too pussified to do that.

He would be sure to say that when he won. When they pointed the camera at his face, he would tell them exactly what he thought. It would be his crowning moment, his "fuck you" to them all.

And he would win. No doubt about that. Teams were for pussies and faggots. He'd been able to skin the wheel and string the kite faster than any team back when they were training. Because he was one man. One strong man. He didn't have arguments with himself, or forget where something went. He didn't have to discuss things, or worry about someone loafing. They called him a machine, and that was exactly what he was, a machine made for winning.

Spin that, Neteno assholes.

Keith had picked a long overland route that looked fairly easy, unlike the extreme sports fucksticks who wanted to go almost a mile straight up, or the geeks who wanted to fly to dry tanks and then chance walking in. The only team he'd worried about was the one with the dot and the slant.

And now they weren't a problem. Keith allowed himself a slow, lazy smile.

No, everything was great. Keith grinned up at the light blue sky. Really not that different from Earth. Not as weird as the photos they had shown him, with the pink skies and all that. He could almost be tramping through the Mojave back home, carrying his old M-16 and looking for shit to shoot.

And that was the one creepy thing. Nothing moved. In the Mojave, shit moved. You'd see a rabbit go tearing-ass out of a bush, you'd see the Joshua trees swaying in the breeze, maybe even an ancient-as-fuck desert tortoise clumping around.

Not Mars. The ground just lay there. There were no plants moving around, no animals darting to-and-fro. The land felt old and scarred and unnatural. The sun didn't seem to be turned up all the way, either. He kept wiping at his header's visor to clear it, but it wasn't cloudy or tinted. That was just the way Mars looked. Because it was farther away from the sun. Farther away from home.

"We have a request," said Frank, from the Can channel.

"What?" They always had requests. Look at this, do that, scratch your ass, pick your nose. But it was usually Petrov who made them. Frank sucked. That John Glenn asshole could talk for hours. Keith frowned.

"The Ruiz team's transpo pod had a landing malfunction. They have no transport."

"Cool." Keith grinned. Two down, three to go. The odds get better all the time.

Plus, the Ruiz team was the one with that bitch Julie. Keith's memory of his beating was still a little too recent. Thinking about the three of them starving in the desert made him smile.

"We'd like you to divert your wheel and collect them."

What? "I haven't even reached my transpo yet!"

"After you get there."

"And you're going to give me extra time for this?"

A pause. "No."

"Then how the hell am I supposed to win?" Another pause, this one longer. "They'll die if you don't pick them up."

"Again, so?"

"Do you just not get it?" Frank's voice edged to anger.

"Do you just not get it?" Keith mimicked. "I don't give a shit. Let them die."

A long pause. When Frank came back on, he spoke slowly, in a carefully controlled voice. Keith imagined him damn near chewing through his knuckles having to be nice to him, and he smiled.

"Keith, we'd really like you to consider this. Even if you don't win the prize money—and you still might—the act of rescue will create its own reward."

"They'll pay me to do this?" Now, that was interesting. Why didn't you say so in the first place, dumbass?

Pause. "I'm sure they will."

"Like, they'll pay me more than fifty million bucks for it?"

"I'm sure our sponsors will be very generous."

"More than fifty million?"

Another pause. For long moments, Keith thought they had given up on him. Good. But Frank started in again as he caught the first glimpse of his iridescent transpo pod, glittering in the distance.

He would win.

"Keith, we've got buy-in from several of the sponsors. We can get you a million. Plus other things. Cars . . . "

"No."

"They'll die. That will be on your conscience."

"They can't prosecute me for it." It would be just like them, to dredge up the fact that he was the only former felon, even though he was pardoned, even though his record was wiped clean when he signed the deal with Neteno.

Long pause. "No."

"I think I'll ignore you now."

"Keith . . . "

Keith looked up at the thin sky, as if to try and see the Can spinning overhead. "A million is not fifty. A million and promises is not fifty. Sorry, no can do."

"You may not win."

"I will win. And you know it."

Another pause. This one longer. "Two million."

"Did you fail math? Two million is not greater than fifty. Give me an offer more than thirty, and they're saved."

"We . . . probably can't do that."

"I . . . probably can't save them," Keith said, mocking his tone. "Shoulda thought of that when you built the damn Can."

Silence. Blissful silence. Long yards passed and the transpo pod swelled in his view. As he reached its smooth, unmarred surface, Frank's voice crackled to life again. "Even if you win," he said. "People will hate you."

"That's all right," Keith said. "I love myself enough for all of them."

"You're terrible."

Yes, Keith thought. But I'll win.

Blocked

"Why can't we just offer him the fifty-one million?" Jere said. They were all in his office, him and Evan and Ron and Patrice.

"Are you kidding?" Ron said. "Have you seen the sponsor bailouts?"

Jere's eyes flickered upwards to his eyeset. Data danced on his corneas. He said nothing. He saw the crater—a fifty-one million dollar hole in their finances. Dancing on the knife-edge, it was simply impossible.

"We're in bad shape," Ron said. "Abysmal shape. Money is rushing back to its safe havens, where everything is peaches and cream."

"So much for adventure," Jere said, bitterly.

"Yeah. So much."

Jere sighed. "So we make the best offer we can afford."

"We can't afford shit," Evan said. "The sponsors are gone or tapped, or they don't trust your ratings. You yourself are Teflon, but you could burn thru at any second. Fifty-three percent thrilled to forty-seven percent outraged, with a polarization scale that has them fighting each other in bars; it ain't exactly confidence-inspiring."

"I can help," Patrice said, softly.

The three guys looked at her, then resumed their argument.

"I said, I can help."

"How?" Jere asked. "Do you have any big sponsors we can tap?"

"No. But I have fifty-one million."

Silence in the room. Three open mouths. If only they knew how much more she had. Patrice struggled to keep her expression neutral. All they needed to know was that she had the money, and she could help them out.

"You're kidding," Ron said.

"No."

"Do it," Jere said. "As a loan."

"I don't care if it's a loan—"

"It's a loan!"

Patrice shrugged. "Okay." She eyetyped in her brokerage account access and looked at the balance. Plenty in the account, even at the terrible exchange rate. Gen3 Bux had fallen against the dollar by 40 percent in the last week.

She got Jere's business account number and eyetyped the transaction.

FAILED TRANSACTION, her eyeset said.

She tried it again.

FAILED TRANSACTION.

Patrice frowned and looked at her balance. Plenty of money. Secure access. What could be the problem? She eyeclicked the MORE INFO icon. Her eyeset showed:

FAILED TRANSACTION

FAILURE TYPE: STIPULATION

FAILURE DETAIL: DISALLOWED BENEFACTOR

NARRATIVE: GEN3 PROHIBITS THE USE OF GEN3 BUX FOR ANY DEBTS OR PAYMENTS TO CERTAIN ORGANIZATIONS, INCLUDING THE FOLLOWING ORGANIZATION: NETENO LLC.

"What's the matter?" Jere asked.

"I can't do it!"

"Not enough money?"

"No. Gen3 Bux can't be paid directly to Neteno. Seems to be a new stipulation."

Ron nodded. "Probably because of the negative publicity."

"Can you convert to dollars?" Jere asked.

A new message appeared:

ACCOUNT FLAGGED. ALL TRANSACTIONS MUST BE APPROVED BY GEN3 INTERACTIVE INC. FOR THE NEXT SEVEN (7) DAYS

"Shit!" Patrice said. "Now I'm flagged. They're not letting me do any transactions."

"It's okay," Jere said.

"No! It's not okay! It's my goddamn money!" She'd go to Bob. She'd get him to release it.

Yeah, right, a little voice whispered in her head.

"I'm sorry," Patrice said.

"I'll call the sponsors," Jere said. "One by one. See what we can do. We have to be able to put something together."

The two other men nodded, but their eyes showed their real feelings.

Experiments

Geoff Smith looked down at the contours of his chest. It was like something you'd see in a home gym commercial, except painted white and covered with sponsor logos. They'd sculpted muscles into his squeezesuit. He'd never noticed it before.

He looked from his own chest to the skintight curves of Laci and Wende, as they performed various acrobatic maneuvers to get their wheel put together. Their transpo pod had come down a little further away than the Can had planned, so they'd run over the rough, uneven terrain for what seemed like hours to meet it. It didn't help that Geoff had to lug the heavy IBM experiments package the whole way.

But now the girls were putting the wheel together, and here he was, Geoff Smith, on an alien planet! And he was going to prove there was life on it! He would do what a million scientists back on Earth wanted to do! He would, with nothing more than an associates degree in chemistry, do what all the Ph.D.s had told him he couldn't do. He would put Martian life under a microscope for the first time! He would look at it with his own eyes! He would be famous! Revered!

Because the big problem was that nobody had ever really looked. They'd tried the carbon-14 tagging trick on Viking, they'd tried spectrographic analysis, they'd even had a little drill and lots of other really silly experiments on the later rovers, but they'd never just taken a sample of dirt, put it on a microscope slide, and looked at it. Because even with all their robots and automation and fancy measurements, they weren't here. Now he was. And he would show them!

"Damn!" Laci Thorens said. She hung from the top curve of their wheel, holding a strut and looking at it disgustedly.

"What's the matter?" Wende Kirschoff said. She was on the ground, assembling the engine into a subframe with the kind of intensity a six-year-old might devote to a paint-by-numbers picture designed for college kids.

"This strut doesn't have the fitting widget on the end," Laci said. "It won't stay in."

"Aren't there spares?"

"Uh, no, I don't think so."

"Look for them."

Geoff hurried off before the girls could rope him in. He remembered Laci's implied threat. They hadn't noticed him yet, and he wanted to keep it that way. They didn't think the way he did. They just talked about women and empowerment and how this'd be a perfect way to show "them" what women could accomplish.

But that didn't matter. With his discovery, he would be so famous that he could name his price.

Geoff set the IBM box in the lee of the transpo pod like the instructions said, digging down enough to ensure it was placed where the sampling tube could penetrate the soil. He was supposed to let it sniff around, suck up a sample, run it through a bunch of tests and processing he didn't quite understand (he knew what an atomic force microscope was, but what was a scanning cantilever sensor, or a tomographic mapping array?) and then take the whole thing with them when they left.

Which was stupid. IBM was doing the same old thing. When all they had to do, really, was give him a bag and a microscope.

So he'd brought his own. It was the smallest and lightest one that he could find. Now it was just a matter of getting some dirt, throwing some water on it, putting it on the slide, and looking for wrigglies.

"There aren't any spares," Laci said, over the local comm. Geoff looked back at here to see if she was looking at him yet. She wasn't.

"Shit. Let me see." Geoff caught a glimpse of Wende's squeezesuit as she hopped up to the top of the wheel.

When he got his thoughts back again, he fumbled the little vial of water out of the tiny pocket of his squeezesuit. The microscope was already out, sitting perched on top of a medium-sized rock, away from the dust and grit.

How had Viking done it? It had moved a rock, hadn't it? And this new one from IBM was digging down. Probably best to just combine both techniques, Geoff thought, and shoved a medium-sized boulder out of the way. The Martian gravity was cool! It made him feel really light and strong. He knew it would be that way, but actually bouncing along and moving rocks like Superman was really a lot of fun.

He dug down into the dust with his fingers, feeling the chill seep through his squeezesuit. At about six inches down, he struck another rock and dug sideways until he had a trench about two feet long and he could dig down some more.

At about a foot down, he hit rock again and decided to call it quits. The dust was clinging to his transparent header, and the front half of his suit was pink.

He took a pinch of dust from the shallow hole and dropped it onto a glass slide. The water had gone frosty around the top, and when he opened it, it started to steam furiously. He dropped a couple of drops on the slide and they froze almost instantly, making something that looked like red ice cream.

Damn, I didn't think of that, he thought. There was no way he was going to see something through all that gunk with the microscope. He remembered that from when he was a kid, and his parents got him a microscope. If you couldn't get light through it, you couldn't see anything.

He sloshed some more water on it and pushed it around with the tip of his finger, trying to get the mixture thin enough to see through. After a couple of tries, he managed to get a thin pink film that looked reasonably transparent in places. Surely he could see something there at the edges.

"Geoff!" Laci said. "Get over here! We need your help."

Damn. They'd noticed him. "Can't," he said. "In the middle of an experiment."

"We need your help or we aren't rolling anywhere!"

Geoff slid the slide into the microscope and looked at the watch embedded in his suit. "We have time." And in fact, they did have almost half an hour left. He thought of trying to explain to them how important his experiments were, but since they'd never listened to him aboard ship, they were even less likely to listen now.

"Geoff, please!" Wende said.

"Wait a minute," Geoff said. Slide in place. Microscope to eye. Nothing but fuzzy grey darkness. Focus. Dark, dark. Sliding into focus. Becoming great boulders. Sand under three hundred power magnification.

"Geoff, now!" Laci said. Her voice was low, impatient, dangerous.

"Just a few seconds," Geoff said. Focus. Ah. Crystal-clear. Scan it over a bit and find a brighter area. There. Ah.

Water crystals. Boulders. Bright light. Nothing else.

Well, of course it wouldn't move. But where was the rounded wall of a bacterium, or the jelly of an amoeba?

"Now," Laci said, and strong hands picked him up. The microscope popped from his hands. Geoff jerked back as he watched it fall, with agonizing slowness, into the dust and grit.

He wrenched out of Laci's grip and scooped up the microscope. It was dusty, but looked okay. He looked through it. The slide was out of position, but he could still see. He reached for the focus knob . . .

The microscope was torn out of his hands. He looked up to see Laci standing in front of him, holding the microscope behind her back.

"Give it back!" he said. "This is important. I'm right . . . "

She punched his header. Hard. He could see the soft transparent plastic actually conform to her fist. It didn't quite touch him, but the kinetic energy of the blow knocked him to the ground.

"Go," she ordered. "Help Wende. You'll get your toy back when you're done."

"Give it back!" Laci raised the instrument and made as if to smash it on a boulder. Geoff lunged forward at her, but she danced away. "No," she said. "Go help. I'll give it back later."

"Laci, this is important!"

"So is winning. Go help Wende."

Geoff knew when he was beaten. He sighed and joined Wende atop the wheel, where they quickly discovered another problem: the epoxy they'd provided for quick repairs wasn't setting in the Martian cold.

"Damn!" Wendy said, when she saw what was happening. "What do we do now?"

Geoff stopped looking longingly at the microscope (now sitting on top of their hydrazine engine) and inspected the problem. The strut was one of the main load-bearers that held them suspended under the top of the wheel. They couldn't ignore it, because after a few good shocks, the structure might collapse and tear the wheel apart.

"Tape?" he said, half-jokingly.

"None," Wende said. Her voice quavered.

Oh crap, he thought. Don't panic. Not now. Not when I'm so close.

"What about the kite?" Geoff said. "Doesn't it share components with this? Maybe it has a strut with the right connector on it."

"It's packed."

"Then let's unpack it."

"What about when we have to fly?"

"We hope the connector makes the trip in one piece. Wende, you want to stay here?"

"No."

"Then show me where the kite is."

She did, and they dug into the bundle of struts and fabric. The components were the same, and many of them were the same length. When Geoff found one with the right connector on the end, he pulled it out and handed it to Wende.

"Just like Ikea," he said.

"They aren't the sponsor!"

"Same idea." *Maybe I can save the mission and discover life too,* he thought. Then he noticed that Laci was frantically tightening the straps that held the little engine in place.

"We're late!" she said. "Check the time! Come on, come on, come on! Let's go!"

Wende grabbed him and had him help set the bottom end of the strut. Then Laci was starting the engine. Near the wheel, his microscope was still parked on top of a rock.

"Wait!" he said, running to get it.

The wheel was already moving. "Hurry up!" Laci said.

He grabbed the microscope and ran back, throwing himself up the scaffold towards the perch by the cabin. The landscape moved by, slowly at first and then with increasing speed. The soft rim of the wheel bounced over rocks and boulders. It was like riding a giant beach ball.

But he had his microscope. Between that and the IBM package, he would surely find something. He would still be famous. And they might even win!

The IBM package! Oh, shit, no! No, no, no! He'd never picked it up.

"Stop! he cried. "You have to go back!"

"Why?" Laci said.

"I left the IBM package. The research one!"

Laci gave him a disgusted look. "How could you be that stupid?"

"Go back."

She just looked at him. A slow smile spread on her face. "Sorry," she said.

Geoff looked back at the remains of their transpo pod, but it had already disappeared over a hill. They were moving. And he was lost.

Bid

"IBM wants a refund of their sponsorship," Evan said.

"Shut up," Jere said, already calculating losses from the IBM experiments package. The replay rights would have to go for a ridiculous sum to offset it. All because of one dumbass geek. They should've given the experiments package to the other starry-eyed loon, like Ron had suggested.

All this shit, Jere thought. I'm buried in it.

Finances so complex that it looked like a three-dimensional topo map of the Alps, with deep valleys to navigate and impossible heights to scale. All moving in real time with the shifting of virtual and international currencies, interest rates, and a thousand other variables and derivatives that Jere could never hope to understand.

The real fortunes, Ron had often said, are now controlled by the people who channel them. They erect the dams, they cut new channels for the rivers to flow. My own little holding isn't even a crumb on the hors d'ouevre plate at the banquet of the true monetary giants. They play with percentages of gross national products, with fractions of the balance of global trade. They've made it a game to devalue the currency and reap the rewards, three or four percent a year, but it was three or four percent a year of the global output of the world.

What could we create with that? Jere wondered. Forget the stupid mansions and cars and parties where everyone applauded and patted themselves on the back. They could have sent hundreds of missions, we could have sent thousands of people, we could have built cities on Mars, like the stuff from Burroughs.

Jere had a moment of crystalline clarity. I would never have thought this way when I started this, he thought. I'm forever changed *forever*. And suddenly, all the money, all the positioning, all the power seemed completely meaningless and empty. They might have their palaces here on Earth, but they'd never looked up to the sky.

Was this what Ron wanted him to see? Was this the final epiphany?

Was *Winning Mars* going to be the crowning achievement of humankind? The final triumph before the frontier closed once again—this time for the last time?

Jere looked at Ron, his face lit by the glow of Los Angeles at night, coming in from the windows of his Neteno office overlooking gray Hollywood. Ron looked back at him and forced his face into something like a smile. Jere could see virtually every muscle moving in his face, he could feel each one pull taut in turn. It was a completely mechanical movement, something that Ron had to think about to do. It was grim and forbidding and wonderful. Jere felt tears begin to well in the corners of his eyes. He blinked them rapidly away.

Without factoring in the loss of IBM's monies, they'd managed to put a couple of million dollars into their buying-out-the-asshole fund. Jere polled his eyeset. It told him that taking any more from his own reserves, or from Neteno's, would navigate them towards one of those valleys that yawned like a crevasse from which Himalayan hikers never returned. Go too far down, and the company would never recover, no matter the changes in the financial markets.

"It's time," Jere said. "Let's talk to the asshole."

"We don't have enough money," Evan said. "He'll never take it."

"Shut up." Ron's voice, now perfunctory. He made his false smile grow fractionally wider as he nodded at Jere.

Jere covered his mouth to hide a grin.

Ascent

They were halfway up the sheer face, and the way Alena was climbing, they were going to die. Glenn watched her almost literally fly up the rock, making twenty-foot jumps from handhold to handhold, reaching out and grasping the smallest outcropping and crevice with fluid grace and deceptive ease.

Dangerous ease, he thought. Climbing in the low gravity seemed childishly simple compared to climbing on Earth. Which meant it was easy to take one too many chances. Easy to get overconfident and make mistakes.

Alena made one last lunge and scrabbled for a grip in a tiny crevice. Her feet skidded and she slid down the face for one terrible instant before catching on another tiny outcropping. Pebbles and sand bounced off Glenn's visor.

"Slow down!" he said. "A fall from here'll kill you as dead as one on Earth."

"We need to keep moving!"

"Alena . . . "

Labored breathing over the comm. "Listen to them!" Alena said. "Laci's team is already rolling, and that psycho guy is too! We're falling behind."

Glenn cursed. The voices from the Can, when they weren't giving orders, provided a blow-by-blow of the other teams' progress. As if it would do anything more than irritate them.

Which is exactly why they're doing it, he thought. To get them doing something stupid. And Glenn knew exactly how that would work on Alena. It would drive her harder. She'd take stupid chances. Because the climbing wasn't fun for her. It was a career. And she always had to get ahead. Telling her they had a different schedule, that they didn't have to roll until the next morning, would mean nothing to her.

Knowing that, in that tiny instant, Glenn could almost hate her. Almost.

Glenn pulled himself up nearer to Alena. She resumed climbing too.

"Let me get nearer," he said. "So we can safety each other."

"We have to keep going."

"The others have more time to roll. We aren't falling behind."

Alena stopped for a moment. "I know, but . . . "

"It's hard not to think it, yeah." Glenn finished for her. He pulled himself even higher. She stayed in place for once. Higher. Higher.

"We'll make the top before nightfall," he said. "Then we shelter and wait it out. We've got a short roll and a reasonable flight. We still have the best chance of winning, Alena."

Pant, pant. He was close enough to be her failsafe now.

Alena looked back, gave him a thin smile, and pulled herself up again. For awhile it was all by the book, then Alena began stretching it a bit, leaping a bit too far, aiming at crevices just a tiny bit too small. With the sun below the cliff, the shadows were deep, purple-black, and the cliff was losing definition in the dying day.

Just the thing to trick the vision, Glenn thought. Something they didn't need. He redoubled his efforts to keep up with Alena, even though he knew it was dangerous, and there were more skids and mini-slips than he cared for.

It was completely different than climbing on Earth. He felt as if he weighed almost nothing, but he couldn't feel the rock at all. Just the cold, through the tips of his fingers where the squeezesuit grew thin. But not thin enough to feel texture. Not thin enough to be able to put your hand on rock and know what you were grabbing, whether it was weathered granite or loose shale, or rock solid enough to bend an old-style piton. Most of the rock was reasonably solid, with a rough, pockmarked finish that looked windblown, and much of the ascent was less than vertical. But still, he worried.

Yet the adrenaline was going, going, going, he was rushing, he could hear the roar in his ears and he felt powerful, omnipotent, charged with energy. It was wonderful.

When they reached a deep crevice in the rock, Glenn thought things were getting better. But here, the rock was fragile and crumbly, and rust-red chunks came off easily in his hands. With the weight of the backpack pulling him away from the cliff face, it was dangerous. More than dangerous. Glenn was about to tell Alena that they should get out of there when she reached up and grabbed an outcropping that looked solid and it broke off in her hand.

She scrabbled for purchase on the cliff face and found none. From ten feet above Glenn, she began to fall, agonizingly slowly at first. Glenn felt his heart thundering, like an engine out of control in his chest. He had a momentary vision of the two of them tumbling out of the crevice to fall thousands of feet to the rocks below. He tested his handholds and footholds, and a small cry escaped his lips when he realized he probably wouldn't be able to keep his grip when Alena impacted him.

Glenn jumped downward, seeking better purchase. Slip and slide. Nothing more. Down once again. Nope.

Down again, and then Alena piled into him, an amazingly strong shock in the weak gravity. Mass still works, Glenn thought, wildly, a moment after he'd lost all contact with the cliff face.

Alena flailed, trying to catch the rock surface as it skidded by. Glenn knew that soon they would be moving too fast to stop, and reached frantically himself. He slowed their fall, but didn't stop it.

Where was the edge of the crevasse?

He looked below him. Right here. But there was one outcropping that looked reasonably solid. If he could catch it . . .

He hit hard with his feet and felt a shooting pain go up his right leg. His knees buckled and his feet slid to the side, away from the outcropping, towards destruction.

One last thing. He reached out and caught the outcropping, keeping one hand around Alena's waist. For a moment he thought their momentum was still too great, but he was able to hold on. Alena skidded to a stop within feet of the opening.

For long moments, Glenn didn't dare move. He could hear the harsh rasp of Alena's breathing. Meaning they were both alive. Alive!

Alena looked up at him with something in her eyes that might almost have been gratitude. He looked down at her and smiled. For a brief instant, she smiled back. He hadn't seen that for a long, long time. His heart soared, and his breath came in short gasps.

Slowly, they backed out of the crevice and continued on up the cliff face. Glenn's right leg roared with pain, and he knew he was slowing Alena down. But she didn't run away from him. She didn't take chances. She didn't say anything at all until they had reached the top, and the last dying rays of the sun painted them both blood-red.

"I'm sorry," she said softly.

He was about to say something, but Petrov's voice blatted in his ear. "What imagery! Pan slowly across sunset."

"Thanks," he said, bitterly, as Alena turned away.

Relief

Jere watched the raw feeds from the slice and dice screen at Neteno, deep in the dark. Paul had been singing popular songs with his own bawdy lyrics for the past hour. So it was still wait and watch. Even Jere's offer waited for the cameras.

At least Glenn and Alena had made it up over the cliff, what,, hours ago? Something like that. When they were both up, he breathed a little easier. Even was out of the room, so there were no stupid comments about how "at least we didn't lose them." Jere didn't want to think about the fallout of a show where they lost three teams out of five. He was sure he could call up predictions on his eyeset.

Keith's voice went hoarse and coughs exploded from the audio channel.

Thank God, Jere thought. Maybe he'll shut the fuck up.

But no. The asshole hacked up phlegm, swallowed it, and resumed singing. Jere cursed silently.

"You can go on now," one of the editors said, in Jere's ear.

"No more naughty nursery rhymes?"

"No. It was a good edit point. We're live on Glenn and Alena, fifteen minutes past. You have a solid seventeen to twenty minute block."

"Put me on."

"You realize this won't be a realtime conversation? You'll have to say your piece and wait for a response?"

"Yes. Do it."

"Done."

The sound of rough singing rang in Jere's ears.

Rejection

Wheeling had been easy back on Earth. The training out by the 395, on the nice smooth sand and little rocks, was no big deal. You could bounce over the flat as long as you wanted, and hardly ever have a problem, unless you were an idiot.

But wheeling was a bitch and a quarter here on Mars. Keith Paul stopped singing and gritted his teeth as he came to another long downhill run. It was scattered with boulders as big as houses and ravines that could catch the edge of the wheel and fuck him up good. He'd already dug the wheel out twice, once when he swerved to avoid a slope that would pitch it over and ended up in a ditch, and once when he got bouncing and caromed over a hill into a ravine.

And man, did it bounce! On Earth, it kind of scooted along, absorbing the shocks with its plastic rim. But here, whenever it hit a rock, it bounced. Sometimes a foot, sometimes a couple, sometimes ten or twenty feet in the air. And that was with you running almost blind, hoping there wasn't anything in front of you.

They probably got some good vid of my terrified mug, Keith thought. Before he started singing. That was smart. Don't show scared. Ever. That was how you got fucked. And the singing was fun. Keith imagined them beaming that into an almighty living room, full of live-in kids with their own kids. They'd like that.

He was making good time across the desert. He'd been up rolling as soon as dawn made the landscape dimly guessable. And he'd been able to keep up a fair clip, even with the setbacks.

Other idiots are probably picking their way along like grandma in a traffic jam, he thought, and smiled. He would take the chances. Even if it was scary. Because he was going to win.

Of course, they didn't want him to win. Frank and Petrov both tried to get him to save the Boo-Hoo Kitty team, aka the No Money team, every hour on the hour. They were like some kind of fucked-up cuckoo clock. They'd promised him everything but a blow job and a hot dog, but the money hadn't changed. Neither had his answer.

Now, he was getting near the kite part of the trip. They'd probably try to talk him into it then, unless they'd found some other suckers.

Almost on cue, the voice. This time it was some new asshole

"Hello, Keith, this is Jere Gutierrez on Earth—"

"Who're you?" Keith said.

" . . . don't know who I am, but I am the founder and CEO of Neteno. Not like I'm trying to show off, I just wanted you to know how important this is—"

"Who. The fuck. Are you?" Like the asshole wasn't going to acknowledge him.

" . . . since there's a several minute gap between my speaking and you hearing. Let me repeat, because you probably think I'm an inconsiderate asshole—"

"What?" Keith said, but Jere had his attention.

"—I have to run through this just once, in one shot, because there's a several minute gap between me speaking and you hearing."

"Ah."

"Let me just start by saying, this is our final offer," Jere said. "And it's a very generous one. Take this offer, and you will be comfortably well-off. And you will be a hero. I will personally use all the resources of Neteno to make you a legend, a star. By the time you come home, they'll be giving you parades, and your hometown will have a sculpture of you up in the square. Or whatever they do. There's probably financial rewards that will come as a result of that too, but I can't estimate or guarantee it. Take this, and you win both ways. But this is your last chance."

"Yeah, yeah, what's the fucking offer?" Keith said. What a fucking windbag.

"By air, you have a good chance of picking up the Ruiz team. It's even conceivable you could win the show, as well. You are currently leading the three remaining teams by a fair margin."

"What's the fucking offer?" *Jesus.*

"If you rescue the Ruiz team we're upping our offer to four million. Plus all the gifts and benefits we've discussed before. Plus the PR campaign to make you a hero. This is our final offer. Let us know your decision. Frank is standing by to hear your response."

Keith shook his head. Fucking windbag. That's the way it always was. Butter up that fucking dry toast before you shove it up my ass.

"Keith?" Frank said.

"Yeah."

"What do you think?"

"I think you're all very bad at math, even your fearless leader." Though, he had to admit, the idea was intriguing. With four million, he could live pretty well if he went to a low-rent part of the world like Mexico or something like that. And as a hero, he could probably get the chicks. Pretty much any one. He wouldn't even have to spend for that.

For a moment, he actually could see himself down there, living on the beach, fishing every day, hooking up with some pretty little senorita . . .

No! Stupid! You're a winner. You're in the lead. Four is not fifty.

Long silence from the Can. Then, Frank: "You heard Mr. Gutierrez. That's our final offer."

"No."

A long, long silence. Keith expected the big man to come back on and plead with him some more. That would be fun.

Finally, Frank came back. "Your decision has been noted," Frank said. He didn't sound surprised. If anything, he sounded tired.

Noted?

"Hey, what does that mean?" Keith said. Like, were they going to try to disqualify him or something? That wasn't in the contract! They said so themselves!

Silence.

"Ass! What the hell does 'noted' mean?"

Silence.

"Fuck you, then!"

Silence. On and on.

Was it possible that he could run this whole thing and not win due to some technicality? Could he take the offer now, or would they try to screw him out of it?

No. No. He was a winner. He was going to win.

And if they tried to take that away from him, God help them.

Contingency

"I'll go back on, offer him eight million," Jere said, slumping over the cool stone of his office desk. He remembered when that massive desk made him feel safe and secure. Now they could bury him in it. Ron, Evan, and Patrice stood in front of his desk, like a jury.

"It won't matter," Ron said.

"Sixteen."

"Run the projections with a sixteen million dollar hole."

"No." Jere already knew what they'd look like. Ruin. Total and complete. A smoking crater. There was no real difference between that and fifty-one million.

"But it's not that much money!" Jere said. His voice was high, cracking.

Ron closed his mouth, blew out a big breath. We don't have it, that breath said. Everything we have is leveraged, and the leverages leveraged. There was nothing to turn into money.

"We could grassroots it like we talked about—"

Ron cut him off. "There's no time."

"But they—"

Ron came over, put a hand on Jere's shoulder. His hand was hard, like the hand of an automaton. Wood. Unfeeling. He squeezed Jere's shoulder hard, once.

The phone rang. The office phone. In all the time Jere had been at Neteno, his office phone had never rung. It was just one of those things you had to have. Nobody had his office number. Jere himself had no idea what it was. Everyone just called through his eyeset. Everyone else was shuttled into, what, some unknown voicemail purgatory? Jere didn't know. He'd never checked.

Ring!

"Pick it up," Ron said.

Jere picked up the old-fashioned handset and put it to his ear. He felt like he was playing a bit part in a movie set in the eighties. "Hello," he said.

"Mr. Gutierrez," a voice said. "I understand you have, ah . . . a financial challenge to overcome."

"Who is this?"

"Ah, now I am hurt." The voice was somewhat familiar, but Jere couldn't place it.

"Who are you?"

"This is Horatio Wood."

"Oh." Jere's hand tightened on the handset, making the cheap black plastic creak. That fucker, the guy who stunk crazy all the way down the hall.

"I wondered if you might want to revisit our proposal."

"No."

A pause. Behind the voice, silky silence stretched, improbable and infinite. And for a moment, just a moment, Jere saw himself saying yes. Because he could get back to Keith and say *Yeah, asshole, take fifty-one, take fifty-five, take whatever, just save the other team*, because the amount Horatio Wood had offered him made that amount look like loose change in a sofa.

"Who is it?" Evan asked, leaning forward eagerly. Jere wondered if he knew who was on the other end of the line. If he had put him up to it. Evan wouldn't hesitate for a moment. He'd make the deal. He wouldn't even blink.

But Jere couldn't get the images out of his head. One of his neighbors had opened a Modern Enlightenment church in his high-rise. Kids went in and out of his condo at all times of the day and night. Kids with shaved heads and brilliant, unseeing eyes. Kids who couldn't be more than fifteen years old. Kids with surgery scars and metallic electrodes sticking out of their skulls. ME had just absorbed eBay, after they tried to ban the buying and selling of their currencies. They'd also purchased CurEx, the second-largest currency exchange on the planet, after there was a flap about their valuations.

The game never changes, Jere thought. Money and power, more and more, never enough. The only things that change are the people pulling the levers.

Like a whisper: *Meet the new boss. Same as the old boss.*

"Who is it?" Evan hissed.

Jere shook his head and waved for silence. Ron grabbed Evan's shoulder and pulled him away.

"Are you certain?" Horatio asked.

It would be so easy. He could say yes. He could save the team. He could save them all.

"Yes," Jere said.

"Yes you want to move forward, or yes, you want to leave people to die?" Horatio asked.

Jere squeezed his eyes shut. He saw three people, laying under a pink sky next to a crumpled lander.

"There is no deal," Jere said.

"Are you certain?"

"There'll never be any deal!" Jere screamed. He slammed the phone down hard enough to crack the plastic handset. He fumbled for the network cable and ripped it out of the wall.

"Who was it?" Ron said, softly.

"Wrong number," Jere said.

He closed his eyes.

Hoping the tears didn't show.

Performance

Last. Dead last. No denying it now. No excuses. No rationalization. It had taken Glenn and Alena far too long to assemble the wheel that morning, far longer than they had taken back on Earth. Blame it on the cold, or parts that didn't want to fit together, or the arcane changes to the engine assembly, but facts were facts. It hadn't tripped the other teams up, as Petrov in the Can (rather gleefully, Glenn thought) told them.

And yet Glenn was strangely content. Just like that one free climb in Tibet, their second time up, when it wasn't about Everest, but about rock that was supposed to be unclimbable, when it was clear they were beaten, hanging exhausted from numb fingertips beneath a thin sun rapidly disappearing behind a front of ominous purple-grey clouds. That moment when he realized they weren't going to make it, that they would have to go back down, that they would have to forget being the first. The stress and the worry suddenly lifted from him. He was suddenly light and free, as if he could do anything.

The only thing more amazing was when Alena, tears freezing on her cheeks, agreed with him. They scrambled down the rock as the icy rain hit. The rain that would have killed them.

They'd made love back in what passed for a hotel with incredible intensity, golden and yellow sparks flying in a perfect night sky, impossible to describe, infinite and endless in a moment's perfection. They'd finally collapsed, satiated, face to face, sweat cooling to an icy chill in the cold room. He'd waited until her breathing had slowed, and lengthened, and deepened, then said, very softly, "Marry me."

Alena's eyes opened. In the dark they were the glassy curves of two crystal spheres, unreadable.

Glenn's breath caught. Had she heard him? What would she think? Would she . . . ?

"Yes," she said softly, and closed her eyes again.

He'd lain awake for a long time after that, looking at the curves of her face, limned in the pale moonlight. Had he imagined it? Had she really heard him? He fell asleep with questions resonating in his mind.

When he woke in the morning, she was already pulling on her gear. Glenn had a moment of sleepy pleasure, watching her slim form, before he remembered his question—and her answer—from the night before.

She looked down at him. The light fell pale and grey on her face. She looked like the ghost of an angel.

"Yes," she said. "I said yes."

"Glenn!" Alena shrieked. "Watch out!"

Glenn jerked back to the present as their wheel caromed off a boulder and promptly went bouncing across a field. He pulled on his harness and leaned outside of the wheel's edge, shortening the bounces on his side and bringing them back on course. They'd rigged the harnesses so they could catamaran the wheel, which allowed them to run full out. Each of them leaned out off the side of the wheel, giving a better view of the terrain ahead than through the translucent dust-coated plastic, and allowing them to shift its direction more rapidly by leaning in and out to shift the center of gravity.

A risk, yes, but a risk that Glenn knew they had to take. Alena wouldn't settle for less. And it might even be better, balancing the time of use with the fatigue on the wheel. If it broke before they were done, they'd have no chance. The shorter time they spent inside it, the better.

Or at least that's what Glenn told himself.

"Pay attention!" Alena said. "A few more inches, and we might have lost a strut."

"I know, I know," Glenn said. "I'm sorry."

"What were you thinking?"

"Tibet," he said.

Silence for a time. "Oh," she said finally.

"Remember?"

"I remember we never made it."

And she was right. A series of storms had kept them from ever trying the climb again. The next year, a guy from the UK had succeeded in climbing the ridge. Glenn had found the printout from the free climb website posted to the refrigerator, when he'd come home from work one night. That was the beginning of the silence. It was, in a way, the beginning of the end, though their marriage limped along for another three years.

Glenn said nothing.

"I don't like losing," she said, after a time.

"Neither do I."

"We don't have to lose if you pay attention."

"I am."

"We're making up time."

"I know."

"The others may have problems with their kits."

"They will."

Alena stopped and shot him and puzzled look. "Why are you so agreeable for once?"

Because I love you, Glenn thought. That's another thing I never wanted to lose.

But again, he said nothing.

There was nothing to say.

Joy

Patrice couldn't drag Jere away from the darkened room of slice and dice screens deep in the Neteno building, so she brought him pizza from Pizza One, the new Italio-Californian place on Vine. His eyes were big and round from the litter of espresso cups in front of him, but the skin hung in dark bags beneath them. His right eye, glazed with eyeset-dazzle, looked far away into space. His left eye focused on her.

"You need to sleep," she said.

"What?"

"Sleep. You know, the bit where you lay down on a bed, close your eyes—"

"I'll sleep when it's over." Petulantly. Like a six-year-old.

"You'll be dead when it's over."

Jere glanced at her, glanced at the pizza. Picked up a slice and mechanically started eating.

Evan snored softly in an office chair in the corner. That was fine by Patrice. Evan would strangle his dog if you offered him a nickel. She liked it a lot better when she couldn't see the strange calculations going on behind his eyes.

Jere's dad was gone too. He was a calculator as well, but she still hadn't figured out what he wanted.

"What are you doing?" She asked Jere

"Huh? Finances."

"I thought Keith was already in his kite."

"Uh. Yeah. He is. But we might . . . " Jere's gaze went away, reflecting strange landscapes. The infogab on the nets chanted for his blood, but they didn't understand. If Jere magicked the money out of Neteno, it would kill the company. And that meant that maybe the contestants wouldn't get picked up in orbit, when they came back. Or they'd be picked up by someone with new contracts for them to sign.

Patrice found out where Jere's mystery call had come from, and what offer he'd refused. The offer that would save everything. But at what cost? Horatio was Evan with a great big tool kit. Where Evan scrabbled, Horatio plowed through. Evan wanted power, but Horatio would really bring the end of the world.

"Marry me," Patrice said.

"Huh?" Jere looked at her. Really looked at her. "Are you kidding?"

"I'm not kidding." Because it was okay. She wasn't YZ any more. It wasn't about the parties, it wasn't about the fun. It was about kids like Amy. It was about taking the chance and doing it right. Jere had taken the chance, and, within his limits, was doing it right. He was the only one she knew who had ever done that.

So she would chance it with him.

"Yes," he said. He picked her up, spun her around. "Yes, yes, yes, I say yes!"

"Then let's do it now."

"Now?" Jere was a kid in school, faced with calculus for the first time.

"Now."

"But—"

"We can do it. It's easy."

"But, a priest, a ring, a service—"

"We don't need a priest, I don't need a ring, and I don't care about a service."

Jere reached turned off his eyeset. He looked at her with eyes big and deep and still. The next thing you say will make or break this, she thought. I'll love you or I'll hate you, depending on what it is. But I'll marry you either way.

"Why?" he said.

Patrice smiled. That why was enough. It said, Why do you want me? I have nothing to give you. Everything is up in the air. There is no prize.

"Because," she said. "I believe in you."

Jere's bloodshot eyes darted left and right. He opened his mouth, but no words came out. She let him sit there, open-mouthed, for a tiny while, before she said, "Come on."

Patrice took him out into the street, where the hangers-on had come to watch *Winning Mars* on the big screens outside Neteno. When they stepped out onto the sidewalk, people stopped and stared. A hush fell. Eyes glittering like marbles in the sunset above the Hollywood hills turned towards them, couples leaned together, whispering Jere and Patrice's name. Gabbers lined up with eyesets pointed, flashing red recording dots.

"What are you doing?" Jere said.

"Marrying us," she said.

She turned to address the crowd. "I believe in Jere," she said. "So I'm marrying him."

A murmur among the gabbers.

"Let your eyesets and flyeyes take this as proof. I take Jere as my husband, to have and to hold, forever and ever."

She looked at him. He could blow it now. He could. It was possible. His eyes quivered with fear.

But he stepped forward, took her hand. He looked at the crowd. In a loud, clear voice, he said, "And I take Patrice as my wife, to have and to hold, forever and ever. Because I believe in her."

The crowd gave a little cheer. Some tourists with old-fashioned cameras snapped pictures. And, Patrice knew, the news was already winging its way around the world.

"What do we do now?" Jere said.

"I have no idea," Patrice said, smiling happily.

Because, just for that moment, everything was right.

Mirage

Geoff Smith felt dazed. Leaving the IBM package behind was one thing, but the slide was inexcusable. If only he could turn back the clock and check the microscope before they'd left! If only he could have remembered to pick up the IBM package! All it would have taken was a glance, and a five-second diversion, and everything would have been all right. He would have both, and his fame and fortune would have been assured.

Now, his best possible ending was winning a prize. Just cash. Only money. And then having to endure the endless interviews that came after it, reporters asking snickering questions about how it was to be teamed with Wende and Laci. Knowing he was the geek, the geek with two nice girls, how did that work, they'd ask over and over again.

Even now, in this instant of time, as they flew over the rugged Martian terrain, it looked like they might actually have a chance of winning.

Chatter from the Can told them what was happening: the felon's kite setup wasn't going well, his lead had evaporated, and every second left him further behind. The action sports assholes had never really been in the running. They'd been slow at everything—assembling the wheel, navigating, assembling the kite—and were many, many minutes behind.

Money, money, money, he thought dreamily, watching the landscape pass below.

He'd hoped to put together another slide as Laci and Wende built the kite, but his water was gone and they wouldn't let him have the time. He'd swapped struts while Laci rerigged the engine and Wende did the electronics checks. And truth was, he didn't really feel like making another slide. Losing the first one had taken all the fight out of him.

Of course, he could scope the dust all he wanted when they were back on the Can, but that would be surface dust, stuff that had been flying around in the UV. What if the dust had to be from a few feet down? Or what if the dust had to be from near the water flows that they had seen from the Mars

Global Surveyor, so many years ago? What if he'd never had a chance at all, and they knew that, and they didn't care? His thoughts whirled like a cyclone, all destructive energy and dark currents.

Wende looked back at him from the pilot's sling and smiled. Geoff tried to smile back, but his lips felt frozen in place. After a moment, Wende turned away and looked at Laci. Laci looked back at him and frowned.

Yes, I know you don't like me, he thought. You've made that abundantly clear. Now turn back around and be a good copilot.

Laci was probably thinking how much faster they would be running if he accidentally fell off. He looked up nervously at his tether, but it was solid and unfrayed.

Movement on the ground caught his eye, and his heart pounded. Movement? He strained his eyes. It was a wispy shivering that played at the edges of the mini-dunes that hid between the rocky fields. Could it be something under the sand, twisting and dancing? Could there be real macroorganisms on Mars, maybe something like sand fleas or worms or . . .

Geoff was about to say something when they whisked over a hill to a larger dune field that was boiling with movement. He made a sound deep in his throat as they were shoved sideways. Wende cried and grappled with the manual controls.

Wind.

Of course. Geoff felt instantly stupid. The wind was kicking up. Even in the thin Martian atmosphere, it was enough to kick up sand and dust.

There was no life underground. Just mindless, lifeless sand, pushed by the wind.

Sandstorm? He wondered, looking at the horizon. But it was the customary light pink, shading to pale blue above. No mass of dust hung like a curtain near them.

His head swam for a moment, and he shook it. His vision blurred and doubled as if his head was a giant bell, just struck. He gripped his perch tighter and held his head still. After a moment, it passed. The landscape streamed by beneath him, soothing and hypnotic.

We've always looked down at the surface of Mars and imagined things. Canals. Faces. Trees. First it was just a red dot in the sky, then named for the god of war. Next, an arid desert world where intelligence clung to life with massive feats of engineering. Then, an incredible fantasyland where all manner of strange creatures hid the secrets of eons past. Then, suddenly, real photography exposed the dead, dry thing they knew it to be now.

But it wasn't dead! He *knew* there was life here. If they'd just let him have enough time, he would have seen microbes. If they'd given him a shovel and even more time, he'd dig up fossils. He knew it! And somehow, he would still prove it.

The landscape changed again from dune field to dark rocks, rectilinear and almost artificial in appearance. It reminded him of ancient Mayan ruins. Like that other guy had said. That guy online, who was always seeing cities in every photograph the unmanned probes sent back. Geoff thought he was a little crazy about it, ancient Mayans and spacemen and stuff like that. Or was it Egypt? Or Stonehenge? Thoughts jittered around in his head in a crazy dance.

Below Geoff, details swam and ran, and resolved themselves again. The rectilinear lines became sharper and more regular. Now he could see individual stones, etched into fantastic designs by the passage of time.

Etched? By what? He shook his head again, and details leaped out: fantastic whorls and patterns, ancient art of the highest order. It wasn't etched by weather. It was etched by intelligence! He was looking at carvings. Alien, to be sure, but deliberate carvings. Someone had done these, thousands or millions of years ago!

Were those patterns he saw in the sand as well? Did they cover ancient squares where people once gathered? For a blinding instant, he could see the entire city as it had stood, towering, over the rough Martian surface, with wise-looking, white-robed people with big golden eyes congregating . . .

"Stop!" he cried. His voice sounded strangely high and strangled.

"What?" Wendy said. "Why? What's wrong?"

"It's them!" Geoff said. "Intelligence! The city below us . . . there's a city below us!"

The two looked down, scanning back and forth with puzzled looks. Probably not even looking down, Geoff thought. Just looking ahead. Always ahead. To the prize. That was all that mattered to them.

"Geoff?" Wende said. "What are you talking about?"

How could they not see it? He could see its lines, etched into the rocks, buried in the sands. There were the remains of an entire civilization below them. "The city! Look at the stones! They're square! Look at the language on them!"

"Geoff, that isn't funny."

A crackle. The voice of Frank Sellers from the Can. "What do you see?"

"A city," Geoff said. "The remains of a city. Stones. Writing! Decoration!"

"Land your kite," Frank said.

"What?" Laci said.

"Put your kite down, now."

"No way!" Laci said. "We're winning!"

"The Roddenberry clause says you have to investigate any overt evidence of life," Frank said.

"Fuck with that! We're not stopping!"

"If you don't stop, it's contract breach."

"There's nothing below us!" Wende broke in. "Just a rock field."

"You have to land. Or you forfeit all winnings." Slow and steady, as if speaking to a child. Geoff had to stifle a grin.

"Shit!" Laci said. Wende grumbled, but they began to fall from the sky.

"Turn around," Geoff said. "The best part is behind us."

Wende wheeled around and he saw it all, the geometric perfection, the ancient city and all its splendor.

"I still don't see it," Wende said. "Frank, can you review our last imagery?"

"Yep," Frank said. "Continue with your landing. It'll take me a few minutes."

"Shit." But still they dropped lower.

Silence for long seconds as they fell out of the sky. Wende picked a relatively clear section of sand and for a moment they all acted as landing gear, running over the sand.

Geoff's legs felt heavy and weak, and he buckled under the weight of the kite. Down this close, he could see nothing. Rocks were just rocks. Sand was just sand. There was no great city.

Like Nazca! he thought. You have to be up in the air to see it. Smart! Real smart! Like the Face!

"Geoff? You all right?" That was Wende. Pretty Wende. Nice of her to think about him.

Frank's voice crackled back on. "False alarm," he said. "I don't see anything other than some regular volcanic cracking. That's probably what fooled you, Geoff."

Fooled? "I'm no fool!" he shouted. He had seen it! He had!

Silence for a time. Finally: "Laci, Wende, what does Geoff look like? Is he blue?"

"No," Wende said. "But he looks a bit funny. Patchy, splotchy. Oh, shit. Does he have a bug?"

"More likely a life support malfunction. Is his suit torn? Is he cold?"

"Fuck him," Laci said, and started the engine again. Wende glanced at her and shrugged out of her harness.

"No," Laci said. "Wende, get back in. We need to fly!"

"It'll only take a minute," Frank said.

"It won't kill him."

"It might," Frank said.

"Then we take the chance."

Wende had stopped shrugging out of her harness, under Laci's hard glare. Frank said nothing. Geoff watched them for a moment, thinking, I saw it! I did! I really did! There was a distant babble on the comm and things got very bright.

Then rough hands picked him up. Wende's face bent over him. "What do I do?"

"Check his suit. He may have torn it."

Wende spun Geoff around, looking at his suit. He tried to think of a snappy retort, but everything was fuzzy. "Stop it!" he said, and tried to twist out of her grasp.

"Nothing," Laci said.

"Check his oxygen," Frank said. "It may be cranked up too high. Funny, that usually doesn't cause hallucinations, but I suppose . . . "

"I saw it!" Geoff said. "I really did!"

He said it would only take a minute, but it seemed to take forever. They did something on the back of Geoff's suit, and he sucked in big breaths of air. His head began to clear.

But when they were all back on board and soaring into the sky, even the Rothman team had passed them.

Face

When Jere and Patrice came back from their short honeymoon at his apartment, Evan was grumping in the slice and dice room. "If only they'd found a city," Evan said. "That'd make this whole trip worthwhile."

"What, did you expect to find the Martian crown jewels?" Ron cracked.

"Who knows?"

"You're an idiot," Ron said.

"Just remember who came up with this idea."

"And the completely bullshit numbers behind it."

Evan stood up. He glanced at Patrice and Jere and rolled his eyes. "You just don't think big enough. We should be selling this as a series! We should be pitching for the next show! Haven't you looked at the numbers? This is the biggest thing to ever hit TV. Ever. This is the Superbowl of Superbowls. This is the holy motherfucking grail . And you sit there, wringing your hands, when you're right on the fucking top!"

"Shut up, Evan," Ron said.

"No. I won't. I shouldn't have to. I've shut up for long enough. I should go out and sell the next show to someone else, right now. You just don't get the power. Not at all."

"If you think you can sell it, do it," Ron said.

Evan looked from Ron to Jere. "Are you formally severing my contract?"

Silence from Ron. He looked down at a program planning screen, as if engrossed in the details.

"Am I released? Because if I am, I want it for the record."

Silence.

"Tell me! Tell me right now!"

"You're not released," Ron said, softly.

Evan laughed. "Of course not. Because you know this is a big idea. You know this is the big deal. You know, if you sell it right, you can do whatever you want with this."

"Shut up, Evan."

This time, he did.

Ron grinned at Jere, looking genuinely pleased. "Welcome home, newlyweds."

"What kind of a fucking stunt was that?" Evan said, humming "dum-dum-de-dum" out of the corner of his mouth, ironically.

Ron moved with more grace and speed than Jere had ever seen him use. In one motion, he stood up, swung, and placed his fist squarely in the center of Evan's face. There was a dull crunching noise, like the foley guys pounding celery, from the dim days of the art. Evan squealed like a girl and retreated, clutching his nose.

"You fucking nut!" Evan said.

"You don't talk to my son like that. Or his wife."

"I'll . . . I'll have you fucking arrested!"

"Try it."

The two old men stared at each other, both motionless. Jere waited tensely, expecting Evan to rush his father. But he just took a couple of steps back. Blood streamed over his hand.

"Go," Ron said. "Have the nose fixed."

Dying

Frank was lying to them again.

Mike Kinsson didn't blame the man. What was he going to tell them otherwise? *Sorry, you're out of luck, best to just ditch the headers and pop off quick.*

"We're still seeing if we can rig one of the returns for remote operation," Frank said. "If we can remote it, we can bring it to your location and you can return to the ship from there."

"How much longer?" Julie whined. "I'm bored."

She and Sam had their arms around each other. The tiny half-dome shelter was still up, but everyone was out of it for the thin grey light of morning. Third day. Last day.

Later, Mike would go and wander around, like he'd done on the days before. Sam hadn't gotten aggressive yet, but Mike didn't want to be around when he did. Julie and Sam were like two teenagers who had just discovered sex, and they were probably happy to have the privacy.

He'd already walked over to the nearby cliffs, turning over rocks, hoping beyond hope to see the tell-tale color of lichen or moss, something that might be able to survive in Mars' hostile environment. He still remembered the first time his mother and father had taken him to the Griffith Observatory in Los Angeles, and they had talked about what life might be like on other planets. Lichens and primitive plants on Mars, they'd said. Maybe. That was about the best they could hope for. Or just bacteria. Things you couldn't see.

It had fascinated him in a way that nothing had ever done, before or since. What if there was life on other planets? What if Mars could be made to support human life? There were an endless variety of *What ifs*.

"We're hoping to have a definitive answer by the end of the day," Frank said.

"What if it takes longer?" Sam said.

"Then we wait."

"We're almost out of food!" Julie said.

"We know. Please do what you can to save food and conserve energy."

They both looked at Mike. Mike looked right back at them, thinking, Like what you were doing wasn't more strenuous than my walk.

He started edging away from them again. What would they do when they found out there really wasn't any rescue coming? Maybe it would be best just to wander off, and stay wandered off. Maybe the Martian night would be cold enough to overwhelm his squeezesuit. Maybe the movies were right. Maybe freezing was a pleasant way to die.

"He's walking away again!" Julie said.

"Mild physical exertion won't hurt," Frank said.

They watched Mike as he walked off, but they didn't come after him.

More lichen hunting. He walked past the cliffs from the day before and came to a place where sand and rocks made a steep slope down into a small valley. Rivulets were cut in the surface of the slope, some still knife-edged.

He remembered old satellite images. Could he be near a place where water was near the surface? He paused to dig into one of the little channels, but turned up only dry sand and dust and pebbles. If there was water here, it was deeper than he could find.

Which was too bad. Because if there was life here, they'd likely find it where there was liquid water. That's what they'd always said. Their best hope for finding Earthlike life hinged on water.

He wandered on. There would be no rescue. He knew that. The returns weren't designed for remote operation. If they were, they would have had one out to them the first day.

He'd keep walking, and see where his feet took him. Until it was time to lie down and turn down the heaters as far as they went. Maybe some real pioneer, fifty years from now, would find his desiccated body and say, *This is the other guy, the one who wandered away from camp. We finally found him!*

Mike shivered. It wasn't a pleasant thought.

But it was better than imagining what Julie and Sam would do, when the final word came down.

Bittersweet

"It's a lie, isn't it?" Patrice said. "What you're telling Sam and Mike and Julie."

Jere turned to her. This is my wife, he thought. It was one of the weirdest things he'd ever thought.

"It—" he began. And stopped himself. "Of course it is."

Patrice looked down. "I want to talk to them," she said. "Before the end."

"I—" He stopped himself again, thinking, I'll wake up to her the rest of my life.

"I'll make it happen," he said.

Honeymoon

"Come on!" Alena said. "Come on, come on, *come on*!"

They were close. The Can had stopped reporting the status of the teams, but Glenn knew they were close. They'd made it from dead last to nearly tied with that Paul guy, when Frank and Petrov started the information embargo.

"What can I do?" he asked, over the local comm.

"I don't know! I was talking to the kite, not you!"

"Will that make it go faster?"

"Maybe!" Alena yelled. "Come on!"

Glenn smiled. There really wasn't much they could do, other than stay lashed up under the belly of the kite for minimum aerodynamic drag? Nothing.

The next one they should make more manual, he thought. Human-powered kites and wheels. None of this motor crap. Or at least have us be able to add our output to the engines. What was the fun in flying, anyway? The wheel had taken some skill and technique, and that was where they'd made up most of their time. But the kite was nothing more than a big powered hang glider. What was the fun in that?

"Look!" Alena said, pointing.

Glenn strained his eyes. Ahead of them, the rocky plain rolled uninterrupted for as far he could see.

"What?"

"The returns! We've made it!"

Glenn squinted. Very far in the distance, he could just catch the glint of metal. "Is that really it?"

"Yeah, that's it! Come on!"

"Talking to the machine again?"

"It can't hurt!"

Alena looked at him, and he saw the girl who he'd fallen in love with, the woman he'd proposed to, all the goodness in her. She was smiling, exultant, her color high and eyes flashing. She was at her best when she was not only competing, but winning. It was impossible not to love her.

She saw him looking and smiled wider. Oh, what that promised!

He shoved the throttle hard against its stops, as if another few micrometers could make any difference in their velocity. It was already full open, always had been. There was only one setting, in the thin atmosphere of Mars.

Where was Paul? If the race was as close as he thought, he should be able to see his kite, bright white against the pale sky. He scanned from left to right, but saw nothing.

And it comes down to this, Glenn knew. Whoever makes it to the returns, wins. The returns went back to the Can automatically. There was no race to orbit.

Another scan. No kite.

Was it possible that Paul had run into trouble? Could they *really* be first?

Karma will get you every time, he thought. Paul should have picked up the Money team.

From ahead of them, a bright flare came from the direction of the return pod cluster. The kite rocked as Alena started violently. One of the returns climbed slowly into the sky, then moved faster, darting upward out of view.

"No!" she said. "No no no!"

"Paul," Glenn said softly. It was Paul. Had to be. Faintly, he heard karma laughing at him.

"How much longer do we have?" Alena asked.

"A couple of minutes. But it's . . . "

"Go faster!"

"It only takes three minutes to orbit!"

"I don't care! Go faster!" Her eyes were brighter now, brighter with tears. Her face was twisted into a mask of anguish.

"Are you talking to me, or the machine?" Glenn said softly.

"Anybody! Anybody who'll listen!"

Glenn fell silent and let the only sound be that of the rushing wind and roaring motor. The return cluster grew ahead of them, big enough so they could see the remains of Paul's kite. It lay there, an almost unrecognizable tangle of aluminum struts and fabric. He'd had a hard landing.

"We lost," he said.

"No!"

"Yes, we have."

When they landed, Alena scrambled to the nearest return pod and began the launch prep.

"Hurry up!" she said. "Come on! Hurry up!"

When the prep was less than halfway done, the voices from the Can came back. This time it was Frank. He sounded tired, and sad, and more than a little disgusted.

"We have a winner," she said. "Paul team is now back on board the *Mars Enterprise*. To our other teams, thank you for an excellent competition. Please travel safely on your way back. There's no need to hurry now."

"No!" Alena wailed. She beat on the low bench of the return pod. Glenn tried to gather her in his arms, but she pushed him away violently. He tumbled out onto the cold sand and lay for a moment, stunned, staring up at the alien sky.

"Glenn?" Alena, on their local channel. Glenn shook his head, but said nothing.

"Glenn?" Frightened.

She came out of the pod and knelt atop him, her eyes red from crying, her mouth pulled taut in worry. "Glenn!" she said, shaking him.

"What?" he said.

"Glenn, I can't hear you! Are you okay?"

"What?" He reached behind him and felt the suit's radio. Nothing. It seemed okay. Of course, he could have hit something in his fall . . . He shrugged and gave her the thumb-and-forefinger "okay" sign.

"I heard you hit, and a big hiss, and I thought you'd broken your header, that I'd killed you." She was crying even more now, big tears hitting the inside of her header and running down towards her chest.

He pushed his header to hers. "I'm okay," he said.

"I can hear you now."

"Yeah, old trick. Frank told me. Touch helmets."

She helped him up. The return pod gaped open like a mouth.

"Let's go," she said, touching helmets again.

"Wait a minute." Glenn looked from the return pods—all four of them—to the sky, and then towards the east, where the Ruiz team was stranded.

Could they do it?

The Can had been talking about rigging one of the returns for automatic flight, but they obviously hadn't. Would it be possible to fly one over to

Money, pick them up, and save them? Would it be possible to fly two? Would they have enough fuel? Could they refuel?

It was worth a shot.

"Alena," he said. "Do you want to be the real winners?"

"What do you mean?"

"There's still a team out there to save."

Alena's eyes got big. She nodded vigorously. She stayed helmet-to-helmet with him as she called the Can.

"Frank," she said. "Let's talk about the Money team."

Show

Evan's bandaged nose didn't get in the way of his presentations.

In the darkness of Jere's office, animated charts showed realtime Viewing Audience, composite Attention Index, Monetization Effectiveness in seventeen different currencies, inferred long-term Buyer Motivation, and Overall Meme Engagement, plotted against historical data from Neteno, their competitors, and even forward-pulled data from the heyday of television. The numbers were impossibly large, towering, everything Evan had bullshitted them into believing from the start.

"Congratulations, everyone. We've set entirely new standards for, well, every metric there is. We are the top, the pinnacle, the best and the brightest. It's that simple."

"We may even make, what, five dollars on the whole deal?" Ron said.

Evan shot him a glance. He was grandstanding for the sponsors, streamed live on all the secure internal networks of the giant corporations of the world. "Given the scope of the program, any positive return should be considered a bonus. What's important is that all sponsors and advertisers received excellent value for their investment. Attention Index times Monetization Effectiveness nets out, even before long-term Buyer Motivation is factored in."

"Which means?" Jere said.

"Which means the stage is set for a sequel."

Jere felt his stomach do a quick flip-flop. Of course, someone is going to die. Probably lots of someones. Even with the Money team being picked up by K2, there was still the matter of Sarimanok.

"No," Jere said.

"Not with long-term historical sequel returns at fifty-seven percent of the original show," Ron said.

"Or a series," Evan said. "Monetization options for a long-term series are very good. We've done it once. All we have to do is keep it running."

"No," Jere said.

"We could move closer-in. There's an opportunity on the moon, perhaps in partnership with the Chinese. Horatio Wood's consumeristians are very interested in financing a permanent settlement—"

"Don't even think it," Jere said.

Evan's mouth clicked shut. "I thought you were the visionary. I thought you were the guys who took chances."

"We did."

"Why not now?"

Jere shook his head. "I know those numbers. I know those charts. And I know that money-happy look in your eyes. We did something very important. Now it's time to step back. That starry-eyed shit that gave us that old second *Star Wars* threequel. The one with that irritating droopy bastard, whatever his name was . . . "

Evan shuddered.

"Point is, this show isn't golden. And we aren't perfect. Leave it now and let them clamor for more."

"Trekify it, you're saying," Ron said.

Evan frowned. "We could do it," he said.

"Shut up, Evan," Jere said.

We're on top for the moment, he thought. And let that be enough.

Winner

"I won, right?" Keith Paul said, breathing the deep stink of the tiny ship. He'd forgotten how small it was. Six months of that shit again. Six months of this stinking aluminum prison. But when he got back, he'd be rich.

"Yeah," Frank said. "You won."

"I'll get the money?"

"Yeah."

"All of it? Fifty million?"

"All of it."

"So where are the cameras?"

Frank ripped off his earplug and pushed away from the comm board. He grabbed Keith's shirt with both hands and pulled him close. The momentum took them off the floor, spinning through *Mars Enterprise's* main crew chamber.

"There are no cameras!" Frank yelled. His eyes were wide and bright, quivering with that adrenaline-fueled, amped-up look that guys got when they were ready to take you apart with their bare hands. Keith had seen that look a few times in his life, and he knew one thing: he wanted absolutely no part of it.

"Nobody fucking cares about you!" Frank screamed, shaking Keith like he was made out of tissue. "Everyone's watching the real fucking heroes now!"

Frank pointed at the live feed from the surface, where the extreme sports fucknuts were slapping the backs of the stupidly named Money team in their crappy little camp. It was like a goddamn birthday party or something. Glenn mugged at the camera, sandwiched between Julie and Alena, giving them all a big thumbs-up.

"I coulda done that," Keith said.

"But you didn't."

"I won."

Frank crossed his arms. "Yes. You did. Confuckinggratulations. You'll get your goddamned money, just like you wanted, but don't expect anyone to care! Now fuck off! I've got important things to do!"

Frank gave him one last shove, pushing Keith into the bulkhead above. His head clanged on metal and he saw stars.

"Okay, man, okay," Keith said, as Frank drifted slowly back down and took his seat.

"Get out of here," Frank said. "I don't want to see you any more."

Heroes

"Look at these showboating dickweeds," Evan said.

In the hushed velvet darkness of the slice and dice room, Evan's words were incredibly loud. Editors, almost used to not seeing Ron and Jere anymore, swiveled and stared at the weary executives. Patrice put her hand on Jere's shoulder, and he reached up to touch it. He felt beyond tired, beyond beaten, lost in some strange nether land.

Instead of *Winning Mars*, they were all looking at the competitive feeds. The slice-and-dice screen showed the story. Fox, Helmers, and the SciFi Channel were all tuned on a crappy little town down in Mexico, where a slim needle was being assembled in a shabby old warehouse. Outside, a makeshift derrick grew from a field of concrete. And some hairy guy wearing a dirty coverall was talking about building a colony ship to send to Mars. He called it *Mayflower II*.

"This is the real show," he said. "Not that publicity stunt they did in Hollywood. We're going, but we're going to stay."

There were shots of wild-eyed engineers and ex-scientists and geeks galore, thrusting what looked like old-time tickets in the air.

"I'm going." One of them crowed.

"I'm going." Another geek with thick glasses.

"And me!" A girl, no more than eighteen, cute in a girl-next-door way.

"And me too!" An old guy wearing a pen-pack.

"And so am I, darling," A moderately-famous internet celebrity.

And on and on it went.

The show talked about grass-roots funding, angel investors, breakthroughs in low-cost spaceflight, and the planned lottery of the best and brightest who'd signed up to be the first to go to Mars and stay.

"They timed it," Evan said. "Perfect. They wait till we shot our wad, then they spring this shit."

But it was nothing, Jere thought. A bunch of nuts talking about open-source technology and happy-happy solidarity and helping each other and crap like that. They didn't have a ship ready. And Jere knew what it would take for them to get it off the ground.

"They knew the ratings would die the instant everyone was back in the Can," Evan said. "They knew it, and they are fucking taking it!"

"What are our ratings like?" Jere said.

Evan shook his head and clicked on the realtime feed. The downward spike was still small, but he could see it accelerating. As he watched, it clicked down a few pixels more.

"Do we have anyone down in Mexico?" Jere said. "Can we get a line on this colony stuff too?"

"No," Evan said. "We weren't ready for this. The fuckers probably talked to every network except for us. Shitheads. By the time we fly someone down, the big story's over. Assuming they'll even talk to us at all."

It's just a news story, Jere thought. One that everyone will forget as soon as they log off. A fifteen-minuter on Facebook.

But he remembered the people, coming down from the hills to stand in front of Oversight. He remembered his face on the big screens at Hollywood and Highland. He remembered getting in front of a billion eyes, and telling them the truth. Because that was what they needed to hear. The truth.

You can go back to the harness, Jere thought. Silk-lined, down-padded as it is. But still a harness. Or you can go forward. These people are going forward. They're taking up where we left off.

He looked at Ron. Ron was watching the competitive feeds. His jaw should be set, his eyes should be hard and glassy. Seeing everything taken. Seeing Neteno slide towards one of those crevasses where their finances would never recover. But Ron was looking up at the feeds, at that primitive rocket that made even the rough, dirty Can look sleek and well-crafted, and his face was soft. His mouth was slightly open. Perhaps, just perhaps, the edges of his lips turned up into a smile.

"We need to announce another show," Evan said. "Now!"

"What are we going to say?" Jere asked.

"I don't know! Asteroids! Jupiter! I don't know! It doesn't matter. We need an announcement, and we need a big one!"

"No," Jere said.

"No? Are you fucking nuts? You're going to let them steal everything we built?"

"No," Jere said.

"What are you talking about?" Evan said.

"I need to get on camera," Jere said, looking at Ron.

"What are you going to say?" Ron said.

"I'm going to tell them the truth."

"Which is?"

"This is what we wanted all along. We planned it this way. *Winning Mars* wasn't just a show, it was a spark to light a fire."

Ron nodded. He did his mechanical smile trick, arranging each muscle in his face in a precisely measured order. Jere didn't find it chilling anymore. He found it very, very sad.

He squeezed Patrice's hand, and thought, I hope I never end up like that. Having to calculate a smile.

In the monitors, the same dirty talking head was going on with that intensity that geeks have, when you activate their center of geekery. He said they wanted to launch sometime in the next eighteen months, to time it for the opposition. He made a very lame joke about having to travel a few million miles farther than Neteno. He looked very excited, and also very scared.

They'll never make it, Jere thought. They'll fucking die up there. All of them. They might not even make it off the launch pad.

But if they do . . .

"Go do it," Ron said. "Go make your legacy."

Jere kissed Patrice and turned to leave. Evan started after him, but Ron caught his sleeve. "No," he said. "Not you."

"It was my show!" Evan wailed.

"Not anymore," Ron said.

Jere hurried out, into the bright hall.

Coda

Mike Kinsson's second going-away party was a lot smaller. Just his parents. There were no banners, no ribbons. Maybe because he still didn't look too good. He was thin, and he still had to use crutches to walk.

"Mars again," his dad said.

Mike grinned. What could he say? They all wanted him, because he'd been there. To Mars. The *Mayflower* guys down in Mexico. The Russians with their *Potemkin*. The crazy fuckers in the Netherlands, now with money from the fragments of the EU, even asked him to crew their *Juggernaut*. Even though he wasn't a real scientist, wasn't a real brain.

It'll be hard, the *Mayflower* guys told him. *We'll probably die. We don't know if we can maintain a technological base, and if our technology falls below a certain level, we're done for. But we're going to try it.*

"That's right," he told his parents. "I'm going back."

This time to stay.

About the Author

Jason Stoddard is trying to answer the question, "Can business and writing coexist?" His work has been seen in *SciFiction*, *Interzone*, *Strange Horizons*, *Futurismic*, *Talebones*, and other publications. He was a finalist for the 2009 Theodore Sturgeon Memorial Award and for the 2005 Sidewise Award. Stoddard was also a first-place winner for the 2003 Writers of the Future Contest. On the other side, Jason leads Centric / Agency of Change. In this role, he's a popular speaker on social media and virtual worlds at venues like Harvard University, The Directors Guild of America, and The Internet Strategy Forum. *Winning Mars* is Jason's first published novel. You can find out more on his website/blog at www.strangeandhappy.com